SLEEPING
WITH
MONSTERS

AMELIA HUTCHINS

SLEEPING
WITH
MONSTERS

Copyright ©April 2nd 2018 Amelia Hutchins
ISBN: 978-0-9970055-9-2

Authored by: Amelia Hutchins
Cover Art Design: Tenaya Jayne
Copy Editor: Gina Tobin
Edited & Formatted by: E & F Indie Services

Published by: Amelia Hutchins
Published in (United States of America)
10 9 8 7 6 5 4 3 2 1

STOP!

Read the warning below before purchasing this book.

Warning!

This book is **dark**. It's **sexy**, hot, and **intense**. The author is human, as you are as well. Is the book perfect? It's as perfect as I could make it. Are there mistakes? Probably, then again, even **New York Times top published** books have minimal mistakes because like me, they have **human editors**. There are words in this book that won't be found in the standard dictionary, because they were created to set the stage for a paranormal-urban fantasy world. Words such as 'sift', 'glamoured', and 'apparate' are common in paranormal books and give better description to the action in the story than can be found in standard dictionaries. They are intentional and not mistakes.

About the hero: chances are you may **not** fall instantly in **love** with him, that's because **I don't write men you instantly love**; you grow to love them. I don't believe in **instant-love**. I write flawed, raw, caveman-like **assholes** that eventually let you see their redeeming qualities. They are **aggressive**, **assholes**, one step above a caveman when we meet them. You may *not* even like him by the time you finish this book, but I promise you will **love** him by the end of this **series**.

About the heroine: There is a chance, that you might

WARNING! (CONT'D)

think she's a bit naïve, or weak, but then again who starts out as a badass? Badasses are a product of growth and I am going to put her through **hell**, and you get to watch **her** come up **swinging** every time I knock her on her ass. That's just how I do things. How she reacts to the set of circumstances she is put through, may not be how you as the reader, or I as the author would react to that same situation. Everyone reacts differently to circumstances and how Magdalena responds to her challenges, is how I see her as a character and as a person.

I don't write love stories: I write fast paced, knock you on your ass, make you sit on the edge of your seat wondering what happens next books. If you're looking for cookie cutter romance, this isn't for you. If you can't handle the ride, ***un-buckle your seatbelt and get out of the roller-coaster car now***. **If not, you've been warned.** If nothing outlined above bothers you, carry on and **enjoy the ride!**

Dedication

For Robert Blackburn, my family, my friend, and, my hero. Without you, I wouldn't be here to write books, or have chosen the path I did. You touched every life you entered in a way that left fingerprints, and made them better for having known you. To the family he left behind, I love you guys. You're brave, strong, and even though you feel broken right now, he's with you every moment of every day. You were his everything.

For Olivia, who lost her heart when God called your husband home, we are with you.

Life isn't promised, so live everyday as if you only have this one.

For Tammie, Gina, Melissa, Tasha and all the other girls who keep me sane during this process, I love your faces.

To the fans and girls in my author group, you ladies rock my socks off and humble me every day.

To my family.

This year has been a ride from hell already, so it's a damn good thing we know how to handle these things together.

Eric, you're my everything. You're my best friend, and even though I spend countless hours writing and being lost inside my head, you keep me grounded.

Also by Amelia Hutchins

The Fae Chronicles

Fighting Destiny

Taunting Destiny

Escaping Destiny

Seducing Destiny

Unraveling Destiny

The Elite Guards

A Demon's Dark Embrace

How to Train A Dragon King - *2018*

A Guardian's Diary

Darkest Before Dawn

Death Before Dawn

Monsters Series

Playing with Monsters

Sleeping With Monsters

If you're following the series for the Fae Chronicles, Elite Guards, and Monsters, reading order is as follows:

Fighting Destiny

Taunting Destiny

Escaping Destiny

Seducing Destiny

A Demon's Dark Embrace

Playing with Monsters

Unraveling Destiny

Sleeping With Monsters

How to Train A Dragon King - *2018*

SLEEPING WITH

WITH

MONSTERS

SLEEPING
WITH
MONSTERS

CHAPTER
one

*In order to find myself, I must first destroy what I have become. What they made me into; someone else. ~**Lena***

My hair whipped against my face as the wind howled from the impending storm that was barreling down on Metaline Falls. I lifted my eyes to the moon, full and red from the smoke from the fires that were burning unchecked in the Pacific Northwest, from Washington all the way into Montana. My eyes burned from the pungent smell of those fires as I waited in the heavily wooded area at the back of the exclusive nightclub.

Music pumped from inside the club; the bass pulsated from the walls and vibrated the ground, stirring excitement from those who'd stood in line for hours just for a chance to be allowed into the kinkfest that happened in the lower levels of Blackstone's notorious club. The front of this place was no different from the back; lines started early and people waited hours in them, uncaring that only a select few ever made it inside without knowing someone or having an exclusive invite.

Immortals stood with mortals, something I'd been noticing more of as I watched Lucian Blackstone and what went on inside this place. I'd asked the coven to investigate him and his club, and instead of taking my concerns seriously, I was warned against meddling in his affairs. No one questioned his motive for opening a sex club in the middle of Little Town, USA, but I did, while the coven seemed to be ignoring the growing demon problem—even though I was sure it had something to do with this place.

I watched a couple as they groped each other, uncaring that others watched and enjoyed the lewd show they were giving. One man had a woman pressed against the building, and from the motion of his hips, he wasn't just kissing her. Others watched, touching their partners, or petting themselves. I closed my eyes, imagining the dream that played on repeat inside my head. The one where I wasn't the voyeur, but the one they watched. I opened my eyes and pushed the memory of it away. Anger shot through me, my pulse quickened, and I exhaled slowly as I calmed my body's response to it.

That music... Every beat was meant to draw you in, dull your senses, make you shed inhibition, and I wasn't so sure that it wasn't magic, or something else hidden in the salacious lyrics or tantric melody. I smoothed the skirt I wore, pushing it down to cover my bare legs as I turned to nod at Kat and Dexter, who waited for the elusive owner to exit the club.

We'd planned this to the smallest detail. There could be no mistakes here. I'd studied Blackstone for weeks now, watching him, learning every detail as possible about him. Nothing went unnoticed as I danced inside his club, catching his eye and holding it for what felt like hours at a time, and yet he never took the bait, never approached me. On those occasions where I would approach him, the moment I got close he would leave the area or the club, as if he couldn't stand the sight of me. It stung my pride, and bruised my ego more than it already was.

I hated that night after night, he filled my dreams with no explanation for why it was happening. All girls fantasize, but I'd used spells to stop mine, and nothing I did halted the dreams or erased the feel of him after the dream had passed. I knew the layout of the club, including the levels below the main floor, and yet I'd never been downstairs. I knew certain details about him that I shouldn't know unless I had been intimate with him. The challenge with discerning between fantasy and memory was I'd never been intimate with him—unless I had and he'd somehow taken those memories from me.

When I'd asked my grandmother to have the coven investigate him I explained what was happening to me, but she'd suggested that I take him for my breeding mate since his line was as old as ours. That hadn't helped me, and only served to frustrate me more. Nothing about him made sense, and she blithely dismissed my worries as if I was crushing on him. I didn't even like this guy; he was an egotistical control freak who waved money around and got what he wanted. I hated that she ignored my fears; as if I was crazy to even think what I was telling her could be true.

The crowd inched forward, and my heart quickened and beat painfully against my ribs. I looked up at the moon, judging the time before I withdrew a vial of sleeping sand I'd created to knock Lucian out. The sand was powerful, but considering how big he was, I'd brought extra, just in case I needed it. I placed a little of the loose sand in the pocket of my jacket and pulled out a small apothecary bottle of Siren's essence. I removed the lid, placed it against my lips and tipped it back, inhaling and taking it into my lungs.

The sounds of the crowd grew louder, an indication that the man of the hour was leaving the building. I watched him as he emerged from the doorway, ignoring those who called out to him. In the last few weeks of watching this man, I knew he always left here with one or several of those hulking men, who seemed to be some kind of bodyguards, or alone. He was hot enough that he could curl his finger and get any girl he wanted, and yet he never did. Everything about him was an enigma.

He was dressed in an elegant bespoke suit, immaculate as always. His long hair was jet-black, pushed away from his sharp features. His strong jawline was etched in marble, a perfect contrast to the hard, sinewy lines of his body. His wide shoulders spoke of raw power, and thick muscles bunched beneath the suit, doing little to hide the raw, masculine form that lay beneath it. Midnight blue eyes lifted to the full moon before he gave the parking lot a quick onceover before pushing his way through the throng of people as if they didn't exist.

Once he was far enough into the parking lot, I whispered his name, beckoning him to me with the lure of the Siren's essence that filled my lungs, making it impossible for him to ignore.

"Lucian," I purred, my voice all seduction, which carried to him on the gentle breeze. I watched as he paused, lifted those bedroom eyes and searched the wooded area bordering the parking lot where I waited. "Come to me."

He began to walk in my direction, but then his steps slowed as our eyes locked across the crowded parking lot. Once he'd reached a certain point, the engine of a van roared to life as Kat and Dexter prepared to block the view of the bouncer.

"Come to me," I said louder, watching over his shoulder as my words carried to a few people in the long line. Shit. "Lucian, I need you to come to me, now."

I released a sigh of relief as he started moving faster, and alternated my focus between him, the bouncers, and Kat and Dexter in the van that were moving towards us. Power sizzled over my body the closer he got to me, and my hand dipped into my pocket, pulling out the sleeping sand. Once the view was blocked by the van and he was close enough, I crossed the distance to him, lifted my hand, and blew the sand into his face. Shock registered across his face before his eyes narrowed, his body swayed, and he started going down.

I moved to catch him, which ended with me on my ass in the dirt with a hulking male cradled between my legs and his heavy head on my breasts. Heat unfurled through me as our bodies made contact and I pushed against him to get him off of me. Okay, perhaps this wasn't planned out as well as I thought it was. I heard the door of the old van protesting as Dexter opened it and hopped out.

"Damn, you move fast," he teased as he tried to lift the sleeping male. "Shit, he weighs a ton and a half," he grumbled as I struggled to get up.

I whispered a spell of weightlessness to help Dexter out and moved to the van, jumping inside as he approached. I laid out a blanket since the back of the van was dirty and covered in rust. Once Lucian was in, I covered him up, leaving his face exposed.

Once the van started moving, I stared down into his slumbering face. Thick black lashes dusted his cheeks and his hair, still perfectly in place somehow, shone in the moonlight that flooded through the windows. I checked his pulse and then lowered my mouth to his, brushing my lips against his as we left the parking lot and sped out onto the highway. Sparks ignited and I gasped as I lifted my hand and touched them where ours had just met.

"Are you molesting him?" Dexter laughed as Kat joined in.

"I'm making sure he's still breathing," I grumbled as a blush spread across my face. "Once we're on the backroad, stay right at the fork. It is only a few miles from there to the cabin; my car is there. You will need to switch out, and then use the decoy spell we practiced. It will buy us an alibi if this goes awry."

"I still don't feel right leaving you there with him alone. What if something goes wrong?" Kat asked as our eyes met in the rearview mirror. "You'll be alone with him, and no one will be there to help you."

"Yes, but tell me, Kat, what can you do to help me? Our magic is limited, the coven is weak, and if we pull on them for anything, we're fucked. No, you and Dexter will leave me there as we planned, because if anyone is going down for this, it will be me and me alone. Besides, what could possibly go wrong?"

"Everything, considering who we just kidnapped," she grouched as her eyes moved back to the road.

"Positive thinking, please," I mumbled as I stared at the man in question.

"I'm positive we're fucked if he gets away," she retorted.

I looked up to catch her eyes watching me, which unfortunately didn't allow me to brace myself as we hit something in the road that sent me sailing forward, forcing me to land atop Lucian. I groaned as I righted myself, regretting the choice of being the one in the back with him. He smelled like sin mixed with sex, with a generous dash of male sprinkled on top of it.

"Just stick to the plan—no deviating unless something happens. If you come back and I'm gone, get back in the car; leave and go home. Don't look for me, because if shit hits the fan, I'll meet you tomorrow as we planned. The diner would be the best place for you guys to go tonight, it shouldn't have a huge crowd even though it's Friday. They also won't hover, which is best since my doppelgänger will only be able to say a few things at most."

"Are we even sure it will sound like you?" Her eyebrows rose skeptically.

"Yes, it is a mirror image of me, but don't let it eat anything. It's not real, so if it orders, don't let it eat or drink, understand?" I peered through the windshield as the cabin came into view. I swallowed fear that crept in at the idea of being alone with this man, but I couldn't back out now—we were in too deep.

Once the van rolled to a stop, I glanced at Kat nervously as our eyes met briefly before I exited the van as Dexter once again struggled with the door. Once my feet hit the ground, my heart leapt to my throat. The cabin was dark, vacant, and staged for the spells I was going to use to draw the truth out of Lucian. I reached back into the van and withdrew my heavy pack as Dexter struggled awkwardly with Lucian's height and bulk as he tried to maneuver him. Luckily the spell of weightlessness was holding up, or I'd probably end up doing the spells right here.

Inside, I flicked my wrist and candles leapt to life, flooding the room with a warm glow and shadows as they swayed with the wind that entered with us. Rain started pelting the tin roof, and a clap of thunder rumbled in the distance.

"I need to remove his shirt before we lock him down," I commented as Dexter nodded and turned to look at me as he scratched the back of his neck. He wasn't a fan of this plan any more than Kat was, but neither of them were having my dreams. Dreams so real that, hours after they'd faded, I ached. Despite their misgivings about what I was about to do, they were here and helping me. Dexter sat Lucian down on the bed and held his heavy upper body up for me.

My hands trembled as I undid the buttons of his jacket and slipped it off his thickly muscled shoulders. I folded it and set it on the chair beside us as I went to work on the buttons of his crisp dress shirt. Once I'd pulled it away from his chest and down his shoulders, my breath caught in my throat. My eyes slid over his tattoos and paused on the piercing. I'd never seen him without a shirt, and yet I knew them as if my tongue had traced every one of them, every tiny detail of them, intimately.

I clasped my hands together to stop the trembling as Dexter lay Lucian down on the bed and snapped one end of a pair of handcuffs around each wrist before snapping the other end around the iron bars of the old bed. I frowned; the idea of being in the middle of a massive storm in an old decrepit cabin with Lucian and a bed was mildly disturbing.

"That's it; he's secure," Dexter said as he wiped his hands on his pants and turned to look at me. "You don't have to do this alone, Kendra."

"Yes, I do. I just kidnapped Lucian Blackstone, and if anything happened to either one of you because of it, I'd never forgive myself. Now go, I have about twenty minutes before the sand wears off, and I have to get the first spell ready," I said as I reached up and hugged Dexter tightly. "Keep Kat safe, and don't come back for at least two hours."

Once he was outside and the door was closed, I turned to look at the sleeping man. I scrubbed my hands down my face and shook my head.

"What the fuck did you do? This was a bad idea," I babbled nervously. I'd just kidnapped Lucian, and I was pretty sure he wasn't the kind of man who pressed charges; no, he'd carry out retribution himself. I was so screwed if this didn't work, or if I wasn't powerful enough to remove the memories of tonight from his mind.

I swallowed and turned to my bag, wondering what he'd do to me. Would he return the favor? Leave me somewhere no one could find me, maybe a spelled cabin deep in the Colville National Forest? Would he handcuff me to a bed and torture me? Probably.

Fan-fricking-tastic!

CHAPTER
two

She's whisky and hellfire, and there's nothing in-between.
~Lucian

I knelt in front of the stones that circled the cauldron, and reached into my bag, pulling out a pouch of glass vials. I dribbled a little of the liquid from each vial on alternating stones, then quickly sealed the rubber stoppers on the vials before pushing them, one by one, back into the bag. I lowered my head and whispered the words that would ignite the flames beneath the cauldron.

The room filled with magic as the rich scent of lavender and herbs boiled in the cauldron. It took seconds for it to reach a boiling point—one of the perks of having magic. I stood up, moving to the bed as I retrieved the other bag I'd left here last night. Inside, I had the gown I'd chosen for purity, washed and cleansed in a mix of lemongrass and flowers from the garden.

I kicked off my tennis shoes and pulled my dress up and over my head, exhaling as the soothing scents lingered and danced with my senses as I folded the dress and laid it next to Lucian's clothes. Unclasping my bra, I tossing it on to the chair, enjoying the freedom it offered. I hooked my thumbs through my panties and pulled the fabric down, stepping out of them. I pulled out the purity gown as my neck began tingling and I turned, still halfway bent over, to find midnight eyes watching me.

I stood up, turning to face him as I held the dress in front of me like a shield. My heart quickened, beating against my ribs as my nipples perked up and goosebumps spread across my flesh.

"Release me," he growled.

"No," I whispered through suddenly parched lips. "I can't do that," I amended as I struggled to sound halfway in charge, but failed.

"Fitzgerald, if you don't release me, I will destroy you," he snapped angrily, his eyes sliding down my body—and I wasn't so sure he meant 'destroy' as in kill me and leave my corpse in the woods for the wolves. "Uncuff me, now."

"I said no," I fumed. "You're not in charge, I am. I have control here." I crossed my arms over my chest before I remembered I wasn't even dressed for this argument, let alone prepared. "You shouldn't even be awake yet!"

"I am awake, and the longer you keep me cuffed, the angrier I'm going to get. I'm also going to guess you don't have the coven's permission or support in this plan of yours. Which means we're alone, and you have no one here to help you?"

I dropped my gaze to his naked chest with a guilty shrug. I turned, pulling the gown on over my head. It barely covered my ass, but it was the only white thing I owned. I tugged at it, trying to pull it down a little further before I turned back to face him. The gown was drenched in magic, and would only be on long enough to protect me from dark magic that might be released at the beginning of the spell that I intended to cast.

"Don't worry; you'll be free soon enough. I have no intention of harming you," I said softly as I moved closer until I was near enough to run my hands down his chest as they itched to do. I met his stare and smirked, leaning in a little closer so that I could appear to have control. "Scared?" I laughed.

"No, but you should be," he growled and suddenly, magic filled the room, thick and powerful, and I felt strong hands grab my arms before I was pulled to him.

I didn't have time to react; one minute I was beside the bed and the next, my body slammed against his and I cried out as my face was smashed against his heated body. A strong arm wrapped around me while a hand gripped my hair and yanked my head back, forcing me to look into those devilish midnight depths. Panicked, I looked up at his wrists, which were still secured in the handcuffs that strained against the iron bars of the bedstead.

"Un-fucking-cuff me," he demanded. His mouth

was inches from mine, and I couldn't stop myself from running my tongue over my lips with hungry anticipation.

"No," I whimpered huskily, wondering if the Siren's essence had yet to leave my system.

"Release me." He smirked and the grip on my hair tightened as his mouth lowered as if he intended to kiss me. "Even handcuffed, I can still kill you, Fitzgerald," he warned. "I'm in control, and right now, we're alone in a cabin, with one of us ill-equipped to handle the situation— and it isn't me."

"And what would you do? Kill me?" I snapped.

"There are plenty of other things I can do to you," he rumbled as he watched me squirm.

I smirked and jabbed him sharply in the stomach before throwing myself backwards, landing on my backside on the floor, legs spread apart for balance as I grabbed and held my head, which I'd just knocked against the hardwood floor of the cabin.

It took moments to even be able to see past the stars dancing in my vision, and when they cleared, thunder exploded directly above us, shaking the little cabin. The wind howled violently as rain pelted the tin roof relentlessly, and I lifted my head to find Lucian hungrily looking between my legs at my naked sex. Instead of covering myself, I smirked. Asshole wasn't immune! I almost wanted to do a happy dance, *almost*.

"Nice try, asshole," I growled as I rolled to my side and stood up. I moved around him, rubbing my head as I watched him. I stared at the handcuffs, wondering how the hell I'd prevent him from casting again, since he shouldn't have been able to in the first place. I whispered a spell, which would hopefully strengthen the chain of the handcuffs. "You're not getting out of here until I get what I want from you."

"What exactly do you want from me?" he gritted out angrily as he watched me with a coldness that sent a shiver running down my back.

"What do I want from you?" I scoffed. "Let's start with the disturbing thought that I know if I kissed those lips, you'd taste like aged scotch with a hint of citrus; or that I dream of you every single night, but it doesn't end when the dawn comes. Instead, I spend hours trying to remove the feel of you from my body. Let's start there."

"Just because you're fantasizing about fucking me doesn't give you the right to do this, Witch."

"Fantasies?" I almost screamed. "Fantasies are dreams of sex you *like*! I don't do that, I have the same dreams that replay in my head night after fucking night!" I scrubbed my hands over my face as I moved closer to him. "This is the kind of sex I've never thought of, even in my wildest imaginings! You hurt me, and I *like* it! You spread my legs in front of strangers and let them watch us, watch me as I come apart in your arms. I can feel you when I wake up, how you stretched my body, how it hurt—and yet you somehow made it so much more than that, didn't you? You would make me wild with need, so wild that I would let you do anything to me, just to please you. But something happens, and then hurt and anger take over. I wake up broken, as if it actually happened. If it changed, or varied at all, I'd call it a dream, but never a fantasy—it's more of a nightmare. I don't like pain, no one does. In my dreams, I relish it, but only from you.

"I think it's a memory, that somehow you did something to me and erased whatever happened from my mind. Either it's a memory, or you've been with Lena and I felt it or shared it through her. One of those two scenarios has to be right, because I've used magic to block the dreams from my mind, to keep you out of my head while I sleep. The dreams actually got stronger after that, as if by trying to keep them at bay, I let something else in. Add that to the fact that there's a ton of pictures in my bedroom that I have no memory of ever taking. Which means I have a big chunk of missing time," I explained as I tapped my head. "Now, there's no one in our coven strong enough or powerful enough to have achieved a mind wipe but me, and I didn't erase my own memories."

"There are ways to go about getting answers, but this isn't one of them. I can tell you how this way ends," he growled thickly.

"And how's that?" I moved closer, as if I was drawn in by his seductive mouth.

"You lose," he replied confidently.

"Even if I lose, it doesn't really matter, does it?" I laughed hollowly. "Either I get my answers and I'm not crazy, or I don't and I go to the coven and ask them to strip my powers. Because as powerful as I am, being crazy would make me a danger to others," I admitted hesitantly.

"You would ask them to strip your powers. You would allow that to happen?" he asked cautiously.

"If I am crazy, or I can no longer discern what's happening to me, then yes. I'd ask them to protect the coven, even at the cost of my powers. I'm not a saint, but I don't plan to be a killer either, and with how much power runs through me, I could potentially destroy the coven. Dark witches are deadly witches."

He didn't look away, but he didn't offer up any explanation as to what I was going through. Instead, he looked at me with pity. I chewed my lip as I watched him.

"I guess we'll be doing this the hard way, then?" I murmured as I turned to the grimoire, a bowl full of black ink, and a spoon that waited for me near the cauldron. "You won't keep your secrets for long, Blackstone."

"That's what you think, but your spells will not work on me," he smirked.

I spun around, marched towards him, and before I could stop myself, I'd slapped him. I blinked, looked down at my hand and then up at him. I'd never hurt anyone before, and yet something about him got beneath my skin, festered, and wouldn't let go. My breasts rose and fell with my anger as his face slowly moved back to meet my angry eyes.

"You're going to regret that," he whispered huskily, his eyes liquid depths of black-blue fire.

"I doubt I'll ever regret removing that smug grin from your face, even if only for a second. Now shush, I need to concentrate."

I turned, smiling as I made my way to the grimoire once more. I knelt beside it and picked up the spoon, then stirred the ink in the bowl with it before I scooped up some of the ink and examined the dark, oily substance as it dripped back into the bowl. Chanting a soft spell from the grimoire, I stirred the ink several more times; clockwise, then counterclockwise as I chanted. Leaving the spoon in the spelled ink, I cradled my hands around the bottom of the bowl, rose, and moved to the small table across the room.

I watched the candles flicker as the cracks in the cabin allowed the air to rush through them as the wind continued to scream outside. Like most spells, this one called for me to be bared to Hecate, exposed so that he, too, would be exposed and forced to whisper truths, unable to lie.

I set the bowl on the table and reached down to the hem of my gown. I chewed my lip nervously as I raised the purity gown over my head and tossed it to the floor, feeling its magic as I whispered the spell to hold its magic to me. I heard his hiss and forced myself not to react. I scooped up the bowl and dipped my fingers into it as I moved back to him and tried not to shrink under his furious glare.

"You could make this easier on both of us," I offered as I held my hand out, threatening him with the ink. "Or I can make you powerless to answer me. I know a man like you isn't used to being powerless, but maybe it will be good for you." I waited and pursed my lips as he watched me through cold, angry eyes.

"If you curse me, there will be no one who can save you from my wrath," he warned.

"Is that so?" I mused, pushing my fingers against his chest as I drew the runes onto his shoulders, across his chest and abdomen. I stepped closer, drawn by the contact, and with my free hand, I began working at the button of his slacks. "I have to remove your pants, so be a good boy and hold still, hmm?" I bent down and set the ink bowl aside, expecting him to fight me; instead, he didn't move. I pulled his pants down and realized my mistake as I looked at what his pants had concealed. I swallowed as I looked up and saw his eyes filled with an emotion I couldn't put my finger on, and then I stifled a groan as I closed my eyes, even though he laughed at me for it.

Who had a beautiful cock? Cocks simply were not beautiful, and yet, his was thick, long, and perfect. I shook my head to dispel that thought and then realized I hadn't removed his shoes yet. As I bent my head down to look at his feet, my cheek rubbed over his cock, and I bolted backwards.

"It's just a dick, Fitzgerald," he mused thickly. I lifted my eyes and blushed from my roots as I realized the object of our discussion was growing!

"Stop that! Stop it," I shrieked, covering my eyes as I pointed at it. "Put it away!"

"Free my hands and I will," he growled, and I frowned even deeper.

"It doesn't need to be growing for this, that's uncalled

for."

"A pretty girl just rubbed her cheek over it," he replied easily. "It doesn't give a fuck about propriety."

I dropped my hand and bit my lip as I turned, looking anywhere but at his cock. I moved closer as my heart raced, my mouth watered, and my throat longed to be filled. I really sucked at kidnapping, and worse, being naked with *him*! Everything that had ever played out in my head decided to become one big porno in that moment, which was the worst thing I could be thinking of right now. My sex heated and my body tightened with unsated need, a need he could easily satisfy.

I lowered myself, refusing to acknowledge his cock as it bobbed a firm *hello* like a happy puppy. I unlaced his shoes and tried to pull them off, but he wouldn't meet me halfway. I backed up, looked at him, and shook my head.

"The book says we have to be naked—together."

"Ask me if I care, little girl," he returned thickly, as if he'd eaten the gravel from outside and it had become lodged in his throat. "This is a dangerous situation you have us in, one I didn't ask to participate in. You're naked, I'm hard. You also suck at kidnapping, but I bet you suck dick a lot better."

"You're an asshole," I snapped, spinning around to retrieve the ink before moving away from him. I dipped my fingers into the warm mixture, brought them up, and painted the matching runes to Lucian's on my body. I tried to ignore his glares and focused on the spell, chanting as I painted my waist and my arms.

I was so engrossed with what I was doing that time held no meaning. I smirked once the last rune was placed and turned around, only to come face to face with a wide, tattooed chest.

I looked up into midnight eyes and screamed.

CHAPTER three

I fucking bit it, so it's mine. ~**Lucian**

Hands wrapped around my throat as I was picked up and pushed against the wall, hard. My head hit, bouncing against it as lights exploded in my vision. How the fuck did he get free? My hands scrabbled against his, scratching his hands as I struggled to get free, but he held me in place as his body pressed against mine.

"Is this what you wanted from me?" he demanded as his mouth lowered to touch against my cheek, his breath fanning my face as he dropped his mouth to mine. Stars exploded behind my eyes, and I scratched him, raking my nails down his sides as I battled to breathe. Tears streamed down my face as I struggled harder, fighting for my life. My lungs burned, and the noises coming from me weren't right. My hands dropped, and my head rolled to the side as blackness threatened to claim me. His mouth brushed against mine, his tongue pushed past my lips, and his hands loosened from my throat as he fed me air. He was feeding me air, his mouth my salvation. I cried out against it, claiming his tongue as I gulped his air greedily into my starved lungs.

He pulled away with a dark, dangerous look dancing in his eyes. "Who has control now?" he taunted huskily as he lowered his nose and rubbed it against my cheek.

I didn't answer him; I wouldn't give him that satisfaction. Plus, it was hard to manage it with the sweet, seductive taste of aged scotch and that fucking hint of citrus filling my senses. I wanted to scratch the look of victory from his face. It was dancing in the endless inky depths of his eyes as he watched me continue to gasp for air.

His smirk deepened, turning as twisted as he was. Lucian grabbed a handful of my hair and pulled my naked body against his. I didn't struggle, I couldn't. I was still trying to figure out how he'd gotten free from the spelled handcuffs and how I'd known what he would taste like. He'd gotten free, his shoes were tilted drunkenly against each other on the floor, and I hadn't heard anything, not a single noise as I painted my flesh.

He lowered his mouth as he jerked my head back, forcing me to lift my mouth to meet his. Right when I thought he'd kiss me again, he threw me onto the floor, roughly. I gasped as I went down, the dull thud of my hands hitting hard echoing through the room as I gasped. He'd knocked the wind out of me, and tears burned my eyes as pain assaulted me.

"I told you that I would win," he growled as he slowly moved towards me. I struggled to wriggle away from him, mimicking a worm crawling atop the soil after a hard rain. "You should have stayed away from me."

"Fuck you," I whispered breathlessly. I screamed as he caught my legs, and I kicked out to escape him. He flipped me over, maintaining his hold on my ankles as he knelt between my legs, not even bothering to hide the lust sparkling in his eyes.

"It turns you on, doesn't it? Not knowing if I plan to fuck you or hurt you?" His voice rumbled through me and straight to my sex as his hand released one ankle to trace his fingers through my folds. He hissed as he found it wet, ready, and turned on by the struggles. I hated myself right now more than I ever had before. What was wrong with me? "So fucking wet for me, aren't you, sweet girl? You want me so bad you're shivering with it, that primal need to spread wide so I can feed you every single inch of me…" The noise he made was animalistic. The tips of his fingers dipped inside and I moaned hungrily for more.

"I hate you," I whimpered as my lips trembled from the adrenaline coursing through me. I hated that he was right, that I was trembling for him, that I couldn't even hide how much I wanted him right now.

"You say that a lot. No, you hate that you don't know why you want me. You hate that you can't control the cravings. Your body knows the truth: it craves what it needs. You like everything perfect, and you need everything to make sense, and that isn't how this world works. You think you're crazy, but what I see? Is a beautiful fucking mess, one that doesn't need her powers bound, because you are not dangerous. Shit, you can't even manage to kidnap one man," he growled as his fingers continued to stroke my skin. He leaned over as if he planned to kiss me, and I smirked as he lowered his mouth. "Next time, I won't let you off with a warning, Witch."

I felt around blindly until I touched a large piece of wood I'd reached for and my fingers closed around it desperately. I brought it up and hit him with more strength than I'd thought I had, considering the awkward angle. The sound echoed around the room and his body went slack. I wriggled out from under him and started to move towards the door, only for his hand to grasp my ankle and pull, knocking me down again. I turned, kicking him in the face and chest as I fought to get my foot freed from his viselike grip.

Angry tears of frustration erupted from my eyes and I screamed with fear as he used my legs to pull me beneath him, trapping me with his massive body. His cock slid over my belly and my eyes bulged as blood dripped from his temple.

"You shouldn't have fucking done that," he snarled. Anger pulsed inside the cabin, mirroring the storm outside. He watched me as I realized just how fucked I was. A sob exploded from me as he smirked, and deadly anticipation shone in his obsidian eyes, mirroring the chaos in the room. His hands captured mine as he pushed them above my head, easily securing them there. My muscles protested as he parted my legs, leaving me open, exposed. I couldn't fight him; I didn't have use of any of my extremities in this position and he knew it. "It was hard enough to walk away from you before you hit me, but now? Now we do it my way, little one," he whispered as he lowered his mouth to my nipple and bit it. I screamed as pain ripped through me, but even as he bit the delicate flesh, he released it, rubbing his tongue over it, soothing the pain. The scream turned into a moan, and my head dropped back, hitting the floor. Pleasure flooded through my system, unfurling the coil that had been building in my stomach. My legs wrapped around him and I closed my eyes against the sensual assault.

His hands released mine as I found his hair, grabbed fistfuls of it, and held him to me as I succumbed to his dark pleasure. My hips rocked as his hand slid between us, finding my apex and sliding through it. Every time, every slow, leisurely pass through my willing pussy, he stopped and worked a circle on my clitoris until I almost reached the precipice he held me on the edge of.

"Bloody hell, you're making it very hard to stay away," he growled as he lowered his mouth to mine, and I claimed it, welcoming it as I continued holding on to his hair. I clung to him like I was drowning in a vast sea, lost adrift in the turbulent waves that crashed down onto me, and he was the buoy I clung on to in order to survive. The noise that tore from his throat was inhuman, and the way he kissed me changed, turning as dark as my soul. "Does it make you wet, knowing I could do anything I want to you right now? Is that why this pretty pussy is drenched?" he growled.

Lucian Blackstone was a hurricane, and I was the land he intended to destroy. He was a category five, creating and wreaking havoc, knocking down defenses as he obliterated me. He ripped me apart, tore me down to my basic animal instincts, and there was no knowing how much damage would be left when he was finished. The worst part was that I wasn't sure I wanted to survive this storm. Some storms were worth dying for just to be witness to them.

He ended the kiss, his mouth still hovering inches from mine. I released one hand from his hair and swung it out, intending to slap him, but he caught it. He pushed it against the floor painfully. I moaned as he stopped his fingers' slow discovery of my body and snatched my other hand from his hair, where I'd held on to him for support.

"I hate you so much," I whispered, because right now, I did. I hated him for what he made me want, what I craved from him. This was wrong; we were wrong to want this. Everything I'd ever been taught said so, so how could I want this, how could I want him?

"No, you don't," he whispered softly. "You don't hate me any more than I could hate you." He laughed mirthlessly, the sound vibrating through our bodies due to our proximity. His mouth lowered as if he intended to claim mine again, but his eyes watched me, staring into me as if he could see inside my little black soul right down to the *very* fucked up fiber of my being. His teeth worried my lip, and I moaned at the slight pain, my eyes growing heavy as he nipped at my lip, already swollen from his demanding kisses. I whimpered from the pain as he sucked it between his lips and ran his tongue over the sore flesh. I moaned, feeling the pain and pleasure to the very center of my core, red hot lust coursing through me. He released my hands, and I raked my nails down his sides, smirking against the satisfying grunt of pain. "You want to play rough?" he rasped, and the sound of his hoarse words made my eyes open, but it wasn't midnight eyes I found waiting for me; they were filled with liquid blue fire.

"Lucian," I whispered as I took in the smile that was more teeth than anything, and the fire I saw in his eyes reminded me of the ancient stories of the blue flames that lit the Gates of Hell.

He kissed my throat as his body rubbed eagerly against mine. His cock rested heavily against my stomach. I moaned as his heated kiss trailed to my shoulder. He moved his hips, adjusting his position until I gasped as his heavy cock slid through the slick heat of my pussy. I writhed against it, using it. I wrapped my legs around his waist, holding him there as I rubbed my naked heat against the thick cock he so freely offered. His mouth continued to suck on my skin, his teeth scraping, nipping before he kissed it.

He rocked his hips, feeding my need and hitting my clitoris until I was screaming his name as the orgasm threatened to rip me asunder, but every time I got close enough, he shifted and pulled his cock away. I didn't care that I was coming undone, or that I was screaming for him to enter me, to take me, to fucking own me. I wanted him in the most primitive way; a way that bares the soul, exposing the darkest needs in your lowest hour. Nothing mattered anymore except getting him to give me what I needed—and now.

Lucian leaned down, as if he intended to kiss me;

instead his mouth touched my shoulder and his teeth clamped down. He bit into my shoulder and all thoughts of coming were gone, just like that. Pain erupted, and I screamed, bucking against him to get away. Then it hit me, and I screamed his name like it was a fucking benediction. It was brutal, coming so fucking hard that I shook uncontrollably as I shattered. I came so hard that when I started to fall back to earth, I realized I had his shoulder between my teeth and it was bleeding, dripping down my chin, and I didn't care because that orgasm hadn't abated as I had thought; it refused to release me. I was literally vibrating so much that his hands cradled my head as it hit the ground with each violent tremor that tore through me. I actually feared that it wouldn't ever end, and I didn't know if I necessarily fucking cared if it did. I was so fucking wet that the only noise inside the cabin was me, screaming as it started to recede. Lights continued to explode behind my eyelids. I wasn't sure if I was dying, coming, or breaking into a million tiny pieces. His sexy as fuck, husky timbre sounded far away as he watched me try to bring myself back from wherever the fuck he'd just sent me to. Hell? Heaven? Who cared, I wanted more. Now.

"That's my good girl," he whispered as he watched me. The moment I thought I was safe, pain ripped through me as he entered my body. I gasped as he buried his cock in my tight sheath, muscles burning and clamping against him. "Tell me you hate me as I make you take every inch of my cock deep inside your tight pussy, owning every sweet inch of you inside and out," he growled.

"Lucian," I whimpered brokenly, unable to protest or

do anything more than hold on to him. "It aches." I was too full, too fast. My body burned where muscles fought to accommodate him, and failed.

"Tell me to stop," he demanded. "I don't do gentle. Are you sure you want to play with me? Because right now, the only thing I want is to ruin you. I want to bury my cock so deep that you always feel it there. You'll feel me there, forever. If that's not what you want from me, tell me to stop now."

"Don't stop," I whispered as I shook my head, which was still cradled in his large hands. He moved them then, grabbing my shoulders as he leaned up and stared down at me. I waited for him to move, wiggling my hips to take anything he was willing to give me.

"I'm going to destroy everything you love while you watch me do it," he hissed as his eyes lit from within. "I'm going to destroy everything you cherish, and then I'm going to fucking destroy you, Lena. You should hate me; right now, you should run from me," he whispered as he watched me.

Lena...

Pain erupted inside my head and tears rolled from my eyes as I blinked past the pain. *Lena.* My breathing grew labored as he watched me coldly. *Lena.* Demons seemed to be watching me from the hellish depths of his eyes. *Magdalena.* My body trembled as he watched me, and his hips started moving slowly, building up speed as I pushed him away, trying to grasp on to that one name, the one I should know. *My name.*

"You son of a bitch!" I scratched him, lifting up, only to be slammed against the floor and weighted down.

"There you are," he purred as he kissed me, and God save me, I kissed him back. My hands pulled at his hair as his hips slammed against me. I held him to me. "Just a few minutes, I just needed a few minutes with you," he murmured, and I watched him.

"No, not again, no... Lucian, please don't do that to me."

"Who are you?" he demanded.

"I'm Lena," I whimpered.

"Who the fuck *are* you?" he growled, and his hands bit into my skin.

"Yours, I'm yours!" I screamed.

"Damn fucking right, you're mine. It's too bad you won't remember this, but I will," he assured me. "Every fucking moment of your sweet ruin, I will relive this a thousand times a day when you are dead and gone from this earth, and long after your last offspring have perished. You have to come back to me on your own, do you understand me?" he demanded, and I stared up at him, not understanding his words as he brought me over the edge of the cliff and sent me sailing into the clouds as a kaleidoscope of colors burst behind my eyes. "You are Kendra..."

"I'm Kendra," I whispered through a moan.

"I miss you, Witch," he growled, something hitching in his tone. He leaned down, claiming my lips and deepening the kiss; a kiss that ruined me more than anything he'd done so far, because I felt it. I felt him. The emotion in his kiss was more than he'd ever allowed me to feel before, as if he was kissing me hello and goodbye all in one kiss. It ended too soon, and I sobbed from the loss of it.

"I hate you," I replied icily as he started moving faster, until my body couldn't keep up. I was going to be sore tomorrow. I opened my eyes to find blue fire staring back into mine; it burned so bright that it hurt to stare into it for too long. I felt the heat from it as he lowered his forehead and rested it against mine, staring into my soul. He was showing me what he was, the monster within, the monster I was sleeping with. His lips curled into a dangerous smile, and I shivered, trembling with the knowledge that he was anything but what he claimed to be. He wanted me to see him, all of him.

"You're so beautiful," he growled, sucking my lip between his teeth. I mumbled, coming around his cock, unable to stop myself from shattering as he stiffened and howled his release to the heavens. Power erupted around us as he peered down at me with blue fire dancing seductively in his eyes. The earth trembled around us as we exploded, and I didn't look away from what I saw, not even as the cabin began to shake with the force of our mutual release.

It started to come apart, and he shielded me. This man who had torn me to pieces, shown me pain and pleasure, was protecting me as the cabin literally crumbled around us. His mouth claimed mine, oblivious to the splintering wood that was raining down on us.

"Lucian," I whimpered as everything around us continued to shatter, and trees exploded and fell to the ground as I held on to him. "Don't leave me."

"You won't remember this in a few minutes," he said softly as he closed off his emotions and we lay in the remains of the cabin in the woods where it had been built; now, it all looked as if an asteroid had demolished it. "You got your questions answered, and then you let me go after wiping my mind," he whispered forcefully, his voice layered, booming against my mind and echoing through it. "You still hate me, because I kind of enjoy this love-hate shit we have going on. But you are Kendra, so say it."

"I'm Kendra," I parroted.

I stared up at him through the darkness of the ruins. My vision swam with tears, my arms dropped, and I lay there, empty and cold, exactly how I felt inside.

"Look at me," he demanded, watching me carefully. "Are you happy?"

"Am I happy?" I questioned. It was an odd thing to ask considering what had just happened. "Something is wrong with me," I whispered brokenly. "Something has to be wrong with me, right?" Fear entered my mind, refusing to release its icy claws. "I'm not right, nothing about this is right. I'm not like this. This was so wrong, how can I like it? My body already craves your touch and we're still connected," I babbled as I turned to look away.

"And I don't even like you!" I sobbed as my body rocked beneath his. "I'm insane. I don't even know what's real and what isn't anymore. Everything is wrong, and I can't stop it. I can't remember if I did something, and everyone else can remember it. My clothes don't even fit anymore, and I don't even *like* them. Whatever grasp I had on reality is gone. I don't even remember being with anyone inside the abbey at the Harvest and yet I pretend I knew who I was sleeping with, but the only thing I can remember when I spell myself, is you. That's crazy. I have to be losing it, right?"

"You're not crazy, you're fucking perfect," he mumbled, raining kisses on my face as he captured it between his hands as I tried to pull away. "Look at me. Listen to me; what we did here? It wasn't wrong, it was beautiful. Does it feel as if I don't already crave you again?" He rolled his hips to be sure I hadn't missed his cock buried in my warmth still. "So what if we fuck like we are going to war; no one else has to like it or understand it. No one else matters but us. What we did, fuck, we do it well together. Someday you'll remember everything. You'll remember us, and you'll know what happens when you try to contain chemistry like ours."

"We blow up cabins?" I asked in a deadpan voice.

"Fuck that cabin, it couldn't contain us." He smiled, but there was something in his eyes—sadness? "When you remember everything, you'll hate me, sweet girl, but I won't care. Because, again, I kind of like it when you don't like me," he whispered.

My breath hitched as a tear rolled down my cheek. "I

don't understand."

"Are you happy?" he asked again, and I blinked.

"You're seriously asking me if I'm happy." I blinked again. "Like right now?" My eyes focused on his throat as he swallowed hard. "I'm naked in the woods with a man I don't even like. We just destroyed a cabin that didn't even belong to us to destroy and you're still *inside* me. I tried to kidnap you and you *let* me! You have runes on your crazy ass *eight pack* that must prevent anything like that from happening. You weren't really unconscious, were you? Which means I am the world's biggest idiot right now, and I seriously feel stupid," I huffed. "We went to war with our bodies, and I mean, not the good kind. I don't even like pain and yet I already crave more from you. I'm pretty sure I just had the biggest, most earthshattering, cataclysmic orgasm of my entire life because you fucking bit me! Who does that? Who comes apart because some guy they hate bit the shit out of them? I'll tell you who: crazy people! Normal people don't do shit like this! I can't get you out of my head.

"I mean, I cast spells to eradicate whatever the fuck I was seeing, but the moment I close my eyes, you're there again, waiting for me! I can smell you, I can feel you and I crave you. Yet this is the first time we've ever touched! The only plausible explanation is I am insane. I have to be, because even now I want you and again, I fucking hate you! So get the fuck off of me, get your dick *out* of me, and leave me the fuck alone!" I snapped, fighting to get away from him. "Stay out of my head! Stay away from me, please," I sobbed.

"You're perfect, you've always been perfect, sweet girl," he crooned, his voice deepening. "We didn't fuck, I never got loose, and you got what you wanted from me. When you wake up, *Kendra*, you will think everything went exactly as you wanted it to. You will not ask the coven to bind your powers, because you're anything but crazy."

"That makes no sense," I mumbled sluggishly; his words were like a drug and my brain absorbed them greedily.

"Sleep. When you wake up, everything will be okay," he promised, and I blinked as my eyes grew heavy. I was exhausted; mentally, physically, completely fucking wrecked.

CHAPTER
four

Alpha females don't need a pack, we choose to have one.
Even the strongest of wolves have weak moments. ~Lena

I stared blankly out the window at the old manor across the field from our house, which used to be empty. Several moving trucks had been parked in front of it, and had been blocking our driveway all day. A week had passed since I'd kidnapped Lucian, and he'd left town the day after. No one knew where he'd gone or what he was doing, but he still managed to drive me crazy. Then I found out he'd bought the old place, meaning he'd be right next door now.

"You stare any harder at it, and it might just catch fire," Kat offered. She was dressed up, ready to head out to Club Chaos.

Pulling my eyes away from the mansion, I gave her a tight smile. "Heading to the club?" I already knew the answer.

"You should come with us; the shipment can wait until tomorrow, couldn't it?" she questioned.

"No, Mom told me that Lucian ordered it for this weekend, so it needs to be filled by Thursday at the latest, and we can't afford to lose his business. The economy is crap, and he is the one keeping us afloat," I muttered, hating that I was defending him. But it was true; since the explosion at the abbey, everything had hit a downward spiral. The tourists who came to the shop were being sent to us by him or by word of mouth from those at his club who had sampled our potions, soaps, lotions, or tea mixtures.

"So you're going to bail on us, again," she complained. "You could just make samples and ask him if you could hand them out on the weekend outside his club. That way you could go inside once they're gone, and I'd have someone other than Dexter to dance with. Love him, but he has two left feet and resembles a fish flopping out of water when he dances."

"I will go with you next time, promise." I gave her a small smile as I turned back to watch yet another truck pull up to the manor. "You know there is always such a thing as *not* dancing and saving your feet that way," I said, laughing as she scrunched her nose up.

"I like him, a lot. My parents, on the other hand, think our line needs a stronger bloodline mixed with it," she frowned.

"You think you have bloodline problems? My grandmother keeps pushing me to approach Blackstone to procreate. Could you imagine? Me and Lucian making a baby," I mused softly, but my body heated, and my cheeks flushed with heat involuntarily as I considered it. "They should trust us to find a match without meddling."

"There's another ball being held. Pretty sure this one is going to be at his club sometime next week," she said excitedly, ignoring me. Or so I thought, until I glimpsed the speculative look in her eyes. "You could approach him, then, ya know, he watches you when you're not looking. And I hate to say it, but you guys would make a very powerful line."

"He has a tendency to run away when I get near him, and you're also forgetting that I don't like him, and I'd have to have sex with him to make a child. I don't think he'd be happy to just donate to the cause—oh, and not to mention, he's refused all offers from every family who has placed a request for his swimmers."

"Semen. Say it with me, s-e-m-e-n," she spelled it out slowly. "Come. Protein-filled frosting, which, considering how he looks, probably tastes like heaven." She snorted with laughter.

"That's disgusting." I cringed and shook my head. "No wonder your last guy can't get over you. What did you do to him, you dirty, dirty girl?" I laughed, smiling until my eyes hurt and my stomach ached from it. "We're horrible creatures, you know. We shop for men to use based solely on their blood and power. Almost like shopping for a sugar daddy, based on his bank account."

"And? Men know what we want from them, it's not

like we're hiding the fact that we want their semen and that's it. Yes, we sometimes keep the men around if we like them, but it's not new. We've been doing this forever, and those we choose from know the rules. And you changed the subject; I know you don't like him, but I'm guessing Mister Owns-A-Genuine-Sex-Club knows how to fuck. So, it's not like it would be a horrible time, and don't tell me you two don't have a 'wow' factor going on—you do. I've seen you looking at him and I see the way he watches you. One night, no strings, and wham! Happy grandma and maybe the most powerful child this coven has ever had cooking in the oven. Everyone is happy. It's not like you'd have to marry him, and you know it."

"You're missing the point. He doesn't want to breed, and I don't want to breed with him—end of discussion."

"The ball, it's a setup, Kendra," she pressed. "There's a reason it's being held at his club, and that reason is because he hasn't been to any of the ones held in the last three weeks, and neither have you. This one is mandatory attendance, to celebrate the solar eclipse happening on the same day that Venus and Mars will be aligned," she hinted.

"Are you serious?" I asked as I slipped into my jacket and turned to glare out the window one last time. "I mean, I knew we'd be doing something for the event since they don't happen very often, but setting me up is a little asshole-ish, even for them," I groaned as I pulled my hair out of the jacket and tied it up into a messy heap atop my head.

"Just think about it? You'd be the most popular witch

in the coven if you land him," she said with a note of hopefulness in her tone.

"I'll see you later," I replied, giving her another tight-lipped smile as I started towards the door. "Kat, be careful at the club. I still don't trust him or his crew. Plus, there's still the demon infestation, which seems to get worse when he leaves."

"I will; we're always ready for the demons," she said, blowing a raspberry at me as she headed out. "Go be the mad scientist and make those love potions." Her voice floated back through the hall as the sound of her footsteps quieted as she moved down the staircase.

I slung my backpack on my shoulder, grabbed my cell phone, and headed downstairs, only to pause as the sound of laughter and music tickled my eardrums. I set my stuff down on the couch and moved towards the kitchen, finding Alden and my mother dancing to the high-pitched, nasal sounds of Bob Dylan. I leaned against the doorjamb, smiling as he clumsily moved her to the beat of the drums and harmonica.

She was laughing so much, her eyes sparkled with it. I hadn't seen her happy in a very long time. Not since we were all together, before Joshua had gone off to boot camp. I should have turned away, leaving them to their happiness, but I wanted this moment, this moment in time to see her smiling, to hear her laughter.

"The girls left," Alden murmured close to her ear, a husky note in his tone that indicated it was time for me to get lost. "I don't know what I want to nibble on more, you or that lamb in the oven."

I turned to leave and cringed as my mother answered.

"Grab the wine, screw the lamb, let it burn. I will let you nibble on me wherever you want… Kendra!" she screeched.

I scrunched up my face as I turned back, my silent retreat noticed. I tilted my head, smiled, and wiggled my fingers in a silent wave.

"We thought you left," she shrilled with a guilty flush that rose to her cheeks, creating a mottled blush. "We heard the door."

"Kat left to go to Club Chaos. I have to go to the shop tonight to make sure the shipment for Lucian's club is ready to be picked up on time." I awkwardly waited for her to dismiss me. They looked like naughty kids caught pilfering from the cookie jar, which was cute in a nauseating way.

"Can't it wait? You should be out there with her, at the club. You're not getting any younger, and rumor has it that Lucian is there tonight," she chided.

"Rumor also has it that you're setting me up with him," I shot back, watching her guilty blush deepen and spread. "Don't do that for me, please. I'm not interested."

"It's a good match; his blood is as old as ours, if not older, Kendra. Your pregnancy test came back negative when the coven cast the sands for you. You have to produce a child soon, you know that. Magdalena is gone and Joshua is dead, so you are the only one who can carry on this line now."

"I know, Mother, I'm aware of my obligations and I am looking into matches, but not with him. I don't like him, and you know it."

She frowned. "You don't have to like him to do what is needed to produce a child. At least consider it, for me?"

"Fine, but don't get your hopes up. Besides, she may come back eventually," I mumbled.

"Who," she questioned softly.

"Your other daughter," I replied sharply with a tight frown.

"You're right, but her powers wouldn't be awakened for a few years, and the coven needs numbers added to it now, magical ones who will eventually receive powers around the same time. Think about it, you will love motherhood." She smiled, her hands wringing the soft folds of her skirt as I nodded—and a flash of mischievous inspiration struck me.

"You know, I'm really not the last in the bloodline that can carry on the line. I mean, you two might pop a little bun in the magical oven if you are up to what I think you are up to," I teased. Alden looked at me sharply and my mother turned about fifteen shades of red. Oh, yeah. Getting a little payback of my own felt pretty good. "Okay, you two crazy kids be good. I won't be home until morning. Lucian ordered enough potions to keep me busy for a week," I grumbled, even though I was thankful. It gave me an excuse to hide. "Love you." I turned towards the living room to retrieve my bag.

"Kendra," Alden called out as I reached for the door.

"Yeah?" I asked, turning to look at him.

"Be careful tonight; the demons are out thicker than they've been in a while. I placed a salt circle around the shop earlier today and added some wards to keep you and your mother safe while you work, but it doesn't guarantee they won't be able to get inside. These ones are stronger than most demons; something is fueling their power—something or someone."

"I'm always careful, Alden. And thank you. She hasn't laughed like that in a long time—but if you hurt her? I'll rip your heart out and feed it to the cats."

CHAPTER
five

Sometimes nightmares become a reality, and sometimes, monsters become heroes. ~**Lena**

I pulled into the empty parking lot of Midnight Emporium a little before nine. We'd picked the new name when we created the branding for the relaunch. Mom and Alden had come up with the idea to add a café that had outside seating, which had bumped the profit margin up. We sold mostly herbal teas that we made to order, or some of the baked goods that my mom and grandmother made on-site in the new kitchen.

It was a typical tourist store in the front, with baubles and whatnots that lined the windows, grabbing tourists' curiosity. The front consisted of non-magical items, with the occasional harmless trinket that was spelled for prosperity or safekeeping. The back was where the real magic was, and where I made soaps, shampoos, and lotions, enriched in magic and herbs.

The shop had barely been above the red when Lucian made my mother an offer. He'd wanted a potion to enhance sexual stimulation. Of course, we'd said yes when he'd named the price he would purchase them for. It was unheard of, but then, I was sure he knew what a pain in the ass they were to brew, and didn't want to deal with the manufacturing process himself. Magic was released during the brewing which went airborne when the magic mixed with the heat from simmering a batch for a few hours, so I'd be a mess distilling them.

I turned off the ignition and grabbed my overnight bag, then slipped it over my shoulder. When I stepped out of the car, I paused as the fine hair on my neck rose. Scanning the dark parking lot, I shivered and rushed for the shop. Once there, I dropped the keys and bent over to pick them up, but felt something touch my back. I spun around defensively, searching the lot, but found nothing. I exhaled as I turned, slipping the key into the lock and entering the store. Closing the door, I reached for the light switch, and murmured the words to ignite the protection candles which were positioned around the store.

I shook my head, knowing I'd let Alden's warning slink around my mind, and was just reacting to it. I hated that we had little to no knowledge of why the demons were here, or why they were converging on this town as if it was some focal point of evil. While the majority of them remained just on the outskirts of town, there were an occasional few that made it past the wards. The other thing was, the demons were unpredictable and tended to show up when you least expected them.

Walking through the store, I righted items that were

out of place or messed up from people picking them up and then setting them back down once they'd eyed something else. It was a never-ending process to keep everything where it belonged. The store was always busiest on the weekend, before and after the never-ending shenanigans at Club Chaos began or ended, depending on your viewpoint. I hated admitting it, but that club brought in the sexually curious who were a lot more open-minded than out-of-towners passing through here on their way to or from Canada.

Opening the door to the potion room, I dropped my bag on the couch and checked the supplies. I left the door open, because being here alone was creepy, but not being able to hear outside the room added to it even more. Plus, brewing in the room was horrible, the heat unmanageable if all of the state-of-the-art stovetops were brewing potions at the same time.

Moving to the couch, I slipped out of my pants and shirt and put on a sexy pair of ruffle shorts and a spaghetti strap tank top that I could easily move in and not melt from the stifling heat. I had resorted to cooking or creating potions at night, since it gave Alden and my mother some alone time, and allowed me to work more efficiently in less clothing. I quickly put my hair in a bun and turned on Ed Sheeran's sultry voice. Music filled the room, and the last bit of stress from the day washed away.

Next, I headed into the very back of the store, where we had a small greenhouse that stored the fresh herbs. Most of them were exotic or foreign to the United States and were a lot more potent if they were grown fresh on site. I piled a basket full of the ingredients I needed and got to work filling the heavy pots. Pouring dried aniseed into the stone bowl, I began crushing it into a fine powder along with cinnamon, cloves, and fennel seed. When it had the consistency of dust, I poured equal parts into the boiling water. Sweat trickled down my neck and back as I used my wrist to push away a strand of hair that had plastered to my temple.

My hips swayed to the music as I ground the dried fruit that would reduce the black licorice flavor of the aniseed. Aniseed was the main reason black jelly beans and Jägermeister found their unique flavor, and it was renowned for its aphrodisiac properties around the world. Cinnamon, clove, and fennel had natural analgesic properties and the fruit I used was pomegranates to help blood flow, which of course added to the pleasure for both men and women.

Once the dust had been added, I placed the seeds of the fruit in and then a spoonful of raw honey and chanted the spell to increase the sexual potency of the potions.

My body ached already, pulsing with the magic from the potion that left me aching for release. Once I reduced the heat to a low simmer, I moved to the couch and retrieved the book I was reading, a naughty erotica that was my guilty pleasure.

I sat down, reaching back to rub my shoulder, which had a knot in it from the tension I'd been dealing with over the last few days. Alden's training was more like military school. It left us mentally and physically drained, and considering he was having us show up three times a week, I was exhausted from the craziness of it all. We trained twice a week in magic, and one day was spent learning to defend ourselves, to fight back. On the bright side, I was learning to harness and control my powers, which hadn't been easy.

I lifted my legs and set them on the arm of the couch as I sat up to fluff the decorative throw pillows behind myself. I rested my head on them and dove into the book as I waited for the timer to signal that the potions were finished. I groaned as I got to a particular part of the book that was filled with sex. I squirmed around the couch, hating that my vagina had a pulse, an honest-to-God pulse that needed release.

Setting the book down and turned to look at the timer. An hour remained. I lay back down and stared at the ceiling, feeling my eyes growing heavy as I fought the sleepiness that was threatening to take me down, but without meaning to, my eyes closed. I struggled to open them, but it felt as if I was being pulled into a dream, as if someone had reached into my mind and dragged me under.

I was inside a nightclub, one I assumed belonged to Lucian, since I'd heard he had several, and there were naked bodies writhing together on the floor, fornicating to the seductive beat of the music that pounded from the speakers.

My eyes slid over the couples in scandalizing positions; the sounds of body meeting body somehow matched the song, which was seducing my body as I stood, playing voyeur to the people in the room.

Searching the room, I found a couple who stared back at me, their frenzied movements slowing as the man pulled his cock from her welcoming heat, slick with her wetness. Silver eyes met mine in naked need, his hand wrapped around his cock as he stroked it, beckoning me to partake in his pleasure. His other hand extended as he watched me, his eyes slowly roaming over my body. I stepped back, away from him, needing to put more distance between me and them, but I didn't get more than a foot away before I hit something hard.

I started to turn, but hands wrapped around my waist as the panic kicked in. My heart beat in a painful staccato pulse, making it hard to breathe.

My brain told me to run, to leave this place, and yet the hands held me in a steel grip. They directed my body until I faced the stage, where a blindfolded woman was tied up as her lover was using her while the crowd watched, spellbound by the scene in front of them. I shivered from the heat of the hands that held me, contrasting against the chill in the room.

I tried to see who held me in place, but something moved on the stage, pulling my eyes with an invisible thread. Lucian stepped from the shadows into view, his shirtless body on display. I didn't move, not as our eyes locked on each other. Everything else fell away, except for the hands that held me. I watched him as he stood there, beckoning me forward, and yet the hands wouldn't release me.

Lucian unbuttoned his pants as I gazed upon him, unable to look away as he freed his glorious cock. I was transfixed, locked into those endless midnight eyes as the hands released me, slid slowly around my waist, and lifted my shirt until my breasts were exposed.

I trembled as the hands held up my arms and slipped the tank top off, dropping it on the floor. The strong hands caressed my breasts, testing their weight as Lucian watched us from where he stood on the stage. I couldn't look away from him, not even to figure out who was fondling me. I felt the hands as they slid down from my breasts and pushed against my shorts. As he lowered my shorts and panties, his lips kissed the curve of my hip and the back of my thigh, trailing his mouth down my skin as he stripped me bare, leaving me naked for Lucian's intensifying stare.

The moment Lucian's heated gaze slid down my body, I was turned, and I peered down into piercing violet eyes framed by thick, lush black lashes. The man touching me was beautiful, terrifyingly so. His long, wavy black hair had been pulled away from his face and was restrained by a leather tie at the base of his neck. He was tall, with a muscular build like a swimmer; a dark seraph, who had come to seduce me.

He kissed his way up my thigh as I passively watched him, and once he stood again, he pulled me against his naked body, forcing me to step out of my panties and shorts.

Marilyn Manson's Sweet Dreams *started playing, and I shivered as the music seemed to steal my inhibitions. My body rocked to the beat, slowly swaying as the man smiled down at me where he'd stripped me for Lucian's intense gaze, knowing I was lost to the magic in the lyrics and chords as the song played.*

The man's hands grabbed my arms, holding them out, much to the excitement of the crowd who now had stopped fucking to watch us. My eyes widened as I took in their hungry looks. I needed to get away from this place before I gave in to the music and ended up in the crowd. I struggled to get my hands away, but his mouth touched my shoulder and I sagged as desire ripped through me.

He spun me around for everyone to see, and then slowly turned my body around again, giving those on stage a delectable view of my ass as he parted my cheeks and growled from deep in his chest. He turned me again, and pushed me towards the stage, giving me no choice but to walk or be trampled by him as he walked right behind me, guiding me.

Lucian waited, his eyes filled with liquid heat as I approached him. The crowd's anticipation was palpable, and mine grew with every moment the song played. Once I was close enough, Lucian held out his hand and I accepted, stepping away from the man who had been touching me.

"You surprise me," Lucian whispered for my ears alone. He pulled me forward and then ran his thumb over my bottom lip. He stepped closer until his heat encompassed me and threatened to swallow me whole.

He didn't smell the same. The fragrance of warm scotch with a touch of citrus was missing. Not that I cared, since it was still heavenly against my senses, disarming them as his mouth hovered against mine. The moment his touched mine, I moaned as desire unfurled deep inside of me. When he pulled his mouth from mine, I cried out from the loss of his heat. He turned me in his arms, forcing my back against his thick chest muscles.

Lucian held my arms out, just as the other man had done before him. He displayed me to the onlookers as he pushed my arms up, encouraging me to wrap them around his neck. His hands slowly slid down my body, until they found my wet pussy, which he rewarded me with an approving growl against my ear as his fingers explored the curves of my naked sex.

"So beautiful," he murmured, his fingers slowly pushing into my body as the crowd watched us. "So fucking tight and wet; is this for me?" he asked, and I nodded. "You're darker than the other one," he hissed as he lifted me without warning, holding my legs open to the crowd as he held me there, balanced on his body.

The crowd quieted with anticipation. He turned me in the direction of a bed I hadn't noticed before, and worry tried to sneak into my thoughts, only to be washed away as the song increased its seductive tempo. Once we were at the bed, he set me down and then shoved me. I bounced on the mattress, and turned to watch him as he crawled onto the bed slowly.

"Do you want to come for me?" His voice was a seductive heat that slid over my body and echoed in my head. I nodded, unable to say it aloud. "Say it, Kendra. Tell me to make you come, to make you mine. You want to be mine, don't you?"

"Yes." The single word slipped from my tongue, echoing through the crowd, who continued to watch us.

He turned my body until I was once again pressed with my back to his stomach as he gave the crowd an unobstructed view of my sex. His fingers slipped through the folds, slowly turning as he hit my clitoris with his knuckles, brushing the delicate flesh.

I could hear the muffled moans of the woman beside us, so I turned, staring at her blindfolded form. She was bound, her hands tied to her ankles, allowing the man who fucked her complete control as he pounded into her body. I felt my body heat at the idea of being so helpless, with no control over what happened.

"I'll fuck you like that," Lucian whispered against my ear. "I'd fuck every part of you until you knew you were mine to do whatever I wanted with. You'd like that, wouldn't you?" I swallowed as I felt something wet touching my pussy. I looked down, finding the man with dark hair and violet eyes staring up at me as his tongue lapped at my sex. Panic shot through me and I tried to back away, only for Lucian to whisper against my ear as he kissed my neck. "Shhh, he won't hurt you. He wants to tastes you, to know what your sweet pussy taste like when you come. You want him to make you come, don't you?" This time, I shook my head. Lucian held my legs apart, giving the dark seraph full access to my body.

I shivered as his violet eyes stared into mine as he kissed and caressed my pussy with his devilish tongue. He was beautiful, and knew what I needed, and yet my mind screamed for me to end his play. My body wanted it to be *otherwise and I exploded as the man pushed his tongue deep inside. He growled as my body pushed against him for more.*

"Just you," I whimpered to Lucian, yet I was rocking my hips against the beautiful man's skillful tongue. My mind knew it was wrong, my body wanted another orgasm from him.

"Your body doesn't lie as easily as your tongue," Lucian growled as his fingers pinched my clitoris, and then pulled my pussy apart for the man, who pushed his tongue deeper, and then pulled it out, only to slowly run it through my folds. "Look at him," Lucian demanded, holding my chin as he forced me to look down at him. "You're so hot, so fucking sexy. You're on fire for us," he growled as I watched the man back away, taking the heat of his skilled mouth with him.

Lucian shoved me aside, and I cried out from being jolted from the delicious haze I'd allowed to engulf me. He turned me until my ass was in the air and my legs were spread apart, and then I screamed as his fingers pushed into my aching pussy.

"Such a bad girl, look at this mess. What am I going to do with you?" He tsked as his fingers pumped into me and his mouth touched the round globe of my ass cheek, kissing it as his nose pressed against it. His tongue slid around his fingers, lapping at the mess he'd spoken of. I trembled as my body started to move, working his fingers deeper into my core.

I wasn't ready when the orgasm shot through me,

violent, yet ending prematurely as he removed his mouth and fingers and slapped my ass, sending pain and heat rushing through me. I whimpered, the waning orgasm still throbbing through my body with the need to finish.

"Bad girl, I didn't say you could come, did I?" he growled, anger lacing his tone. He turned me over, my face inches from his cock as he stared down at me with fury in his eyes. "You don't come unless I allow it; now clean the mess you made." He pushed his cock against my lips, as he grabbed my hair and forced his thick cock into my mouth. I gagged as it hit the back of my throat; tears filled my eyes as I adjusted to his size and the saltiness of his pre-come. He wasn't gentle and right then, I didn't want gentle. "That's a good girl, take it all," he encouraged, pushing deeper into my mouth as I relaxed my jaw to accommodate more. "Look at me," he growled, and I looked up, finding his grin sinful—and there was something darker than usual in it. Something that bothered me as it registered in the back of my mind.

He pulled out and rubbed his thumb over my lips as he pushed me back down, moving his body between my legs as his mouth clamped against my sex. His noises were of approval, and I cried out at the heat his mouth delivered as his fingers slid over my ass. I was so lost in his sinful mouth that when he pushed a finger in, I jerked in surprise.

"You haven't been fucked there yet, have you?" he laughed, sliding it in and out as I tightened against his exploration. That was a weird question for him to ask. I was coming undone and he knew it; my body tightened and the moment I should have exploded, he pulled out

and pushed me down as he leaned over me. "Answer me."

"No, I have not," I whimpered, and then he turned my face until I was watching the woman on stage as his cock slid against the mess he had created.

"Isn't she beautiful? Watch as they make her come for me."

I watched as one man pushed his cock against her mouth as the other stepped away, his cock dripping come as he left the stage, another taking his place immediately. She opened to them, her body pushing and pulling as one entered her from behind while the other pushed into her mouth without stopping until his cock was buried to the base, deep in her throat.

"She can take three at a time now; she's quite the pleaser. They beg me to fuck her, to abuse her sweet pussy and throat. She's mine now; she does anything I tell her to, anyone I tell her to. She doesn't watch anymore, doesn't feel anything unless I allow it. You will be like that soon, begging me to let them fuck you. Never knowing who it is who enters your pretty holes, and yet willing to take who I tell you to."

"Lucian," I pleaded, unsure what I was asking, but his fingers had been teasing my sex as he spoke, and I needed to come, to find the release I knew he could give me.

"Call me Luc," he demanded angrily. He sat back, staring at my glistening sex, wet from the need to come as the woman who was now screaming had. "I'm going

to fuck you, do you want that?" His fingers pushed inside of me, forcing me to spread my legs wider to take more of him. "Do you want me to fuck you until my cock caresses your womb, planting my seed so deep that it can't be removed?"

Seed? I swallowed a moan as he withdrew his fingers as he leaned over to kiss my lips, drawing my mind back into his haze of heated pleasure. When he pulled back, he pushed me to the edge of the bed, forcing me to watch the woman who was still pleasuring the men she was with. My head hung off the edge, and I lifted it to watch as Lucian knelt between my legs. His cock pushed against my pussy and I closed my eyes, knowing that soon he'd be buried in my welcoming heat and I'd get to come.

I heard his laughter and opened my eyes as I struggled to sit up, only to find vinelike things crawling over my skin. I whimpered as they caressed me, sending the feather-soft kisses over my flesh. His cock rubbed against my wet slit, entering it slowly as I watched the vines that were attached to him slowly entwining my body. Skeletal wings exploded from his back, and I gasped at the strangeness of it. His eyes, a shade lighter than true indigo, turned red, red as the flames that licked the walls of Hell. I dropped my head, unable to hold it up as the vines caressed my clitoris and wrapped around the peaks of my nipples, creating a maelstrom of sensations that threatened to consume me.

I turned my head to the audience, blanching as I took in the blood and gore. Women and men were tearing each other apart. Literally. I shook my head and turned to look at the other woman on stage, only to discover they'd removed the blindfold, and my own eyes stared at me. I was the woman on stage? I blinked and lifted my head, finding an inhuman creature between my legs as he watched me absorb the fucked up chaos that was playing out around us.

His huge, skeletal black wings expanded and vines ripped from his body without him reacting to the pain as blood seeped from where they'd escaped. They writhed as they left his body, slithering onto mine with a pleasure I couldn't ignore. They caressed my pussy, rubbing my clitoris as he rocked his hips as the tip of his cock remained cradled in my pussy.

What fucked up shit was this? I dropped my head, trying to ignore what my eyes were telling me and focus on what my body felt: white-hot pleasure. It was everything. I needed to focus on it, and nothing else.

My eyes opened against my will as I heard my name being called. It was being screamed. I blinked at my reflection, who was now screaming at me as Lucian laughed wickedly while pushing further into my body. Something pushed into my mouth and I swallowed, unable to stop myself as it pushed in deeper.

Pain erupted as everything happening registered at once.

I struggled to sit up, only for my hair to be yanked back down as the man who'd tasted my pussy appeared in front of me. He made me look at Lucian—who wasn't Lucian at all.

An Angel of Death stared back at me, his features

twisted into smug satisfaction as he watched me struggle to get away from the monstrosities that were trying to enter my body through my skin. Not vines; they were alive, like he was.

"Scream," he demanded as he pushed in deeper. "You let me in, so now you belong to me. No one can protect you from me, not even him. *I own you both." He buried himself in my body and I trembled as I exploded around his cock. Muscles burned, tightened as my body clenched against his cock, milking it as the orgasm tore through me. "I own you both, and* he *can't save you now." His laughter filled the room, drowning out the music as he watched me struggle against him. "My sweet girls, so fucking beautiful," he snarled as he pumped harder into my body, as if he was running out of time.*

"Wake up!"

The words tore through my mind. Another orgasm ripped through me as something slapped against my face. I felt myself being pulled in two directions, as if something was trying to get me away from this creature who gave me pleasure.

I winced as blood trickled from my nose and then gasped as water was doused on me. I blinked, watching as the winged creatures stared into my eyes with sickening amusement. I was being grabbed by rough hands, and then water was poured over my head, ice-cold water.

"Wake up!"

The voice boomed in my ear, ricocheting through my

body and mind. I blinked, watching as my dream lover was forced from my body violently by blue flames. The blue flames hit the red flames as they erupted, protecting me from the searing heat. The sound of laughter echoed in my ears as hands held me up, forcing me back to reality.

"Bloody fucking hell, wake up!"

Something slapped me and I blinked, the echo of the orgasms still clinging to my body. I whimpered as I felt everything. The ice-cold water, the thing stuck in my throat, and the cock which withdrew, followed by the echo of his laughter.

I bent over, throwing up until I felt the thing that had slipped down my throat. I pulled on it, forcing it out as I retched up everything in my stomach. It was endless. I stopped, unable to get it out as pain ripped through me. Strong hands reached down, uncaring that saliva and blood were escaping along with the writhing creature, and yanked it out of me.

I looked up into terrifying midnight eyes and screamed. I slammed against the shower wall hard, my naked body a mixture of pain and bruises with the ghost pain of seductive fingers that played upon my pussy.

"Did he fuck you?" came a snapped question and I trembled until my teeth chattered violently.

"It was a dream. Just a dream," I whimpered as another orgasm threatened to consume me. This wasn't happening, right? I buried my face in my hands as my body shook and my knees buckled. Hands grabbed me, catching me before I could fall, and then the orgasm ripped through me and I sobbed at what was happening to me. I was coming in Lucian's arms from a nightmare in which he'd just played a starring role.

"I'm going to rip his fucking spine out through his mouth," he growled as he held me carefully, as if I was some delicate flower that would wilt.

A sob ripped from my chest as he moved me back into the other room, touching my stomach as he pushed my legs apart, and then looked up at me with ice-cold, midnight eyes. I looked down, finding lacy red marks all over my legs, torso, and breasts, and then lifted my tear-filled eyes back to his with accusation written in them.

If it had just been a dream, why was my sex swollen and sore from it? Why had I just tossed my cookies and thrown up God-knows-*what* in the bathroom?

"Get dressed, now," he gritted out as he stood and turned away from me as if I was some vile creature he couldn't stand the sight of.

CHAPTER
six

*What the fuck do you mean I wasn't dreaming? ~**Lena***

I was seated on the couch, wrapped in a blanket, as Lucian recounted the delicate position he'd discovered me in to my mother and Alden. He told them that he'd stopped by the shop to pick up his order early since normally I was done before the requested time. He'd explained how he'd found the door unlocked and walked in to find me in my more-than-compromised situation.

Thankfully, he'd skipped some of the embarrassing details, such as how I'd been naked, which I still couldn't understand, or that I'd been throwing up something… weird.

"And you're sure it was a demon?" Alden asked, and Lucian nodded with a look that passed between them that worried me. "Dream demons are almost unheard of these days; humans are who they prefer to go after, since witches can normally ignore their presence in a dream state."

"Normally, yes," Lucian explained patiently. "But this one had to have had something she wanted, something to draw her to him."

Or someone.

"They can't do anything unless the person who is dreaming wants what they are offering them." His tone turned condemning as he spoke.

"So what you're saying is that I wanted to be…that I wanted to have sex with him?" I asked sharply, and glass shattered. I turned my head in the direction of the sound and found Lucian glaring at me with a look that could easily kill. I lowered my eyes to his hand which had blood oozing from where the glass had sliced through it.

"Oh, my," my mother murmured as she jumped into action and grabbed a tea towel to wrap around his hand. "I can heal it," she offered, and my eyes were drawn back to his angry black-blue glare.

"It's fine, I have runes active. It will be healed shortly without aid." He continued to glare at me. "Did you fuck it?" he snapped angrily, and my mother's eyes darted nervously from me to Lucian.

"It was a dream," I gritted out. I hated that I still felt that creature's touch on my skin. I hated that I remembered every lurid detail of it. I hated that the man sitting in the armchair across from me looked just as the supposed demon did.

"Keep telling yourself that and you may end up believing it."

"If it wasn't a dream, it wasn't my fault! Dreams aren't supposed to be real, that's why they are called dreams!" I argued.

"How do we protect her?" my mother interrupted, ending our argument.

"She has to fight him; but before she can fight him, she would have to *not* want to fuck it first."

"I didn't want to fuck him!" I growled as I stood up and glared at him. He moved stealthily like a panther, until he was towering over and glowering down at me.

"You had to have or he wouldn't have been able to get to you!"

"I didn't want *him*!"

"Then what could he possibly have done to convince you to fuck him?" he shouted, shaking the planters.

"He didn't do anything. It was you," I whispered coldly. "You were the demon, Lucian. I fucked you. I let you use me, touch me, and play with me. If it was a demon, I let him fuck me because I thought it was you."

He swallowed and seemed to deflate a little as the fight left him. His eyes closed as he rubbed his hands over his face as if he was exhausted.

Lucian grabbed my hand and I shuddered, remembering him holding me through the violent orgasm that he hadn't given me, yet he'd cradled me through it, holding me as I cried into his chest.

When I just continued to stare at his hand, he dropped it. He resumed his place across from me, and I quietly sat down as the room remained in deafening silence. I wanted to scream and cry, but mostly, I wanted to figure out why it had targeted me in the first place.

"Why me, why would it go after me?" I asked softly.

"You're powerful, fertile, and unmated. You have yet to choose a partner to procreate with, so you make an easy target. Demons like him, they like to breed because then they have total control over the one who carries their unborn child and the child itself once it has been born."

"So you're saying that when he said seed, he meant he wanted to impregnate me?" I swallowed against my rolling stomach as the color drained from my face.

"Well, he couldn't achieve that goal unless you agreed to it," he snapped, and I grimaced at his damning words. "You need to tell me what happened, and start from the beginning."

I stared at him and then looked at my mother and Alden. I blushed and moved my eyes back to Lucian. "That's not going to happen."

"Leave us," he demanded, and my mother and Alden stood up, yet waited for my direction.

I chewed my bottom lip and nodded at their unasked question. I was going to tell Lucian everything. Every time the coven had an issue, he was the one they went to anyway. If what he said was true, I'd given myself to a demon that had looked and sounded exactly like Lucian did, which meant the demon knew him. It had taken his form to get me to succumb to it, which said a lot, since no one knew I had a huge thing for this man.

Once the room was cleared, Lucian stood, moving to the sideboard, and picked up a bottle of scotch before twisting off the cap. He poured the amber liquid into the glass and returned to me, quietly offering one of the crystal tumbler glasses. As I took it, he sat on the sofa, way too close for comfort.

"What did he look like?" he asked, his penetrating glare seeming to drill a hole into my head as he stared at me while I gazed at the doorway my mother and Alden had just disappeared through.

"You," I replied softly. "The first thing I can remember about the dream… It began with me walking through a club, one I assumed was yours. I was trying to leave, but someone grabbed me, and when I looked at the stage, you were there. It was like I had no will of my own and was just going with the flow. The man who grabbed me…I let him take off my clothes. I let him do it because I thought you were watching me, and I wanted that to happen, I guess. I let him take me to you, and then you showed me to everyone, and I let you. I'm such an idiot." My voice hitched unevenly. "The one who grabbed me…I let him…I let it, it do things to me. I let it because you wanted me to." My voice trailed off in a whisper as I covered my face with my hands, hating myself as I told every lurid detail, right down to what I felt coming undone for the creature.

Once the story was out, I waited for a few moments for him to say something. When a few more moments passed without any of his devastatingly hurtful comments, I turned my eyes to Lucian and found him studying me silently. He looked angry, hurt, and violent, a weird combination considering everything that had happened and everything I knew about him.

He stood up and moved away from me, as if I was some dirty little thing he couldn't get away from fast enough. "You shouldn't have let him touch you," he snapped.

I turned in my seat and looked at him incredulously. "I didn't know it wasn't you touching me," I argued.

"You should have been able to see through it. What type of music was playing in your dream?" he growled.

"Marilyn Manson, *Sweet Dreams are Made of This*."

He stared at me, nodding. "The beat, it called to you?"

"It was like it went through me, taking away the part of me that wanted to run. Any time I got scared, the music got louder or the beat got faster. Once it had, he would touch me, and I would refocus on him. I wanted him, though—no matter what was playing, I wanted him to have me."

"Him, or me?" There was a pain in his eyes that I didn't understand.

"You, Lucian," I admitted, albeit hesitantly. "I wanted you for some crazy reason."

"Because you lust after me, and he's a creature who feeds off sin. Lust is a big one for demons."

"You know who he is, don't you?" My eyes narrowed as I carefully observed every nuance about him.

"Yes," he spat out as though he tasted something nasty, and I swallowed hard.

"Who was it?" My voice wavered and sounded breathy. He regarded me for a few moments as he considered his words, and when they came, it was as if he had leveled a wrecking ball right at my body.

"Lucifer." His voice was so clear, there was no way I could mistake what he just said. I shook as tears filled my eyes and burned as they slowly slid down my cheeks. "You fucked the devil, Kendra."

"He didn't finish, and I didn't agree to carry his seed, or whatever the hell it was," I replied as nausea burned my insides.

"You took him in your mouth; you let him enter your body. You all but signed your soul over to him; it doesn't matter if you agreed or not at this point. He's marked you now, which means I have to undo it."

"How?"

"That's what I have to figure out. Until I do, you do nothing alone. You definitely do not sleep alone. Lucifer got to you once, he will do it again. You're fertile, which is just an additional inducement for him to try for you again. Your child would be powerful, but a child from you and him…" He paused, staring at me as the tick in his jaw hammered angrily. "That would be a child more powerful than you could ever imagine."

I shivered as a sob sounded from the doorway to the kitchen. I turned in that direction, and saw my mother covering her mouth as tears streamed down her face. Alden held her as he stared at me.

I'd had sex with the devil; because shit around here wasn't crazy enough, why not screw Lucifer?

"How do we prevent him from finding me?" I turned away from the horror I'd just seen in my mother's eyes. "Is there a spell, or some sort of devil's trap? Is there any way to prevent him from getting to me?"

"Me, you use me. He won't chance having to wait the nine months to know if the child you breed is his or mine."

"Excuse me?" I blinked, wondering if I hadn't heard him correctly.

CHAPTER
seven

*So, that happened. ~**Lena***

I stared at my reflection in the mirror as I prepared for bed. I'd showered and scrubbed myself until every part of my body was red and sore. No matter how hard I scrubbed, those phantom fingers still touched me in sinful ways. I glared at the weak girl in the mirror, wondering why she would have done something so stupid, considering she hated Lucian. I picked up the vase that sat on the counter and threw it at the mirror, closing my eyes as the glass shattered.

I picked up one of the jagged shards and then dropped it as I stared down into the fractured reflection that stared up at me. I was a mess, and now that my mother and Alden had left me alone with Lucian, I felt lost. They'd most likely done it so they could run and tell the coven what I'd allowed to happen, and to hopefully prevent it from happening to others. I was a defensive mess who wanted to be anywhere else but here right now.

Getting the broom and dust pan to clean the wreckage that seemed to symbolize my life allowed me a chance to get my head in a better space. I slowly cleaned the glittering shards, only to have the illusion shattered moments later as I made my way down the hall from the bathroom. I paused as I noticed Lucian leaning against the doorframe of my bedroom, watching me with amusement dancing in his eyes.

I crossed my arms and considered changing yet again. I was wearing a black nightgown, one that offered little to the imagination, but in retrospect, I never shopped with the thought of someone sleeping with me. It had little bows sewn into the hemline and matching ones on the spaghetti strap top. All of my normal pajamas were filthy since I spent so little time here, and most of my time was wrapped up in training or working in the shop.

"Are you okay?" he asked softly as I neared the doorway of my room.

"I'm fine," I snapped, unable to stop the self-loathing that consumed my mind.

He straightened, eyeing me as if I'd said my hair was on fire, instead of being fine.

I pushed past him, moving to the bed we'd be sharing tonight. It was midnight, still too many hours until dawn, and my mother had suggested he sleep in my room, to protect me from being seduced by the devil. As if he wasn't just another version of the devil, except this rendition in the flesh?

"Stay on your side of the bed," I warned. The moment I said it, I eyed the twin bed and scowled at him. "This isn't going to work."

"It will work." His tone carried more confidence than I felt. He pulled off his shirt and my mouth went dry. His muscles rippled in the dimly lit room, and I ran my tongue over my lips as I turned away from him. "We'll just have to get up close and personal, which is fine since I have to touch you to keep the monsters at bay. He can't get to you if you're grounded."

"Grounded?" I asked hesitantly as I turned around just in time to watch him slipping into a pair of sweats that did little to hide the fact that he wore nothing beneath them.

"If someone is holding on to you, he can't pull you to him. It's one of the basic laws of physics, so as long as I am holding you, he can't have you."

"So all I have to do is find someone to sleep with me every night and I won't need you?" I raised one brow in question.

His mouth jerked into an angry smirk. "If they're strong enough to fight the devil himself to keep you, sure," he mused with a cocky grin.

"You're so sure that that is who I was with?"

"Get in bed, you're wasting my time," he replied thickly as I kicked off my slippers and stared at him. I looked up as I started to roll my eyes, only to find a huge red devil's trap that had been marked on the ceiling above my bed. It took the fight out of me; reality was such a bitch.

I did as he asked, slipping beneath the covers and then shivering as he did the same, our bodies connecting as he pulled me close and cradled my head on his arm. We fit perfectly, like two puzzle pieces that had once been lost, and were now being reconnected.

I inhaled his earthy masculine scent and closed my eyes, knowing sleep wouldn't come easily, not after the last dream I'd had.

"You'd fight the devil for me?" I murmured as I opened my eyes and turned to face him, which was a huge mistake. Our lips were mere inches away, his breath fanned mine, and I licked my lips as I stared into his eyes, endless zeniths that answered my question.

He smirked. "Some people scare the devil," he whispered as his eyes lowered to my lips. The tick in his jaw came back, as if he was considering right where my lips had been earlier. "Other's become his playthings. Don't be that one. Be the one he fears. Now go to sleep before I show you the difference between him and me."

I turned back away and then jumped as his arm wrapped around my waist, just under my breasts. I could hear my heart pounding in my ears, feel it beating wildly inside my chest, which meant he could too. His nose was in my hair, smelling it, and I could feel the heat pouring from his body.

"This isn't going to work," I grumbled as I sat up and rubbed my temples. I could feel his eyes on my back as I sat there, hating the idea of sleeping next to a man I hadn't even realized I wanted until I'd kidnapped him. Then, as if I was being punished for lusting after him, I allowed Lucifer to pretend to be him—which, hey, turned out hadn't been a dream.

"Look at me," he growled, and I chewed my bottom lip before I turned and looked at him. "You're not the first to get tricked by him, and you won't be the last. You can't stay up forever, so lay your ass down before I hold you down until you sleep."

"Just fucking *try* it," I snorted. I was picked up and slammed down, flat on the mattress. His heavy body pinned mine to the bed and a sexy smile played across his lips as I stared up at him in shock.

"I don't try anything, little girl. If I say I will do something, plan on me doing it. Don't challenge me, because I like to win," he murmured as he lowered his mouth to mine, as if he was testing what I might do.

I lifted my lips to his, not kissing him, but needing to know the difference. Maybe he understood what I was doing, maybe he didn't. I inhaled deeply of him as I opened my eyes to find him watching me with an intensity that made me shiver.

I wasn't convinced it hadn't been him in my dream. He'd felt so real. I'd noticed similarities, but there'd also been subtle differences. I licked his lips, needing him to open to me, but he didn't. Instead, a guttural growl escaped from deep in his chest and he rolled off of me.

"Go to sleep," he snapped.

I rolled away from him, hating that I'd even tried anything with him. What the fuck was wrong with me? He was part of the reason whatever had happened to me happened. I'd assumed I was with him, no one else. I'd wanted him so bad that I'd allowed my guard to lower, and it had landed me here, in my bed, with this man cradling me as silent tears rolled down my cheek.

"Sleep," his voice boomed, echoing in my mind, and I didn't fight him. I couldn't. My eyes closed and my body sagged as I succumbed to his demand.

~Lucian

I was going to destroy Lucifer. Rip him apart, bit by bloody fucking bit, until nothing remained. I'd entered her shop, surprised at the sweet noises she'd been making. My cock had reacted, growing hard with the need to fuck her until she couldn't move afterwards. The same shit which had been haunting me since I'd fucked her in the shack where she'd taken me to last week.

Then I'd heard other voices, and seen red. I'd pushed through the front doors, finding the one to her brewery room open. She'd been on the couch, naked, her body writhing as she touched her sweet bean, flicking it with urgency. I'd pulled back, watching as her body moved and her noises drove me to the brink of insanity—up until she'd whispered Luc.

Many had called me that before, but then I'd smelled sulfur, noted the way her body was moving, as if she was actually being fucked. The vine had slithered from between her lips and my stomach had dropped at what I was playing witness to. He was fucking *my* Lena. He'd gotten to her somehow, discovered they were twins and he'd somehow gotten her permission to enter her body.

Holding her as she escaped him without throttling her had been an act of supreme willpower. I'd wanted to show her the dissimilarities, to make her feel me to her core so that she never mistook the difference again, because somehow I'd known he'd used my image to get to my girl. He'd die soon enough, but right now…right now I had to prevent her from falling into his hands, which meant I had to stay close without getting emotionally attached to her.

"This is unexpected," Hades' deep voice whispered through the room before his form solidified from smoke.

I turned, locking eyes with his violet ones that skimmed my profile before moving to Lena's scantily clad form; lingering at the place where her hip had been exposed as she'd kicked off her blankets. Without thinking, I moved my hand to pull the sheet over her, covering her from the burning curiosity in his eyes.

"She's not worth starting a war. Call off the bounty you placed on Lucy's head."

"Fuck you, Hades. He wants her because she's mine,

because of what he thinks she has. That alone should fucking scare you, considering what would happen if that asshole gets his hands on the seal before we do. Consider this, friend: I am older than both of you. I am eternal, more than immortal and never-ending. I don't think the little asshole is searching for the seal just so he can have a friendly game of hide and go seek; from what I have heard, he tires of being tethered to Hell. He can't remain outside of Hell for more than a few hours without his strength weakening. He wants to open the gates, but he hasn't figured out how to.

"Now, he's creating minions to help him from outside. He meant to place his bastard in her belly tonight. Had he done so, he'd have more than a stepping stone into this world. He'd have a son strong enough to demolish the Gates of Hell and accomplish his goal without the seal. Do you seriously think their God would be merciful if his entire flock was murdered or possessed by demons? Lucifer is merely a child to us, one that needs to be knocked on his ass to be shown where he is in the chain of command. The other Gods have already noticed his demons are here, wearing humans as if they are fucking Halloween costumes. Sooner or later, he will get the war he wants."

"What if the sky falls?" Hades shrugged, his eyes narrowing as he watched me. "We've dealt with other people's problems for long enough. Let them clean up their own fucking messes."

"Do you think this round is just about him wanting a little more room to move around in? How long before the old Gods and the New Gods declare war on each other—

or us, for that matter? That seal he is searching for won't just unlock this world to Hell, it will open every world. Every world, Hades. Only a few beings know what that entails. You damn well know we're not ready to fight those creatures again. Besides, if they come, it means we lose everything we've worked to achieve here. There will be no place or no world where we can hide from them. That seal is the one thing keeping them where they are. So either help me, or fuck off."

"You know whose side I am on: I've been beside you since the dawn of man," he snapped. "Speaking of sides, I think it is best you hear it from me rather than one of your little spies: I tasted her tonight—"

Faster than he could blink, I flew from the bed, snatching him up and pinning him to the wall; my eyes burned blue fire as I snarled, inches away from his throat.

"I should destroy you."

He laughed, staring me down as I held his throat in a death grip. "I parted her sweet pussy and she rode my face, coming on it so prettily. She does make the most divine noises, doesn't she? And she tastes of heaven, which none of us can get enough of."

My hand tightened and yet the asshole continued to smirk. I measured my words so there would be no question about how I felt about what he had done. "She is mine and mine alone, and if you want to continue your sorry existence, you will shut the fuck up about what you did to her."

"Why? If I hadn't made her pussy wet, hadn't made her come hard for me, she'd be pregnant right now. I placed a nice contraceptive spell over her precious womb with my tongue as I licked her so he couldn't plant that seed she so blindly agreed to host. I knew which twin he'd pulled into Abbadon. I knew she was yours, and while I could have stood back and watched him do as he pleased, I improvised. I presented her to him, the devil himself. I stripped her bare, kept her calm and controlled her mind so he wouldn't rip her apart or rape her. He would have; he would have done the same things to her that he did to her sweet sister until she stopped fighting him.

"Now that her sister carries his child, she's nothing but a broken toy that has been given to his minions to use. So yes, I made damn sure it didn't happen to your girl, and bought you some time to get to her." He eyed me critically as I let go of his throat and backed away from him. "This sentimentalism isn't you. You don't care about her; you care about the idea of her. You are the monster who is called upon to slaughter hordes of monsters. You are death, and yet here you are, with another mortal. Fragile, weak creatures that have an expiration date that starts counting down the moment they draw their first breath." He made his way to a frilly armchair and made himself comfortable in it; his large frame dwarfed the absurd thing, yet he managed to look at ease as he crossed his long legs and looked at me expectantly.

"She's different," I bit out angrily, hating that I cared. She was a fucking weakness that I didn't need or want, and yet couldn't kill.

"This isn't you. You have spent too much time on

this mortal plane and you are starting to sound like one of them. You need to wake the fuck up and see what is happening around you. Faery is pouring into this world and their Goddess, bless her sexy tight ass, can't stop it from happening. The Horde King, nope, he can't stop it, either. Demons are already here, they've been in this world for a millennia and no one fucking cares but us. Where are the other Gods? They're not here, not breaking a sweat to save any of these weak creatures. No, just us. You keep fighting this, but it's never-ending, and personally, I'm damn tired of watching you fall for a mortal as you lie to yourself that you haven't. I've watched you kill Katarina's incarnations too many fucking times. If you plan to change the cycle, you have to change how you approach your problem. After that, if you plan on playing with the mortals, find one worth dying for. This game of cat and mouse is endless, and that's because she is mortal and you are so much…more."

"Magdalena isn't Katarina," I barked, and saw a taunting smirk lift the corners of his mouth. I struck, watching as it faltered ever so briefly.

Blood trickled from the corner of his mouth and he swiped at it with his thumb before licking it clean. Hellfire danced in his violet eyes that were transfixed on mine. "How can you be so sure?" he began slowly as he settled back in the chair.

"If I was Katarina, I would have sent Lena in to keep you distracted. She seems to do just that, doesn't she? But if we're honest, their pussies taste nothing alike." His jibe was meant to pull anger from me. Instead, I smirked, watching him with indifferent coldness. He sighed and shook his head, knowing that he wasn't going to get me to admit what he wanted me to, and shifted tactics. "Luc upped the ante tonight; just be glad I happened to be there when he pulled his little stunt. I cast my spell to protect her from what he wanted her to see. He wanted her to see the chaos playing out around her. I fed her an illusion of lust. I played music inside her soul with my touch. She never noticed that she was ankle-deep in blood as I marched her perfect little ass to the stage. She didn't notice that the crowd was ripping each other apart because they can never find release in that place."

"Do you know if he has taken Kendra through the Hell Gates yet?" I asked, narrowing my eyes on her sleeping form.

"He's kept her moving in different levels surrounding the gates for a few weeks now. Hidden right on the edge of the realm, not deep enough to tell if she houses the seal, if that is what you were wondering. If she did house the seal, there would have been a shit-show that none of us could have missed if he crossed over with her." He glanced at me speculatively. "Now that he's tasted the fire in both of them, he won't stay away. Not when he knows that there are two of them; not when he knows he got the wrong sister first and that you hid the other."

"You could have stopped him from fucking her," I growled as I moved closer to Lena.

"Sure, I could have. I just love having sudden bouts of stupidity that would make that little fuck boy suspicious of me." He rolled his eyes and shrugged his wide shoulders. "I gave you enough time to get to her, and so what if he got his dick into her? I just slowed him down and got in the way so he didn't get what he really wanted, and I knew you wouldn't be far away. Luckily, you pulled her out before he could make her a corpse. He would have, just to make sure you lost. Make no mistake, Lucian, this is a game to him. These girls are no more than pawns. This one got lucky; her sister is the one being tortured because Luc thought she was your lover, while this one suffered nothing more than a little sexy time in the arms of the devil. By the way, when she remembers who she is, and what you have done, do you think she will so willingly trip and land on your dick? Or will she hate you as much as my wife hated me? It could go either way; she's a whisky kinda girl, they tend to be born of fire. That's something you and I will never understand, never can since we are the flames that both birthed and burned them. You and me, we're not so different. We both have an affinity for wanting women with complications, now don't we?"

"You struck a deal, one you didn't have to make. It prevented chaos; at least you get her for six months out of the year. It could be worse."

"Oh yes, and such a sweet fucking deal it is, isn't it? For the other six months, I have to be creative and get my kicks where I can. It took a lot of creative ingenuity and I had to swallow a fuck-ton of my pride to get her to stop hating me," he said as he pointed his finger at Lena's sleeping form. "You took her choice away from her, erased who she was without her consent. When she regains her memories, and she will, she will hate you. Sure, you can always keep her as a fuck toy chained to your bed, which is fun for the first couple decades, but trust me; fighting them every day gets old quick. You think I agreed to Atum's deal because Demeter was having a massive hiss fit, or that I have a fucking heart for all those humans she killed because she was pissed at me? I assure you, I don't. I was just like you, addicted to the fight in their eyes. The spirit in their soul, but captivity smothers it; extinguishes the flame and the fight. Then all you have left of them is a pretty, broken doll.

"No, despite the lies those storytellers told, I didn't let her go back to her mother because I knew she missed the sun or because she wouldn't stop crying. I did it because I'm a selfish prick and I figured six months at a go was better than none. One thing I can promise you is this; what you're doing now won't work, it never does. Your story has a little twist from mine, though. Yours is on a loop; the moment you love her, she's dead. You were not created to be loved, or to give love. You are what you are because you're the coldest motherfucker they could think of to become it. Do me a favor; if you win the game this time around, stay away from the witches and find someone who can't be used by those who cursed you?"

"She doesn't die because I fall in love with her." I grimaced and stopped myself from rolling my eyes at his stupid speculation.

"Doesn't she? You fell in love with the first one; three days after you admitted it, she was murdered—by you. And she keeps dying with every reincarnation. One of you falls in love, and she dies. If she loves you, she dies; if you love her, she still dies. Do us a fucking favor: fall in love with someone who isn't associated with this fucking curse so that you can know what it feels like to have love and get it back and not have her die. Maybe then you'll come back to us as you once were."

"Leave," I snapped, hating the truth that escaped his mouth. He was right, which meant I had to push Lena away before I killed her, or worse, cursed her to my soul.

CHAPTER
eight

Each player must accept the cards life deals him or her.
But once they are in hand, he or she alone must decide
*how to play the cards in order to win the game. ~**Voltaire***

1897

My hair whipped against

my face as the wind in the Rocky Mountain Basin howled.
The storm lingered, threatening to let loose in the open
meadow where some members of my coven lay dead, or
dying. I was bathed in their blood, my chemise pink from
it. My wet hair whipped against my face, cold in the chill
November air. I tilted my head back, letting the light from
the full blood moon bathe my face as it did the meadow I
moved through like a wraith.

I scanned the faces of the dead closest to me, stopping
as I took in my sister's lifeless gaze. Unlike the others, her
death had hurt me. I'd loved her. Luckily, the evil inside
me had turned off my emotions as I'd taken her soul into
mine. It had whispered to me long ago, foretelling of the

man who would come to destroy me, and I'd listened to it with bated breath.

It had told of my past lives, showing each one in vivid detail that brought their pain to me, letting me feel the love they'd shared with a monster, one who had ended each of their lives. I'd watched him through the centuries as he'd seduced and then murdered them, but it had been me who had played the voyeur as he'd taken each of them. I knew his touch, his taste, and everything they knew about him.

The moment Lucian had entered our town, I'd known it was he who sought the soul of the cursed witch who lived inside of me. He'd whispered in the ears of the coven, and my sister, Flora had succumbed to his allure; she'd taken him between her legs and accepted anything he told her as truth.

Together, they'd spread news of what I had inside of me. This utterly beautiful darkness that was real. It spoke to me of past lives, and how to end this deadly game, once and for all.

I'd started taking steps the moment the evil within me had told me what was coming, and how this game needed to end. I'd placed things at the farthest reach of our community. I'd packed up everything linking me to the cursed soul and made the long journey to the Guild. I had bargained with the elders and they agreed to help me. I'd hidden everything there, including the grimoires that had been passed down through the bloodlines, trinkets that each had owned, journals of each life lost, along with the coven's tales of cursed witches.

The Guild Elders assured me that everything I found was hidden, locked away and sealed into the catacombs of the Guild. The one place no one in our own coven or he would ever think to look.

Like pieces of a game, everything was set up, placed perfectly for the next rebirth to find and use against him. He'd been searching for me, the one who had been reborn with the cursed soul of his beloved Katarina inside of her. The darkness had whispered her secrets, and with those secrets came her memories.

It was a love that always ended in death, a love that should have never been. In every rebirth, he seduced the unlucky woman. He turned her into a mindless being so lost in love that she allowed her to death to occur. Some had gone to him blindly, some had fought him; all ended up in love with him. In the end, no matter how hard they fought, every one of them ended up dead.

Each one had added a curse to his soul; one had made him unable to sire children. Of course, she'd had to include a way around it, as so many curses included some sort of exception to them. So far, he was childless, as had been my sister when I'd killed her. Another had cursed the soul to carry the essence and souls of those he had killed, figuring together, we were stronger.

What a mess that was, considering they all whispered inside my head, insistently. I could hear their voices, feel their emotions, even the love Katarina had for the monster she had fallen for. My curse, my curse wouldn't do anything to him. I was the first reborn witch who planned to curse his beloved Katarina.

I wasn't stupid enough to believe that I would survive where others had not. I knew death had called for me, whispering my name upon the stars, and I welcomed it. After they'd marked me, they'd taken everything away from me. My love, the man I'd given my heart to, had been slaughtered at the order of this monster who hunted me, and that monster was ultimately responsible for the dead and dying who now littered the meadows.

A few from the coven had distracted me, as the others had gone to my house to murder John, the man I'd loved with every piece of me. We'd planned our lives out, children to fill our home with love, and they'd taken it from me. I'd rushed home, only to find what was left of him inside our cabin. Written on his body had been a message from his murderers to meet them here, beneath the moon in this sacred place where the leylines gathered and crossed.

It had done them little good, considering I lived and they were nothing more than fodder to feed the worms.

The rest of the coven must have been confident that these fools would best me and had hidden in town or the abbey. Instead of hunting them, I'd started preparing for retribution. I'd called to the salt from the lines to gather and create the hexagram the evil inside of me had instructed me to make. Next, I'd started the fires that created a circle around me and the area I needed to work in. The fires burned brightly, fueled by the remains of those who had been sacrificed here and strengthening me and the curse I intended to inflict on the monster who'd taken everything from me. I'd prepped the cauldron, flames licking its sides as it began bubbling with the ingredients I'd collected as

I waited for Lucian to come.

Because he would come, he always did.

I grabbed the dagger and pulled my blonde braid forward, sliced it off, and threw it into the boiling cauldron. It sizzled, sending a thick putrid plume of smoke into the air. I sliced the palm of my hand as a twig broke, alerting me that the monster was here.

The shadow took form, and I watched as he knelt beside Flora's corpse. Two of the witches who had not succumbed to their injuries called to him as he rose from her lifeless body and I smirked, flicking my wrist as he moved to one who had yet to die. The moment he reached her, I flicked it again and enjoyed the sound as their necks broke, smiling as I felt their life forces fading away as they added to my growing power. He lifted those midnight eyes and locked gazes with me across the open field, and I smirked coldly as death stared at me.

He prowled towards me, his strut perfectly matching a cougar as it hunted its prey. I could feel his anger. The subtle pulse of raw power he exuded and gave off when he entered a room slithered through the protective barrier and across my skin.

I murmured the spell to ignite the barrier as I remained still, watching his fluid, graceful movements.

"You didn't have to kill them to get my attention," he growled, and I laughed, clapping my hands as he neared.

"You think I killed them for you? They didn't die to get your attention. They died because they thought to do your

bidding. You turned them against me, and so their lives ended here. You did this; you brought them into this, so their blood is on your hands. Not mine, monster," I hissed as I glared at him from beneath my lashes. He walked over to the dead, unaffected by their brutal deaths—but then again, in the past, so many of us had died at his hands. He was the monster in this story, not me. "Besides, had I wanted your attention, I would have spread my thighs as my sister did for you. Isn't that how this works? You fuck me, and then you destroy me."

"They were trying to save you, as was I this time," he snapped, his eyes burning with the anger that I felt.

I could sense the truth in his words. Unfortunately, no one had asked me if I wanted to be saved. Now, I craved death, because I'd be with John, at least until the souls were forced to be reborn into the next incarnation. Instead of speaking to me, they'd believed him as he'd whispered lies in their ears, telling them of the darkness which controlled me, and yet it hadn't. It told me truths, showed me a path to escape the creature who stood before me. They'd tried to leave me defenseless against this man, this creature who hunted me through space and time just to kill me over and over again.

He'd told them I needed to be saved, but he had no idea that I enjoyed the darkness. I craved this thing inside me, the seal that kept balance between the worlds. Did I trust it? No, I trusted no one except John. I knew I was being used by the seal to fight this monster in front of me, and yet I didn't care. I wanted to end this game, to put a stop to it once and for all. The next time he killed me, it would be over. There would be no rebirthed soul, it would *cease to exist. I planned to hurt him as much as he'd hurt me by killing John.*

"Ah, beautiful Katia likes the darkness she harbors, doesn't she?" He studied me as he walked around the circle, looking for a chink in my defenses. Those eyes of his seduced, they bored into me and tried to lower my defenses as I watched him, spellbound by every step he took. His gaze slid down the tattered remains of my chemise and I shivered at the heat that pooled in his inky gaze. His eyes feasted on my breasts that had been pushed up by my corset, heaving with every breath I took. "Come to me, and I'll show you pleasure unlike anything your poor lover could have shown you."

"You're afraid of what I hold inside of me, are you not?" I needed to change the direction of the conversation, as my body heated for him. It responded as if it knew he spoke truths, but then it probably did. I housed his lovers inside me; each one had succumbed to him at least once. "Is it because it shows me what you truly are? Or because it told me how you enjoy seducing, then murdering us after you've enjoyed yourself?

"Tell me, Lucian, what will you like most about hunting me down; the excitement of the kill, or fucking me as you end my life? I know all about you because I listened to it, and the women before me who you slaughtered. Did you want me to fall hopelessly in love with you so that we could play out this deadly game again? Or do you prefer I just take off my clothes and let you have me?" I pushed down the straps of my chemise, exposing my shoulders to him. "That's why you killed my John, wasn't it? Because he stood between us, and I loved him." I reached for the

bloodied ribbon that held the chemise together and pulled it free. Slowly, I moved closer to him as I exposed more skin than was proper.

I reached around, slowly loosening the ribbons that held the corset up, one by one, undoing them until I was before him in nothing more than the chemise. I dropped the corset to the ground and bent over, grasping the hemline of the slip and pulling it over my head to expose my naked body to his heated eyes.

My eyes held his in open challenge, knowing he wanted me as I wanted him, but it wouldn't be love we made. It would be war. How I could want him after what he did—well, it didn't make sense. He'd brought us to this time and place; he'd put me through hell to make sure this confrontation happened.

I stood inches from him, naked as the day I was born into this world and drawn by the fire I saw burning in his eyes. He watched my movements; they were slow, calculated, made to bring his attention to my naked form. The fire from the protection barrier licked my skin, and yet I cared little if it burned to the bone. His eyes did little to hide his hunger as he slowly moved them down my body until he brought them back up to hold mine.

"Come to me, Katia," he crooned, his body calling to me, but his eyes... His eyes searched my soul, finding every flaw, every desire, playing it like a fiddle. "I'll help you; you want me, don't you?" He started to unfasten the gold buttons of his dashing blue undress coat. He'd come to us in the guise of a soldier, a deserter who did not think our country should be involved with the conflict between

Spain and some of its colonies. Our town was isolated and news was hard to come by, so our coven had glutted themselves on his stories of the outside world. He'd played on our sympathies by telling us that his coven was no more and he longed to belong to another. Lies, all of it lies to ingrain himself into our tight-knit community.

I slid my hands down my sides, watching as his eyes followed their subtle descent. Once he removed his coat, he pulled the white shirt over his head, revealing runes that covered his chest in utter perfection. I moved my hand over my pussy, watching as the muscle in his jaw clenched.

"I don't want to be saved," I murmured. I stared into the flames inside his eyes; they burned midnight blue. "I like how I am, don't you?" I taunted as I grabbed my breasts, squeezing them as he watched me. "Do you think I'm pretty?" I tilted my head as I gazed into his eyes defiantly.

"You're beautiful, Katia," he growled as he stepped back. "Let me touch you," he pleaded as he worked the buttons of his breeches.

"I don't think so," I said, turning to dismiss him and walking back to the cauldron. I retrieved my knife from the ground and, over the boiling pot, sliced through my palm so both matched. Then I slapped my bloody palms together, twisting my hands as it sent droplets into the boiling potion. "Do you know what happens to a witch who kills those she is bound to?" I didn't bother to turn towards him as I spoke, for fear that he would be more than I could resist. I was testing his knowledge of witches *since it had to be vast, considering he'd stalked me through generations, always hunting the same coven.*

"She will be cursed by Hecate," he snapped, once more pacing the circle as he watched me, like an animal, stalking prey that was just out of his reach.

"And if she's already cursed?" I turned and observed him as he paced around the circle, the hunger in his eyes deadly as he took in my naked form. The curses of my past lives were now visible, brought forth for him to see. My flesh marred, glowing with every curse he had placed upon me. "Do you know the answer or not?" I mocked as I drew the words and runes of a new curse upon my body in blood. "You should know the answer. Are you not the one who enjoys this game, Sir Lucian?" I asked with a one-sided smile. "The curse will be intensified, so any curse she used on herself, or those that someone else cursed her with, in this case, that's you, are tenfold what they were when she is reborn."

"Don't do it," he growled as he stopped in front of me, his naked body luminous in the moon's light. "Come to me, now, or you will die," he growled.

"I'm already dead," I laughed. "I was dead the moment you walked in and spread your lies to anyone stupid enough to believe them. John, though, he didn't deserve what you did to him. That was your mistake, Lucian. You shouldn't have touched him. You see, I was content to play your game, but you had to go take the one thing I loved the most away from me." I grabbed the ladle and poured some of the bubbling liquid from the cauldron into a vial.

"He deserved everything that happened to him and more," Lucian returned, stalking my naked form as I moved around the cauldron, dropping in the remaining ingredients so he wouldn't be able to identify the curse I'd made. "He wanted you because of something you have inside of you, not because he loved you. He didn't marry you; he only wanted a child from you. He wasn't even human anymore; a demon possessed a human so that he could come to you and appear mortal. Once he'd gotten you pregnant and the child had been born, he would have slit your throat."

"He loved me," I whispered defensively, as if I was trying to convince myself as well as the monster prowling nearby.

"You were fucking a demon, Katia. One whose sole purpose was to get between your pretty thighs and impregnate you," he hissed as he knelt down, touching the circle that protected me. "Once he'd ensured you were pregnant with his child, and it had been born, you would have died by his hand. So yes, I had the coven kill him. I enjoyed giving the order, too. I heard that John bled for hours, and he never once thought of you or cried out your name as he lay there, dying."

"You were jealous, and if he was a demon, then you are no better than he was." I turned away from him so he couldn't see the tears in my eyes. My hands trembled as I stood there with the vial in one, smoothing over my skin as if I'd still worn the chemise with the other. I pushed the pain away, burying it so deep inside of me that it was absorbed by the seal so I could focus. "You wanted her to be me, didn't you?"

I nodded in the direction of Flora's corpse. "You wanted it to be me you were fucking, and you couldn't have me, could you? In every life I lived before, I was yours. Except this one. In this one, I was already his. What does that tell you?" I asked with a soft smile playing across my lips. I tipped up the vial, intending to drink it, which would render the circle broken and let him in, but his voice stopped me.

"That I should have fucked you anyway, and you would have forgotten all about him, sweet witch. You're right, you are mine. It matters little what you come back as, because when you do, you are mine in every way. You love me, even now. You don't like it, but you do. You crave me, don't you?"

"I hate you, and I know that once the circle is broken, I am dead. But know this, Lucian; when I die, it will be with purpose. I have watched you kill them all, every single one of them. I have watched you manipulate their families. I have seen and heard the lies you spread about all of my incarnations. Most of them didn't discover what you were doing until it was almost too late. I learned from them. I know what they did and where they failed. This time when I die, it will set wheels that you cannot stop into motion."

I'd moved to the edge of the circle and watched as he knelt in front of me on the wet grass, his breath fanning my naked pussy as he stared up hungrily. The heat of it shot through me, rendering me stupid with how much I needed him to touch me. It had to be killing him to be this close to me, and yet I was so far out of his reach.

"I want to taste your sweet pussy—let me," he whispered huskily, his tone filled with need. "I want to hear my name on your lips as I take you further to the heavens than that demon could ever get you to reach. He was a monster, one who only wanted a child from you. I'm a man. One who wants to show you what heaven is like. I want to feel your body against mine, feel it trembling as you find your pleasure. Let me have you," he crooned seductively.

I lowered myself in front of him and smiled coldly. "Touch me," I called softly, my own voice mirroring his need, yet I was in control. "Come get me if you can."

"Come closer; let me show you what your body was made for. Let me love you."

"I had love, you took it away," I bit out, and his eyes narrowed ever so slightly. "You, you're not a man. You are a monster who hunts me through space and time. You always leave my corpse behind in a pretty glass box covered in runes that you hope will stop my curses when you've finished. That's not love; love is giving yourself to someone and discovering they're flawed, but you love them anyway, because you make them a better person. You don't know what love is. You, Lucian, will never know true love. You want her because she discovered what you are, because she preferred death over your touch. You hunt her because you're a monster."

We stood up slowly together, eyes fixed on each other until we were face-to-face again.

"You still love me every time. Every time you come

back to me, Katarina. You are mine, and when you love me, you give me every piece of you. You hold nothing back from me. That darkness inside of you? It binds you to me. It is what brings you back to me. Your love, though, your love cannot be forced or taken; it's given, because no matter how much time has passed, you are mine. Your love is the purest thing you have, and when you give it, you move mountains to protect it."

"I am Katia, not your Katarina! I loved him, not you. I loved him more than I could ever love you! He didn't want me dead!"

"He did, he wanted your body to bear him a child, and then he'd have cut your throat while it suckled your breast. He was a vile being, lower than anything that exists here. And you fucked him! You are mine, every part of you belongs to me, and you gave it to a demon!"

I lifted the vial and stared at him.

"Put it down, now," he demanded as he watched me. "I can save you. We found a way to separate your soul from the seal, which means you can live. The seal is the reason Katarina ran from me. The seal weaves lies to try and get free. Please, Katia. Let me save you. Let me end this," he murmured, never taking his eyes from mine. "Once it's removed, you are free to be reborn without me; you can live the life you deserve. You will do more damage than just cursing your soul if you kill yourself, and you know it."

"The hell with you and your curses. I already told you, I don't want to be saved. Whatever this thing inside

of me is? It hates you. It hates you as much as I do. It wants revenge and so do I. You also fear it, so I think I will keep it."

"It's evil," he whispered as his eyes tracked the vial I held close to my mouth.

"I know it is," I agreed. "So am I. It's also the one thing you fear, and I own it. So why would I give it back? It terrifies you, so for now, it's mine. I know what curses my predecessors cast against you. They whisper to me all the time, delighting in what little torments they could leave you with as you killed them. Let's see if you can guess what I have added, shall we? One cursed you so that you could not create children—a nasty curse, that one. But considering how handsome you are, that's almost a shame. Wouldn't it be a boon for you if there was an exception to that curse? Perhaps my curse could counter that one under the right circumstances. Or there's already an exception to that curse, and the one I have casted ends this once and for all in a way you cannot possibly foresee?" I taunted.

"Touch me, Katia," he growled, his steps mirroring mine as I began to pace the circle with the vial clenched in my bloodied fist. When I didn't respond, he nodded to my hand. "What's in the vial?"

"What do you think is in it?" I smirked when he cursed under his breath. "What's the matter? Afraid I will steal your kill?" I smiled as I paused to frown at him, close enough to kiss him. "Obviously she's here with me because I find myself wanting to taste you. John always said it was a waste of seed and the cock only belonged in

one thing, yet I crave you in my mouth. So, she must be here, ghosting in my soul. Because I don't want you, never will. Neither will the next; in fact, she'll hate you. I've more than made sure of it."

"Tell me what you did," he demanded. His hand pushed against the fiery barrier of the circle, and I watched as he struggled and almost succeeded in reaching me. I stepped back, narrowing my eyes on his.

I brought the vial up, tipped it against my lips, and drank the contents. Tears filled my eyes as I considered what I had done. I turned, taking in his naked body as he prowled, moving back and forth as his eyes watched the flames flare around the circle. No one had wanted me for myself in this life. John wanted a child, because once born, it would hold that which he had wanted most in this world. Lucian wanted her, the one he'd loved so long ago. My coven had chosen him over me, and in the end, I would die alone.

I dropped the vial, listening as it bounced off the ground. I lifted my eyes, staring up at the full moon as it reached its apex, high in the sky. My curse wasn't much, but it was enough to give the next one a fighting chance against him. A chance to end this. My eyes slid back to Lucian, watching as he paced, naked, bathed in the moonlight in utter male perfection. I could see why she had loved him. I knew why they were all besotted by him until the end as their life force ebbed away. He was everything a woman would want in a man; strength, power, virile, and he'd never age. His body was sleek, hard, muscled, and covered in runes that seduced the eye of anyone brave enough to look. I dropped my gaze, *watching as the flames around the circle died and he lifted his midnight gaze to mine as a dark smirk tugged at the corner of his lips.*

He moved with purpose, crossing the now nonexistent barrier, and then slowly, ever so slowly moved around me as his hand touched my body, creating a storm of emotions inside of me. His touch set me on fire, and I knew I didn't want to desire this man. He'd taken from me, and yet I wanted him to lay me down and do what he wanted, which was utterly sinful. Instead, he circled me slowly, prowling around me like some naked beast ready to claim its prize. He strutted, making sure the hair on my nape stood up at his close proximity, and I waited, I waited for him to land the blow that would end my life. It didn't come.

Instead, his fingers slowly drifted down my sides, sending heat unfurling inside of me. I was covered in blood, and yet the moment his hands touched me, I forgot who or where we were. His lips touched between my shoulder blades, kissing his way up the base of my spine.

"Turn around, Katia," he whispered as he kissed the curve of my neck. I turned, watching as he backed up. "Tell me what you did. If you tell me, I will be able to help you."

"I don't know what I did," I said woodenly, waiting for him to respond in violence. His hand raised and he backhanded me, sending me to the ground with a punishing blow.

He knelt beside me with his cock hard, his hand slowly touching me where he'd hit me. His eyes watched me and something soft took hold. "Tell me what you did. I don't want to hurt you. Too much depends on what you did, you understand that, right?" Despite the violence he had just used against me, his tone was still that of a lover.

"I can't," I whispered, and cried out as he grabbed my hair and pulled me back to my feet.

"You'll tell me, you always do," he growled as he pulled me flush against him. "You feel that?" he asked as my body rubbed against it willingly. "Your demon made love to you, but me? I want to destroy you. I want to take you so hard that you know you are owned, so that when you come back, you'll still feel me, here." He pulled me away and slid his fingers inside my slick flesh. "That excites you, doesn't it? My dirty little girl, so dark and deadly that she isn't even safe from herself," he hissed coldly. "Tell me, Katia, when your demon lay between your legs whispering sweet nothings, you craved more, didn't you? You had no idea that it was me you craved."

"Go to Hell!" I snapped.

"Hell doesn't frighten me, it cannot contain me. Come on, Katia, fight me," he demanded as I struggled against him. "I like it when you fight me, remember? Did she whisper that to you as well?"

"You didn't at first," I hissed back. "Tell me, what would you do if you only had one more chance to save her? Because that's what this is; you're trying to save her from what she did. But think about this, I didn't curse you. I cursed her," I laughed as he swallowed convulsively and shoved me to the ground. "I figured it out: the way to

hurt you? Is to hurt her. You will try to save her, but you won't be able to, no one will. You will love her, and the moment you do, her clock starts ticking. Every one of us will be with her, but they won't love you anymore. She won't love you. Next time she is reborn, she will win this game. We've made sure of it."

"Tell me what you did, or I will make sure the reminder of your life is nothing but unnamable pain," he warned. When I just smirked at him he shook his head and knelt between my legs. Never taking my eyes from his, I parted them. "Last chance, Katia."

"I can't tell you because I don't know," I whispered. "I spelled myself to forget what I cursed. I spelled myself to know of a thousand possibilities, but I do not remember exactly what I cursed anymore. I saw what you did to all of them. The way you manipulated and seduced them before you killed them. You think I'd trust myself not to beg you?" I laughed, feeling him as he settled himself between my legs as he captured my hands high above my head and forced me to arch my back. His mouth crushed mine with a fervent need that I matched. Unbridled lust ripped through us and, wanted or not, I needed his touch as the poison and curse burned through me. His tongue pushed past my lips, sucking mine as they met in primal need, unaffected by the chaos that played around us. Lightning lit the sky as thunder clapped and shook the ground. I craved him.

I craved him like a prostitute craved silver to feed her babes who waited hungrily at home. I moaned, unable to deny what he did to me when he touched me. I could feel his throbbing cock as it slid between my legs, poised to take what I freely offered. He laughed coldly, the sound unintelligible, but not wholly human.

"If you won't tell me, then beg me for mercy. If you know the past, then you know what I am capable of. Beg me," he demanded. He pushed inside, and I cried out against his mouth, moaning as he filled me until I hurt, yet craved the pain.

I smiled coldly as he witnessed the seal taking control of me, changing my eyes to the color of his soul; black. Thick black lines raced over my skin as the power of the seal surged through my veins. A knife materialized in his hand as he raised it and clenched his fist around it. I brought my hands up to stop him, but too late. The knife sliced through my hands and plunged into my chest. I screamed as he pulled out and stood up, ignoring the fact that I was no longer it, the evil which lurked inside of me. I struggled to my feet to face him.

"Let her go!" he demanded.

"It did," I gasped as I brought my palms up, gagging as I took in the bloody gash that had cut to the bone and flayed me open. When he moved towards me, I whispered his name and he stopped, his hooded eyes blinking slowly, as if he was waiting. Waiting for her.

"Katarina," he whispered.

"We are all here, my love," I replied, unable to stop the darkness as it swirled to life once more.

"Gods," he growled as he rushed to me, knocking me down as he entered me hard, moving at a pace that wasn't

human. As he chanted words I couldn't understand, words that sounded older than time, his body took mine, sailing over the moon and through the stars as I shattered against him. With a gasping and ragged breath, he found release.

"Lucian," I warned, unable to stop it from controlling me. A voice that didn't sound like mine emerged from my mouth. "You're making this too easy. You think I'd let her go?" it laughed, changing my features to hers. I rolled away from him, unable to stop it from using me to speak to him. Pain racked me, consuming my mind as it took full control. "You have been trying to put me back into that box, and I have no plans of going willingly."

"Gods damn you," Lucian snapped, retrieving the blade. "I will find a way to destroy you."

"No, you won't. There is no way that this ends with me being destroyed or going back into that box. You won't kill her again. She knows what you are and what you do to her every time she is reborn. Next time, when you find her, it will already be too late for you. The gates will open and she will be free to be reborn as I have promised her in a life without you in it. You see, she's not going to be the same when she returns. She will be faster, stronger, smarter, and hidden until she is ready to play the game. You loved her, which means she is a weakness which can be used against you."

"I'll be prepared, creature, I always am," he snarled as he jumped, slicing me as, once more, the seal disappeared, leaving me to feel the bite of the blade as he cut me to ribbons. I fell to the ground as my blood flowed and his feet kicked, hitting my spine until it snapped, and

with it, blissful nothing as he ended my life.

I awoke from the nightmare, gasping for air, and turned in bed, only to see Lucian watching me. I launched myself from the bed, covered in so much sweat my nightgown clung to my curves. I crawled across the floor, to the wall, and crumpled against it, staring at him.

"Bad dream?" he asked coldly.

"You, you killed me," I whimpered as if he'd really driven that knife through me. I brought my hands up, holding them out as I looked at them, and then pulled away the top of my nightgown to examine my body. "Holy shit, that was fucking terrifying!"

"What happened in your dream?" He looked out the window as he stood up and turned to face me.

"I killed people, and then, oh God, I killed my sister, but it wasn't *my* sister. And you, you were naked, stalking me around a circle of fire. Naked, like, dick swinging in the wind naked," I babbled as I lowered my gaze to the dick in question. "Then when the circle broke, you killed me. You, you…" I looked out the window as the sun started to rise, then back at Lucian, who had gone as still as a statue.

"You should get dressed," he growled, and I blinked at his cold dismissal.

"That's it? You ask what happened and then nothing?" He'd turned from warm to cold faster than jumping in an ice-cold pond in winter.

"I said get dressed; it was a nightmare, Fitzgerald, what do you expect me to do about it?" he snapped angrily.

"Nothing, nothing at all," I muttered as I pushed from the floor and stood on shaky legs, which he noticed. "Last night I had a dream about fucking Lucifer, and everyone panics. Tonight, it's about you. So maybe the dreams have something to do with you and nothing to do with me."

"Careful, Fitzgerald," he warned, his expression glacial.

"No, no, I don't think so, Blackstone. Last night you offered me a solution; today you're as cold as the iceberg that sank the Titanic. If that solution is you, I think I'm willing to keep the dreams. After all, it wasn't so bad being fucked by the devil, considering you're a close second." I was pushed up against the door with his hand wrapped around my throat, my head bouncing against the wood. I cried out as I brought my hands up to his and gasped for air.

A knock sounded at the door and my mother called my name softly. I started to reply, but his hand tightened until I couldn't do anything but glare at him. We listened as her footsteps retreated down the hall.

"Do not fucking tell me I'm worse than he is or I will give you a damn good reason to think I am. You think I fucking care if you think I'm a monster? I promise you, little girl, I will fuck you and then destroy you in the same night. I'm not a nice man, but I still am a better choice than he is. I'm there when shit happens because, believe it not, I am trying to protect this coven since they seem hell-bent on fighting demons when they have no fucking clue how to accomplish it. You think I don't know about you and your little group of demon fighters? When you get in over your head and they seem to run away from you? It's not you they fear, it's me. When you and your little playmates got in over your head a few weeks back, who the fuck you think stopped the demons from tearing all of you apart?

"Remember, Fitzgerald, they ran *away* from you even though you were on your ass in the dirt. It wasn't you and it sure as dick wasn't the old man downstairs that they feared. You need me, like it or not. You don't have to like it; fuck, I prefer it when you don't. Now, get fucking showered, you have places to be today. Try not to slip and land on Lucifer's dick while I'm away."

He pulled away and I slapped him hard, bringing my hands up to my throat as he backed away from me.

"Yeah, I like it rough, too, little girl," he growled as he turned, taking long strides as he left the bedroom. I slid down the wall and glared at the door long after he'd closed it.

CHAPTER
nine

I am not looking to escape the darkness; I'm finding myself in it. ~**Lena**

I sat on the couch with my legs under my ass, watching reruns of *I Love Lucy* with my mom and Alden as the doorbell sounded merrily throughout the house. Alden jumped up and hurried to the foyer, and I could hear him opening the door.

A few moments later, as I drummed my fingers on my thigh, I looked up and froze as I caught sight of our guest. Green eyes found mine, smiling before they moved to my mother and then back to me.

"Babe, Kendra, this is Adam," Alden announced as he cleared his throat and looked at us uncomfortably.

"Pleasure, ladies," Adam seemed to purr as he entered the room. I righted myself and slid my eyes over him, because if sex walked on two legs, it had just walked in through my front door and was waiting for my mother and me to respond to his greeting. He was tall, like well over six foot, with long dark hair the color of mahogany, and muscles that went on for days.

"Hello," I mumbled, wishing I'd taken a little more time with my appearance. But we'd been watching Netflix and chilling with Lucy all night, so I had been pretty comfy in my baggy sweats up until he'd arrived. "Sorry, we weren't expecting company," I admitted as I stood up awkwardly and smoothed down my sweatpants. At least they were Pink brand, and light grey that went with the baby tee I'd made to sell that said, "Witches eat Snitches," across the breasts.

"That's okay, you still look good enough to eat," he smirked as he slid those green eyes down my body with a hungry look in them. "Just here to talk to Alden for a moment."

"Is anything wrong?" my mother asked, worrying her bottom lip as her eyes darted from Adam and settled on Alden. They made puppy dog eyes at each other and I made a gagging noise that stole a laugh from Adam, which only made him even more boyishly handsome.

Something pulsed in the room and I swallowed as my body awakened with a violent need. I eyed Adam, who almost looked as if he was waiting for some kind of reaction from me. I licked my lips nervously and tried to pull my eyes away from him.

"Maybe we can double date later, ladies?" Adam suggested with a sly wink at me. On another man, the gesture would look smarmy. With this man, I was imagining panties thudding to the ground around the state.

"Are you from his coven, his old coven?" my mother inquired, and I noticed Adam's lips tightening, as if something about what my mom said was funny.

"You could say that," Adam nodded, but the way he said it made me question it.

Something was off here. Yet the more I looked at him, the more I just wanted to rip off my clothes. It was all wrong. I tore my eyes away from him, trying to make the pulse that had just leapt to life between my legs stop. He wasn't a witch, not with those eyes he was trying to hide. I turned back to him in time to see the tattoos on his arms pulse and undulate briefly over his skin. Fuck me. I shook my head to clear it as Alden asked my mother if he could use her office; the moment she agreed, I beat feet through the kitchen and out the back door.

I ignored the fact that I wasn't dressed for the chill in the air, or the fact that I was sneaking around my house to figure out what the fuck was going on in it. I paused as I pressed myself against the house and glanced at the driveway, wondering absently what kind of car he had come in.

A guy like that wouldn't be driving around in a lime-green Gremlin or a Volkswagen bug. For starters, I doubted he would fit in one of those cars unless he was folded, but I was curious as to what he would drive.

There was nothing. I was about to head back inside

when a window a few yards away from me opened, and Alden glanced around nervously as he placed new salt just outside on the ledge as they spoke. I waited for his head to move back inside, and then snuck as close as I dared to it. As my heart beat wildly against my chest, I tried to quiet my breathing so I could hear what they were saying.

"The Guild is almost finished, yet there's still rooms inside the catacombs we can't get into. So, if you know what's inside of them, you need to start talking," Adam said softly, and I froze.

"Couldn't Olivia get into them like she did with the room that had those grimoires in it?" Alden's voice was smooth, as if he wasn't discussing treason against our coven in my house.

"We haven't asked her yet, considering she's pregnant and Ristan is being an overprotective asshole. He'd probably rip my heart out and eat it if I even suggested sending her in right now. Synthia is planning on asking him, but she's been rather busy. All things considered, I didn't want to bother them if you already know what's inside there. Plus, now that the leyline witch is out of there, it's safe to start gathering the little ones to live and train there again. Syn wants it up and running soon; seeing that other Guilds are falling, those children will have nowhere to go."

"Has Synthia figured out what Lucian wanted from the catacombs yet? She made that deal with him without considering what it might have been first, and that worries me." Alden's voice turned stern, as if his own words disturbed him.

"No, but you know he'll get it. Eventually. She won't break her word to him."

"No, no…once she gives it, she will honor it. God help us if it is something that threatens this world and yours, Adam. I worry about what he's searching for, and how it will affect the Guild or this coven. Not to mention, the other night, Lucifer made another move that would have been almost as disastrous as his last one was. Do me a favor and keep an ear out, let me know if you hear anything. I'll pour through the files you brought me last week; see if I find anything in them."

"You do that," he said. "Lucifer, huh? Sounds like a fucking mess you have here, old man. You need us, you know how to reach us."

"Adam, use the door. The house is warded and spelled against every creature possible. These witches are smarter than most."

"Fine," he groaned, and I heard the window close, as the door opened to the hallway. I moved towards my car, hiding in the shadows as the man stepped from the house, walked into the driveway, and then disappeared.

I stood there, staring at where he'd evaporated into nothing. As if he just ceased to exist. I leaned against the car, staring at the mansion across the way before I turned towards the backdoor. I had barely made it through the door when I heard footsteps heading in my direction, so I dropped onto all fours on the carpet.

"Kendra?" Alden called out, and I answered him, as he came around the corner and found me, pretending to examine the carpet where it had become threadbare in places. "Everything okay?" he asked.

"Only so much Lucy a girl can handle," I lied with a tight grin.

"Don't think your momma would agree with you on that one, kid," he smirked, and studied me closely. "Lucian was a gentleman last night, wasn't he?"

"Perfect gentleman," I agreed. "Condescending asshole, but he kept his paws to himself." I pulled myself upright and dusted off my hands. "I'm going to go out tonight with Kat and Dexter, so I'll just go on in and shower, if you want to tell Mom?" I didn't want to face my mother right now. Hell, if anyone could tell I was lying, it was that woman.

"You sure? Lucian said you shouldn't be out alone."

"I won't be alone. I'll be in his club with my friends." I grinned brightly.

An hour later, I was walking up to Layton, who was tracking me with narrowed eyes. I paused in front of him, giving him a lopsided grin.

"I need to speak to your boss," I stated boldly, expecting to be let in.

"He's busy," he growled, dismissing me coldly.

"I'm not here for pleasure, it's business," I replied

icily.

He gazed back at me, his eyes roving over my curves, and what I was wearing seemed to be a footnote in his perusal. The dress was a double-slit maxi dress that looked damned good on me, and the top just happened to be a tube top, which meant no bra—which, apparently, he seemed to like. "Could have fooled me; ain't no witches coming looking for business in a dress like that unless they're in the *business* of looking for trouble. So tell me, Witch, you here to fuck or fight, which is it?"

"Neither," I replied primly as I narrowed my eyes on him. "Where is he?"

"He's below. You got the balls to go down there for your *business*?" he drawled as his eyes remained fixed on my breasts.

"You think I won't?" I snapped, and he smirked.

"Go in; he'll find you when he is ready to," he growled as he lifted the red rope so I could pass through.

"Thanks," I quipped, not caring if it sounded more like a *fuck you*.

I entered the club, hearing the fast tempo of a song that seemed to flow through me. I looked around, scrunching my nose as I took in the crowd, which looked more 'other' than human as they danced and moved to the beat. The vibe inside the club was sin, mixed with something darker.

I moved deeper through the crowd, pushing my way

through until I got to the hallway that led below. Tonight it wasn't blocked off. Normally there were men stationed at the entrance and you couldn't get through. I looked around to be sure no one was watching, and smirked as a group of girls started down it; I caught up to them, blending in.

We moved down the stairs to the lower level, and I paused once we reached the dance floor. It was filled with half-naked men and women, all dancing to the hypnotic beat.

There was something beautiful and sensuous about the way they moved; it wasn't anything like I had seen at the awkward high school dances or bars that catered to the college crowd. Their movements pulled me in and mesmerized me. I swallowed the urge to remove my dress and join them, forcing myself to go deeper into the secrets that lay in this level which we'd been forbidden to enter.

My eyes scanned the room for cameras, ducking my head as I passed some. I entered a winding hallway that branched in three different directions. I was about to go one way when I spotted Adam, who held hands with a girl as they walked deeper into what looked like a never-ending hallway. How the hell was this place so big?

I followed them, keeping enough distance that they didn't see me. When Adam abruptly turned, I was forced to enter a dark room to avoid being seen. The door was opened just far enough so I could hear what they were doing. Was he really fucking her in the hallway?

Shit. How the hell was I supposed to get out of here if

they were fucking? I moved further into the room, finding random sex furniture and toys set up throughout it. It even had a table big enough to hold a body. Weird ass shit. I moved to the glass wall that looked a lot like the one in Lucian's office, but this one looked like tempered glass. I got closer and saw a group of people on the other side that looked like they were waiting for something.

They looked scared, almost terrified, but why? I heard a door open and watched as Lucian and Spyder walked in, both shirtless as they approached the group.

"You broke the rules tonight." Lucian's voice cut like ice shards through the group as a bloodied woman I hadn't seen earlier moved into view. She was cut in several places, her body a mass of angry purple bruises. "Now, why don't you tell me why you thought you could fucking do something like that in my club," he demanded.

"Fuck you, you're not king here," one snapped. "She liked it, she screamed for more."

"Is that so? It didn't look like she was enjoying it to me." Spyder tilted his head with a dangerous glint in his eye.

"Fuck you, too, shadow. You think we'd be here if we weren't allowed? It's a new world, there's a new king coming. You won't be here long," another snarled, and I frowned, daring to look at Lucian, who smiled wickedly.

"You think he can take it from me?" Lucian challenged.

"He took your whore right from under your nose, didn't he?" the guy taunted, and I watched as Lucian grabbed the guy's throat with one hand and his shoulder with the other before literally tearing the man in half.

My hand flew up to my mouth, stifling the scream that tried to escape. My elbow hit the window and I stepped back, watching as one by one, they were killed in a manner that couldn't even be considered remotely human. Horror movie, yes; human, not so much! My leg bumped something, and the sound of glass shattering on the floor made me look up down and then back up, only to find enraged midnight blue eyes locked with mine.

I spun and ran from that room of death as fast as I could go. My heart thundered in my head louder than the music that boomed inside the club. My feet moved faster than they'd ever moved before, because I'd just watched them kill someone, people, like, ripping them to fucking pieces. Lucian hadn't even broken a damned sweat! Who did that?

I exploded onto the first dance floor, pushing people out of my way as I rushed through it and up the stairs to the upper level. I hid among the dancers, catching my breath as I made my way towards the door, but he was there, less than a few feet in front of me, waiting for me with a cold look in his eyes. He was the only one not dancing, staring at me as everything else moved around us.

I turned my head, intending to go out the side door, but somehow, he'd appeared there. Metallica's *Enter Sandman* cut off the other song playing, and I felt my body trembling as he started towards me. I pivoted, scrambling back the way I'd just come from. I moved through the crowd to the next floor, finding him closer than I thought he could be on the other side of me. I spun around in a circle and then ran in the opposite direction, closing the distance between me and the staircase that led upstairs. I had almost reached it when he stepped out of the throng of bodies and blocked the exit. I turned again and hastily pushed my way back through the crowd, back in the direction I'd come from. He was hunting me, chasing me back down into the underground rooms of his club.

I hurried through the hallway without looking back, kicking off my shoes as couples embraced in the long winding hallway, oblivious to the monster chasing me, rounding a corner, planning to take the stairs up to the offices, but the moment my foot touched the stair, I looked up, only to find him slowly coming down the stairs. He was no longer covered in blood, which was insane because I'd just watched him slaughter a bunch of people.

What the fuck?

I twisted in the direction I had come from and ran blindly, looking for anywhere to hide from him. I rounded another corner and as I dashed towards the closest room, every door slammed shut. All except one, which had BOSS emblazoned on it. I sprinted inside and slammed the door behind me. I moved to the back of the room, where I found a floor-to-ceiling glass wall, I examined each side, trying to find whatever might make it work and let me out of this room. I touched it, and nothing happened. I pounded on it, and wondered if there was anything in the room that might break through it, but the moment I turned my head to look, I was slammed against the glass.

Midnight eyes ate at mine as he pushed me against

it and grabbed a handful of my hair as he pulled my head back. "You shouldn't be here," he snarled. He was pulsing, his power vibrating, filling the room with raw current. "Not tonight, not when I need a release from what you did with the devil."

"My coven knows I'm here, Lucian," I whimpered as his mouth touched my throat and a growl rumbled from deep in his chest. He rubbed his nose over my cheek, allowing his heated breath to fan my flesh.

"You think they can save you from me?" he murmured as his fingers cradled my neck. "No one can save you from me tonight, no one." His mouth touched my shoulder, and then he pulled the top of my dress down, ignoring the scream that ripped from my throat as I pushed him away from me.

"If I don't go home, they'll know I'm missing," I babbled as I struggled to pull my top back up as I danced around him. I started backing away as he prowled closer, shaking my head. "Lucian." I held my hands out to ward him off. "Please," I gasped as my legs hit something soft, yet firm, and I fell backwards.

He loomed over me, shirtless. Beautiful in a terrifying way that left me both breathless and dumbfounded, which made me realize I was no better than the witch in the dream I'd had about him. Maybe that was why I'd dreamt it.

"Please what, Witch?" he growled as his arms reached for my legs. I scrambled, backing up on the bed as he smirked and stalked me across the mattress. "Please wreck your pretty pussy, or please let you go? I only have it in me to do one, and letting you go isn't really an option."

"I have to go," I squeaked, trying to figure out how to get around him, but there was no way to do it without throwing myself off the bed. "Before someone notices I'm gone and comes looking for me."

"I don't think so; you told Alden you were coming here, so they know where you are. You're out with friends, isn't that right, Adam?" he asked over his shoulder. "Won't be home until late," he finished, not bothering to look guilty as he watched me squirm. My eyes moved to the door, where Adam leaned against the frame, watching us.

"You! You set me up!" I accused, and snapped a deadly glare at Lucian. "You set this up, why? Because I lip off to you? Because I don't take orders well?"

"Because you let Lucifer fuck what's mine, and I don't like sharing my toys," he snapped, pushing me onto my back as he followed me down. "There's also your flagrant disobedience and unwillingness to follow my rules. You were warned to stay away from the lower levels repeatedly and yet you refuse to listen. Just because there wasn't a guard posted doesn't mean I don't know everything happening inside my club." He claimed my mouth, hard, demanding I open to him.

I moaned against him, bringing my hands up to cradle his face, uncaring that we had an audience. He pulled back as he stared down at me. "Before this night is over, I am going to fucking make sure you know the difference between me and Lucifer. There will be no question as to who is fucking you from now on," he warned, pushing his sex against mine, forcing me to wrap my legs around him until our bodies were flush. "You're so fucking beautiful. So utterly fucking perfect," he purred as his tongue swiped against my lips, coaxing them open even further.

My body was ablaze with a need only he could fix. I whimpered his name as he pushed my dress down, his hot breath fanning my nipples as he laughed coldly. I was oblivious to everything else happening around me as he lifted himself up and pushed my dress down, and pulled it off of me then he was back, kissing me until I was making noises with how much I needed him to fix the ache he'd created.

Lucian pushed my hands away from him and I moaned, struggling to touch him, but then his mouth lowered, catching my lip as he gently bit into it. I cried out, feeling my body respond as it arched, and my nipples hardened, desperate to be sucked.

"I need you," I whimpered, unmindful to anything but him. I wasn't even sure why I needed him only that I did. He kept saying that I was his, and I couldn't even bring myself to argue it. I'd never been his before, but I wanted to be in ways I didn't understand.

"Soon," he promised, glancing beyond the bed as he once again lowered his mouth against mine. My feet were yanked from around him and I stilled, feeling hands on my ankles, both ankles. I pulled away from him to see what was going on. He watched me as a wicked laugh rumbled through his chest.

"What are you doing?" I whispered as an uneasy feeling took hold when I saw Bane and Layton securing my ankles as I struggled against them. Swiftly they moved to secure my wrists. I slowly put it together, and my body trembled as I looked around at the men who looked down at me. This wasn't what I wanted or needed. I stared up as Lucian sat back, exposing me to the men. My panties were all I still had on.

Bane tightened the rope through the loops in the restraint cuffs on my wrists and as he straightened up, he glanced down at me with a hungry look in his eyes. I was tied to the posts of the bed, which were too thick to break or get away from, spread out and vulnerable as they watched me squirm.

"What the hell are you doing?" I demanded.

"Claiming you," he smirked, stepping away from the bed.

"Let me go!" I spat, fighting against the ropes as I struggled to get away. "I will kick your fucking asses!" I knew it didn't matter what I said or did, because it wasn't as if I could actually kick their asses—yet.

Layton cleared his throat, clearly amused, and tipped his head at Lucian. "It's going to take a little while to get everything prepared, you want me to get the others in here?"

More?

Fuck this.

I whispered a spell, but nothing happened. I chanted it inside my head, over and over, as tears began to slide down my temples into my ears. "What the fuck do you think you're doing to me? You won't get away with this shit," I warned.

"Don't worry, we won't do nothing you wouldn't like, pretty kitty," Spyder murmured as he emerged from the shadows, as if he'd been there watching the entire time. "The others are already on their way. She's already hot, don't want to keep her waiting, now do we, gentlemen?"

CHAPTER
ten

I'd go to hell and back for you, walk through fire, and do anything to protect you. Even this. You. Are. Mine.
~Lucian

I thrashed around, fighting to get away from them until Lucian called Adam over. I paused, glaring at the man who no longer concealed the telltale markings that identified him. His tricolored eyes slowly moved over my exposed breasts. His smile was sinfully beautiful as he sat beside me, and slowly and lightly caressed my ribs with one large hand, leisurely exploring. I chewed my lip as I felt his hands, sending shockwaves through me.

"Get on with it, but get your fucking hands off of her," Lucian growled in warning.

"You want her to stop fighting, I need to touch her. This shit doesn't work through the air like that for me. I'm not Ryder. I just transitioned less than a year ago, so if you want her mindless with need so she agrees with what you want from her, back off. Or find someone else. I'm not exactly on board with this as it is, because the whole consent thing is sort of out the window with this crap," Adam said, not touching me until Lucian nodded.

"For what has to be done here, it is consent enough." Lucian gave him a 'get on with it' gesture.

"You son of a bitch!" I cried as I put it together. Adam was Fae, but not just any Fae. His tricolored eyes and pulsing brands said he was royal Fae, and royal Fae could fucking make you do anything they wanted. "Don't you do it!" I shouted, but his hands skimmed my sides, sliding over them, and my eyes rolled back as pleasure tore through me. I lifted my back, fighting to remember *why* I was struggling. I shook my head, screaming profanities and fought against the ropes.

"Damn, she's fierce," Adam murmured as he pulled his hand back and I growled. "I'm going to need to kiss her, because she's not letting me in. It's going to take more than my touch."

"Try again," Lucian ordered, pushing the hair away from my face as he watched me with an impassive look in his eyes, as if he was trying to detach emotionally from what he was ordering Adam to do to me.

"I'm going to rip you apart, asshole! Let me go!"

"And let him get to you again? I'd rather cut my dick off," Lucian smirked. "Which isn't happening," he clarified when I grinned ferally at his answer. "You like my dick."

"I've never even had your dick to know if I like it or not!" I growled back at him.

"I'm about to remedy that," he murmured as he watched me.

I felt both of Adam's hands caressing me and I screamed in frustration as I fought the Fae, hating that it was taking everything I had to hold his touch away from my mind so he couldn't do whatever the fuck it was they did. I was winning, right up until Lucian leaned over as his hand slid into my panties and his mouth brushed against mine.

I yelped, moaning against him as my struggles to keep him at bay faded and my need for him grew to an explosive level. I whimpered as his fingers flicked my sex, pulling growls from every man in the room, as if somehow they knew what he had done. I felt Adam's fingers as they caressed my nipples. Lucian released my mouth, and my eyes struggled to remain open.

"Fucking hell," Adam groaned as he pulled away as if I was a fire, one he'd ignited and couldn't put out. "She's a spitfire," he muttered as he scrubbed his hand down his face as if he was trying to ignore the tent in his pants, and I wanted it, I wanted them all.

"No, no please," I begged. "I'm going to rip your cock off, asshole." I lunged at Lucian, and no one had expected it. I bashed my head against his, catching him off guard, and he smirked, the motherfucker smirked at me!

"Jesus," Adam whispered and moved off of the bed,

probably trying to avoid getting his head butted too.

"That's…unexpected, but fun," Spyder smirked, sitting on the side Adam had just vacated. His hands touched my navel, gently tugging on the dangling piercing. He moved, sliding to where my head was, and sat behind me. I smelled sage and other things burning as candlelight bathed the room in its glow. He pulled my hair away from my face, rolling it under my head as I rolled my eyes to watch him. "I want to fuck you, what do you think about that? In fact, we all do, kitty. Think you can take us? Maybe tag-team a few of us?"

"Let's start with your cock in my mouth so I can swallow it after I bite it off, asshole!" I cried as I tried to slam my head back against him, but he caught it, lifting me; in fact, they all moved together as if they'd just been waiting for his cue, pushing me up so he could sneak behind me as others readjusted the ropes that held me. Spyder cradled my body with his, holding my back against his naked chest as Lucian watched us through hooded eyes.

"I see why you like her," Spyder purred against my ear. "Adam, kiss the bitch so we can move this along, yeah?"

"No," I whimpered, moving my head from side to side as tears dropped unchecked. "Lucian." There was nothing in his eyes, only anger as he watched me beg him. "I didn't fuck him! I thought it was you I was with!" I shouted hoarsely, which caused everyone to pause and look at me. "It was supposed to be you."

"It doesn't fucking matter who you thought you were with. You fucked the devil, and you know what happens when you let him in? He doesn't stop—he can pull you into purgatory, fuck you and you end up pregnant because of it. He can slit your fucking throat and it's over, you die. So this? This is happening. You are mine, and he won't get to you again, ever. Understand? Be a good girl, kiss the pretty boy. I told you, I'm not your fucking fairytale, I'm your nightmare."

"I'm not yours and I will never be, asshole," I whimpered and my head was turned, and Adam was there, seizing my lips as I pushed myself backwards, only to feel Spyder's erection as Adam claimed my mouth. He didn't just kiss; he fucked with his tongue, dipping it in, slowly caressing mine until I was leaning against Spyder, and rubbing my ass over his thick cock as if I was inviting him to play. When Adam pulled away, I groaned, whining from the loss of the heat he'd given me, only to take it away.

"She's ready now, she won't fight it anymore," he murmured with something akin to sadness in his eyes. "You fucking owe me, remember that. Next time, leave us out of whatever the fuck this is. Not sure what calls for this many half-dressed dudes and one dainty female, no matter how strong her mind is." Adam turned and looked angrily at Lucian before he shook his head and seemed to vanish from the room.

"Good kitty," Spyder purred as his hands released their hold on my waist to squeeze my breasts as he kissed my ear. I moaned, never looking away from Lucian, as if my life depended on keeping eye contact with him.

Lucian glanced away and moved to the table, leaving me alone with Spyder as the others gathered around the table, adding something to a goblet. Spyder's fingers continued to pinch my nipples, tugging on them as I closed my eyes and dropped my head against him as I inhaled the smell of him and the room. Masculinity mixed with magic. Spyder didn't stop; he held me there as I struggled to open my eyes as I saw the other men, one by one accepting a dagger that slowly moved around the table. Each made a small slice in their palm and blood dripped into the goblet, until the dagger reached Lucian, who made his offering and brought the cup to Spyder. He glared down at Spyder, who growled as he played with my breasts.

"Give your hand to me," Lucian ordered, and Spyder lazily extended his hand out, even though Lucian held a wicked looking blade in his hand, which he drew across Spyder's palm until I could see his blood, glistening like rubies as it dropped into the goblet. After a moment, Spyder pulled his hand back and I couldn't see a single mark on it as it descended to torment my nipples again. He was keeping me in the moment, locking me into whatever the Fae had done to me, making me want his cock even though I only wanted to hurt him, or them.

Lucian settled between my legs, pushing them further apart to accommodate his wide frame. He took a generous sip from the goblet and I could see the blood on his lips, blood that was contributed from every man in the room. Lucian touched the rim of the goblet to my lips. "Drink," he ordered softly, and it was a compulsion I couldn't ignore. The taste exploded on my tongue, not of a coppery tang, but of erotic musk, wine, sage and a hint of frankincense.

He then dipped his finger into the goblet and as his eyes captured mine, he slowly withdrew the bloodied digit and began making markings on my stomach as chanting erupted in the room. I swallowed as magic slithered over my flesh and my body heated. I shut my eyes as my head sagged against Spyder, who kissed my neck as he chanted huskily along with the others.

My eyes opened as I felt my panties being torn off, and a whimper of fear left my throat as I discovered Lucian painting the scrap of cloth with their blood. He watched me as I watched his hand, his thumb grazing my clitoris, and I cried out as Spyder's hands moved to the backs of my thighs, holding me open to Lucian as he continued drawing runes over my body.

"Naked little pussy," Spyder growled, his hot breath fanning my ear as Lucian moved around, making his markings. "Bet you taste like you need to be fucked—taste her for us," he demanded as Lucian's gaze moved over my shoulder. Was that anger in his eyes? He didn't like them seeing me like this, or he didn't like Spyder giving him orders? Fuck him. The next words from Lucian's lips stunned me.

"She tastes like chaos, mixed with the beginning of a storm. She fucks like a hurricane, wild with need so raw and demanding that she cannot be match. And when she comes, she roars like a fucking beast killing its prey. And when she breaks apart, she's a beautiful fucking mess. Find your own; she's mine."

"She's ours now, Lucian," Spyder corrected, slipping his hands closer to my sex as he pushed his fingers through the heated folds, which were wet, but it wasn't from him. His finger pushed into my depths and I arched for him, needing release. I felt Spyder shiver behind me as he pulled his finger out of my body and once again slid it through the slick folds as Lucian watched us. Lucian and his fucking words, the man slayed me. "You want us to guard her, you know the cost. You know what it will take to protect her from him, and we have no reason to want her to keep breathing, except you. Take it or leave it, because there's no other way around it. Lucifer is going to know what we did; he didn't think you'd do this because you don't like to share. If we don't use it all, he will get to her again. Decide."

Midnight eyes held mine and he nodded. I felt them all getting closer, even with the Fae haze mixed with the spell being cast upon my skin. I didn't want them in me; my body wasn't something to share. I didn't care what he did, as long as he didn't let them have me.

I watched as Lucian slid onto his belly and began kissing my flesh as the others moved closer, and I struggled to understand what was happening. I felt their mouths touching me, licking my stomach and breasts as Lucian latched on to my pussy and I cried out, sensing Spyder would join soon, even though he alone kept me upright as the multitude of sensations threatened to make me explode. I felt his mouth licking my shoulder as I held eyes with Lucian. Spyder bit into my shoulder and I screamed; pain burned and then, just as fast as it started, it turned to pleasure.

The others joined in nipping and biting and I couldn't tear my eyes away from Lucian as his smile turned sexy as he licked my clit. I gasped as I realized what he intended to do; even as he nibbled at my slick pussy, he was watching me with them. Only they weren't fucking me, they were biting me and sending something into my system. Layton moved in close to my sex, and I caught a glimpse of fang just before he struck. As each one licked and bit me, the site where they bit flared and sent erotic sparks shooting through my entire body.

I felt Spyder release his hold, even as he moved slightly, sending my limp body falling against him until someone else grabbed me. Then he was back, opening my jaw as he held the goblet to my lips.

"Drink, or I'll ruin this ass," Spyder growled. "It's tempting me with how sweet it is, and I'm not sure you wouldn't enjoy me fucking it hard." I struggled against him, but he laughed. "Aww, kitty, you inviting me to fuck it?" He pushed his hard cock against my back, holding me against him as the others started licking my body in one brutal assault, sending my body spiraling over the edge as Spyder held me through the orgasm.

I felt Lucian's teeth against my thigh, close to my sex and I came undone as Spyder continued to hold me through it, even as Lucian released my skin to go back to working my pussy with his dangerous tongue. Spyder's hand slid down, parting my flesh that Lucian was ravishing, slowly working his fingers against my clitoris. "You feel my cock?" Spyder murmured against my ear. "It wants to be buried in that tightness. You'd let me fuck it, too, wouldn't you?" The goblet was back, resting against my lower lip, waiting.

"Drink, now," Lucian growled as he nibbled my clit, sucking it as the orgasm subsided. I opened my mouth with a moan and drank what Spyder poured down my throat. I gagged and yet I continued swallowing until the last dregs were gone, licking my lips clean as Lucian smirked, his husky laughter vibrating against my body. When I'd finished swallowing the remaining potion, my body heated until sweat pooled between my breasts. I trembled as my body shook, as the men backed off, and stood around the bed, waiting. "Good girl, now tell me who you belong to and fucking mean it."

Spyder's lips brushed the back of my neck softly, his fingers departed from my pussy and he slowly moved away from me as Lucian loomed larger than life over me. His eyes drilled into mine as the meaning of his words hit me. Him or Lucifer, those were my choices.

"You," I whispered without hesitation. His mouth touched mine as his cock pressed against my opening.

"You are mine now until forever," he growled as he watched me tremble. His mouth curved into a devilish grin as he pushed inside of me as his men witnessed what he was doing. "Say it." He rocked his hips as a loud moan of anticipation left my lips.

"I am yours, Lucian," I moaned, dropping my head as he pushed deeper into my body. I cried out as he filled me, not caring about the audience surrounding us. "Now, until forever, I am yours, Lucian."

"Good girl, now scream it so you never forget it," he demanded, pushing in hard as he ripped the ropes free and pushed my legs against my chest as he fucked me. I screamed as I felt him inside of me. He was claiming ownership, but it wasn't just of my body; he wanted every single part of me, including my soul. My very essence.

His men began chanting again and I detonated, my back arching off the bed as I felt them there with us, as if they shared this intimate piece of us even though they hadn't touched or joined in as he fucked my soul. Lucian grabbed my hair, flipping me over as he pushed my legs apart, pounding into me with his inhuman speed as they chanted faster and faster, until my head dropped, only for him to grab my hair and pull my head back until he claimed my mouth with his hungry kiss.

Sex and magic filled the room. Dark sex mixed with black magic, and I had willingly agreed to be his, to be theirs. My mind was returning and I pushed back, joining into the foray that we called sex—and no, I didn't give a shit if they watched me be dominated in the bedroom. I was on fire, and he was the fuel that burned inside of me. I turned over, slapping him as I pushed him down, earning a grin from him.

"There's my girl," he growled as I slid slowly down his thick cock, leaning over to bite his lip as I growled my approval. I raked my nails down his chest and heard the men around us groaning as I lifted and once again, slammed myself down until I exploded around his thick cock, only to be shoved down and captured against the bed as he smiled down on me. "Now, to punish you for not knowing the fucking difference, and to make sure you damn well never forget how I feel inside of you."

I wasn't sure how many hours had passed, or how long we'd fucked, but I was sure I'd never forget it. I turned over, exhausted and sated, and stared at him with heavy eyes.

"Such a naughty little girl, sweet Witch; you wanted them, didn't you?" he murmured huskily, still hard and inside my body. "You're mine. There's no one who can reach you now, no one who can take you away from me. You can never run from me because I will find you. You. Are. Mine."

"Suck a dick," I groaned.

"That mouth of yours," he laughed as he pushed in deeper. "It's useful; let me show you what for."

I woke up sore as shit, unable to move. I groaned, pushing myself up off the bed, and looked around the room. I got to my feet, taking in my bedroom, blinking as I looked around it. It couldn't have been a nightmare; nightmares didn't leave you wincing when you walked, and damn, I was grimacing as I made my way into the bathroom.

I finished with my bodily needs and stared at myself in this mirror. I pulled up the Hello Kitty pajamas and glared at the multitude of red marks from where they'd bitten me. Proof of what those assholes had done.

Moving to the shower, I turned it on as I slowly got in and slid down the wall, where I sat and thought up ways to set them all on fire. There wasn't one part of me that didn't hurt, or at least ache. I remembered everything from last night. I quickly washed, using the new shampoo I had made, and then dressed in a skirt, without panties since I was too sore to even attempt them. I was going to fucking murder him.

I made my way to the front room, fully intending to find my mother and explain what had happened last night. Only, the moment I reached the bottom of the stairs, she wasn't there. They were. Lucian and his men smirked, cocky as shit as they watched my slow, painful gait.

I didn't make eye contact because I couldn't; after what they'd done to me? I just couldn't. I searched the room again and moved towards the kitchen, only to have something pull me backwards, which had moved faster than my mind could comprehend.

"Sweet girl, you're ignoring us now?" Lucian purred, and I growled, baring my teeth like some rabid dog.

"What the fuck did you do to me?" I snapped. "You think I won't tell my coven what you did? What you *all* did?"

"What did we do to you?" he murmured with a faux innocent tone as he inhaled the smell of my hair. He held me there, exposing me to the room full of men as he held my arms out. My midriff was exposed, and Spyder smiled at it as his eyes left it to hold mine.

"You know what you did!" I said.

"We protected you from Lucifer," he whispered against my ear as his nose nuzzled it. I wanted to close my eyes so they wouldn't see the angry tears building as I remembered them all kissing and touching me before they gnawed on me like a bone. "You let him in, not us. You were open to him, and you let him fuck what is mine, so we made you ours. All of ours, and now, now he can't touch you," he murmured smugly.

"And you had to do that? You couldn't have warned me, or at least tried to talk to me about it?" I snapped as I pulled my arms away from his and turned to face him. "You had to fuck me to accomplish the spell, or was that just you being you and needing to claim shit?" He slowly walked forward, forcing me to move back.

"That was included in the spell. You see, when you claim something as we have, it normally constitutes being fucked, hard. And you were fucked hard, weren't you?" His voice was deceptively soft as he moved forward, slowly pushing me towards the men. "Tell me, can you still feel me inside of you, claiming you, wrecking that tight pussy?" He smirked as a blush heated my cheeks. "Thought so. I told you, you'd damn well know the difference between us, little girl. When I fuck, I make sure you hurt in a pleasurable way you won't forget. He plays, torments, tortures, and discards his broken toys; I own, and I take care of my belongings." His voice dropped dangerously. "I let you keep your memories. You saw what I do, so go ahead, tell the coven. The moment they make a move against me, they die. You want a monster, I can be it. You think what you saw last night was bad, I can make it look like child's play. Don't make me show you the monster in your bed, little witch. You won't like him."

"You can't kill the coven," I warned as anger pulsed through me.

"I can, and I will if they find out what you saw, or if any of them learn about what *we* did together. Make no mistake; you joined in the fun for hours. That's dark magic. You reek of it," he laughed, pushing me backwards, where I landed in Spyder's lap with a cry of pain. He pulled me against his body and growled, and my eyes lifted to Lucian's, who had discovered I was rocking commando today as Spyder lifted the hem of my skirt. "Someone's sore." Lucian smirked as Spyder caressed my thigh, close to my sex.

"We enjoy killing, but we enjoy fucking more. Tell them, and I'll make you watch as they are slaughtered while I fuck you; I think you'll know pain and pleasure on an entire new level, kitty. I have tasted you and to be honest, I understand why he fucking craves you. You're sweet, but you hide a dirty side that drives me crazy. So please, please tell them, because once you do, his protection ends and the real fun begins," Spyder growled as his fingers traced the crease of my thigh, inches away from where my sex was bared to Lucian's heated gaze.

I struggled in his lap until I felt his cock growing against my backside, realizing he enjoyed it more if I resisted. I stopped, arching my ass away from him as he laughed huskily against my ear.

"Too easy," he murmured gently as he kissed my

neck. "You taste of sex and magic, and a hint of whisky—and honestly, you look a lot better tied to a bed, naked. So don't go and fuck up, because if you do, it's where you will stay."

"Fuck you," I whispered hoarsely.

"No, but you whisper our secrets to a soul and that's exactly what I will do to you," he promised. "Now, be a good girl and don't do anything stupid. We are everywhere, watching you." My skirt was smoothed down as one hand slid down my thigh, the other touching my shoulder, and it burned the moment he did. "You smell good, almost good enough to eat."

I stood up sharply and scrambled away from him until I bumped into Lucian, who smiled as I fumbled for words. I turned away from him with crimson cheeks and watched the backs of the men as they filed out of the house. I swallowed a sob as I turned to face Lucian, who raised a finger to run it down the side of my face.

I remembered being with him, all of him. I remembered begging him to do things to me, bad things. *Begging*. As in, I pleaded and did things to him just so he would give me what I needed, and still, I'd hungered for more. They had watched us all night, and every time we detonated, they'd come a little undone along with us.

"What we did…" I couldn't finish as heat blossomed on my face and tears lingered in my eyes.

"We fucked, you and me. You didn't fuck anyone else, and you won't, ever again. Get over it; even animals fuck when they're in season and right now, you're the animal and I am the wolf hunting you because, make no mistake, you are in season. I told you I wasn't a good guy, I told you I was the one protecting you, and so I am. I fixed your problem with Lucifer, but it wasn't for free. You let him in. Not me, not them. We paid a price to fix what you did, and therefore, you are mine. Understand? And the next time you think about exploring my club, you'll do it with me, or you won't like what happens. Break the rules again, and you will be punished, and it won't end as well as this turned out."

"I'm supposed to find a mate. I have to get pregnant, so unless you plan on having a child with me, I will be up for selection at the next event. And you...you didn't," I paused, staring at him while I tried to delicately ask if he'd worn anything.

"Didn't use protection?" He laughed as he watched me panic. "No, I didn't, and I won't with you. You will tell the coven that you are mine, or I will tell them that we fucked, and that we will continue fucking. One of the two will happen, because you are not fucking anyone else. Not unless you want to see them at the end of a sword, without a head."

"You're a bastard," I hissed as I stepped away from him as he moved closer, forcing me up against the wall.

"Save the names for in the bedroom," he laughed as he pressed me against the wall. "Kiss me, and fucking mean it. Pretend like your pretty little life depends on it, because it does."

I lifted my mouth to his, slowly running my tongue over his lips as I moaned against him. My tongue slipped between his soft lips, capturing his. A growl tore from deep in his chest as he lifted me, pressing my pussy against his cock, tearing a cry from my lungs as the soreness he pressed against burned.

What was it with this man? He hunted me down, moving in ways no witch could, and yet I couldn't stay away from him. I wanted him, wanted everything about him. I wanted him to fuck me right here, right now, and he knew it. I wrapped my legs around him, grabbing between us to free his cock, until a cough sounded from elsewhere in the room, and then another, followed by laughter.

I pulled away from him, staring into his condescending midnight eyes that smiled at me in triumph, struggling to calm my body's response to him and forcing my breathing to level out. I bit my lip, leaning my head back against the wall as he let me slide down him, right until his fingers slid through my sex with my mother and her boyfriend mere feet away from us. I smothered my face against his chest, inhaling his earthy scent as I fought to calm the storm he created.

"What is this?" my mother chirped, and I groaned. "Is this why you didn't come home last night until late?"

"She's mine," Lucian said firmly. "Let your mother know that I've claimed her as of last night and I intend to breed with her." He watched me as I skewered him with a glare that promised a thousand deaths. "A Fitzgerald and Blackstone will make a very powerful child indeed, won't we, sweet girl? Probably the most powerful in the coven's history," he murmured before he removed his hand and kissed my forehead.

"What about *him*?" she asked barely above a whisper.

"He can't touch her anymore." His eyes bored into mine, watching me as he spoke. "I used an old family spell to protect her and claim her. She's bound to me now, and closed off to Hell forever." I smirked coldly as I remembered his 'family' spell, which had consisted of a Fae and a room full of half-naked men licking and biting me.

"I will make the announcement; the coven will be thrilled. It's unexpected, but I don't think I could choose a better mate for her. That is if you breed, of course."

"I agree, as does she," he said softly, lowering his mouth to mine in a chaste kiss, which sent butterflies into a rage inside of me. "I'll see you soon."

"Hold your breath while you wait," I whispered softly, for his ears alone.

"Don't make me spank your ass, little witch," he said loudly enough for them to hear, causing my cheeks to turn redder than they already had at being found with his hand in the cookie jar. Literally.

CHAPTER eleven

Oh the secrets we hide in this web of tattered lies. ~*Lena*

Pacing in my room was becoming a bad habit. I'd been doing it for over an hour, probably punishing myself for what I'd allowed to happen last night. I still didn't know why I went to his club, for starters.

Perhaps it was the conversation between Alden and Adam that rattled me, or it could have been to spy on Lucian and finally get some answers about the crazy that surrounded him and was influencing everything in my little world. Bottom line; I knew that, for whatever twisted reason it was, he had something to do with the Fae showing up at my house.

I'd heard talk of the Spokane Guild, that it was being rebuilt after it had been rendered into a pile of rubble. I had also heard about the Seattle Guild falling, though there was no word on that one being rebuilt. The news had covered both stories about the battles at the Guilds. Both battles had fingers pointing to the Fae as the logical bad guys, yet there seemed to be something bigger going on behind the scenes with the Guilds, something the media wasn't telling us about.

Then there was Alden. He had invited the Fae into my home and seemed to be quite friendly with him. No, he was more than friendly with him; he was almost paternal to the royal Fae rat-fink who stripped me of all of my defenses and left me open to Lucian and his depraved band of merry-men. Alden, the man who had been training us to use our magic. Alden, who had been guiding our coven, knew a lot more than he let on about Lucian and what was happening with the Guild, a place our coven was forbidden to go to. Alden, the big fat traitor who was currently shacking up with my mother!

I grabbed up a picture of me and Lena and threw it against the wall, watching as it shattered in a gratifying shower of glass. I walked over to the remains and plucked the photo out of the glass remnants. I shook it for sharp fragments and noticed a map drawn on the back of it.

Sitting on my bed, I studied it for a few moments, and then a thought struck me as I slowly surveyed the other pictures. When we were kids, we'd left hidden messages everywhere, but the important ones we'd hidden in plain sight.

One after the other, I removed the photos from the frames and turned them over to find hastily scrawled notes, then lined them up on the bed until I had a full message. I swallowed fear as I figured out what it meant. My heart pounded as I studied the notes side by side on the map.

Taking one last look around the room, I grabbed my pack and stacked the notes into a neat pile before sliding them into the pack. I slipped on shoes, heaved the lightweight pack onto my shoulders and made my way to the door, but hesitated for a moment as I held the knob. I pulled it open and moved down the hallway, listening as laughter sounded from my mother's bedroom.

Satisfied that she'd be busy for a bit, I crept down the stairs as quietly as possible, glancing furtively around the room, but found no one. I moved a little quicker to the front door then out to my car. I slipped the bag from my shoulders and tossed it into the passenger seat before sliding into the car myself.

Nothing was as it seemed here, and everything felt wrong. I felt like I'd slipped into a Twilight Zone episode, one with body snatchers. I'd replayed Lucian murdering people over and over inside my head, memorizing every minute detail, right down to those people in the crowd not being human; they'd been other. No one said anything when I was being chased; no one moved to help me. As if they were used to scared people running for their lives in the lower levels of the club!

The sun was setting as I pulled out onto the road and looked in the rearview mirror in time to see another car pull onto the asphalt behind me. Lucian had warned me that his people were everywhere, watching me, and I had learned the hard way that he never made any meaningless threats. If he said he was watching, I could count on it. However, I was a girl, and he had guys stalking me. I could literally bore them to death, make them lower their guard, and then sneak away.

I spent the next several hours meandering around the mall, indulging in chocolate and perfume samples while window shopping, then headed to a bookstore that was closer to where I really wanted to be. I spent a couple more hours looking through books as the clerk watched me as if she feared I was going to finish the one in my hand. I made my way to the cash register and placed the book on the counter, nonchalantly peeking out the window to see Bane waiting in his car with an unknown passenger.

"That's it?" she asked, pushing her perfect librarian glasses into place as she made me feel like a naughty kid reading one of her mother's saucy novels. "You sure you don't want the others that you read half of?"

"No, no, they didn't hold my interest. But this one did; thank you so much for asking!" I grinned cheerfully.

"Can't say I blame you; they do lag a bit, but that one speeds up in the middle." She pointed to one of the books that had a bodice-ripper type cover, surprising me. I looked out the window again and she watched me speculatively. "They have been out there this whole time; friends of yours?"

"No, not exactly," I snorted. "Friends of my very-unwanted boyfriend, I guess you could say."

"There's a back door," she offered. "Not that you

could get your car without being seen, but it would give you some time before they figured out you were gone. I had an abusive piece of shit once. Sent his buddies to push me around when I broke it off with him. Us girls, we stick together, am I right, sugar?"

I stared at her as I considered it. The Guild was five blocks away from here. I could make it there on foot in minutes if I hurried. I still wasn't sure how I would get in, but I didn't intend on not getting in at this point.

"Please. That would help me out greatly, but I'll need to come back through here, if possible," I whispered quietly, and she nodded as she finished ringing up the book before pointing out a few shelves and talking about other books, as if she was helping me find something else. She rounded the register counter, and I followed her to the front of the shelves, where she began randomly pulling out books and describing them to me before we moved around to the back shelves, which we couldn't be seen from the front windows. I exhaled as she set the books down and hurried to the back door, pulled it open, and peered down the dark alley in both directions. She didn't stop there; she moved across the alley and rapped her knuckles on the door across from her store.

"Roger, open up, sugar," she called, and when the door opened, a thirty-something man stepped out, smiling from ear to ear as he looked over the busty store clerk. Without missing a beat or an ounce of charm, she began talking fast. "This girl needs some help, she's got a hot one on her tail; let her out through the front for me?"

"Anything for you, Carla," he crooned before he

looked at me and blinked, his eyes slowly traveling down my body with interest.

"Now, Roger, don't you be doing that to her, she's been through enough. Just let her out, please?" She shook a chastising finger under his nose.

"You got it, but you will owe me," he grinned, and I narrowed my eyes on him, unsure I wanted to leave poor Carla in this guy's debt.

"I can just walk around the buildings," I offered, but she shooed me through the door.

"Now, I already told ya, we girls got to stick together. And Roger here has twelve-plus inches in his pants, so I don't mind him at all. A girl has got to find it where she can. Lord knows they don't make them all the same. No brains, all cock on this one. He's just how I prefer them, these days. No hard feelings, sugar, but you know I'm in it for the cock already."

Laughing, unsure I should have, but unable to stop it from bubbling up, I hugged Carla quickly then followed Roger, who informed me it was more like thirteen or so inches and he was willing to show all of them to me if I wanted to check. I passed, slipping out the front of his shop with a quick wave and a sneak peek at his crotch before dashing into the next alley.

I jogged from alley to alley until I skidded to a halt as I rounded the last corner and came face to face with the forbidding sight of the Spokane Guild. The soft glow of the streetlights reflecting off of it showed me that it really had been rebuilt and was a lot bigger than I expected; huge, in fact. Lights were glowing from some of the windows and I saw that the front was guarded by a couple of tall and forbidding-looking males that I didn't have to go far out on a limb to guess were Fae.

I pushed the book into the pack, exchanging it for the map. There were arrows pointing to the back of the Guild on it, and I chewed my lip as I lifted my eyes and saw a familiar blonde as she and a dark-haired male moved around the front of the Guild.

Eyeing them suspiciously, I moved around the back and hunted around in the dark until I found the storm drain marked on the map that would give me access to the catacombs. I slipped through it, holding my breath along with my pack so I didn't make any noise as I entered the stygian interior. I scaled down, ignoring the obnoxious odor of mold and musty stagnant water as I reached another ladder.

I climbed through a pile of rubble, one that had been mapped out, which meant the map was right. I clicked on a flashlight and looked at the map again. What the fuck had she been thinking coming here after it had been attacked? Her notes said she'd been coming for months, and yet the Guild had been damaged a lot longer than that.

I moved deeper into the sewers and finally into the outer edges of the catacombs as the notes instructed, then paused, taking in my first sight of the inside of the Guild. This section was still broken, rocks and concrete blocks that had once been walls littered the floors. Dried blood coated them like macabre paint, as if this was where the

Guild members had fallen, then later been moved away for burial. My heart clenched for those who had died here. I pushed those thoughts away as I stepped past the rubble and deeper into the Guild.

I snuck down the dark hallway, following the arrows until I had to change page. My heart beat wildly as I discovered another hallway that led further into the labyrinth under the Guild.

Once I reached the floor I was looking for—thankfully without landing on my head—I turned off the flashlight and whispered the spell to see in the dark. It was a great spell, but unfortunately quite unpredictable. The leyline here was strong, strong enough that I wouldn't cause a ripple by tapping it. I moved soundlessly through what I presumed had once been a library, holding the map at my side as I followed the picture inside my mind.

I passed what looked like a medieval altar room and stopped at the entryway of it. It was old and reeked of death, as if this had once been a place of sacrifice to the Gods of old. A shiver snaked down my spine as I stared at the door, covered in wards. Heavy wards, like the kind you didn't mess with because it could bring the entire place down on your head.

Lena was officially fired.

I carefully picked my way through more rubble, wondering why they hadn't fixed the lower levels as they must have done with the upper levels.

My first sight of the catacombs almost made me turn

around and run; this section was worse. Every door had runes on them, and the deeper I got into the rabbit warren of tunnels, the more I wanted to leave this place. I could see traces of dried blood, as if some of the witches from the Guild had hidden deep inside the catacombs the day this place fell.

I paused outside a door, holding the map up to look at it. It was marked with blood, familiar blood, and yet instinctively I knew it wasn't of my line. I felt it calling to me, so I placed my hand on the door, which opened it. What the fuck?

From outside the room, I peered in at the rows of books and rolled-up scrolls of parchment that filled the shelves. In the back were old wooden tables, along with decrepit old chairs.

The moment I stepped into the room, a ghostly figure appeared, staring at me. It was a beautiful woman, created in the image of what we were taught was the Goddess, Hecate, and yet somehow I knew she wasn't the Goddess. I held my breath as I stepped closer, eyeing the door behind the figure.

"And so you've come," it said. "Blood of my blood, and line of my line, I am released from this time."

"Say what?" I asked, and watched as the door behind her opened as she disappeared. "Because drugs are bad, kids." I groaned as I rubbed my temples and moved into the hidden room, pulling the door closed behind me as I whispered a spell to ignite the candles inside the room.

I gasped as I took in the ancient items inside the room. Jars of herbs and other items were interspersed with books on the shelves. I reached out, touching one of the vials that had liquid in it, and watched as fluorescent blue writing appeared across the label. I snatched my hand away from it, afraid I'd set something off, but as I pulled my hand away from it, the other labels all began to glow with the same iridescent blue writing. I moved to the next thing, which was a small box, where I found a cameo necklace that looked as if it had been crafted in the early 1700s. Pressing the tiny mechanism on the side, the locket sprang open and a dark-haired woman stared back at me, her lush lips full as she pouted at whoever had painted her image. I put it back and continued perusing the items. Turning in a circle, I noted the wards inside the room were of the same color as the writing that glowed from the objects, as if it was projected there.

My eyes followed the lines that zigzagged through the room until they landed on a stack of grimoires. I shivered and stepped closer, pulled by the glowing handwriting that was scrawled across the grimoire on the top of the pile.

I looked around the room once more and took the last step that brought me to the books. My hand darted out, grabbing the first from the pile. I dropped my bag as I knelt in front of the pile and opened the leather-bound cover to the first page. Everything inside of me said to close it and back away, but I couldn't. I was drawn to them as if an invisible line connected me to them.

A violent tremor pulsed through me as my fingers touched the first page. My eyes grew heavy as the air inside the room grew thick with magic. As I watched letters rose from the page, slid across my flesh, and disappeared into my skin. My arms glowed with the fluorescent letters as one after another left the book and vanished into my body. I couldn't stop myself, not until every grimoire was empty and sat in a pile beside me. I brought my hands up, wiping away the tears that refused to stop as every word and story entered my mind. Ancient spells swirled around my mind—and worse. The stories that belonged to the owners of the grimoires whispered through my mind as well.

It hurt; emotionally my mind screamed with their pain even though it wasn't my own. Each one had predicted their own death, as well as whose hands it would come by. Names and dates were missing, yet somehow I knew more than just the details of their lives; I knew their pain. I stared at the last book, noting it hadn't been a grimoire, but rather a yellow-paged journal. Upon the page that lay open were my tears as I'd cried as each word had played like an audiobook as it entered my mind. I stood up, putting the books back into a neat pile and stepping away from them.

I turned and looked at the other small box on the shelf, blinking back tears as I made my way to it. After removing the lid, I held another crude locket in my hand. This locket was older; it had something written on it and yet I couldn't make out what it said. I put the top back on the box as I slipped it into my pocket and then I touched the next item. Memories that weren't mine rushed through me. I removed the lid from the next, touched it, and the next, and so on, until I had touched every article in the room, and pulled the memories from them.

I righted the room, putting everything back where I'd found it, and then silently slipped from it.

I now held the grimoires of at least six witches inside my soul. Minutes, that was how long it took me to gain the entire lifetime of magic from each grimoire. Not only that, but I held treasured memories from them; love and fear tingled inside of me, and it felt foreign. None of it made any fucking sense, yet it somehow felt right.

My feet moved as if they were controlled by someone else. I turned into the next room, stopping in front of a coffin that was covered in beautiful craftsmanship. The wood was etched with a story of curses, and the strangest sense of déjà vu shivered down my spine. I ran my fingers over it, searching for the memories it held, but there was nothing there. The more I touched it, the more the hair on my nape stood up. Whoever had etched the carvings had done so with love, taking their time.

I turned away from it, forcing myself to go. A wall of skulls met my vision and I jumped back, hitting the coffin with my hip. Watchers? I moved my eyes from them to the coffin, swallowing an uneasy feeling. Creepy.

I shivered and as I did, I heard voices. I stiffened, eyeing the coffin and wondering if I had the balls to hide inside it. *Not even going to try it.* I flattened myself against a wall, whispered a spell, and blinked, standing still as people rounded the corner. I braced to fight, knowing I wouldn't win, but they walked right by me.

I almost exhaled, but instead I stood as still as a statue, listening to them.

"Something tapped it, Ristan. I felt it, you didn't?" the blonde asked, and I stared at her. "It's still here, whatever it is. It feels…not right. Not whole. Powerful—I'm telling you, something is here."

"I would have felt it too, Flower, and I feel nothing. I feel you, and I feel me. Maybe it was Adam, his magic tends to linger when he sifts. He hasn't perfected it yet, but we all know he's been through the wringer."

I moved quietly, watching each place I stepped until I was back in the room with the altar. I had just entered it when the blonde appeared in front of me, with a sword drawn from thin air. I ducked right and crouched on the floor as she swung the sword in a wide arc, peering around the room as the other guy with long black hair gave her a golf-clap. I squinted at them, trying to get a better look at whatever weird shit was going on with his eyes.

"Congratulations, you killed air," he laughed.

"Stuff it, Demon, something is here."

I crawled on my hands and knees, rounding the altar until I rested my head against it. I heard her shoes, sexy as hell high heels that tapped as she rounded it and swung her sword inches from my head. I held my breath, holding my spot as she moved around it, staring at the spot.

"If I'm right, it's a witch. A powerful one at that, which means she might be hiding here, needing our help," she mused as she pushed the sword into the holster on her side.

"I doubt she'd ask with you swinging that thing around like She-Ra on steroids. I mean, pretty sure she'd assume you were team Skeletor about now. Come on; if you don't feel malice, she isn't evil. She's probably terrified and hiding down here, so let's give her some room. She'll see we're team He-Man soon enough."

"You and your movie shit. We need to get you more Blu-Rays soon."

"Blu-Rays are so last year. I have Demon on Demand, which is a step up from Fae-per-view."

I held my breath until they'd left the room, and for what felt like an eternity after they'd gone, I remained in place. I slowly got to my feet, searched the area, and prayed that the invisibility spell I'd somehow cast was still working. I rushed out the way I'd come, not stopping until I entered Roger's shop as I shed the spell. He smirked, coming around his counter wearing a pair of shorts instead of the jeans he'd been wearing before. I eyed the clock and saw that I hadn't been gone more than an hour and a few minutes. It had seemed like several had passed.

"I need to get back inside Carla's shop, now," I blurted as he nodded.

"This way, little lady. All the pretty girls are always in such a hurry around here," he grumbled. Once I was in the alleyway, he opened the door and I heard Bane's voice. I held my finger up to my lips and looked around, finding the bathroom, and hurried in, quietly closing the door behind me.

I listened as Bane's heavy feet pounded on the floor as I flushed the toilet and opened the bathroom door while fixing my shirt. I eyed him, narrowing a glare on him as I stepped out of the bathroom. I growled, and he smirked.

"What the hell are you doing here?" I snapped.

"Following your sweet ass for Lucian, you? Tell me, who the fuck spends this much time in a bookstore; my Gods woman, three fucking hours!"

"Book shopping, *alone*. Which means, doesn't matter if it's five or ten hours, because I'm *alone*," I replied as I moved to the pile Carla had left on the chair, then moved to the register and set them down, smiling at Carla.

"Find everything you needed?" she asked me, as if I hadn't spent the last hour or so *not* in the bookstore with her, curled up with books.

"And more, let's just hope my newfound love has big shelves," I joked.

"If a man expects to please a woman, he needs to please her mind first," she giggled, and Bane snorted behind me.

"If a man wants to please a woman, he parts her pussy and fucks it with his mouth until she's begging him to stop. After that, he fucks her for hours until she's, again, begging him to stop. Then, then he claims her mind, because once you have her body and her mind, that soul is yours."

I stared at him as the cashier sighed.

"His isn't twelve inches; more like five," I snickered, and she laughed at the disgruntled look on his face.

"The fuck you say," Bane growled as he eyed his jeans.

"I do love my inches," she winked.

CHAPTER
twelve

Along comes a Spyder, who wants to be inside her.
~Spyder

I lounged on my bed, unsure if I really wanted to go out with Dexter and Kat, especially after the shit that had gone down with Lucian. I felt more confident now, knowing I had countless spells within my grasp, especially since no one else knew it. I'd spent most of the day mentally turning the pages and perusing the spells I'd never dreamt existed.

Even though I tried to ignore it, the dream of Katia replayed in my head at least three times today, as if something wanted me to remember it. The mere idea of Katia trusting the Guild with the grimoires and journals I now had bothered me. Why had she run to them? The Guild was the last place she should have entrusted with her secrets, and yet they'd hidden them in a secret room. Why? Why would they go above and beyond for a witch who wasn't part of the Guild? It made no sense, and every new piece of information I learned made everything more confusing.

Nothing made sense anymore, nothing!

I'd had sex with Lucifer in a dream, which hadn't been a dream after all. It had led to Lucian and his men claiming me, and I wasn't an idiot. I knew it had been more than just an act of protection—it went deeper. Spyder's bite still ached, and anytime I touched it, my body responded in ways it shouldn't. Lucian had bitten the inside of my thigh, and it continually ached as a reminder of what had happened.

I'd scoured the coven's archives yesterday for anything resembling what they'd done to me, and yet there was nothing even close.

I moved away from the bed, glowering at my reflection in the mirror. I pushed the lace strap of my nightgown to the side. It revealed an angry red bite that had yet to fade. It pulsed and burned as I ran my fingertips over it. I glared at the bite then lifted the gown to expose my inner thigh, where Lucian's was, was bright red, as if he'd just bitten me a few minutes ago. I dropped the hem of the gown, grabbed some clothes, and shuffled out of my room and down the hall to the bathroom, intending to scrub my skin raw to remove the feel of them nipping my flesh. None of the other bite marks were visible, only Spyder's and Lucian's, and both throbbed with a direct line to my lady bits.

I hated it, but worse, it felt like they'd placed some supernatural LoJack on me. Then again, if I had to pick between the devil and them, I'd pick them.

Once I had showered, I changed into a billowing skirt with a lacy top. I pulled my hair into a ponytail and dabbed a little rouge onto my lips before a knock at the door pulled me from all of my confusing thoughts. I hesitantly moved to it after checking to make sure my shoulder was covered, hiding the evidence of the delicate situation I'd endured.

"You need to pack, now," my mother stated briskly as she pushed her way into the bathroom and shooed me out of there, into my room.

"Um, excuse me? I'm going out with Kat and Dexter tonight," I explained as she moved to my bed, where she sat with a frown marring her beautiful features. For her age, she looked younger than she actually was. She sure as shit didn't look old enough to have me as her daughter.

"No, you're not. The coven has requested your help, and I have taken the liberty of agreeing that you would. There's a witch in Portland Oregon who is in trouble. I need you to do this, and saying no isn't an option, Kendra. Our numbers are low. Your grandmother believes she will be a useful addition to our coven."

Her gaze drifted from me to the broken picture frame that still lay on the floor. The glass shards reflected the sun that entered the room from the window, and her eyes darted from the missing picture frame to the one remaining framed photo of Lena and me. Her blue eyes watered before she wiped at them and turned to look at me with resolve in their beautiful depths.

"I miss her too," she whispered as she stood, pulling a piece of paper from her pocket, along with a little bag of herbs. "These will aide you, and I packed a few strands of Siren hair in the pouch should you need it. You merely place it on your tongue and, for a short amount of time you will inherit the Siren's ability to charm with words. Hopefully you will not need it, but you won't be alone in this endeavor. Lucian has sent someone to guard you in his absence. As he has agreed to breed with you, he has the right to ensure your protection."

"I never agreed to be his."

"You slept with him without protection. Had you used something, the coven may have considered your thoughts on it, but you didn't. Until we know if you carry his child, there is little we can argue considering the bloodlines involved. This match, well, it would be welcomed if a child was produced from your union. With the low numbers, we need the next generation more than ever. I can see no reason for arguing this match right now, not unless you know something about him that we don't?" she asked, pointedly.

"No," I said, remembering what Spyder had threatened. "I just don't like him very much, nor do I trust him."

"And yet you slept with him?"

"I did," I admitted. I wouldn't lie to my mother. Not any more than I already had. She deserved better from me. I bit my tongue, knowing that the lies I told protected her from Lucian and his men.

"It doesn't sound like you enjoyed it," she pointed out crassly. "Is he not pleasing in the bedroom?"

"Mother," I groaned.

Was he not pleasing in bed?

She sounded like she just escaped from a Victorian novel. The man was a beast in bed, and probably some sort of sex God, but that was beside the point! "Who am I going to get from Portland, and why me?" I asked, changing the subject.

"Your grandmother said she's from one of the original bloodlines, but her family broke ties years ago. There's an address on that note I gave you a place where the witch lived; you should start your search there. If you can't find her with the info we provided, scry for her. Be careful, daughter mine. Use whatever is necessary to bring her back, but not at the cost of your life. Spyder is out front, when you are ready," she murmured, stepping closer to hug me tightly. "If he tries to stop you from reaching her, use the Siren's hair to make him see things your way."

"I don't need a babysitter," I stated.

"No, you don't. But you are my daughter. You're the granddaughter to the highest-ranking member of this coven, and that makes you a target, whether we like it or not. Lucifer himself has tried to reach for you, so I'm glad you won't be alone. Alden agreed that sending you out alone would be reckless, and you are the only one who can carry on this bloodline. I will take no chances with your life."

"Then send someone else," I grumbled.

"No; your grandmother chose you for this, and so you will do as she has requested."

"Fine," I groaned in irritation as I rubbed my temples. "How long are we scheduled to be gone for?"

"Until you find her and bring her back to us," she answered softly as she pulled me in tight for yet another hug. "Pack quickly; there's three thousand dollars on your credit card, use it if you need it. If anything happens, do what you must but try to conceal it, we do not need attention drawn to the coven." With that, she left the room, leaving me to puzzle at her whirlwind of confusing words and emotions.

I packed quickly, stuffing the pouch and a few other things into my pack, along with extra clothes in case we were gone longer than necessary. My feet shuffled hesitantly towards the window, peering down into the driveway to find Spyder looking up at me with a lazy grin on his lips. Ice blue eyes held my gaze as frown tugged at my lips at the sudden burning in my shoulder. I shook my head as I moved away from the window and made my way out of my room and down the stairs.

This wasn't a good idea, nor did I relish searching Portland for one single witch who might be in trouble. Talk about a needle in a haystack.

I exited the house and slowly approached the driveway as Spyder pushed off the hood of a sleek, black Audi R8. His smile was all teeth, which did very little to stop the wild tempo of my heart as I got closer to him. The last time I had seen him, I'd been on his lap, feeling his unmistakably hard cock against my ass.

"Hey, pretty kitty," he purred smoothly, smirking as he moved to the car door, holding it open for me. "Be a good girl and make this trip easy on us, or you know what I will do to you. Lucian isn't here to protect you this time. I take no shit, and if you fuck with me, keep in mind, I *will* fuck you back…hard."

"Where is he?" I ignored his heated gaze. I pushed my bag into the car and climbed in, trying to disregard his choice of words and what they made me feel.

"That's none of your fucking business. If he wanted you to know, he would have told you himself, and he didn't. Instead, you got me here to hold your pretty little hand."

"Whatever," I growled as he climbed in the other side. I adjusted my skirt, wondering if I shouldn't go back inside and change before we left. Portland was a long drive, and I needed a layer of protection against this man.

"You wearing panties, kitty?" he asked with a dark look, his eyes slowly moving to slide over my legs.

"Keep your eyes and your hands to yourself, asshole," I warned. "This trip is business, only business." I dismissed him as the countryside blurred past the passenger side window as we hit the highway.

"I claimed you, kitty cat, so sheath your fucking claws or I'll show you what it means to be claimed by someone who doesn't want you. That attraction you have to Lucian, I feel it for you now. I sure as shit didn't want it, either. You, however, went and rode Lucifer's cock, so here we are. Sometimes you have to do what is needed for the greater good, and other times, you help your friends out even if it is going to make them hate you. In this case, it's a little of both. So get the fuck over it. I have."

"You didn't want to help him?" I questioned lamely. I slid my eyes from the passenger window to his cold face.

"Want to? No; you're not worth the fucking trouble. I don't want to crave that pretty pink pussy. Yet I do, and watching you get fucked the other night? I'm addicted to the idea of being the one fucking you. Everything about you is calling to me—your scent, the curve of your spine—but then, that's the spell working, dark fucking magic. You're not my type; I like to break my women and watch as they fight to put themselves back together. I like to tear them apart, to shatter their mind with nothing more than what the Gods gave me. Tell me, kitty, you ever feel torn apart until you no longer care who you are, and don't care who is taking you as long as you get that next orgasm?" His eyes tore away from the road to stare me down.

"Only when you guys held me down," I swallowed, turning away from him before he saw the need growing in my eyes.

"You wanted to fuck me, didn't you?" It wasn't a question, it was a statement.

"I don't know what I wanted, or what you guys did

to me," I replied icily. "You drugged me, you let the Fae touch me, kiss me, feeding me his powers until I was mindless. So that wasn't me in that bed, it was someone who couldn't stop herself. The thing I don't get is why anyone other than Lucian needed to claim me. And I sure as shit didn't want that, either." My voice had dropped to a throaty whisper, unable to hide the hunger in my timbre as I remembered the heat of his touch.

"There are two things Lucifer fears: me and Lucian. He isn't wild about the rest of the guys, either. He knows what he is dealing with. You have our marks on your skin now; if he tries again with those marks on you, we'll feel it before you even know he's reaching for you. If he has the balls to make a go for you again, we may have to step up the claim on you. Lucian doesn't like it, but you really need both of our scents on you."

"And how do I get that?"

"You're a smart girl, figure it out."

"Indulge me, Spyder." I waved my hand at him magnanimously.

"I'd fuck you, kitty, putting my scent with Lucian's. Mixed together, Lucifer wouldn't waste his precious time on you. He sure as fuck wouldn't wait around to see who the baby daddy would be, now would he? He needs minions, but he wouldn't wait nine months to see which one of our sons crawled out of your body."

"That won't happen," I hissed as a shiver snaked through me. His hand moved to my thigh as he grabbed

Lucian's mark, pinching it until I gasped and leaned my head against the leather headrest. I struggled to push his hand away. He wasn't even paying attention to the road or the cars on the other side of the highway. I grew flushed, excited as he held on to the mark. My eyes grew heavy and I moaned, spreading my legs even though I didn't want to. My nipples turned to hard pebbles and he growled at my reaction.

"It's that fucking easy," he warned as he released me and moved his eyes back to the road. "I marked you; you're mine now too. I can fuck you, anywhere, anytime I want you. The difference is, I don't really want to, and Lucian does. Now, be good because this car isn't big enough to fuck you in and my dick is already throbbing from being this close to you without being able to sate its fucking attraction."

I grabbed for my bag and pulled out my iPod and earbuds, setting them on my lap. I looked away from him, ignoring his gaze I still felt burning my flesh. I hated that I'd been weak against his touch. Why had Lucian sent me with Spyder if he knew this would happen?

"Does Lucian even care that he sent us out together with this—condition?" I asked offhandedly.

"I don't pretend to know what he is thinking. I do know that he's busy or he'd be here himself. But yes, he does know that we are connected now; he's fully aware of what happens when that spell is used—once the claiming has begun."

"Has begun? It's not over?" I perked up, staring him

down.

"My claim is finalized when I fuck you. Until then, I'm in a perpetual state of need only you can fix—so fair warning, I'm hoping you fuck up, because after watching you fuck him, I'm needing a piece of you and I don't really care which piece it is."

"I'm not fucking you, so stop it already," I muttered.

CHAPTER thirteen

That's not my shadow, he's my darkness. ~**Lena**

The ride to Portland was uncomfortable. No matter how much I ignored it, I felt what Spyder had described. I had to force my mind to focus on other things, such as scanning the mental pages inside my head to try and find a spell that would erase the claiming spell. I doubted it would be as easy to erase as using a simple spell.

Lucian had fucked me so many times that I'd stopped keeping count that night. They had watched us every time, in every single position, and I hadn't cared. Not that it had bothered them or me, not until I'd replayed it in my head. Then I'd been a little more than embarrassed, but they didn't seem to mind watching what Lucian had done to me.

The Audi pulled up to the hotel and I stepped out,

grabbing my bag, which I started to toss over my shoulder when Spyder grabbed and took it from me. He retrieved his own from the trunk before he moved to the valet and spoke to him as I waited.

Keys were handed off and then we were moving up the walk to the luxury hotel. The scent of roses hit me as the doors opened, revealing an impressive entryway in hues of white and blue. Large murals were painted on the walls and ceiling.

Once we reached the counter, Spyder handed the bleach-blonde concierge a card, which seemed to perk her demeanor up. I was praying that Lucian had had the foresight to know that I wouldn't be able to afford the room service in this place, let alone a room.

"Is *he* joining you?" she murmured seductively. The husky undertone in her voice scraped against my nerves. "He was so—*generous* the last time he was here," she giggled as she fanned her reddening cheeks.

"No, he's busy, Ana. It's just us," he said in a bored tone.

"And will that be one room or two, Spyder? She doesn't seem like your normal type." She pointed her nose in my direction and didn't seem to care that I was right fucking there hearing her.

"His suite, please, which of course you will charge to his card," he grumbled, and I frowned as he stretched his neck as if he wasn't enjoying this any more than I was.

"Two rooms," I spoke up from behind him, frowning

when he turned those icy eyes on me with an angry glare.

"One fucking room, kitty," he snapped as he moved away from the desk. "Send up room service," he called back over his shoulder.

"What would you like?" she shouted back.

"Two of everything on the menu," he muttered just loud enough for her to hear.

I followed him, smothering a yawn as we hit the elevator. I leaned against the side, watching him as he studied me beneath his lashes.

"You should have gotten two rooms. We are not sleeping on the same bed," I grumbled tiredly as I chewed my lip. No way in hell was I getting that close to him, not with these mixed emotions and the inability to prevent them.

"I call the shots here," he muttered as he stepped closer, and a knowing grin quirked at the corner of his mouth. "Ever been fucked in an elevator?"

"No, and I don't plan to start now," I warned. "Besides, there are cameras." I pointed at one with a raised brow.

"You like to be watched," he smirked. "You like people to see what they can't touch."

"I don't like to be watched," I said confidently, but wasn't really sure if that was the truth or a lie. I'd been turned on by them watching us, and it hadn't had shit to do with what the Fae had done to me. "This is a bad idea."

"Liar," he taunted as the doors opened up and we stepped into a room that was decked out in expensive furnishings and crystals. It looked like a high rollers suite in Vegas instead of something you'd find in the Pacific Northwest.

From the entrance of the suite, I could see that the doors to the bedroom were open and the bed was huge. Sheer fabric with small crystals sewn throughout it hung from the square wooden frame above the bed. There were chandeliers in each room. Nothing in the suite deterred my eyes from slowly moving back to the bed with trepidation and fear as I noted it was the only bed in the suite.

He moved into the bedroom, dropping our bags beside the bed. He slowly turned around, looking at me as if he was contemplating saying something, and then thought better of it.

I walked deeper into the room and snuck a peek at the balcony and hot tub which waited invitingly outside, with steam spiraling up through the chilled air. Rose petals floated in it, probably having drifted from the trellised vines of roses that surrounded the balcony. I turned in a circle, taking it all in.

"This is a normal room here?" I mumbled.

"No, this is Lucian's personal rooms when he's in Portland. I found it fitting to use it, since I'm here with his girl. Might as well use his room with her," he replied casually. As if he hadn't just thrown a barb at me.

I rolled my eyes and then looked at the clock.

Midnight; we'd made great timing, but it left little time to find the witch tonight and be able to turn around and head home, which sucked. It meant I'd be sleeping here, with him. Alone. I looked at the couch thoughtfully and started towards it, wondering if the room had extra blankets.

I'd no sooner reached it when the elevators opened, revealing two carts full of food trays and a bellboy, who peeked at Spyder sheepishly, as if he feared him.

"Put it in the entryway and get the fuck out," Spyder snapped, sending the already timid kid scrambling to get away from him as fast as he could. He pushed the carts into the room and then pushed the button to close the elevator doors several times as he watched us with huge, cartoonish eyes.

I looked longingly at the silver platters as my belly growled, reminding me that I hadn't eaten in hours. The aroma was inviting, and my mouth watered in response.

As soon as he was gone, I spun around to find Spyder watching me thoughtfully. He nodded towards the food as he brought his phone out of his pocket and spoke into it. He'd dismissed me with nothing more than a nod of his head.

I strode to the trays, finding an array of delicious smelling meals. I decided on a plate of lamb and rosemary potatoes, along with a plate of what looked like chocolate silk pie. I set it down at the table and went to the mini-bar, pulled out a bottle of champagne, two flutes, and walked back to the table. With a defiant glare at the door Spyder must have disappeared behind, I popped the cork with a sharp twist and poured the bubbly into one of the flutes.

I had just finished polishing off most of the meal, along with a third glass of champagne when Spyder entered the room again. I swiped my finger into the pie and scooped a dollop of chocolate and whipped cream up, licking it off my finger, and moaned at the heavenly taste that exploded on my taste buds.

A masculine growl brought my gaze up to lock with his as I swallowed the creamy goodness, slowly pulled my finger out, and hated the guilty flush that spread over my cheeks.

"Gods, what the fuck was he thinking?" he groaned as he rubbed his hand over his face and turned away from me, making his way to the couch.

I slid the champagne away from me and forced myself not to bang my forehead against the table. I stood up, pushing the chair away from the table, and wobbled on clumsy feet to the bed, pulling out a note from the pack and handing it off to Spyder.

"Take me here, please," I pleaded, and then thought about how I sounded as I swayed, and started to giggle. "I'm drunk enough that I can break in without feeling guilty."

"Fucking lightweight," he grated as he looked at the address and then back at me suspiciously. "Why here?"

"It's where the witch was or something, and no, I don't know why or where it is. I only know my mother said to check it out while we were here. Maybe it holds a clue to where she is so we can get home faster."

"Bloody hell," he growled as he grabbed my jacket from my bag and tossed it to me. "Come on," he muttered beneath his breath as he strode to the elevator and pushed the button. I followed behind him like a puppy dog as we exited the hotel. The car was waiting, as if they'd predicted he would need it.

I slid into the passenger seat and the car shuddered as he closed my door with more force than was needed. We drove in silence, with him looking at me oddly every few minutes. It took a lot longer to reach the address than I'd thought it would.

Of course, the address hadn't been *in* Portland, which I would have realized had I looked before giving it to Spyder. The address was for a small apartment complex that was located in a small coastal town, which had a cozy vibe and was just a couple blocks away from the ocean.

I got out of the car and started forward, feeling Spyder's immense presence behind me as we made our way down the sidewalk and past the little gate of the apartment. I double-checked the number before I tried the door, and found it locked.

"Crap," I mumbled, already over the buzz of the alcohol in my system. I hated being at a disadvantage in this state.

"Move," he growled as he shouldered the door, the lock giving way easily. We walked quietly inside the tiny vacant apartment, and I paused. I blinked rapidly as I looked around the tiny room.

One minute it was empty and the next I could clearly see myself in this room, with lit candles on almost every available surface, poring over books that were stacked on the table and music played softly in the background. A black kitten sat in my lap, purring as I rubbed behind its ears.

"What the fuck?" I spun around to find Spyder studying me.

"Yeah, what the fuck is about right," he muttered as he moved deeper into the empty one-bedroom apartment, which wasn't even big enough to fit him, much less his presence, which swallowed up the rest of the room.

There was a card on the mantel, which he took down and read. I moved closer as I watched him wad it up and turn to look at me. "You better not be playing games with me," he warned.

"Why would I be playing games with you?" I glared as he snorted and stepped back. I moved around him to the window seat and opened up the curtains as I stared out at the ocean. I closed my eyes and envisioned a dark figure out among the surf amid a storm. I opened them, and looked out at the darkened sea. "I think I've been here before," I mumbled. "That's weird, right?" I clamped my hands over my ears as pain tore through my head.

"You've never left Haven Crest to come this far west, kitty."

"I know that, but this is—familiar." I rubbed my head

and moved away from the window. "This was a bad idea; if she was here, she erased all evidence of it," I mumbled as I took about three steps to the bedroom, pushed the door open, and found it was empty too. "We should go back to the hotel and rest." I spun around and headed towards the door.

"Any other places you plan on dragging me off to tonight?" he grouched, and I shook my head as we walked out of the apartment and he pulled the door closed behind us.

"No, not tonight," I muttered as we made our way back to the car. It didn't seem to take as long to get back to the hotel, and he pulled up under the valet canopy and dropped me off with a curt nod before speeding off, leaving me alone.

Feeling a little disheartened, I made my way back to the room and eyed the tub on the balcony with a speculative gleam in my eye. Did I dare? Knowing he probably wouldn't be back for at least a few hours, I smirked. Yeah, I did. I kicked off my shoes, shimmied out of my clothes and retrieved a towel.

I opened the doors to the balcony and dropped my clothes and the towel on the chair beside the tub. I tested the water with my fingers and gingerly slipped into the heated tub, groaning as it relieved the aches and pains. I pushed myself up against the side. Staring out over Portland's cityscape that was much larger than Spokane's, I saw thousands of lights dancing in the night, sparkling against the coming dawn.

Once my skin began to prune up, I stood up, staring out at the city as my nipples hardened as the crisp air stung my skin. I turned, sensing I was no longer alone. Spyder waited on the other side of the glass doors, staring at my naked figure hungrily. I slipped back into the water quickly as he glared at me.

"You weren't supposed to be back for a few hours," I said out loud with shock as I brought my arms up to cover my boobs.

"And you weren't supposed to be naked," he returned angrily, stepping backwards, as if he needed to put distance between us. He spun on his heel, headed back towards the bedroom and retrieved his bag, then marched to the elevator. I stared at him while he jammed his finger repeatedly against the button as he continued to stare at me with a hungry look lingering in his wintry, icy blue gaze.

Once he disappeared behind the doors of the elevator, I stood up immediately and grabbed a towel, then moved briskly to the bedroom. I slammed the doors closed behind me as my heart hammered wildly.

I grabbed my bag and dressed into pajamas, combed my hair, then retrieved blankets from the bed and a single pillow before I moved to the large couch and made a bed, crawled into it, and pulled the blanket up to my chin, never taking my eyes off the elevator as I waited for Spyder to return.

I awoke, sort of, to arms wrapping around and lifting me from the couch as something solid held me.

I felt myself being moved onto the bed, but instead of waking up I smiled as I lifted my mouth and kissed warm, masculine lips. My hands cupped his strong face as I pulled him to myself, claiming his mouth and welcome heat against mine. He pulled away, and I whimpered at the loss of his warmth. I felt weight pressing against the bed, and then it was gone.

"Lucian," I whispered before sleep claimed me again.

CHAPTER
fourteen

*Whatever it takes, even dancing with the devil, I'll come for you. ~**Lena***

The next morning, I awoke with a start as something crashed against the wall. I lifted my head groggily, then slowly wiggled out from the blankets and shuffled into the other room. Spyder glared at me as I yawned.

"Get showered; we find this witch and we get the fuck back to Metaline Falls so I can be rid of you," he rasped angrily. His eyes were bloodshot, and his hair was mussed, as if he'd been running his fingers through it all night.

"Fine," I nodded, still fighting sleep. "What the fuck triggered you?" I snapped, but his glare stalled any other argument I might have had.

"Get in the fucking shower and lock the door, kitty.

I'll be back," he snarled as he punched the button and refused to look back at me.

"I'm going, asshole," I growled as I moved back to the couch and then eyed the bed with confusion. "Did you move me?" The sound of metal crunching drew my eyes to him. I looked around the now empty-room, which was bathed in shadows. The doors to the elevator opened, but no one was there. "Spyder?" I called out as a shiver raced down my spine. I glared at the now-ruined room service cart and frowned.

I shook it off, grabbed my pack, and locked the door to the bedroom and escaped to the bathroom to shower. I quickly undressed and took in the large shower that was about as big as my bathroom at home.

I stepped through the glass doors and turned the water on, feeling a sensation of warmth as it feathered over my nipples. I paused, closing my eyes as the water started raining down over my hair and skin. I reached for the soap and removed it from the paper. I quickly lathered every part of my body that I could reach, and as I rubbed the soap over my pussy, pausing as a wave of warmth and lust surged through my body, moaning loudly, unable to stop it from coming out. I felt something, like warm hands touching me, but the moment I turned around to investigate, there was nothing there, and I wondered if I was losing my shit. I sat on the small bench inside the shower and parted my legs as my clit throbbed like a heartbeat that begged to be touched, needing release. I let the water run over my body as I pushed my fingers inside my wet sex, clenching against them. My eyes lifted to the shadow that moved on the other side of the glass, and I closed my eyes against it.

It didn't take much; the tension of being here with Spyder and feeling this wild craving was sending my body over the edge. I pushed two fingers inside, spreading my legs further apart as I rested my head against the shower wall as the other hand stroked my clit slowly. I exploded without warning, no building pressure, just euphoria as it rippled through me.

My moans were muffled as I brought my hand up, holding it over my mouth as something slid through my naked pussy, pushing against the wet folds as it dipped and pushed inside. I cried out as my body tensed and arched for more. Something flicked against my clitoris and I shuddered as another orgasm began to build. I started to look down to see what was happening, and everything stopped as if I had imagined the pressure and entrance into my body. I stood on trembling legs, letting the steam from the shower comfort me.

I was going insane.

I was a little twisted, but who cared. I had needs, and had Lucian been here with me, I probably would have used him to fulfill them. But he wasn't here, and I wasn't sleeping with Spyder just to scratch my itch. It wasn't something he could fix anyway; only one man could assuage the ache he created inside of me, which sucked to admit.

I quickly finished my shower and dried off, and pulled on a pair of ripped jeans which had black lace peeking from where the holes were. I slipped on a comfy oversized sweatshirt and ran a brush through my hair. I glowered at my tired reflection before leaving the room, and found Spyder sitting at the table, staring out the window with his finger pressed to his lips.

"Feel better?" he taunted, and I considered becoming one of those birds that hid their heads in the ground as I wondered if he'd heard me in the shower.

"Refreshed," I stammered as I laid my bag on the floor and pulled out my kit. I set the map down on the large round coffee table and sat on the floor in front of the couch. Mother had mentioned that if we couldn't find the witch at the address to try scrying for her.

"What are you doing?" he grumbled suspiciously.

"Scrying for the witch so we don't have to drag ourselves through every Gods-forsaken place in Portland," I answered softly as I shifted to my knees and bent over the small table. The shirt exposed his bite, which didn't go unnoticed by him. He moved closer, sitting next to me as I set out what I needed for the scrying spell. I paused, and glanced over my shoulder to where he sat. He grinned wickedly, noting that I squirmed with his proximity. Before I could say anything else, he slid down beside me, sending my heart palpations into a crescendo.

He leaned over my shoulder, forcing me to look back at the map as I picked up the crystal, which was attached to a magic chain. I whispered the spell and held the crystal over the map, where it began rocking back and forth as it searched for the witch. I felt his mouth hovering inches from where he'd bitten me and my concentration snapped.

My head jerked in his direction before thinking, and I found my lips smashed against his. I stared him down, wondering what would happen if either of us moved an inch. My mind warred with right from wrong. I pulled away from him, crying out as the bite mark burned red hot on my shoulder. It pulsed and sent waves of pain through my body.

"It's only going to get worse." His head dipped close and his mouth moved gently against the bite, kissing my shoulder as my head rolled back. He pulled away as if I'd burned him, or as if he'd forgotten himself momentarily. His breath fanned my skin and I bit my lip to keep the moan that bubbled up at bay. He stood up and quickly put some distance between us. I gazed at him from beneath my lashes as he made his way to the mini-bar and pulled out a little bottle of Jack Daniels, biting the cap off and chucking the empties into the little trash basket. "The longer we suppress it, the more it builds. That ache, the one in your shoulder where I claimed you, I have that same fucker in my chest. It throbs for you and you alone. I fucking hate it, and yeah, I hate you a little because of it."

"How long will it be like this?" I frowned, lifting my eyes to meet his.

"That's the thing, kitty. It never ends," he laughed coldly as he downed another bottle. "One of us would have to die, and sometimes the bond doesn't end there. It's not white magic binding us, it's dark. Why do you think you were in a dark room with blood being taken from all of us? Lucifer could easily kill you, but there are a lot of bad things he would do to you before he did you in. We gave you our protection, but it wasn't free. I'm not a fucking saint, and this cost me a lot, more than just the need to fuck you. That's why you're ours now, not just his. If I decide to act on these feelings, do you think he'd stop me?" He snickered coldly as his question danced on every nerve ending throughout my body.

"And he agreed? Lucian would share me with you and the others?" My voice hitched as pain tugged at my heart and did little to hide the growing panic I felt.

"They can't claim you like we can. When we claim, it does more than just mark you. It claims your soul at the same time. Lucifer won't fuck with us. You don't have to worry about him anymore; you're ours to protect now, kitty." His voice was filled with lust and smoke.

Spyder's eyes began to glow the color of freshly polished rubies as a dark smile spread across his lips. I paused, gaping at him, swallowing hard repeatedly as I gathered my courage. Once they'd changed back to the icy blue, I picked up the crystal, forcing myself not to tremble as if his little display of otherworldliness hadn't just shaken me as much as it had.

"You obviously want me to know that you're not like me, I get it. You also don't want me to know what you are, which is fine. If you did, you'd tell me. I also know witches can't mark other witches, because free will is huge and fucking with it is frowned upon. Breaking it curses you. All magic has boundaries, even dark magic. That means none of you are what you're pretended to be. Yet he's fully claimed me, and on top of that, he also agreed to breed with me. That means I will end up carrying his child sooner or later." I paused, glaring suspiciously as I studied him.

"Unless of course he can't breed, in which case, his mark and yours will be removed, Spyder," I sighed heavily as I shook my head. "I have a bloodline to continue, and I want to be a mother someday. In fact, with everything happening around us, I've realized how fragile life is, and every day I have it drummed into my head from the coven how important it is to carry on my line. I mean, look at us. We are in Portland hunting down a witch because the coven thinks she is in trouble and can be of help to us in some way. We live in very dangerous times."

"So if he can't have kids, you'd just find another dick, just like that?" He drained another bottle and tossed it into the growing pile in the basket.

"We are not a couple," I replied softly. "He's fucked me. It didn't mean we changed our social media statuses to 'in a relationship,'" I snorted as I made air quotes with my fingers. "Now, let's take a special note of how he fucked me. That wasn't normal sex, and nothing between us has ever been normal, has it? He says he did it because I was in danger, but that doesn't mean he really wants to create a life with me and I wouldn't force anyone into it, so the entire point is moot. Then add in the fact that he doesn't really like me, and I don't like him. That's a mutual understanding, which makes my brain itch when I even think of having a child with him."

"He wants you and if he fucking offered, you can believe he means it," he growled harshly, as if I had offended him. "He isn't used to wanting anyone. One thing you should know, though, kitty: If I didn't think he really wanted you, you'd be spread out on that bed with me, twelve inches deep in that naked little pussy. You think I'm enjoying fighting this? I don't; I hate not just taking you as everything inside of me is screaming to do right now. Only reason I'm fighting this need to fuck you is because of Lucian, he's my best friend. So do us all a favor, try talking to him before you consider tossing him aside for some limp dick that couldn't begin to fucking scratch your itches. Because, let's face it, no witch alive could soothe that fucking ache we created inside of you. You're a dirty little girl, which is just the way we fucking like them. One who needs to be ruthlessly fucked, hard and often. Now fucking scry away, because I'm about done playing house with you," he ordered and then hesitated, as if he was contemplating saying more and when he did, it was said gently. "And, kitty, if he can't give you a powerful child, I sure as shit can."

"You would do that for him? Because I'm not sure we'd work out, Spyder," I laughed, trying to lighten the mood.

"I'd do anything for him. Anything he asked of me, even snap your pretty little neck."

I swallowed hard and regarded him through narrowed eyes as the crystal continued to move across the map. His spiky hair was black, but it moved as if it was trying to blend into the shadows he tended to stand in.

"That would solve the little claiming issue we have." I smiled as he gawked at me and then laughed outright, revealing a dimple. He looked younger smiling, and I realized I'd never seen him genuinely smile before. This man was a killer; it was etched in the lines of his face, and it shined from deep within him when he looked at you.

The crystal stopped and slid down, and I glanced at the area. There was nothing there, no buildings, no nothing that was marked on the map other than a mass of caves and heavily wooded area, marked in the terrain.

Spyder stepped forward, staring at the map. "Bloody hell," he breathed out with a chuff as he lifted his liquid blue orbs from the map to mine. "Fuck that. We're done here, get your shit. We're going home."

"No, we are not! I can't go home without her." I squared my shoulders as I stared him down.

"You think he's going to let this go if I take you into that club?" he challenged.

"What the hell kind of a club is it?" I dropped the bravado a tinge. After all, it was a club in the middle of nowhere, which said a lot about it. I wasn't even sure how he knew it *was* a club since the map only showed a lot of caves, and rough terrain.

"The kind where you would be my pretty little plaything, kitty," he purred thickly. "The kind where they'd expect me to fuck you right there in front of everyone." He moved close enough to me that I stepped back. "You think you could pretend to be my plaything for a night? Because that is the type of club that hellhole is."

I swallowed and nodded. My hand slipped into my pocket, knowing why my mother had given me the potent

Siren's hair; because if Spyder wasn't willing to take me, and if I had to, I'd use it. She'd said whatever it took, and now I knew she hadn't meant against others, only him.

"I can be your fucking huckleberry if I have to be. Whatever it takes," I whispered, hoping my voice wasn't shaking as much as I was inside. "Just help me get her out of there."

"And if Lucian loses his shit over this?" he asked as his mouth lowered to mine. "Who takes the punishment?"

"I will," I said, lifting my mouth until my breath fanned over his lips before I allowed them to touch his, ever so slightly. "He likes to punish me anyway," I whispered as I stepped away from him. "You can tell him I drugged you or spelled you to do as I said."

"You think he'd believe that?" He laughed, but it was hollow. "He's going to be livid." He moved into the bedroom and punched the code to the safe in. I followed him into the bedroom, holding the Siren's hair in my fingers, ready to use it if I was forced to.

He took a few things from the safe, closed it then turned around and moved towards me. He smirked, gazing down at me as I held his icy eyes and slowly held up a jeweled necklace as if he was challenging me.

"Lift your hair and turn around," he ordered, and I hesitated. I rotated slowly, giving him my back and lifting my hair as I stared his reflection in the mirror that faced us on the wall. He brought his hands around my body, touching my skin as his fingers rubbed my collarbone as he slid the necklace around my throat.

No, it wasn't a necklace; it was a collar for a submissive. I swallowed hard as I shivered at what it meant. Once it was clasped together, he didn't move away. His lips touched the side of my neck, right above the jeweled band. I didn't look away from him, knowing he was testing me. If I pulled away now, I failed to do as he said, I'd end up using the hair on him and his way was easier, less messy. "Grab your things; we have to go get you a dress."

"Right now?" I asked, staring in the mirror at the sparkling collar.

"It's only a collar, kitty. Every pretty pussycat should have one," he said huskily as he strode away from me. "Just don't let Lucian catch you wearing my collar."

"He hasn't placed his on me, yet."

"Careful," he warned. "I'm hanging by a thread, and you're about to fucking cut it. Both of us would regret something like that happening, so let's go before you end up on that bed, tied to it."

"Okay," I stuttered breathlessly, scooting away from him and fleeing the bedroom to the elevator, where I pushed the button several times. "I don't have much cash with me." I glanced over my shoulder at him.

"Don't worry about it; we're shopping with Lucian's card." He smirked at me as we waited for the doors to open. His hair seemed darker than before, black as it blended in with the shadows; even the small gauges in his ears seemed darker. I wondered what the hell he was, that he literally became a shadow.

"That's not something I really want to do," I said, turning to enter the elevator as the doors opened.

"Didn't ask your permission, did I?"

"How much money does he have?" I asked.

"Enough."

CHAPTER
fifteen

She's got more than chaos in her eyes; she's got fire in her soul. ~Spyder

I stood in the mirror of the upscale boutique he'd dragged me to. The saleswoman had been more than happy to assist once Spyder had pushed into the boutique behind me. Up until then, she'd eyed me like a bug she wanted to squish with her red-soled heels. She licked her lips and made a production out of the most expensive clothing that they had in stock once Spyder had mentioned Lucian's name.

"This dress isn't even supposed to be seen until spring, but for you…" she flirted openly.

Spyder smirked; his eyes seemed to slowly caress her figure before they moved to the dress. It was sheer, baby blue, and looked like something you'd wear on a honeymoon, instead of to a sex club. He took it from her and handed it to me.

"Go try it on," he ordered, and I rolled my eyes as he turned to her and crooked his finger. I ignored him and headed into the dressing room, slammed the door, and stripped off my clothes. I removed my bra once I'd made sure the dress had enough support for the girls and left my panties on. Good thing I'd done laundry, since they couldn't be seen through the sheer fabric.

I turned in the mirror, noting the thin straps that crisscrossed over the shoulders and laced down the back, leaving the area just above my ass bare. I tilted my head, and then eyeballed the door as noise sounded from the other side.

I opened the door and hesitated. Spyder was on the couch which was positioned right in front of the dressing room. His head was back, and the woman was sucking his cock without any care of discovery. My eyes slid to the front door and saw the open sign was facing me. She'd at least had the sense to lock the doors.

I stepped back, which alerted Spyder to my presence, and instead of looking away from me, those bedroom eyes held mine as her head bobbed over his cock. She moaned as he pushed her head down as far as she could go, holding her there as he gazed coldly at me.

I should have looked away. I should have slunk back inside the dressing room to hide. Instead, I watched as he lifted his hands and slid them into her hair before lifting her head up, exposing his thick cock to my prying eyes. I swallowed, taking an involuntary step backwards, away from him. He'd said twelve inches, and he hadn't been bragging. If anything, he'd been modest in his calculation.

His eyes slid down my scantily clad body which had heated, because hey, I was a woman and I wasn't immune to him. He shoved her back down without warning and she cried out, her protest muffled around his cock as I wondered if she had any gag reflex at all. He smirked as I grabbed for the door of the changing room, my shoulder burning with pain.

I leaned my head against the wall, hating that I'd stood there like an idiot, watching them. Why had Lucian sent us together? He knew we would be like this, he had to know. I closed my eyes, listening as she cried out, no longer muffled by his cock. I heard skin hitting skin and the screams of pleasure as she took what he so freely offered her. His grunt sounded, and I opened my eyes, staring at myself in the mirror as my shoulder began to buzz with hotter pain.

"That was, that was wow," she whimpered breathlessly as she struggled to catch her breath.

"Get dressed and find her some shoes. She can't go barefooted."

"We just…you want me to wait on that whore after you just fucked me?" she huffed.

"She's not a whore, she's my kitty." His tone was dangerous, as if he was daring her to say it again. I heard shuffling, a terrified scream, and then heels clicking as they moved across the floor. I shook my head, not wanting to know what had just happened.

I took the dress off, and was standing in nothing but

my panties, feeling pretty stupid and out of place when the door opened. I grasped the dress in front of me; he didn't say anything, and he didn't have to. I felt it, the need to give in to what we both felt, even if it was just a spell. I was so kicking Lucian's fucking ass when we got back from here.

"She wasn't you," he murmured as he leaned his head against the wall and nodded to the scrap of fabric in my hands. "Put the dress back on; we can leave from here. She's getting shoes to go with it."

"I don't have make-up here," I admitted absently, wondering why it even mattered.

"You're fucking beautiful the way you are. You don't need that shit on your face—and leave your hair down." He stepped closer, uncaring that I was almost naked as he trailed his fingers down my cheek. "I know, I felt it too," he admitted. "I hate him a little every time the mark on you burns." He rubbed the area of his shoulder that was the mirror of where he had bitten me. "What the hell was he thinking?" He backed away from me as he adjusted his pants.

"These should fit her," the saleswoman hissed, throwing the shoes into the dressing room. Startled, I jumped and dropped the dress as if we were under attack. Spyder growled and turned to leave the moment it dropped.

I slipped the dress back on, lacing up the back before I slid my feet into the heels. I took a quick peek in the mirror and stepped out of the dressing room with my own clothes over my arm. I moved across the room to the register, where Spyder waited for me.

"Fifteen-thousand-and-seven-hundred, even," she huffed as she glared at me. "You may want to invest in breast enhancements if you're going to dress her in couture; there's not very much there."

My stomach dropped, but not at her words. Who the hell bought a dress costing that much?

"Her breasts are perfect, you should see them bounce when she rides a cock," he growled, winking at me as my cheeks heated. Of all the comebacks, he had to say *that*? I mean, I knew he watched, but he didn't have to point it out.

I moved away from them as she huffed and puffed and rang up the dress. I wanted to cry at the price, argue that it was too much, but he'd ignore it—besides, Lucian deserved it.

The moment I stepped away from them, I pretended they didn't exist as she jotted down her number on a business card and slid it across the counter to Spyder, who lifted a brow in question.

"Call me," she said in a thick voice.

"You weren't that good," he snorted, grabbing the receipt, my bag of clothes, and leaving the card behind as he left the store.

I didn't say anything as we sped away from the store. I didn't know what to say. I mean, I'd watched him with her, and he'd watched me. It had been both awkward and a little hot, which also bothered me.

"You jealous?" He turned off on an old highway and stared ahead at the road. "You shouldn't be; she meant nothing."

"You mean nothing to me," I growled, pissed off more at myself than him. I *was* jealous, and he wasn't even mine! How dare I feel anything, or hate some unnamed woman for having him. I had no right to feel it. She didn't deserve my hatred, because he was a free agent and she'd done nothing wrong, other than being a petty bitch who would fuck a strange man at the drop of their pants.

He smirked wickedly as he accelerated the engine. "Noted."

"That came out wrong."

"No, you mean nothing to me, either. This mark tells us something different, but neither of us actually feels what it's telling us. It's good you know it, because honestly, I'd rather break your pretty neck than shove my cock down it."

"You're an asshole," I breathed as I turned to look out the window.

"I never said I wasn't an asshole, kitty. I won't lie to you. Nor will I fuck you unless Lucian says I can, and if he does, I *will* wreck you. That I can promise you. What I did to the bitch back there wasn't even a warm-up," he taunted coldly. "Do me a favor; stay the fuck away from Lucifer so he forgets you exist. That way you don't have to worry about that bite."

"I didn't go looking for him the first time," I seethed.

"No, but you didn't see through the glamour to get that it wasn't a dream and he wasn't Lucian, either, and we all know you could have. You allowed it to happen, which is something you won't do again. The mark won't allow you to go to him; it will make sure you know who and what the fuck he is."

"Whatever," I mumbled as we pulled into a parking lot packed full of cars. In the distance it was as if the club was part of the mountainside. "What the hell?" I angled my body to find Spyder studying the club.

"Something is off," he muttered under his breath. "You stick to me like my cocks inside you. Got it?"

"Got it," I whispered as we parked and got out.

We started up the path which led to the club. The people waiting in line were off too. Instead of looking excited about getting a chance to get into the club, they looked vacant. As if they weren't really interested at all about getting inside, or didn't care either way. Where people at Lucian's clubs exuded excitement, this one reeked of fear.

Once we reached the front door, a bouncer blocked our way. Spyder pulled out his wallet and thumbed through a stack of hundreds before holding a wad of cash out to the man.

The man eyed it and smiled coldly as he removed the

red rope and swung his hand out in the direction of the pulsing club.

"Nice mortal you got there; she's your problem. If she dies, there's no reimbursement," he warned.

"Nothing will happen to her," Spyder snorted. "My property is mine to protect."

"Yeah, sure, asshole. She's sweet; we like to break the sweet ones."

"This pussy only fucks me, see this?" he asked, yanking on my neck. "Claimed, in every sense of the word. I tell her what she does, who she fucks, and right now, that's me until I say differently," he growled threateningly.

I didn't say a word or argue what he'd said to the guy. I'd watched the couples inside Lucian's club the last time I'd been in there. The ones who wore collars didn't speak unless told to; they didn't argue with those who claimed them. They did as they were told, and who they were told to do. They were every dominant's dream: docile, domesticated, and subservient. Pretty much everything I wasn't.

Once we were inside the club, Spyder pulled me to him as a man with beady, glassy eyes approached us. Spyder held my tits, crushing them with his hands as I stifled a groan as the pain hit me.

"Beautiful," the man breathed, reaching out a hand to touch my hair.

"Do not touch my property," Spyder warned coldly.

"I have three; you can have them all for the night if I can have her?" The man's hand moved, touching my hip until Spyder growled.

"She's not for trade," he rumbled threateningly. "She's new, still being trained to serve my needs."

"I like them like that, their skin is pure still. I'll pay you very well to watch as you break her."

"I'll find you if I change my mind," Spyder said, dismissing the man as he pulled me with him through the throngs of people. Once we were lost in the crowd, I spun around into his wide chest as he pulled me closer, acting on instinct. He smelled exotic, addictive, and anything but human.

We were being watched by the bouncers, huge creatures that eyed us suspiciously as we swayed to the heady, sultry music that played inside the club. Spyder's hands slid to the base of my spine as he watched them.

"Kiss me, kitty," he urged softly as his mouth lowered to hover next to mine.

I swallowed hard as I tried to think of a way out of kissing him. But, I'd told him I could do this. It wasn't as if it would mean anything. We were playing roles here. One's meant to save a life, right? I lifted on my toes to connect our lips and shock waves rushed down my spine as we connected. His lips rubbed against mine before his tongue pushed past my lips, claiming my tongue. He tasted of sin, sin mixed with leather and expensive spices. I moaned against him as he deepened the kiss, and then pulled back, staring into my gaze.

I mumbled incoherently trying to figure out what to say as I fought against the mixed emotions the kiss had caused. "What did he mean by *break her*?" I blurted, swaying to the music as I stared into his eyes. He smiled softly, as if he realized what I was doing and allowed me to ignore what we'd just done. It had worked though; the bouncers had moved their attention away from us. But my eyes seemed unable to stay off his lips, wondering how I'd felt as much as I had with him.

What the fuck was wrong with me?

"He whips and fucks his females until they are nothing more than a bloody mess on a whipping pole. He's an extreme sadist, but where most draw a line, death is his line. The tattoos on his left arm are those he released to death. The ones on the right are for those who lived."

I shivered as I ignored the tightening in my throat. I wasn't meant for this world. I wanted to find that man and rip his throat out. I doubted the women had been willingly tied to any pole knowing what their fate would be. I was relieved when we started moving again.

I followed Spyder further into the seething mass of people who danced body to body. It forced us to push through them to get where we could find somewhere to sit down. By the time we reached the middle of the dance floor, which was pretty far into the club, my head started to pound and my stomach roiled. Pain shot through me and my hand, which was in Spyder's, slid free as I started to fall backwards. He caught me and held me against his side as he began to shove people out of his way.

"Something is wrong," he noted, and I nodded. Heat unfurled inside of me as I clung to Spyder like a lifeline. I felt sick, and my head pounded with the music. Once we cleared the crowd, I covered my mouth as the nausea swirled in my throat with a painful pulse.

"Bathroom," I whimpered as saliva built in my mouth. "Now," I beseeched.

He rushed me in the direction of the bathroom, pushing the door open as he helped me inside. Once he'd stepped the first foot inside, he was pushed out by an invisible force. He tried again and the door slammed shut in his face.

I rushed to the stall, unable to wait as I tossed my cookies, violently. Once I had nothing left in my stomach, I headed to the row of sinks, washing my mouth out and patting my face down with the wet paper towel as a stall door opened and a redhead stepped out. She had vivid green eyes, which sized me up and down as if she knew me.

"You finally made it," she grinned at me as she washed her hands. "I feared you wouldn't after you didn't show up last night."

"You're the witch?" I stepped away from the sink to look at her. She didn't have a mark on her that might indicate any kind of trouble or distress. She wore a beautiful gown, white for purity, which seemed off inside this particular club.

"I am. I'm Tiffany, Tiffany O'Hara."

"You couldn't find a safer place to meet up?" I asked with a shake of my head, and she gave a small shrug.

"Places like this are *in* these days. We should go, though, we're not safe here. They enjoy witches a little too much in places like this."

"You think?" I hissed, marching for the door and opening it wide.

Spyder looked pissed. His eyes looked me up and down for injury before he grabbed my arm and started towards the front door.

"I found her," I announced briskly with a tilt of my head in her direction.

"I don't care if you found her, we're leaving, now," he snapped.

I took in the bedlam of the club. Clothes were coming off, and couples were fucking right out in the open. I kept my gaze on Spyder's back until *Sweet Dreams* started playing and my blood ran cold. I pulled against Spyder's arm as an illusion of wings caught my eye. One minute he was there a few feet from us, then the next he vanished like a mirage, only to reappear a little closer to us without wings.

A man with black hair and vivid indigo eyes watched me with a knowing look in his sinful gaze. I felt my body heating up as he moved towards us in a brisk pace. Spyder yanked on my arm, swiveling to see why I'd stalled.

"Bloody hell," he growled as he shoved me behind him, but it was too late.

Lucifer moved in a way that hurt my head. One moment he was across the crowded room, and the next he had a hold on my arm and was yanking me towards himself. Pain shot through me as his fingers curled around my arm, biting into my flesh. Black, skeletal wings exploded from his back as barbed vines shot from his fingers, wrapping themselves around and through my arm. I screamed and tried to pull myself away from him as I struggled to remain in Spyder's arms.

"She is mine!" Lucifer growled coldly.

"Fucking try to take her from me, asshole," Spyder returned with a dangerous glint sparkling in his eyes.

One moment I was being ripped in two directions with demons descending on us. The next, Spyder detonated with power—raw, uncut power that slammed the air out of my lungs as if he'd pulled the air from the room itself. The runes which covered his arms lit from within and his hair lifted in the air as he let out an earsplitting howl as demons exploded into black clouds of ash around him.

He had power glowing from his fingers that must have been holding Lucifer to the ground. I gawked as I gasped for air, afraid I'd pass out from the lack of it. Lightning flashed and zigzagged around the club as thunder rattled it. Lucifer on the ground shook with it; blood oozed from his nose and eyes as Spyder held him there with his power.

I struggled to get up, but I couldn't move. No one

could. Whatever the fuck Spyder was, he had brought the entire club to the ground with ease. My hand lifted, touching his leg as darkness threatened to consume me.

Silver eyes looked down at me, blue flecks mixed in the mercury depths. His hair was bluish white, as if someone had stolen the pigment from it and given him some hellish, stylish highlights. I dropped my hand, my head flopped to the floor, and my eyes drifted to Lucifer's. He no longer actually had eyes, just blood oozing from where they should have been.

What. *The*. Fuck.

Spyder reached down and yanked me up as he moved. I pointed at Tiffany, who looked like she was also about to pass out from the power in the room. He grabbed her hand and dragged her with us into the dark night. Once outside, I greedily sucked in air. Tiffany sputtered, wheezed, and coughed as she sucked in her own.

Spyder set me down carefully, holding onto me as he pulled his phone from his jacket and punched the buttons with his thumb. "Now," he demanded, his voice mixed in layers of anger and unease. I looked back at the doors of the club, noting that even those outside hadn't been spared. Spyder pushed his phone back into his pocket. Tires squealed, and I watched as a black Land Rover pulled up and someone got out. Spyder tossed the Audi keys to whoever was in the Rover, and pushed me to the passenger side of the Rover, opening the door and lifting me into the seat.

I watched in numb horror as he pulled the barbed

vines from my skin, and pressed his mouth to the damaged flesh as he sucked against it. I closed my eyes against the imagery as black pus oozed from where he'd pulled the first one out.

"Fuck, fuck!" he shouted as he pulled several more out. Brilliant light flashed and blinded me for a moment. Once my eyes adjusted, I could see the light was emanating from his hands as he slid them over my torn skin, healing it as he methodically touched every injury. The light dissipated, and he returned to the normal dark, angry Spyder I was used to. He pulled back, and slammed the door closed. Bags were tossed into the Land Rover from the Audi before it sped out of the parking lot.

I turned, looking at Tiffany, who appeared calm, as if we hadn't just almost died. She looked too calm, and I wondered who the hell she was, and how my grandmother had found her. I spun back around to watch Spyder as he climbed into the driver's seat and slammed his door.

We sped off, tires squealing as the club doors exploded outward. I struggled to turn and look behind us as Lucifer stood in front of the club, watching as we drove away.

My heart hammered as his eyes bored into mine; even in the distance, I knew it was me who he was looking at. I swallowed, unable to break eye contact until Spyder pushed me back and touched the side of my face.

"He can't follow us," he muttered. He glanced in the rearview mirror to check on Tiffany. "You better explain what the fuck you were doing there, or you can get out and wait for the fucking demons to find you. Now," he demanded. "What the fuck were you doing in outer levels of Hell with the devil?"

I felt my blood turn to ice as images from the dream came flooding back. *That club.* I'd been in that club before, on stage. I'd been fucked there! Tears burned my eyes and I stared at Spyder, knowing he'd just saved my life.

"Hell?" I whispered. "Mortals can't enter Hell," I continued, watching him. "Only souls can, right?"

"They can if they are invited, or if they remain on the outskirts of the Hell Gate, but that one wasn't normal. It's been altered."

"I wasn't invited, I was taken there." Tiffany licked her lips nervously. "I sent a distress call through the leylines. I had to get out of there; you have no idea what they do to witches in that place." She sat back and closed her eyes. "I am a witch of the original bloodlines; your coven had no choice but to heed my call."

"Fuck your blood, and fuck you," he snapped; fury seemed to emanate from him. "And you, you scryed for it. Witches can't find Hell Gates. They're hidden from your kind for good reason."

"Well, I found it," I bit back angrily. "I only scryed for her, not the Gates of Hell, Spyder!"

He had been about to say something, but he paused, and pulled his phone out of his pocket. He held it up to his ear for a moment, then shouted, "What? Yeah, I know you fucking felt it, we all fucking felt it… No, fuck you.

She took me there, you can fucking ask her why we were there… No, it's not my fucking problem. You can ask her when she gets to you. I didn't want to babysit her in the first fucking place. No, of course I didn't, it was wide fucking open. Yeah, I know it's a fucking problem, this entire fucking situation is one big fucking problem, but who's fucking fault is it?" He turned, looking at me before he snorted into the phone. "Yeah, I'll bring her to you." He hung the phone up and we drove the rest of the way in silence until a few miles out of town.

"I need to go to the abbey," Tiffany said softly as she smoothed out her skirt. "I must reach it before the solar eclipse today."

Today? I looked at the clock on the dashboard that said it was five in the morning. What the fuck? I turned and looked at Spyder, who glared at me.

"Hell moves differently than this world. One minute in there can be a week out here, depending on what is occurring in it."

"That's insane," I said hesitantly. "We weren't in there that long!"

"We were—it just doesn't feel like it. You were inside the bathroom a while, plus, it took us a few to work through the crowd, among other things we did. There's no perception of time in Hell. If you're sentenced to an eternity in Hell, you are sentenced to their time, not this world's."

We pulled up to the abbey around ten in the morning,

and I watched the doors open as my mother stepped through them. Her eyes skimmed over me and went to the witch in the backseat as she exhaled a sigh of relief. I frowned as Tiffany exited the car and rushed towards the group of witches who came out to welcome her.

The SUV started down the driveway and I looked back, locking eyes with my mother as we sped off towards Club Chaos.

CHAPTER
sixteen

I thought he'd hit all my buttons, turned out, he's just getting started. ~**Lena**

We pulled up at the club and saw a crowd of people milling around outside, which was weird considering what time it was. I must have had a confused expression on my face, as I caught Spyder gazing at me oddly.

"It's the solar eclipse. Lucian's clubs tend to draw in those who believe in the supernatural powers of these events," he explained to my unasked question. "There are mysteries around the eclipses that not even your coven or the Gods themselves can start to understand."

"So they come to Lucian's club because they're crazy?" I laughed nervously.

"Even witches believe that the solar eclipse holds powers beyond their comprehension. Then again, life is full of mysteries that aren't ours to understand."

"That's deep, Spyder," I murmured as his icy blue eyes narrowed on me.

"Let's go, now," he growled as he opened his door and stepped out, ignoring the gawking girls who walked by us, fixated on him as he opened my door. He was a gentleman, at least. I got out of the car slowly, trying to brush off the curious glances from the crowd wandering around the club as he grabbed our bags out of the trunk. "Don't piss him off when we get inside, kitty. He's already bent out of shape as it is that we walked into a pocket of Hell."

"We didn't know it was," I said defensively.

"No, but I should have known better," he snapped angrily and slammed the trunk closed. It seemed more like he was mad at himself and not at me.

"I don't see why he's upset at all." I tried to walk a little faster to keep up with his long strides. "We didn't get hurt, we got Tiffany out of there, and we all lived."

Spyder gawked at me incredulously. *"Are you out of your ever-loving mind?"* he almost bellowed at me. "We went into a shit-show and you got hurt. Yeah, we got that fucking witch, and we were just fucking lucky to get out of there." He scrubbed his face angrily and took a deep breath trying to reel his temper in. "Just keep going." He motioned towards the doors, where Bane waited for us.

"Here come's trouble," he mocked with a smile as we got closer, and held the doors open for us to pass through.

"He's waiting for you in his office."

"Come on." Spyder pushed a couple of guys who got too close to us out of the way. I followed close behind him until a hand snaked out and grabbed my arm. I spun around and before I could even take a breath to yell at the guy Spyder was already in action.

With one hand on the huge man's throat, Spyder pinned him to the wall. The man's feet kicked at air as Spyder's nose hovered dangerously close to the man's. "Do not fucking touch her again or you die, understand?" he growled coldly, sending a wave of chills rushing down my spine. "Leave this place, now." Spyder shoved the sputtering man away as he gasped for air and nodded his agreement to leave the club immediately.

"I can handle myself," I whispered, wishing I could hide from all the curious glances.

"A lady shouldn't have to handle anything when she has someone willing to protect her," he said softly as we resumed our trek through the crowd towards the stairway that led to the offices overlooking the club.

I followed his stiff back up the stairs and down the long hallway until we were in front of Lucian's office. The thick wooden door was cracked open already, so Spyder pushed it open as I straightened my shoulders and prepared to face the storm.

Soft, classical music greeted us as we made our way into the office; Lucian faced away from the door, standing at the wall-to-wall window at the back of his office as he gazed down at the club below.

Once Spyder had set our bags down, Lucian turned and his eyes glittered dangerously at me. I swallowed as his eyes slowly slid down the length of me, as if he was looking for a single scratch or hair out of place. They stopped at my painted toenails and roamed back up until they zeroed in on my neck.

"You fucking collared her?" he snarled, looking over my shoulder at Spyder.

"We thought we were going to a sex club, Lucian. I sure as shit wasn't letting her waltz in there unclaimed," he scoffed.

"What the fuck were you thinking?" he demanded, aiming those sinful blue-black eyes at me with enough fire in them to burn my clothes off.

"I didn't know it was *that* club," I sputtered. "I scryed for that witch just like my mother told me to, rather than hopping all over Portland for the next few weeks, and believe it or not, it didn't say *Hell* on the map, or common sense would have kicked in and I would have skipped it. As soon as I found where she was, I gave the location to Spyder and we headed out."

"After charging a few items to my card?" he bit out.

"That wasn't my idea," I huffed. "And you know what? You're not my father. You don't get to bitch at me because you feel like it. I'm a big girl, and I can handle myself!"

"You should have had a father who cared enough to yell at you!" he roared, and my spine straightened as my eyes narrowed on him. "Instead, you had that piece-of-shit excuse of a father that couldn't even stand up for you."

"Excuse me?" I glared at him as his breathing grew labored.

"Get out," he snapped over my shoulder, and I heard Spyder leaving the room, the door closing after his retreating footsteps.

"What the fuck would you know about my father?" I asked carefully.

"More than you, it would seem," he snapped. "You could have died." He smoothly changed the subject so fast I almost didn't catch the shift.

"But we didn't, did we?" I retorted angrily. "You have no right to shout at me. My loyalty is first and foremost to the coven; they sent me there to get something, and I did it! My loyalty isn't to you, nor have I ever pretended otherwise, Blackstone."

"You're done taking chances with your life, little Witch," he growled, and I blinked as my head started to hurt. "Do you have any idea how fucking helpless it felt to feel his hands touching you, knowing that I could do nothing to protect you?" He stepped closer, trailing his fingers around my throat as he unclasped the collar, then twisted it into an unrecognizable sparkly lump.

"Would you have cared?" I snapped as his eyes burned with liquid blue flames. "You sent Spyder with me. Alone.

You knew we were connected and yet you sent us there together, anyway."

"You think I don't care? You think I wanted to send you with him? I didn't, nor should I care about you, and yet I find myself stuck between wanting to kiss you or strangle you. I was busy here, dealing with matters that needed my immediate attention, so yes, I sent you with him. I should wring your fucking neck and wash my hands of you. But it wouldn't be that easy, now would it?"

"Fuck you," I swore as I stared up at him. "You have more mood swings than anyone else on this planet!"

"Maybe if you'd stop throwing yourself into Lucifer's arms, I wouldn't!" he shouted as he grabbed my arm and moved us towards the couch.

"What are you doing?" I demanded as he dragged me unwillingly along with him.

"Teaching you a fucking lesson," he snarled as he sat on the couch and pulled me over his knees. I blinked and turned my head to look up at him as I felt the air on my ass as he lifted my dress. His hand cracked sharply against my ass before I fully guessed his intentions, and I screamed as pain burned across my derrière. I twisted, but he held me there, locked onto his lap as his hand slapped my ass over and over again. Tears slipped from my eyes as I cried out with each punishing slap of his hand against my rear.

"You motherfucker!" I shrieked as anger pushed through me, outrage riding on its heels.

The moment he stopped, I was up, moving away from

him to the other side of the office. "You have no fucking right!" I tried to ignore the pain that shot through me with every step. "You son of a bitch!" I picked up a vase and hurled it at him. It shattered against the wall too far away from his head. I picked up another missile and threw it at him as he took long strides towards me.

"Little girl," he warned.

"Screw you!" I flung the glass paperweight on his desk at him as I rounded it, remaining just out of arm's length. "No one spanks me!"

"I just fucking did!" he roared as he pushed the desk aside and grabbed my arms. "You have no right to take chances like you did. Lucifer would take you to the darkest pits of Hell and do what he does best. Do you understand me? He'd ruin you and then, when he'd had his fill of you, he'd send you to me in pieces!"

"How the fuck was I supposed to know it was Hell? Do you think that if I'd known what that place really was that I would have gone? I'm not fucking stupid and I don't think Spyder would have deliberately served me up, either!" I shirked as I tried to yank my arms free.

He slammed me against the wall and pressed his forehead against mine. His lips touched it so softly that I wasn't sure I hadn't imagined it.

"I hate you," I whimpered as I closed my eyes.

"You can hate me, because you have to be alive to hate me," he murmured as his hands released my arms and slowly moved to the V of the bodice of my dress. The fabric ripped right down the middle with the force of his hands. I pushed him away as I glared at him with tears swimming in my vision.

"Don't," I snapped coldly as I turned, intending to walk away. But this was Lucian. My brain never worked around him, and typically my body betrayed me. I barely made it two steps away from him before he jerked my body back against his, and all rational thought fled the moment his hands cupped my breasts.

"You're mine." It was a statement of ownership. A declaration. Anger pulsed to life as he watched me as a hunter would its prey. His hands slid up, grasping the shredded bodice that left the curves of my breasts exposed, and ripped the dress the rest of the way. "All of you, little Witch, belongs to me," he purred as he pulled my body flush against his own.

He walked me backwards towards his desk, leaned over, and swept his arm across it, sending what little remained on it crashing to the floor. He hefted me up, gripping my hips as he sat me on it. My legs wrapped around his hips, forcing him closer as his mouth crushed against mine.

My hands untucked his shirt before ripping it open, sending buttons raining to the floor and desk as they snapped in my haste. *Skin*, his skin in particular, did things to me. My hands roved and rubbed over his hard lines of muscle. I groaned as his lips left mine, hesitant for him to stop.

Thinking was dangerous. When my brain worked, I

knew right from wrong. When his mouth touched mine, he made the lines blur enough that I didn't care.

Never taking his eyes from mine, he shifted back and unhooked my legs, unbuckling his belt and sliding it free from his pants. I took advantage of his movement to shed what little remained of the dress that still clung to my shoulders.

Lucian feasted on my naked figure and I smirked, knowing he wanted me as much as I wanted him. He held the belt in one hand, pushing my hair away from my face before he wrapped it around my throat and slid the end of the leather strap through the buckle gently until it was snug. I swallowed the fear it elicited because excitement of the unknown took precedence.

He applied a little pressure as his lips touched mine again, softly. The contrast was heady. I gasped as I struggled to catch his kiss, one he held just out of reach as he slid me further onto his desk. He laid me back, sliding my panties off without a protest from me. His hand slid through my sex, finding it ready. His fingers pushed inside as the belt tightened. I arched into his touch, rocking my hips as his fingers explored the depths of my desire.

He kissed the heavy globe of one breast. "So fucking beautiful," he growled, then kissed the other before nipping gently against my nipple as his tongue curved and teased the raised skin. He slowly kissed his way down my belly, leaving a heated trail as his mouth found my clitoris. I cried out, jolting from the desk as the belt tightened even further as his teeth scraped across my delicate pussy.

His mouth sucked my pussy until I spread further apart and arched for him, giving him full access to my most private parts. He pushed another finger inside, filling me until I cried out as he stretched my body. My head dropped back against the desk as he released his hold on the belt, pushing his mouth harder against my sex as he took me sailing over the edge. I cried out his name as wave after wave of pleasure rushed through my body, then whimpered as he pulled his mouth away and glared down at me as I writhed as the orgasm ebbed.

"Lucian," I whispered, barely able to get any words out as he continued pushing his fingers into my body.

"Don't talk," he ordered angrily. "You piss me off when you talk. I shouldn't feel anything for you and yet you make me want you, make me feel this need to protect you and I'm not this guy. I'm not your fucking prince; I'm the dragon who slays the weak-ass prince as he tries to rescue you. You are a weakness, one I can't afford." He picked me up and then tossed me onto the couch, spreading my legs as he pulled me to the edge, working the buttons of his expensive slacks. "I want to destroy you in the most beautiful way, in a way that would ruin you for any other man. To make sure you know that no other male in this world would stack up against me," he purred as he pushed into my body without mercy.

I whimpered, ignoring his words as he lifted my legs, spreading them apart as he drove his hard cock deeper than he'd ever been before into my core. I pulled away, only for him to capture my hands and hold them against my belly as he pumped his hips.

Seether's *FMLYHM* exploded inside the room. It poured from multiple speakers that lined the walls. I dropped my head, watching as he stared down at where our bodies joined together. He pushed my arms away, wrapping his hands around my hips as he picked up speed. I cried out from the heady, addictive mixture of pain and pleasure as he fucked me without care or thought. He was too big, yet we fit like two pieces of a puzzle that had come together to become one.

I felt my body clenching around him, demanding he give me more. I felt the world teetering around us as I toed the edge of cliff once more, but right when I was about to detonate, he pulled out, shuffled my body around, and placed me on my stomach with my face buried into the couch. My legs were parted, placed on either side of his legs as I felt him rearrange the belt. All at once he was there, pulling against the belt as his cock entered me again.

I exploded without warning. My body shook with the force of it and I felt him tensing as he pulled harder on the belt, stealing my air as he fucked me from behind. His other hand slapped against my tender bottom and I arched into every thrust, every sensation he created, and then once again, my body succumbed to white-hot pleasure that held me locked in limbo as I drifted in the clouds.

I'd expected him to finish with me. Instead, he pulled one of my legs over his shoulder, spreading me wider as he situated me onto my side, more exposed as he pinched one nipple, thrusting into my body again.

I cried out, unsure I could handle him in this position,

but he wasn't asking. He was taking and giving when and what he chose. He held absolute control as he pushed in slowly and left my body slower than he'd entered it. I stared into his eyes as my body tightened, arched, and gave him what he needed. Everything I had. I gave him control—I gave him me.

I watched him as his body stiffened and a moan slipped past his lips as he pushed harder, coming undone with my submission. His eyelids grew heavy, languid as he continued to hold mine, and his body seemed to glow from within. The runes on his stomach flared up with a golden radiance, as if lit with a power from within him. My hand lifted without thought, slowly trailing over his body as he emptied his cock into me.

"What the fuck did you do?" he demanded after a moment had passed, and I blinked as I tried to guess what I had done wrong now. "What sort of magic is this?" He pulled out, leaving me bereft without his heat as he stared at the glowing runes.

"What?" I whimpered, still unable to speak through the dryness of my mouth. "What the hell do you mean, what did I do to you?" I demanded, confused as to how any of it was my fault.

"What the fuck did you do to me, Witch?" he snarled and pushed away from me as he stood up. I frowned up at him in confusion as he yanked his pants up and fastened them.

"I didn't do anything to you," I huffed as I followed him up, naked and bared to him. Clumsily, I unfastened the belt from my neck and tossed it at his feet. "What the hell is your problem?"

"You will tell me what you did, or I will rip the truth from you." His growl was barely audible as he stared at me as if I'd done something to hurt him.

"I didn't do anything! We *fucked*! That's it, I didn't use magic on you. Is that what you think? That I cast some spell on you?" I asked, horrified that he would think so little of me that he would believe that I would cast magic on him while going at it like rabbits.

"Those runes don't react unless someone spells them to, Witch," he taunted as if I was stupid, and I gaped at him, completely at a loss for what to say.

"I didn't do it, so find someone else to blame," I snapped angrily as I marched to my bag and started digging for a change of clothes since he'd ruined mine.

"You will tell me what you did before I allow you to leave here," he ordered, and I swung around to face him, intending to tell him where to stick it when a knock sounded at the door.

I shook my head, hating his bipolar ass at the moment. I hadn't done shit to his fucking runes, and I couldn't have even if I wanted to. I wasn't adept in runes, and they scared the shit out of me. I had barely gotten my panties up when Spyder burst into the room.

"We've got a big fucking problem downstairs…" He paused, and I felt the heat of his gaze as he admired my red cheeks. "That's a pretty pink ass, kitty," he said silkily.

"What's the fucking problem?" Lucian demanded, as if he didn't care that my panties didn't cover much and Spyder could see his handiwork all over my ass. Heat flooded my cheeks as I ignored them, dressing in a pair of joggers and a tank top. I pulled my shoes out of the bag and slipped my feet into them, then spun around to find both men regarding me for a very different reason, I was sure.

"The coven is downstairs," Spyder began, taking in my angry frown and the tears swimming in my vision from Lucian's accusations. His icy blue eyes shifted between me and Lucian before he expelled a breath and turned to Lucian, only to explode with a curse as he took in the glowing golden runes on his stomach. "The fuck?"

"Ask her," Lucian snarled, opening a closet I hadn't even noticed before and pulling out a new dress shirt. "Seems our little witch is playing with dark magic," he declared angrily. "She's been learning to cast and remove curses, apparently."

"I didn't do shit." I pulled a hairbrush out of my bag and yanked it through my snarled hair. "We fucked. It's as simple and easy as that. I didn't use magic, and I sure as shit couldn't chant a spell between screaming your name and coming undone on your cock. If I had, you'd have heard it. Wouldn't you?" I demanded impatiently while shoving the brush back into my bag.

"Dark magic doesn't always need words, Witch."

"I'm done with this," I bit out, hating him. "I'm done with you blaming me for shit that I couldn't possibly have known about or done. You think I'm to blame? Fine, whatever; stay the fuck away from me. Problem solved." Fresh tears slid down my cheeks as I headed towards the door.

"You're not leaving," he growled.

"Try to fucking stop me, Blackstone," I seethed as I turned to face him with a cold, dead stare. "You want a war? Because that is what you will get if you try to keep me here."

I hefted my pack over my shoulder and exited his office, not giving a shit that I looked freshly fucked, or that the entire coven was below, waiting for me. I didn't look back to see if they were following me; I knew they were. I felt them to my core, as if their fucked up ritual had done more than just claim me.

"Kitty," Spyder called from behind me, but I didn't stop.

I walked faster until I reached the steps, taking them two at a time to get away from them. I needed distance, needed to get away from them and stay away. My head pounded, my entire body ached, and my heart cracked with his accusations. To spell someone was huge; to do it during sex was just fucking cowardly and dirty. I would do almost anything for the coven, but I wouldn't use my body to get what I wanted. That was just wrong on a level I didn't want to even imagine.

CHAPTER seventeen

*I'm coming back, are you ready? ~**Magdalena Fitzgerald***

The moment my feet touched the main level of the club, I paused and managed to pick the coven out of the crowd as they waited impatiently. My grandmother wasn't with them, but my mother and the rest of the coven with her looked terrified. I pushed through the throng of people to get to my mother and tried to ignore what I must have looked like right now, or that I ached with every step that led me closer to her.

"What's wrong?" I demanded, wondering what could have upset her this much. Her skin was pasty white, eyes wide with fear as she leveled her matching blue eyes to mine and shook her head as tears filled her eyes.

"The Gates to Hell are open," she cried over the music as tears streamed down her cheek. "The town is burning, and people are dying. We tried to find the others, but there was too many demons."

"What? What are you talking about?" I replayed our drive through town as we made our way here just an hour or so earlier. "I was just in town, everything was fine."

"I was coming to find you when the fires started, and then they converged on the town. I don't know how many got out of there, but from the looks and damage the monsters left behind, I wouldn't assume very many. It's bad, really bad. The coven has cast sanction wards and doused holy water inside and around the abbey to prevent them from coming inside. I need you to come with me now," she sobbed. "You have to come with me—it's time, baby."

"This is insane." I shook my head in denial and noticed that the others in the crowd looked just as frightened as my mother and the coven did. How could the Hell Gates have opened?

"Come with me." She held out her hand and I slipped mine into hers as we started towards the doors. I paused, hesitating as I looked back at Lucian. If anyone could help us, it was him, but would he?

"Go," he demanded coldly. The ice in his voice shot through me, radiating through my heart and soul. I swallowed hard and nodded. Turning my back on him, we picked our way through the club and out the front door. We blinked against the bright afternoon sunlight and I noticed there was a reddish cast over the sun and I caught a faint whiff of the acrid scent of smoke from the fires in town.

I exhaled as we started towards the cars, and from the corner of my eye, I noticed we picked up an escort. Spyder walked silently beside me as some of Lucian's men flanked our sides. The coven would run. They always had in times of crises. It was a fallback crutch, one used through generations to maintain our way of life.

I didn't look back, knowing that if I did, he wouldn't be there. If he was, would I still go? I wanted him; even though I hated him most of the time, I wanted Lucian Blackstone. It was as difficult and as simple as that.

A car door opened and I slid into the backseat, keeping my eyes on the seat in front of me as I waited for the door to close, but it didn't.

"Kitty, stay safe," Spyder ordered gruffly as he knelt down beside the car. His hand slipped between mine as he held them tightly. "Stay inside the abbey, do you understand me? What's coming, it's not going to end in this town. It's going to be in every town around the world. This is some end-of-days shit going down right now."

"Will he fight them with us?" I choked out, not bothering to look at him as tears of anger welled in my eyes.

"I don't know. I don't even know if we can fight what is coming. Hell Gates don't just open, something triggered it. Someone took something through a gate recently and opened them. That means there is no barrier between earth and Hell. No one is safe anymore. There are no rules to this game, no referee here to stop them." He bent his head, kissing my hands as my mother watched. I chewed my lip as I considered what he'd just told us.

"Lucifer is coming," I whispered, closing my eyes as the first tear fell.

"If the gates are open, he's been freed to do as he pleases in this world. Stopping him isn't going to be easy and it's going to get worse before it gets better."

"We have to go." My mother slid into the passenger seat and turned to me. "We have to get to the house. There are a lot of books belonging to the coven there; we have to protect our history from them."

I nodded and turned to say something, but the door shut and Spyder was already walking back towards the club. The car ignition started, and we sped out of the parking lot onto the highway.

"Once we get to the house we stay together, or close to one another. Do you understand?" My mother's voice was fairly calm, considering the situation.

"Yes," I said softly, but my mind was back at the club, at Lucian's anger over a curse being removed. Wouldn't that have been a good thing? The man gave me emotional whiplash. Not to mention I couldn't just control myself and *stop* fucking him. It was as if my body didn't care that he was a total asshole; it wanted what it wanted, and that was him.

"I need you to go into the cottage and retrieve the books hidden over there for me while I get started in the main house," she said. "Kat and Dexter will go with you and watch your back so you can get the books from under the floorboards. Do not waste time; we don't know yet if the demons are heading this way or if they just attacked the town. We aren't prepared to face them."

"Lucian can help us," I said softly, sensing her frown as we drove towards the house. Even from this far out of town, I could see the fires burning, as well as in the hills surrounding the town, which had houses scattered through them. "He can kill them. I saw Spyder take down Lucifer; he can do it again. Lucian and his men aren't witches, that much is for sure. Whatever they are, they can fuck them up. They can save the town."

"The town is as good as gone, daughter mine. The gate opened in the middle of town and hundreds of demons poured out of Hell from it. The lives…the poor, innocent lives." She paused as a sob tore from her lips. "We couldn't get close enough to see them, much less protect them, so we left them to their fates. Being helpless is a horrible feeling."

We pulled up to the house and I stared at the old cottage. Our great-grandparents had built as they'd worked on the manor and now it was mostly used for storage.

The car stopped in front of it and I got out, waiting for a moment as the car pulled away and another one pulled in behind it. I quickly glanced back to see Kat and Dexter getting out of the car as I made my way up the steps of the cottage, stopping dead in my tracks as memories assaulted me.

Lena's memories?

A scene unfolded in front of me. Joshua and Lena playing on the porch; running from each other as great-grandma sewed an old, worn pair of coveralls for great-grandpa. I placed my hands on my head and I turned around in a circle, searching for myself. Why was I seeing it through Lena's eyes?

"Kendra?" Kat startled me, placing a hand on my shoulder as she turned back to look at Dexter. "Let's get inside," she offered, moving up the stairs. I noted both were armed with razor sharp athames. As Dexter pushed the door open, I walked past them.

"Hey, we need to check it first," Dexter cried out.

I ignored him and glared at the couch, which was empty. My eyes swept the kitchen and found a vision of Lucian in nothing but a towel as he leaned against the kitchen entryway. I swallowed, feeling the heat that pulsed through me at the sight of him. I gazed at the ghostly figure, a memory of Lucian who made himself at home in the little cottage, unabashed to only be dressed in nothing more than a cheap towel, which hugged his hips.

I shook my head firmly, trying to dispel the image or memory.

"Are you okay?" Kat murmured, observing me intently as I slowly brought my eyes to meet hers before I answered on a hiss of breath.

"I'm fine, everything is fine," I growled angrily.

I moved into the bedroom, looking at the bed as I made my way to the section of the room I needed. I pulled the bed out and scooted around it, pulled the floorboards up, and set them aside. I reached in and pulled out a few books and the photo albums, and paused as I reached deeper. Beneath the albums were pages upon pages of notes scribbled. I stared at them, knowing them as if I'd written them myself. I withdrew them from the hiding place and set them on the bed. I flipped through the pages, endless scribbles written in the early morning hours that had once been hidden with the sun's rising rays. I swallowed as pain tore through my head. Memories flashed inside my head and I swallowed the cry that threatened to rip from my lips.

A cat jumped onto the bed and I paused, observing it as it pushed its head into my chest, demanding I pay attention to it.

Luna?

I closed my eyes and swallowed down the fear that pulsed through me. Someone had played with my mind, but they hadn't made me forget anything. They'd *erased* me and overwritten me like I was some sort of computer. Anger vibrated through me as I spun around to face Kat.

She'd been studying me from the doorway, as if she had been expecting this. Tears slid from my eyes as memories flooded back into my mind and were held up to the light of day like treasure. My hands trembled as I tried to work my mouth, but nothing came out as Kat waited and observed me on the edge of a nervous breakdown.

"Welcome back, Lena," she said softly. "It's about fucking time."

"You knew?" I demanded.

"We've known for a little while now, but the mind is a tricky thing. You can't force someone to remember something unless they are ready for it. You know who you are, but the rest…it comes back over time. Mine took a little longer than the others, but you, you took your sweet ass time coming back to us."

"Who did this to us?" I asked, watching her as she shrugged.

"That part remains blank to the entire coven. There hasn't been any way to identify what happened, not magic or otherwise. Just faceless creatures, but we think Cassidy and Helen had something to do with it, because my memories have those two locking us inside the abbey."

"What happened at the abbey?" I started putting the floorboards back into place.

"You have to remember what happened, we can't tell you. If we do, it could fracture your mind. Like I said, the brain is tricky." She scrunched her nose up and leaned against the doorframe. "It will come to you, though hopefully not all at once, because Laura had hers all return at once and she's…different now."

I placed the books, albums, and papers on the bed and began stacking them so I could carry everything easier. "Different how?"

"She's straight fucked up. She screams all day and all night. She doesn't stop, not even when her voice is gone. She sounds like a banshee wailing for the dead coming.

Hell, with the gates open, maybe she was trying to warn us of what was happening."

"We need to go," Dexter interrupted as he appeared next to Kat and noted the tears that trailed over my cheeks. "It's going to be all right, Kendra."

"She knows who she is." Kat patted his shoulder. "Who she really is," she elaborated.

"Jesus, took you long enough, girl. Thought I was going to have to start dropping hints everywhere to get you to come out of it." He hesitated.

"Who else knows?" I scooped up the stack of books and papers and handed them to Kat, who looked relieved when I took her athame.

"Pretty much everyone," he murmured. Dexter glanced around nervously and motioned me towards them. "But really, we got to get the fuck out of here. I heard chants coming from the woods. We don't have long before the demons are here."

"Demons chant?"

"I guess they do when they are calling for our blood," he muttered as he moved with us towards the front door. Once there, we ran to the main house, and Dexter threw open the front door. As I moved into the room and found droplets of blood spattering the floor, walls, and furniture, I slowed, and my gaze rose to the stairs.

"Cover my ass," I whispered as we moved as one up the stairway. Once we reached the top of the landing, I sniffed the air, smelling the putrid sulfur and the copper tang of blood in the air. There was no noise; nothing. It was eerily silent; my feet made no sound as I approached the first room, peering in. Empty.

The scent grew stronger at the next door. I peeked into the room, and saw my mother on the floor, crawling towards the door as a tall, emaciated creature with white eyes twirled a dagger in one hand. I looked around the room, noting the others who had been with my mother looked lifeless. The creature looked evil and held a form close to a human, and yet something slithered just over the surface of its skin, shimmering thick black lines of evil that told me he was anything *but* human. I stepped from the doorway into the room, knowing my mother wouldn't be able to fight it off, not alone.

His eyes rose, as if he was assessing how tasty of a meal I might be. Saliva dripped from his lips as he watched me saunter in. "Pretty," he hissed.

"Kendra, run," my mother whimpered.

"I'm not the running type." I pulled power to me, sucking it from the air and pulling from the ground as I tapped the nearest leyline. I felt it in my bones, raw, electrical current that threatened to consume me. "Where's your friends?" I could feel the lightness of the power as it pulsed in my words.

"They'll be here soon enough," he growled, unaware that I'd pulled enough power into my body to light up the entire state of Washington.

"Pity, they'll be too late," I pouted. I brought my hands up to direct the power and let it loose, watching as his eyes widened with the amount of power I shot at him. His body jerked, exploded, and I winced and threw my body over my mother's as the entire house trembled around us. "I got you." I winced at the pain that raced through my body and the scratchiness in my throat. When I looked up, there was nothing left of the creature other than black ashes where he once stood.

We stood up on shaky legs. I hugged my mother's slight frame tighter as she trembled against me. I'd let loose too much power at once and was in no better shape than she was. I let her hold me for a moment longer before I pulled away.

"Kendra," she cried. "You should have run away, you could have been hurt!"

"I'm not Kendra, Mom. I'm Lena. I'm Magdalena Fitzgerald." I allowed my name to slip off the tip of my tongue for the first time in a long time, and it felt good.

"We have to go now." Her voice was weak as I supported her until she could get her bearings and stand on her own.

"Help me with her," I said, needing to get the others up. Once Dexter had accepted the slight weight of my mother and freed me from keeping her upright, Kat and I made our way to the two still figures lying on the floor. I knelt down, checking for a pulse. "She's gone," I murmured as I closed her eyes. I glanced at Kat, who sadly nodded her confirmation that my mother's other friend was dead as well. I grabbed a blanket from the bed and placed it on the floor, intending to use it as a shroud for their bodies.

"Lena, no, they'll awake soon," she said softly, terror coloring her features. "There were three demons here; two are missing. I think they're inside Meg and Sheila; I don't think it's a good idea to bring them with us."

"When we get back to the abbey, we need to look up how to ward ourselves from these things." Mentally, I had already started flipping through the grimoires, trying to locate what I needed. "I think there are some wards we can use like tattoos that prevent them from getting inside of us, so this sort of shit doesn't happen," I muttered. "Let's go before they wake up."

CHAPTER eighteen

I'm not afraid of the darkness anymore. Inside it, I have found who I was born to be. ~**Magdalena**

Several days later, I found myself sitting in the corner of the great hall of the abbey with my knees against my chest. This room was the gathering center of the coven. Meals and celebrations had taken place here over the years, and now it was our sanctuary.

I frowned at how quickly the memories were coming back. I had kept most of my memories from being with Lucian, retained from when I'd thought I was my sister. I also had memories from before, which seemed to flow and ebb as they entered my mind. I'd been unable to put all of the memories into a linear direction for the first few days, and then, as time passed, my dreams mixed with what I now knew had been real.

I was a fucking mess of anger and hurt that I wasn't

able to process. I rested my head on my knees as I watched the young ones mop the floors with holy water as the older kids replaced the salt in the windowsills.

That was how my grandmother found me when she was finally allowed out of the council chamber with the rest of the coven elders. She sat beside me and patted my leg as she sighed.

"You're angry because we didn't tell you," she murmured thoughtfully as she rested her hand on mine.

"I'm angry because I should have known. All of the clues were there, and I ignored them. I really thought I was going insane a few times, when in reality, it was someone fucking with my memories," I sighed and angled my head so I could see her better. "Grandmother, we're not strong enough to fight those demons alone."

"No, and the Guilds which stood against those who would harm humans can't help us right now." She nodded her head in solemn agreement. "But he will fight for you. You're strong as well." She patted my hand. "You're my granddaughter. I know whatever is blocking you is painful, but you're stronger than you think. Our line has a long history of fighters. You, my sweet Lena, you hold power inside of you, great power. You had him, you can get him again."

"Lucian won't help us now." I grimaced and focused on my chipped nails. "He thinks I've undone some great curse that was cast on him, or cast one on him, who knows what he thinks. He hates me right now."

"You cannot remove a curse unless you cast it to begin with," she said firmly. "Only the witch who cast the curse can remove it; unless you somehow triggered the loophole to his curse, you had nothing to do with it. Every curse has a way to be undone; it's just a matter of finding and using it."

"You think he will believe me? He said some pretty terrible things and acted like he hated me."

She smiled knowingly. "I think he hates Kendra. He never seemed to care for her before, and you're not Kendra anymore. You're Magdalena Fitzgerald."

"You sent me into Hell to get Kendra and didn't even bother telling me it was her I was saving," I accused, hating that she'd been the one to give the order. "You didn't trust me, or you would have confided in me more than you did. Instead, you left me in the dark even after we'd returned. Imagine my surprise when Tiffany's disguise dropped and I found out she was really my twin sister.

That was about as surprising and fun as getting hit upside the head with a baseball bat. You also sent me into Hell, which sucked. Did you even know where you were sending me, or were you just willing to sacrifice me for a chance to get her back?" I snapped angrily, hurt that they'd sent me to Lucifer, which could have gone down very differently if Spyder hadn't been with me. If he hadn't been there, I could have easily traded places with Kendra.

"We had to be sure you were on our side. Much has happened since Lucian Blackstone arrived, and he is an unknown to us. However, you are one of us, Magdalena. You always have been; even when you left us you still felt us, just as we felt you. We felt that she was in trouble, but we assumed, as we were meant to believe, that it was you who had been taken. As we planned to retrieve her, things started coming back, and the attack on the abbey surfaced in some of our memories. You were the strongest witch we had when it was attacked, so you were the ideal one to go and get her. She summoned us through the leylines; magical ties don't end when you leave one world for another. You having a connection to her also made you the perfect one to find her. You couldn't be fooled by magic, not when the bond you girls share is so much deeper than any magic this world holds. We could only discover the general area of where she was being held, but you, you found her and in much less time than we had hoped for. But no, we didn't know where we were sending you into, only that her life was hanging in the balance. You freed her, and right now, it's all that matters. With how many perished in the attack, every witch is needed if we intend to survive this."

"Grandmother, the bond hasn't been the same between Kendra and I since the attack happened." I gave her a few moments for it to sink in, and when her face crumpled with the magnitude of what could have happened because of their misplaced faith, I knew I had made my point. "Will we run?" I sighed as I leaned my head back against the wall.

"There is nowhere to run to this time." She craned her neck, glancing around the hall, and nodded to Alan, who was a little older than I was and had just been awakened with the last group of witches. He grabbed a remote and turned on the big-screen TV.

All of the channels seemed to only be showing the news. He stopped on one channel, where a reporter was giving a detailed accounting of the unexplained cases of the dead coming back to life inside the morgues, as if a mistake had been made in several parts of the country. Towns had been set ablaze with no explanation, as if riots had happened without rioters. To the outside world, it looked as if hate groups had popped up in sporadic locations and had created chaos. Some cities had countless people who had gone missing. Families held up missing persons posters as the news camera passed by them. Some bodies had been found in strange locales, torn apart in grotesque ways. None of these people had any idea that Hell had been unleashed upon them, and there was no known way to close the gates.

"Turn it off," I hissed as I slid my feet to the floor and faced her. "You think he will help us, that he *can* help us?"

"The Guild is no more, not in the state of Washington anyway. The nearest one is in California, and they have not responded to any calls for help. It's possible that it too fell in whatever war they are waging against the Fae. As of right now, we have to assume Lucian isn't a witch. Whatever he is, he's deadly.

"We need to know which side he is on in all of this. From what you told us, he may be able to kill these creatures, like you did. None of the covens we are in contact with have killed a single demon yet. Only you, Lena." She gave me a weak smirk and patted my hand again thoughtfully.

"Dark magic." I hesitated, because I knew what I was about to try and convince her to allow us to use was forbidden in our world. "You fight demons with dark magic, because they are powerful. If we change some of us to dark witches, we could fight them."

"But you are light and you've killed one already. Who told you of such a thing?" she scoffed. "It's unheard of to even speak of such a vile thing inside these walls."

"No, no, it's not. We have books about it in the lower levels. I've read some of them before. We are not the first witches to face demons, and we won't be the last, either. There is a book based on the history of the witches of Salem, who faced a situation much like we do now, Grandma. They fought demons, and they won." I kept my voice low, just in case someone might overhear. "They turned dark to defend the coven, but they remained bound to their coven, and it prevented them from becoming evil. There are runes which can be inked on the witch who turns, ensuring she or he remains one with the coven. I know the rules, but we are fighting for survival, just as those witches had to do back then."

"That was a different time, and most of those witches didn't survive being turned after those events unfolded. Most were sacrificed to save the coven. If we tried and lost more witches, we would be in more danger than we already are. Dark magic is deadly, not only for the witch who uses it, but for those around her. It plays with your mind, and takes a piece of your soul every time you use it. It's forbidden for a reason."

"Grandma, people are dying. There's no place we can go that we will be safe." I waved my hand at the great hall and the witches wandering around it, trying to find something to occupy themselves with. "This works for now, but how long will it last? Eventually, they'll figure out where we are. Human bodies don't last long; witches are a much better host for them because we live longer than the humans do. Our magic makes them stronger. We aren't safe, no one is. If we go down, we need to go down fighting."

"I want to try something on you, Lena. After that, I want you to see if Lucian is willing to help us, or if he knows how to shut the gates. I know you don't want to go back there, but you have to. If the abbey is breached, his club will be our last hope for survival."

"You want to use Club Chaos as a last resort? You do know it's a sex club, right?" I asked.

"Life or death situations turn the sinister things grey and I find the name quite fitting, all things considered."

"What did you want to try?" I asked, following her up as she stood. She appeared older than she had in a long time.

"Come with me," she whispered.

I stood outside Club Chaos with a few of the witches who had been brave enough to make the trip with me. Not that my grandmother—sorry, the High Priestess—had given them much of a choice in the matter. My stomach twirled and flipped until I felt as if I was going to toss my cookies right there on the cold pavement. I took a deep breath and pushed the door open, boldly walking in; the presence of the witches following me gave me a measure of comfort and confidence I knew I was going to need.

Lucian's dark head was bent over a map that was spread out over the tables they'd pushed together. The Fae were here, along with a few others that weren't Fae, but weren't human either, who looked up and observed us curiously as we approached them. Midnight eyes glittered dangerously as he noticed me.

"Go home, Kendra," he growled.

"The coven needs to know if you will help us fight," I replied harshly, forcing myself to remain detached.

"I said go home." He dismissed me with a wave of his hand and bent back over the map.

I chewed my lip as I watched him, wondering how much I should tell him, if anything. He knew; he knew I wasn't Kendra and yet he'd left me to believe it was so.

"I can't go home without an answer," I blurted, and he lifted his dark head, glaring at me.

"Go home, Kendra. I won't ask you again," he snapped.

"I said I couldn't, not without an answer. Say no, it's okay. We don't really expect you to stay and fight with us anyway." I folded my arms in front of myself as I challenged him.

"You think you can stand against what is coming?" he laughed coldly. "The armies of Hell have been unleashed into this world, and the walls of the other worlds are crumbling. You think I care about your coven? I have bigger fucking problems at my door, Kendra."

"Fuck. You." I smirked as I saw his eyes narrow and his mouth curved into an angry frown. Everyone in the room stopped talking and paid attention to the drama unfolding between myself and Lucian.

My eyes slid over the pile as I focused on the rest of the room, and I saw some of the grimoires from the secret room stacked haphazardly on the table beside the maps. *Empty grimoires.* Synthia seemed to be sizing me up, and I tilted my head, returning it. Men stood beside her, beautiful men, and a pretty little redhead, Olivia. I remembered she'd been kind to me before when the Fae had first shown up here.

I looked back to face Lucian, only to find him closer to me than he'd been before. I craned my head up to see him better and smirked as he glared at me.

"You have exactly an hour to get back to the abbey before the sun goes down. I suggest you use it."

"And I don't care what you think I should do anymore, Lucian. You mean nothing to me," I replied coldly as I stuck out my hand and, with the smallest burst of power, called the grimoires to open for me. Olivia gasped as the pages broke free of the bindings and started sailing through the air, filling the room as they ignited one by one in little puffs of fire, burning as they drifted to the ground.

"What the fuck do you think you're doing?" Lucian demanded.

"They're not yours, or theirs. They weren't left inside the Guild for you or them, and you know it. Those grimoires were blank anyways. But don't worry; I have them," I laughed, pointing at my head. "Here. Where they are safe," I smirked as anger pulsed from Lucian.

"*You* were the one creeping around inside the Guild," Synthia said, and I leveled her with a cool look of interest.

"I was," I admitted. "You should know better than to mess with another witch's grimoires. Touching another witch's history can turn you inside out," I said, tilting my head to stare at Alden, who had joined us from the back of the club. My stomach twisted, and I struggled against tears. "You? You too? It all makes perfect sense now." No wonder he was meeting up with royal Fae, he was friends with them. They were all working together. I took a deep breath and pushed my way through the pain clenching around my heart.

"Kendra," he began, as if he intended to come up with some excuse for why he was here among the Fae and Lucian.

"I'm not Kendra, I am *Lena*!" I snapped, magic pulsing through me as I stepped back, moving closer to the men and women at my back. "You knew who I was too, didn't you?" I demanded, turning to find Lucian regarding me with no emotion on his face. "You are not here to help us at all, are you? You're here to destroy us. The Guild, the Fae, and whatever the fuck you are…we're just fucking collateral damage, aren't we?" My voice shook as tears blinded my vision. "How easy was it for you to erase me, and Lucian, did you even stop to consider what it would do to me?"

"Lena," Alden pleaded, and I spun on him, pulling magic around me.

"No! No, don't you fucking Lena me, you're with them! I trusted you! You knew who I was, and you did nothing. You are not just a warlock, you are an elder and you're one of them. You stay the fuck away from me and my mother. Did you ever even love her or was she just a means to stay close to us? You're all fucking evil."

"It's not like that," he insisted, and I saw Synthia edge closer to him protectively, as if I was a lit cannon about to explode.

"Not like what? Not like you erased what happened at the abbey and made us forget what really happened. You let us blindly go about living when so many had been murdered—and you!" I turned my rage on Lucian. "You let my sister be raped and tortured by Lucifer when it was me he wanted. He wanted to use me to hurt you. It should have been me! I should have been allowed to save her since you just left her to that monster!" No one said anything. I shook my head and eyed him as I stepped closer. "I want Luna back, and then I want you to forget I exist, which should be pretty fucking easy for you, seeing as you did it before. My grandmother thought you would fight for us, but I told her it was stupid to assume you were on our side."

"You would have died trying to save your sister from Lucifer," he growled. "But not until he had done everything he did to your sister to you. And this time, I am sure it would have been far worse."

"Probably, but that was my choice to make, wasn't it?" I replied coldly. "You didn't even give me a chance before you decided what to do, and when you did, your cure was erasing me from this world. You took away everything that made me who I am. My tattoos, my memories of the pain I've endured—and you had no fucking right to do it. You erased Joshua," I uttered as a sob bubbled up and my chest heaved. "I can't remember him or the pain of his loss, and I know you took it from me. People are what they've endured. Pain we survive is what defines us. Memories keep those we love with us, and you took it all away from me. It may come back, it may not; I don't know because you decided to play God in my world. You keep telling me I need you to protect me, but I don't. The coven thinks they need you to protect us, but again, I don't. I don't need anyone in my life that can erase me so easily," I laughed numbly, numb to the pain that threatened to rip me apart.

"You can't keep the grimoires inside of you, Lena," Synthia said softly. "No one is strong enough to keep the memories and magic of that many witches inside of them. Not without going mad."

"Aren't we all just a little mad?" I tilted my head as I took a good look at her. She was ethereal, beautiful, and she wasn't Fae. She was more. "Besides, who wants to live forever?" I laughed coldly. "Haven't you heard? It's the end of the world and we know it, and I feel fine." I laughed coldly again, pulling a line from *R.E.M.*

"You may not feel the grimoires inside of you yet, but the stronger your magic gets, the stronger they will grow until you lose control of them. Grimoires are living things. They can communicate with those who wield them, past and present. That's why most witches won't touch another witch's grimoire."

"We must have had the same teacher." I turned angry eyes to Alden. "I can control them."

"Not unless you're a dark witch," she growled.

I smiled as she narrowed her purple eyes on me.

"You can't turn, not and remain with your coven."

"I wonder how you can know so much about us, seeing as you come from the Guild." I wiped a few of the traitorous tears away and smiled grimly at her. "Our coven isn't like yours. Yours runs towards danger, ours runs away from it. This time, though, there's nowhere to run, is there?" I glanced at Lucian and let out an irritated huff. "Had we known what was happening, we could have hidden ourselves, but someone intervened and prevented that. Now, now we're utterly fucked without the fun part. It's okay, though, because I know what to do to save us. When you have nothing to lose, you have nothing holding you back."

I spun on my heel, heading towards the door as the

others followed me. At the door, I stopped as I laid my hand on the exit bar and looked over my shoulder.

"I want Luna back. You can deliver her to the abbey; leave her at the door and she'll find me. Then you can go back to pretending I don't exist anymore. I plan to figure out a way to get rid of the marks you and your men cast on me, so hopefully you'll no longer feel the need to protect me. I will erase them from my body so that whatever connects us is gone, just as I want you to be from my life. I forgive you, but I will never forget what you did to me," I seethed, somehow keeping my dignity intact. "I suggest you leave, though, since it might become hard to decipher friend from foe as we get ready to fight demons. Have a nice fucking life, Lucian." I waved back at him as I pushed the doors open and slipped out of the club.

I'd barely made it to the car before I was pushed against the door by an angry Lucian. His eyes were midnight, the color of a starless night. "You think I fucking wanted to do it? I had to protect you. You would have died in a manner more horrible than you can even imagine, and I couldn't fucking live with that," he gritted out coldly.

"You weren't protecting me. You were being a selfish prick. You knew we would run and you didn't want to give me up. I know why you did it. You knew the coven would run from this, and they should have been able to. I wouldn't have run from you, I'd have stood beside you and helped you get my sister out of Hell, but you didn't give me the choice, did you? No, you took it from me and you erased me. I remember that night and everything you said as you turned me into her, every detail of it.

"You thought I was weak, but I wasn't. I could have loved you, Lucian. I could have been your *everything* and you mine, but you don't want that, you want me destroyed. You've said it since the day I met you and I should have listened. Congratulations, you destroyed me. That Lena you erased, she's gone. I'm not the same as I was, and I sure as fuck don't need you anymore. You made sure of it when you decided for me. You told me you would ruin me, and so you have." I pushed him away from me as the others converged outside the club to see how our drama played out. "Watch your back, because we are no longer friends. Us? We are nothing, just as you wanted us to be from the very beginning. You're Lucian, the one who destroyed me, ruined me, and I'm just the girl who let it happen."

"I need the pages of those grimoires back," he grated.

"Take them, then," I smirked. "Cut my fucking head off and take them back. The only way those pages can be returned is if I die, truly die. So kill me, Lucian." I glared at him defiantly. "Do it, I won't even fight you," I chuckled as I held my arms out, offering him my neck. "No? Didn't think so," I laughed coldly as his eyes sparkled with anger.

He swallowed as he took note of the resolve in my eyes. I was done being his fucking chess piece, one he moved when he needed to make a play. I was a Fitzgerald, born of the original bloodlines, granddaughter to the High Priestess, and I was no one's fucking toy anymore.

CHAPTER
nineteen

*Pain changes people, but it's okay. I like who I am becoming. ~**Magdalena***

My hand slid over Luna's glossy coat as she purred in my lap. She'd been scratching against the door, and once the coven figured out that she wasn't a threat, they brought her to me. I checked her for any sign of neglect, and instead found a very healthy, very fat cat who had obviously been pampered. I'd opened the cat food which had been in a bag that was sitting just outside of the wards. Evidently he'd been feeding her a kitty version of caviar, something I'd never be able to afford. He'd spoiled my baby, which tugged at my heartstrings and pissed me off even more. She'd been wearing a shiny new collar, which I wasn't so sure didn't have real diamonds in it.

At least she'd been happy to see me, which was how I ended up with her in my lap, stroking her glossy coat as I thumbed through journals from the abbey's library, written by witches who had died over a century ago. The first witches to be housed in the abbey had written down just about everything, yet it was really nothing at all. The journals held no clues about demons, or how to fight them. They spoke of farming and the herbs that grew wildly around the abbey and other boring shit.

I tossed the last journal onto the large pile and picked up Luna, disturbing her and ruining her nap. She growled as I held her up before nuzzling her neck. As I pulled away from her, I noticed a little message capsule attached to her collar. I pulled the removed note from the capsule and stared at it a moment. Setting her down, I considered opening it, and then, as the butterflies erupted, thought better of it and pushed it into my purse. Lucian was a rabbit hole, one that sucked me in no matter how hard I tried to ignore it.

Too many things were going wrong right now, and my personal issues—and my libido—had to take the backseat to it. Considering everything happening, I didn't have time to worry about him or the array of emotions that man made me feel, which were mostly rage and the need to strangle him, followed solely by the mortifying and conflicting need to fuck him into next year.

I stretched and bent down to retrieve the journals as Luna growled at the door. I twisted my head towards it and tried to concentrate on listening for whatever it was that Luna might have heard. I hefted the heavy load and made my way to the door, slowly opening it and peering out into the hallway.

Nothing was there: the entire hallway looked

abandoned and no noise filtered through it from the kids playing or otherwise. I closed it and went to my dresser, yanked the drawer open and pushed the books inside. I bounced onto the bed beside Luna and my mind wandered to Lucian on its own.

I got where he was coming from; I probably would have died if I had attempted to go after Kendra. It didn't change what he'd done. He'd erased every trace of me coming home. Then he'd taken my memories of Joshua away. Grandma had worked strong magic to bring back many of my memories.

Then, there was the horrifying truth of what he'd allowed to happen to Kendra by covering up the fact that she was missing, taken by Lucifer. I knew firsthand what kind of sick, twisted shit he was into.

She'd been with him for months, and even though she didn't admit it, I knew she blamed me. There was coldness in her eyes when she looked at me. She moved away from me if I got too close, as if she feared me. She was my best friend, and I'd lost her because Lucifer had wanted me and taken the wrong girl.

Kendra still wouldn't speak of what she'd endured to me, other than screaming at me if I asked her. There was a wedge between us, one I wasn't sure I could easily fix. She told Grandmother of how she'd been called Lena by Lucifer, how he'd boasted of impregnating Lucian's girl. She never told him the truth of who she was; some of the suffering she'd gone through. If I'd known, I could have tried to find a way to trade places with her, or tried to save her.

No matter how much I tried to push the guilt away, it ate at me. Lucifer had wanted me, but why? What had Lucian done or taken from him that he'd torture an innocent girl and impregnate her? The coven had confirmed her pregnancy test, which meant Lucifer had succeeded in what he'd set out to do to me, except that he'd taken the wrong twin, and to protect me, Lucian had erased me. There was no record of me ever coming home for the Awakening.

In fact, there was no record of me being in this small town, not since Joshua's funeral. I waited for the familiar pain to rip through me, and yet it didn't. I couldn't even recall his face. I got up and padded over to the mirror. I looked tired, empty. My blue eyes seemed duller, my hair was a mess, and I didn't care. I pulled at the neck of my shirt to get a better look at the bite that graced my shoulder, and I winced.

I still had the one from Spyder, but it wasn't his that ached in the twilight hours of dawn. It was the one on the inside of my thigh, close to the apex of my sex, which pulsed with need. It had been a little over a week since the doors to the abbey had closed, and yet I still felt his presence with me every minute of the day and long into the midnight hour.

It shouldn't have bothered me inside the abbey because nothing should have been able to reach us through the protection spells and wards that covered every inch of this place. Runes that had been painted on little rocks littered the ground outside, ones meant to keep all kinds of creatures away from us. Everything was meant to keep evil out, and yet I felt something inside of me growing as the anger I felt pulsed with a life of its own. I felt like a prisoner inside this place, unable to breathe or feel.

He'd ruined me, as he said he would. I'd fallen for him somewhere between meeting him and him erasing me. I'd fallen a little in love with the monster who had said from the very beginning that he'd destroy me. And the worse part of it was that I'd let him. I'd wanted him to, and something inside my soul still wanted him.

I stepped away from the mirror and glanced at Luna, who watched me with a bored look as she cleaned her paws. I grabbed my jacket and the journals from my dresser and headed out of my room, only to find Kendra standing across from my door, leaning against the stone wall as she glared at me.

"Kendra," I whispered, narrowing my eyes when she didn't respond right away. "Kendra?" I repeated, louder.

"Hmm?" she said absently, moving away from the wall as her eyes gained focus. "It is a beautiful day outside," she mumbled before she turned away from me and headed down the winding hallway.

Shaking my head, I made my way through the corridors of the abbey to the library, placing the books I'd brought back on the *return* table before moving to the older section. My fingers slid over the bindings for each book, hesitating on one where the leather was older, more distressed than its neighbors. I pulled it from the shelf and stared at the ancient scrawling.

I moved to one of the benches and opened the pages,

knowing it held dark magic within its ancient bindings and there would be more consequences for using any of the teachings in this book. I knew the older witches in our coven were investigating the usefulness and effects of harnessing dark magic, and every day more questions arose of what would become of us.

The news had begun reporting fewer deaths in the mainstream media, and yet we knew without the reports that hundreds had been killed, and in their place were demons.

Murders were up, husbands slaughtering their families and disappearing into the night without a trace. Some reports included entire families going missing, and yet they'd left not a single trace of where they'd disappeared to.

For those of us who knew that Hell was wide open, it wasn't surprising. Human hosts only lasted a little while before they began rotting, so the need to find a new one would continue unless the demon found a body that could last longer. That meant we were becoming their main targets.

Messages were coming in from other covens via magical routes, such as scrying, or ink appearing upon pages next to one of us here at the abbey. Witches were now being targeted because of the ability to permanently house a demon.

We'd sent out instructions for tattooed spells to protect them, but some refused to cast the simple ward on their body. Maybe they didn't believe us, or maybe they knew there was little hope living through Hell on earth.

Heels clicked across the library floor and I lifted my gaze from the ancient tome as my grandmother approached. She looked exhausted, but not many of us were getting sleep with everything we knew was happening outside the walls of our sanctuary. Hiding didn't mean obliviousness to the deaths or chaos that reigned outside our doors. It did, however, mean we couldn't help them, either. Shit, we couldn't even help ourselves right now.

"Magdalena," she murmured softly as she sat on the bench beside me. "You said Alden trained you and a few others in magic that our coven traditionally doesn't teach, correct?" She peered around us as if she was afraid we'd be overheard.

"He did," I said quietly. He wasn't on our side, but what he'd taught us wasn't child's play, either. He'd taught me how to contain my power, to tap the leyline without being detected by others. He'd trained us to defend ourselves, as well as fight, which I was thankful for, even if he was now the enemy.

"Do you think you could get inside your mother's shop and retrieve some of the items on this list?" She handed me a neatly folded sheet of paper. "It's imperative we be well supplied if we intend to hold up here for much longer."

"You want me to go out there?" I clarified carefully.

"I don't want you to, but we have little to no herbs for spells and you know where they are inside the shop. I will send others with you, but to survive, we must be prepared to face the demons should they discover how to penetrate the wards. Not to mention, Lucifer himself may try to get inside to get to your sister now that she carries his child."

"You think he cares that she's pregnant with is child? He wanted minions to do his bidding here. Now he no longer needs them. He's here already, and I doubt he cares much that he will be a father."

"We can't know what he will do, and the fact that he is here means we must be prepared no matter what, no matter the cost."

"And yet you still fight against witches turning dark to protect us?" I wondered if her mindset about the dark witches was changing. This was as good of a time as any to test her resolve.

"I am considering it, but there's a price for my agreeing to allow such a thing. It's a price I'm not sure I can live with or make. We will talk more on the subject when you return. Right now we have to get supplies, or nothing will matter once they breach our defenses."

"I'll go," I answered calmly, somehow managing to hide the fear pulsing through me. Outside was dangerous; demons were filing out of Hell and into our world with every passing moment. The stories of old told of armies of them coming out to slaughter the living, and that's exactly what was happening.

"I knew you would, but not alone. Take some of the others who trained with you. There's safety in numbers.

To cut down on time, you should split up into groups once you reach town. It should cut down the time needed there, and if something should happen to one of you, Goddess forbid, we won't lose you all or all of the supplies. I'll give you a few more lists of what we need that you can give the groups. The others, while important, can fail; yours, however, cannot. They are needed the most, you understand me?"

"Understood," I mumbled as I grabbed the book and pushed away from the table. "We knew it was needed when we started training with Alden, just not that it would be imperative or vital to our continued existence. At least not at the time, anyway. I also knew you wouldn't approve of it. I'm sorry for not telling you straight away," I admitted softly, guilt tinging my cheeks.

"Your mother knew what was happening," she scoffed with a gentle wave of her hand. "She isn't as blind as you think she is. In fact, she knew who Alden was but had yet to figure out why he was here. How do you think you got so smart? It's in the blood," she smirked with a mischievous twinkle in her eye. "But, much like you, she had little control over what her heart did after she met him."

"I don't love him," I interrupted icily, holding on to the book tightly. "He erased me, Grandma. The rest of you had your memories changed to alter events. For me, he erased my memories of people, of events, and the past few years of my life. He took what made me, me, and stole it from me. I don't remember much about Joshua anymore, and that is something that aches deeper than any other wound."

"I gave you back certain memories, but some are harder to grasp because you are not ready to. You blame Lucian for his meddling, but I can see his reasoning. You wouldn't have stopped fighting to save Kendra. You'd have died trying to save her, and for that, I am grateful for what he did. He couldn't stop what happened to us, nor am I convinced that he could have saved Kendra from what Lucifer did to her. But he did save you. He reset us, and because of that, we lived. Had we run as the rules dictate we do, we'd be clueless of the evil that has entered this world."

"How can you say that? He took our memories. He took everything from me! Everything bad that happened, he erased it! Everything that made me into who I am is gone! I feel empty, devoid of emotion, and I'm terrified that I can't get those memories or feelings back."

"They will." She patted my shoulder. "You're angry, but not because of what he did, because of how he did it. You're hurt and you have every right to be, but there are bigger matters to worry about now. Right now, the humans are being slaughtered and they are oblivious to what is happening. There's no Guild to protect them, or us. Lucian may not be a witch, but he is something strong, and right now, we can use all the help we can get."

"We don't need him," I grumbled. "We don't even know whose side he is on in this fight."

"He protected you from Lucifer with ancient magic, granddaughter mine," she insisted fiercely as she gave me a reassuring pat. "Not many know magic as old as what has been used to protect you from that monster. It's older than any of our tomes date back to, and they go back to our first generation of witches. If he is enemies with Lucifer, then Lucian Blackstone is one we have to have on our side, no matter the cost."

"And if the cost is me?" I asked, wondering what her answer would be.

"Then you will pay it for the sake of the coven. At least until we find something else he wants more."

CHAPTER
twenty

I do not live in darkness, it's within me. ~**Magdalena**

We moved to the doors, ignoring the people who watched us with a foreboding look. As if it would be the last time they saw us alive. We had very few weapons, and even less protective gear on. To say we were ill-prepared to face demons would be the understatement of the century. My jacket was black, as well as the jeans I wore. I had borrowed boots from Kat, who had a large uncanny quantity of shit-kickers. Luckily, we wore the same size shoes.

My pack was tightly secured, and the list of herbs was tucked away in my pocket. The more we waited for the doors to open, the more nervous I got at the idea of facing demons. The marks on my body singed with pain as I moved closer to the door, as if warning me to stay in the safety of the abbey.

"You ready for this?" Dexter asked as I approached, staring him down with little confidence. He was dressed in black as well as the others, with a larger pack held over his chest that hung empty on his back.

Would I fail him if we were faced with demons? I'd taken down a demon, but it hadn't been easy. I couldn't save them all, not if we faced a horde of demons. One, yes, I stood a fighting chance against, but that wasn't what waited outside those doors. What if last time had been a fluke, and I couldn't really stand on my own against them? It was the unknowns that worried me the most. Was Lucifer waiting for me? Did he still want me to use against Lucian, and if he did, if he caught me, would Lucian even care at this point? If he got to me, I feared what he would do. He'd messed Kendra up bad, so bad that she wouldn't even talk to me. Instead, she hid in the library or in the archived files we had, reading. She was a mere ghost of the vibrant woman she'd once been.

"None of us are ready for this, but we don't have a choice," I uttered as I watched Kendra enter the room, her gaze slowly puzzled over the hunting party and our shabby gear. She blamed me; she'd even admitted it to a few others. He'd done things to her while screaming my name, and yet she'd protected me still. Now… now, she had pushed me away, and I didn't blame her one bit. She'd screamed at me when I'd asked her about Hell, saying that it should have been me instead, and yeah, I agreed. Guilt ate at me, tore and twisted my insides when her stare went vacant as if she was reliving some event she'd endured.

I'd let Lucian into my life. I'd slept with him, and it had

cost Kendra in the end, which was on me. Our connection had been severed; somehow in her leaving this plane for Hell, it had been cut or she refused to use it. It mattered little now, since she barely spoke more than a few words to me in passing if I was lucky, and those words held no meaning. It was almost as if she didn't even know me, as if I was nothing more than a stranger.

"I will open the door and once you are outside, it will be sealed again. Once you return and are inside the runes that surround the abbey, we will open them for you to come back inside. That won't change unless your plan changes. Understand me; they will lock you out if it is too dangerous to open them. If that happens, go to our house and activate the wards in the basement," my mother said, visibly struggling against anxiety as she stared at me. "If you can't get the supplies we need safely, leave them and come back. They're not worth your life," she whispered as she hugged me tightly. "We will find another way to get them, do you understand?"

"Failure isn't an option. We will succeed and we will come back safely, I promise," I replied, pulling away from her. "Talk to Kendra, see if she will open up to you about what happened."

"You've tried and she refuses to say more on it," she returned softly, staring into my gaze.

"She blames me, and she should. You didn't hurt her as I have—try, Mother. She grows more distant with every day that passes."

"It's only been a week and a half, she needs time to

heal," she retorted. "The things she must have endured…"

I winced and nodded, unable to answer because I knew what she'd endured. I'd been there, watching her on stage as she'd taken multiple creatures inside her body. They'd beaten her, used her and raped her until she had become compliant. That much I was sure of. I'd taken Lucifer inside of me, thinking he was Lucian while she'd been mere feet away from me, enduring what should have been meant for me. Kendra was gentle; she was soft and unable to endure such things as she had. I was dark, twisted, and would have been able to sustain it.

The door opened and I slipped through it without another word. It was dark and cold outside the abbey, a sign that winter was closing in on us. No stars sparkled high above us in the onyx sky. Only dark clouds loomed above, obscuring their welcomed light. I stood inside the runes, searching the tree lines for any sign of danger. Shadows played across the darkness and I swallowed the doubt and fear as I stepped over the runes, knowing my mother watched me.

The others waited, as if Lucifer himself would jump out of the bushes and consume my soul. I spun around, eying them before I withdrew my old athame and started in the direction of the woods. The old trails through the trees were the best route, since we'd be covered by thick brush and no one would expect us to come through them to reach the town. Assuming demons had coherent thoughts beside bloodlust and body jumping, which we were no wiser about.

"This should be fun," Dexter said as he stumbled over

a fallen tree and righted himself. "They're insane, sending us out."

"They're not insane," I grumbled as my foot caught a root and I paused to kick it free. "They're desperate to survive, and we are trained."

"By someone who may or may not be on our side," Kat scoffed from the other side of me. I turned, looking at her. I understood their fears; I had my own.

"He trained us to be like those he taught inside the Guild. I've seen one of them in action and she's pretty badass. There are a lot of things we are questioning right now, but fighting and what he taught us to defend ourselves doesn't belong on that list. He taught us to fight, so use it. You have magic; you were born with magic and it runs through our veins. We can do this, I know we can. I have faith in you, all of you, so stop second-guessing yourselves. They sent us because we are their best hope right now. We're out here for the coven, to keep us all alive."

"We're scared," Kat said softly as she wiped at her eyes.

"We're all scared, but we are stronger than they are," I replied loud enough to be heard by those who watched us and listened. "They are not used to our world, and they have no idea what we are capable of. They are unknown to us, but so are we to them. They may know witches, but they don't know us."

I started forward, ignoring the words of agreement

that followed my speech of encouragement. It sounded good, but it was as empty as the woods we stood in. It took us over an hour to trek through the thick terrain, over the dead or dying frost-covered grounds as the night took hold of the land and winter's icy grip tightened its hold over the Pacific Northwest.

I stood on the edge of the forest, staring down at the town we'd once called home. Houses were burned to the ground while others stood pristine against the violence that had rocked the sleepy little town. I tilted my head, hearing nothing except the waterfalls that roared in the backdrop of the night.

"Do you hear that?" I asked, waiting for Kat to speak up, ever endless with chatter. She was silent; tears streaked over her cheeks as she looked at the destruction our town had endured.

"Nothing, there's nothing," she whispered, choked up with emotion.

"No demons, either," Dexter announced. "It looks abandoned," he pointed out.

"Looks that way, but we should assume it's festering with them. They will look human, so anyone you come across you must assume is now a demon. There's a Hell Gate in the middle of town… If anyone did survive the first onslaught, I am sure they are gone now. I don't imagine they hung around to become fodder to the fires of Hell. I'm unsure where it is, but should something look unfamiliar, stay away from it."

"You were born to lead," Kat pointed out as we marched towards the shops on the outskirts of town. "You're good at it."

"Yeah, if you consider the blind leading the blinder into battle something to be born into," I muttered. Once we were within running distance of the shops, we paused, hugging the buildings. "Okay, get in and get out as fast as you can. Once you've finished, head for the woods. We will regroup there."

"And if we find a demon?" Dexter asked.

"Kill it," I replied carefully. "They're not alive, neither is the body they have possessed. From what we know, once they enter it, they either feed on the soul until it's consumed, or they extinguish it. Do not hesitate; hesitating will get you killed." I pulled up my hood and nodded to them before I slipped from the protection of the building and headed in the direction of our store.

The town was filled with deafening silence, and the closer I got to the store, the darker it became, as if the shadows were following me into the shop. The door to the store was pulled from the building, and I had to step over what I assumed had once been a human to get inside. It was a sunken husk of meat, as if the demon had eaten it from within until only the shell of the person remained. I stalled, staring at the old woman whose sunken, lifeless gaze stared up at me.

Mrs. Carson, the baker who had always come over to get coffee from us even though her shop sold it inside.

I rubbed my eyes and looked around for something to cover her up with, finding nothing. I stepped inside the shop, pulling a tapestry of the moon down and slipping it over her. Life wasn't fair; it was never those who deserved to die who did. It was those who were kind and goodhearted who God took from us, leaving the nasty fuckers behind.

The moment I moved inside, I whispered the spell to light the candles, unable to see in the darkened shop. It was empty, with trinkets strung everywhere, as well as potions that were shattered on the floor. The power grid was down, had been down in town since the moment the demons had entered it. As if something about the gates opening had short-circuited the grid.

I removed my backpack and entered the back of the shop, searching through the plants that looked moments from withering and dying as the last traces of magic pulsed through them, keeping them alive. I pulled buds from plants, placing them into large Ziploc bags before I eyed the smaller room.

I whispered the spell to light a few more candles and extinguished the one out front, leaving the door open in case anything entered. This room had no exit except the one I'd come in. Unlike the others, this room was secured for the plants to breathe, but also to keep the chill winter winds from killing the tropical ones. Not that it had mattered much without power to keep them alive. Luckily, they were clinging to life with the magic I'd used to grow them. I slipped packets of seeds into the bag, since we couldn't grow them again without more. I'd plucked roots and other things to be able to use magic to replenish our supply when these ones ran out as well.

Once I'd finished placing them all into the secure bags, I zipped the pack and slung it over my shoulder. I twisted around, listening as a shiver ran down my spine. I could hear crying—a child? I slowly moved into the next room, whispering the spell to light the candles.

I could see tiny feet sticking out from the counter up front. I shoved down the urge to rush to it. I slipped closer, placing the bag on the floor as I made my way to the child. I had almost made it to her when I was rushed from the side, thrown against the wall with red hot pain that engulfed my head as my ears rang. I reached for the athame but something was thrown at me and I didn't have time to dodge it. Pain erupted as blood dripped from where the glass had shattered against my head.

"That's enough," a smooth, deep voice growled as I struggled to get back up. A piercing blue gaze locked with mine the moment I regained my balance. A silent scream bubbled deep in my throat as I faced Lucifer, who smirked at me, as if he was tickled he'd found me again. "You surprise me, sweet one. You're either stupid, or braver than your sister. You don't strike me as being stupid. How is my little bun in the oven, anyway? Does she miss me?"

"Go back to Hell," I growled, wondering what the fuck I could do to prevent him from taking me with him.

"Now, why would I do that when I just got here? I'm pretty happy here," he said softly as his gaze skimmed down my body. "You look better naked. This century's clothing is not flattering at all. I prefer the dresses; so much easier to get to the goods, wouldn't you agree? In this outfit you almost look normal, and we all know what you hide beneath isn't normal. I must confess; I'm not sure what it is he sees in you. You look nothing like her at all."

"You should go before I get pissed off. You only want me because it would piss him off, but he doesn't fucking care about me. You're wasting your time here. I don't belong to him or you," I snapped as I wiped away the blood that threatened to drip into my vision. "You two, you think you can just say someone is yours and they are, but this is the real world. It doesn't work like that. You both need lessons on how to date, or ask a girl out."

"It works exactly like that when you're as old as we are, sweetheart," he purred as his gaze slid to where my hand held the athame. "Tsk, tsk, Witch," he clucked as his lips tipped into a seductive smirk. He brought his hand up, sending me sailing against the wall where the shelves still stood; they gave under the pressure as my body slammed against them, sending the items raining onto the floor below. I screamed as pain tore through me when something stuck into my side. He held me there, in midair, my feet dangling off the floor. I watched helplessly as he moved closer as he dropped his hand, leaving me unable to touch the ground or even move as he closed the distance between us.

His nose pushed against my sex and I growled as I fought to get free. Whatever he was doing, it left me paralyzed, unable to move so much as a muscle. His nose grazed and rubbed against my sex and he laughed as his gaze rose to mine with laughter in their ocean-hued depths.

"You smell like heaven, intertwined with the depths of hellfire," he groaned as he pushed against it harder. "You have secrets of your own, don't you?" he asked, and I stared down at him with loathing and hatred. "Or, you are unaware, which means he is as well," he chuckled. "Fucking priceless; it's working better than even I assumed it would. Are you aware of what this means for you?" He laughed harder, as if whatever the fuck he said made any resemblance of sense.

I couldn't answer him. I couldn't move my lips. One minute I was in the air, pressed against the wall with slithering power that threatened to choke me, and the next I was on my hands and knees at his feet in the glass and other debris.

"Fuck you!" I snapped, coming up to hit him, but something smashed through the window of the shop before I could. His head turned and his minions moved to investigate, leaving only a few who stood arranged around the shop with him.

"No, it's I who fucked you and you liked it. You are perfect for sin, un-fucking-educated on dick, but we can blame that on the creature who is grooming you to be his whore. I wonder, has he told you what he is?"

"I don't care what he is."

"Yes, you do, it's in your eyes. You see, I own sins, and lying is one of them. You need to know what he is, what he wants, and how you fit into his world. You don't.

Fit into his world, that is. You're nothing but a mere blink of an eye to creatures like us. You help us pass the time."

"You should leave," I offered, pulling magic from the leyline. I pulled until I felt it pull back, knowing I was taking too much at once. I didn't care. I wasn't dying here. I was bruised, bloody, but I was alive and staring Lucifer down. I let it loose, letting the power pulse through the shop as the minions screamed and bellowed as their skin sizzled. Bones popped, skin sagged, and the nauseous smell of burning flesh filled the store.

He didn't get touched, at all. He watched me, uncaring that I was killing his men as power pulsed from my fingertips as I whispered the spell over and over until my head pounded and blood dripped from my nose.

"You're not normal, after all, sweetheart. You're… different," he mused as he watched me. He suddenly grabbed me, pulling me to him as he spun us around. His hands wrapped around me, turning me until I faced the door of the shop with my back pressed against his.

Lucian stepped into the shop, Bane and Spyder flanking his sides. I watched them as the magic pulsed through me; anger sizzled in the air, palpable as the animosity erupted hot enough to bring the entire shop melting down around us.

"Let her go," Lucian said barely above a whisper.

I felt my body sagging in relief, but it was short-lived as Lucifer rubbed his nose against my neck. He purred against my ear, watching Lucian as he moved a little closer. "Take her from me if you can," Lucifer challenged. His hand pressed against my neck and I closed my eyes against what I assumed he planned to do. He had an audience now, and if he wanted to kill me, it would be while Lucian watched him.

"Let her go and I will consider letting you live," Lucian warned, his eyes holding mine the moment I reopened them as his words registered. He could kill him? What the fuck *was* he?

"You think I am afraid of you? You had your chance in this world, you gave it up. Now you want it back? Why, because you fucked up and lost the seal? It's too late to fix it now, I've won," he snickered as his lips touched my cheeks. "She's sweet, but that's not why you like her, is it? You taste the wickedness inside of her, don't you? I tasted it, and it's delicious. Did you know she came for me? Screaming for more?"

"Because she thought you were me? You must feel accomplished," Lucian replied coldly, his tone carrying death in every syllable he uttered. "Yet the moment she knew it was you, it ended, didn't it? Always second in every fucking thing you do; must get tiring, always losing?" he purred.

Okay, what *the* fuck? Getting the creature at my back angry while he held my life in his hands? Not okay. I swallowed down the words as I watched Lucian wipe invisible lint from his expensive suit. He looked bored, uninterested with the entire charade. His eyes held mine and spoke without having to say anything.

"What the fuck are you doing out of the abbey?" his glare demanded.

"I don't need you to hold my fucking hand," I glared back at him.

"You seem to be doing a splendid job of holding hands with Lucifer at the moment." His eyes narrowed.

"It's a hiccup, I got this," I smirked.

"Yet here you are, in his arms." His frown tugged at the corners as he watched me.

Lucifer tugged me closer, placing his arms around my chest as his hands tested the weight of my breasts. I stared at Lucian, fighting for calm as he continued to grope me. I stifled the cry as he applied pressure to them, taunting Lucian to make a move as he fondled me blatantly in front of him.

"You sure you got this, Damsel in Distress?"

I lifted my arms, wrapping them around Lucifer's neck slowly, as to not alert him or make him hurt me. I stared Lucian down the entire time, watching as his jaw ticked angrily. I leaned into Lucifer's body, feeling his inhuman heat as it pulsed against me. His lips touched my neck, sending heat unfurling to the pit of my stomach, and my eyes grew heavy. Lucian stiffened, watching me as I kept my gaze locked on his. Lucifer's hands slid down my side and I moved, grabbing his neck as I bent my body, using the momentum to send him sailing across the floor into a set of shelves. He never struck them; the moment before he should have hit them, he vanished.

I stood there, shocked it had actually worked and unable to move from the spot I was rooted in until Lucian moved, making a grab for me. My power sizzled, unable to find an outlet as it had continued to build.

"Let it go," Lucian warned, watching me as he got closer to me.

"I don't know if I can," I admitted, jerking away when he moved to touch me. I was a live wire, an explosive device set to go off. I'd tapped the line, pulling on it even when it tugged back. I'd taken too much; the black piles of what had once been demons were proof of that.

"Kitty, stop being a pussy and release it," Spyder demanded, coming up on my right side as he watched me. "You took too much; if you don't let it out, this store is going to be nothing but a burned mess. You don't want that, so fucking breathe for me and let it out."

I trembled as the power grew, unable to stop it as my hair rose from the static charge that was pulsing through me. Items inside the store started to float in the air around me. My body burned, hatred pulsing to life as I imagined all the demons had done to this town, and I opened my mouth too fast, only to have Lucian's lips pushed against mine. My mind whirled; the slight pressure had been enough to end the spell that had danced on my tongue. His hands touched my cheeks, erasing Lucifer's touch with their tenderness.

When he pulled away I exhaled, but the power still wouldn't release. It intensified until I swayed on my feet with the force of it as it filling my veins.

"*Sleep, Lena,*" Lucian whispered as he pushed his forehead against mine. The air whooshed from my lungs as my head dropped onto his shoulder and my eyes closed.

CHAPTER
twenty-one

*When you can't find the bright side, find someone to walk with you in the darkness. ~**Magdalena***

I awoke to someone shaking my arm. I blinked, taking in the magnificent colors of the dawn as it took control of the sky. I turned my head, finding Kat staring down at me before she moved her gaze to someone who stood on the opposite side of me, staring down at where I lay in the grass. Lucian watched me; his midnight eyes sparkled with amusement as he knelt down to my level and watched me as I struggled to remember what happened.

"Time to get up, sleeping beauty," he murmured as he nodded to someone else behind me. I tilted my head, finding Spyder there in the shadows. He stepped out, handing off a flask, which Kat accepted and twisted the top off of. She pushed it against my lips and I drank deeply before sputtering as the Jack Daniels burned its way down my throat.

"What did you do to me? Where's Lucifer?" I demanded.

"You kicked his ass, kitty," Spyder chuckled, but it was cut off as Lucian gave him a warning look.

"You want to explain what the fuck you're doing outside the abbey?" Lucian demanded sharply.

"To you? No, not really," I grumbled as I sat up, grabbing my head when my vision swam. "I don't have to explain coven business to you anymore," I pointed out as two of him danced in my line of sight. "Besides, I don't even like you."

"I told you to stay inside the abbey," he growled.

"No, I believe you said something along the lines of I cursed your penis with my vagina by using magic, or something to remove a curse," I mumbled as I took in the battered and bruised faces of the witches I'd brought with me. I did a mental headcount and grimaced. "Where's Tara?" I muttered, pushing through the spinning in my head to gain my footing. I swayed as Lucian reached out, holding me up until I jerked my arm away from him.

"She hasn't returned," Kat answered as she stood up to stare at me. "Is it true? You took on Lucifer?" she whispered, as if the men beside her wouldn't hear it.

"Not exactly, I just used the defense moves we learned over the summer," I grumbled as I rubbed my temples. "How long was I out for?"

"Few hours, but we weren't sure we should wake

you up yet," she admitted as her gaze slid back to Lucian before coming back to mine. "You were pretty out of it. You were leaking power, which was kind of scary. They said you pulled from a leyline and didn't stop when it gave warning? Wasn't that the first thing we were taught, Lena?"

"Yeah, well I was facing down the Prince of Darkness and some lackeys, so I had to pull as much as I could to make sure I got out alive," I explained delicately. "You guys were attacked too?"

"A few of us; some of us heard the others being attacked and aided them to get free of the demons. We searched for you and Tara but they kept coming so we got out when Spyder came for us and told us you were with Lucian. We didn't find Tara, though."

"And there's been no sign of her yet?" I asked, knowing alone she wouldn't stand a chance against the demons.

"No, and we were told we couldn't leave you," she huffed as she turned to Spyder and hiked a thumb in his direction, indicating him as the culprit. "He said he'd tie us up and leave us hanging from the trees as demon bait if we even tried to go looking for her before you woke up."

"I'm going," I said, turning to my bag only to realize I didn't have it. I exhaled and shook my head. "I have to get the herbs anyway. I can't leave them behind, the coven needs them."

"You're not going anywhere," Lucian warned.

"You're not my boss," I shot back, anger radiating from my pores. "You can't tell me what I can or can't do here. The coven is trying to survive alone, and in order to do that, we need those herbs and supplies. Tara was collecting medicinal things; her bag will have to be collected as well. So either come with me or step aside and let me do what I have to."

"You shouldn't be out of the fucking abbey, let alone traipsing through the woods. You are fucking clueless to the monsters that are topside now, Lena," he sneered angrily.

"Then educate me, big boy," I countered, crossing my arms over my chest as I stared at him and then faltered as heat entered his stare, as if I'd said something else.

"You're not going alone," he returned carefully. "You have, what, twelve barely awakened witches who wouldn't know the difference between a demon and a fucking harpy. You can't cast on cue let alone on the spot; shit, you can barely tap a line without almost killing yourself. So no, Lena, you're not going out there."

"Lucian, I may not be strong enough to save her, but I'm going one way or the other. Tara is alone. She's probably hiding in one of those stores waiting for us to come get her. I'm not leaving without her, so either help or leave. Those are your options right now," I seethed as I stepped closer to him, squaring my shoulders as I dug my heels in. I wasn't leaving anyone behind.

"They're fucking demons, Lena, ones that can smell humans and their fear, and witches? Sweeter than humans, you call to them with it. You think they haven't found her already? She's a fucking beacon to them," he argued, until he noted I wasn't giving in. "You are the most stubborn, irritating witch in existence," he snarled as he stepped closer to me.

"You say it like I care, which I don't," I smirked as I turned to the group and away from the man who was even now crowding my space with his heady scent. "You guys head to the abbey, have them prepare for us in case we come in hot. Have the healers on standby as well, in case she's bad off."

"You think she's even still alive? She's been gone hours. You could end up hurt trying to find her, and she may not even be alive," Dexter debated.

"I'm not counting her out yet, neither should you. If it was you out there, any of you, I'd come for you too. I wouldn't stop looking until I knew your fate," I replied carefully with a calmness I didn't really feel. My heart had sped up, my temples throbbing with the fear I felt of going back into town, but I couldn't leave her. "Go back to the abbey where it's safe, and stay together no matter what happens."

Grandma had been reckless, and wrong. She'd told us to split up to increase the odds of some of us making it back alive, and yet if we'd stuck together, we'd all be on our way back to the abbey safe and sound. There was protection in numbers.

"Spyder, go with them. Make sure they get back to the abbey in one piece."

"They know how to survive," I replied crisply.

"They are walking back without you, the most powerful witch of the group. He'll keep them safe while you and I go find the missing girl."

I watched them retrieving their bags as they slipped them onto their backs and started out of the little clearing Lucian had brought me to before gathering the others. Spyder and Lucian shared a look before he took up the tail end of the group as they made their way back to the protection of the abbey.

Lucian jerked his head in the direction of the group. "Why would you even bring them out of the protection of the abbey?"

I snorted and shook my head at him. "You don't get it, we're alone. You fucked us," I laughed hollowly. "They could have been in a bunker. Instead, we're fucking sitting ducks for demons. They might as well put us in an amusement park and pick us off one by one. Why are we out here? Because if we plan on surviving, we'll need supplies to do so. You don't have to help us; like you said, it's not your fucking problem, it's ours. You made it clear that you wanted nothing to do with me, so you tell me, why are *you* out here?"

"Because no matter what has happened, you're not going to Lucifer to be used against me. You think I care if they die?" he asked, hiking his thumb in the direction the team had just walked off in. "I don't, but you? You are being hunted, and he almost fucking had you. You think he won't cut you up and send you back to me, piece by bloody fucking piece?"

"Would you even care?" I scoffed. "You placed me in his path, and then you allowed him to take my sister in my place. Instead of trusting me to be strong enough to handle it, you erased my memories. Do you know what he did to her?" I demanded, fighting the angry tears that burned in my gaze. "She won't even speak to me now, no more than a few muttered or screamed words, and then she walks away from me."

"She'll get over it," he growled.

"You have no remorse, do you?" I whispered as I stared at him.

"For protecting you? Absolutely fucking not," he murmured as he closed the distance between us. I stepped backwards and shook my head.

"We don't have time for this," I muttered softly as I turned towards town and started the trek back.

"You can hate me if it makes you feel better, but no, Magdalena, I'm not sorry she took your place. He would have ruined you. If I was given the choice again, I'd do the same thing to protect you from him."

"Why does he even want me?" I asked, refusing to turn around and look at him as I stumbled over downed trees and branches. We weren't close to the trail we'd followed from the abbey. This one was more jagged, and turned in directions that added more time to the hike back to town.

"I don't know," he muttered angrily.

"Bullshit," I growled, finally turning to face him. We'd just cleared the last large tree and entered a thicket that had rushing water beside it. "The devil doesn't come hunting without reason. He sure as shit doesn't seek one witch out to torture without a reason. You said it was to hurt you, why?"

"I took something from him," he admitted.

"Something?" I pressed as I continued to watch him.

"I took someone he loved," he growled as he ignored my wide-eyed look.

"And now he thinks you love me?"

"He watched us fuck, Lena," he laughed coldly. "Whatever he saw as we fucked that night in the club, he assumed you were mine and meant something to me."

I shivered at the reminder. "He watched us together," I huffed out a deep sigh and swallowed as I closed my eyes. "You think that was enough for him to think you love me? You must fuck a ton of women; I mean, you own a sex club and you have women panting after you with their tongues rolled down to the floor. What was different about us?" I asked, watching him as his jaw ticked with anger. "Had to be something you did," I said thoughtfully as I tapped my chin, recalling that night. My body heated as the memories swam inside my head.

"You were no different from the others," he said coldly, and just like that, a bucket of ice-cold water was splashed over my head.

"No? Then why wasn't he after the others instead of me?" I demanded. "I mean, he somehow escaped Hell to get inside the abbey. Of course, it was Samhain, so the walls were down a bit to allow the dead through. But then, he didn't go there for anyone else you fucked, he was looking for me."

"Walk or I turn around and take you to the abbey," he demanded.

"What the fuck was so special about me to make him come after me?" I returned.

"Nothing," he hissed as he pushed past me and started on the trail that led into town.

Once we were a mile from town, I paused and stood still. The smell of sulfur was thick, assaulting my nose with its putrid scent. I had been about to open my mouth and point it out when Lucian slammed into me, taking me to the ground with a bone-jarring thud as something flew over the top of us and bark flew from the tree as it gave way and slammed into the ground next to us with a deafening sound.

"Lucian," I whimpered as the sound of feet thundering over the wet forest floor met my ears.

"Lena," he smirked as his forehead rested against mine. "Scared?" he murmured as his lips feathered over mine.

"Shouldn't we do something?" I asked, unsure why he

seemed so calm considering there was probably an entire army of demons heading straight for us.

"Who says I'm not?" he muttered as he inhaled my scent into his lungs. "You smell fucking delicious."

"It's just wild berry and chamomile shampoo," I rambled off as I shivered against him, inhaling him greedily. His woodsy scent made my senses swirl as the rich, musky aroma curled my insides with need. Lucian was raw, infused with earthy scents that seemed to work against me.

"Lena, close your eyes for me," he whispered as his lips pressed against my forehead. I held them shut tightly as I felt his body lifting from mine, leaving me cold without his heat. On the ground, I lay there, paralyzed without his warmth to feed me strength. I listened to the sound of feet meeting the ground and then something else joined in. A new sound erupted in the forest. I rolled onto my stomach and pushed off of the ground, getting back upright as I stepped over the newly fallen tree and took cover behind a larger one.

I leaned my head against it as the sounds intensified, growing closer to my location. I turned my body and peeked around the tree as my fingers bit into the bark as I watched a whirling blue light moving through the demons. I shivered as, one after another, the demons fell into smoldering piles of nothing but ashes and sulfur. When the last demon had fallen, Lucian shimmered to a corporal form and his blue glowing gaze held mine as he moved towards me.

"I told you to close your eyes," he growled angrily.

"I cheated a lot as a kid playing hide and go seek," I babbled as I stepped backwards needing distance between us. "What the fuck are you?" I whimpered as a tree barred my retreat.

"Does it really matter what I am?" he asked softly as his stare landed on my lips.

"Sorta, I'm in the woods alone with you and we've done things," I hissed barely above a whisper. As if someone would over hear me and start laughing at me, which would be my luck.

"Done things? Like when you swallowed my cock?" he mused cockily as he tilted his head a bit. "Would knowing what I am change what we've done?"

"Here's the thing, you got really angry when we had sex and your runes disappeared. That means something, right? The coven intended to have a ball that night, inside your club. You know why? Because the solar eclipse aligned with Venus, which means fertility. Those runes of yours, they vanished as it happened, not before it, not after it. Exactly during the eclipse," I explained in a firm tone, somehow managing to keep the utter panic from filling it. I watched his gaze darken as he stepped closer to me. "You knew that, though, didn't you?"

"You're not pregnant with my child, Lena. I can't have kids," he snapped coldly.

"Noted," I said. "I didn't say I was, but what *if*? Then knowing what you were would matter to me, wouldn't it?" I challenged.

"Let's move, Witch," he growled, grabbing my hand before I could yank it away from him. I followed him closely, hating that the simple touch of his hand against mine sent butterflies fluttering through my stomach.

"Why do you need the grimoires?" I asked, trying to think of things to talk about to calm the nervousness inside of me.

"Not your concern," he replied, not stopping as we trudged through the once again thick brush. "Why'd you take them?"

"Not your concern," I shot back as I nearly tripped over an uprooted sapling. "Who's Katarina?" I asked.

I was pulled against him before I even knew what was happening. His lips pulled back from his teeth as he growled at me. "How do you know that name?" he demanded coldly.

I tapped my head. "First book inside my head is hers," I admitted carefully. "You are after them; you should know whose they were or who they once belonged to, or you wouldn't want them, now shouldn't you?" I smirked as he released his hold on my arm and I stepped back, putting distance between us. "You know what they hold, or what you think they hold, so tell me: Who was she and why does it repeat her name through generations?"

"It's your history, Lena, not mine. You tell me," he challenged as he pulled a branch up to let me pass.

"I think she's the cursed witch, the one the monster hunts," I said, studying his posture and body language. He gave nothing away. "She's reborn and then he comes for her."

"And you think I'm the monster?" he asked, turning to stare at me with his hands fisted at his sides.

"No; she does reference L a lot, but my money is on Lucifer, so is she who you killed?"

"I didn't say I killed her, did I?"

"No, but this is you we are talking about, and I know you have a tendency for hiding dead bodies in your backyard. I did mention that when my memories came back, *all* of them of you came back, right?" I goaded, reminding him of the body I'd once accused him of burying. "I think you took the witch from him and he is trying to pay you back for it with my head."

"You think too much, and this isn't something I care to fucking discuss with you, Witch," he growled, turning to leave me standing alone as he tromped over bushes. I struggled to follow him and then turned my head as I heard a noise.

"Lucian," I said, trying to catch up with him. He didn't slow down, not even as I tried running through the thick brush and fell into a hole where a tree had once grown its roots. I closed my eyes as I tried to hear the noise again, turning towards it. I could hear Lucian getting further away; his footsteps continued as I pulled myself out of the dirt and looked around.

"Lucian!" I shouted, and then I heard it. The whizzing of something as it shot through the air and moved towards me. I hit the ground, crying out as the tree that I'd been about to climb over splintered, sending slivers of it into my skin as I lay there, unmoving.

I heard feet moving, and then grunts of pain, as if something was tearing them apart. I brought my hand up and wiped away the blood from where the wood had cut me. I didn't get up this time; instead, I waited until Lucian loomed over me and I glared up into his glowing stare.

"You're the worst bodyguard ever," I muttered as I got up.

"You're bleeding," he growled.

"It's a scratch," I hissed as he tried to look me over. "I called for you."

"I know," he said gruffly. I couldn't tell if he was mad at me, himself, or both. "You should have stayed behind me."

"I tried, but my legs are shorter and I can't leap over trees like you," I said as I stood up and ignored his hand, which he'd offered. I searched the brush for any sign of danger, pausing as the bright white straps of my bag came into view. "Tara!" I screamed, moving through the brush with ease as I raced to her as she turned and looked at me. I stopped as the damage to her face came into view.

Her eyes were blackened from abuse; angry bruises covered her face and arms, and cuts from claws bled freely. Her pants were covered in blood as well, as if she'd been held and tortured.

She didn't say anything. She made it to me and rushed into my arms as sobs rocked her body. I didn't ask if she was okay, because I knew she wasn't. I rocked her as Lucian watched us, taking in the damage to her body.

"She could be possessed," he pointed out.

"We are protected from it," I whispered as I pulled away, looking at her green gaze and bright red hair. "You're okay, you will be okay."

"I thought you left me," she whimpered as her nose started to bleed. "I thought they'd catch me again and do…that again," she sobbed.

"They won't touch you again, ever," I vowed firmly, even though anger pulsed to life inside of me. "Let's go home, Tara."

A few hours—and a lot of stumbling to keep her upright—later, we made it to the abbey. I was exhausted, yet relieved to have made it back. Lucian hadn't said much since the last attack or finding Tara, other than to tell us to watch our step every once in a while and placing his hand behind my back when I faltered. It sucked admitting that if he hadn't shown up when he had, we probably all would have died tonight.

Everyone was outside as I helped Tara pass over the wards and handed her off to my mother. Lucian and Spyder stood just outside the wards and I paused, watching him as he took them in. His stare lifted, as if he'd felt me watching him. I grinned as his glare narrowed on me.

Yes, I'd helped place them, and I'd used the ones from the grimoires inside my head.

"Lucian, a word?" my grandmother called out as a Land Rover pulled up into the driveway of the abbey.

"For you, Sarah, anything," he said, but he made no move to pass the wards. He stood firm just outside of them, forcing her to step beyond the protection I'd erected. I watched in silence as she moved to him and then, together, they moved even further away, out of hearing distance.

My heart sped up as I waited for her to return. I heard Kendra speaking to the others, her tone low and muffled. I turned, watching as she smiled and nodded to the other girls, who all spoke excitedly. As if something had had happened to help her in my absence from the abbey? Her gaze lifted and held mine briefly before they moved past me and settled on Lucian with a wide-eyed look of shock.

Lucifer had taken Lucian's form, and yet she continued to stare at him with something I'd never seen in her eyes. Hunger? Hatred? I wasn't sure. She'd been through so much. Guilt washed over me as I turned my gaze back to where my grandmother was, watching as she shook hands with Lucian before making her way back to me.

"What was that about?" I asked as I tried to ignore Lucian as he folded his tall frame into the Land Rover before it drove off without so much as a goodbye.

"I'm adapting to the times," she said with a sad smile. "Come, we must prepare for what must be done soon."

CHAPTER
twenty-two

She's batshit crazy and she's mine, or, she used to be.
~Magdalena

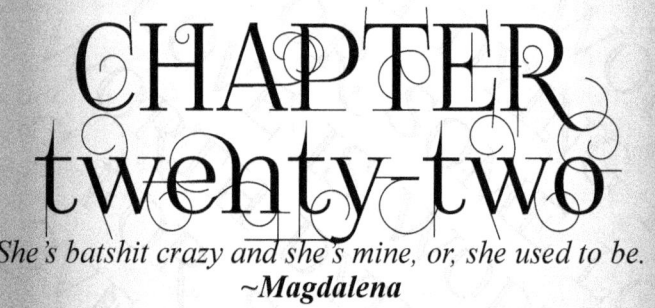

A couple days passed with the abbey in a bustle of activity as everyone moved around, doing daily chores and helping to create potions. I sat in the window seat again, watching the wards that protected us from the demons outside.

I'd spent countless hours trying to get Kendra to just talk to me, and yet she continued to put more distance between us. Not even doing communal chores together urged her to speak to me. She had, however, begun talking to everyone *but* me.

I stared out the window and didn't hear her approach until her hand touched my shoulder. I looked up at her in surprise.

"Kendra," I said softly before looking around at the

now empty room.

"I need you to take me somewhere," she said sternly as she folded her arms across her chest.

"We can't leave," I scoffed and creased my brow at her request. "It's too dangerous to leave the abbey right now."

"You owe me for what happened," she snapped heatedly. "You will take me where I need to go, and you won't ask questions."

I looked at her in confusion and then shook my head. I stood up and stretched. "You know we could die out there, right?" I asked carefully.

"You're powerful," she scoffed. "It's all everyone is talking about. How special you are, how much you've done, and what you will become someday."

She hated me. It was in her tone, in the way she glared at me. Guilt assaulted me and I looked at the almost-empty room, which only had a few people milling about.

"I have to get a few things first," I stated, staring as she nodded and fixed her skirt. "You may want to change into pants and actual shoes."

"I don't have any here." She glared at me expectantly. "But you do."

I started towards the rooms, which were down the first set of hallways. Once there, I opened my door and let her inside. I pulled out clothes and waited as she examined the pants and shoes I had placed in the bed.

"What do they say I will be?" I asked, trying to make polite conversation.

"They say you are with Lucian Blackstone, even though he should be considered an enemy to the coven. But then, I know that better than most, considering what happened to me. Lucifer called me your name every time."

"Every time what?" I asked.

"Every time he forced himself inside of me," she whispered, and I winced. "Those here think you will be the next High Priestess, because you hold so much power inside of you."

"Is that so? Too bad I don't want it," I grumbled as I moved to grab a few things, which I slid into the backpack just in case we didn't make it back tonight.

"Why would you not want it?" she asked in disbelief. "To even be boasted about as a possibility is an honor."

"An honor for what? Being locked up, being hidden from others when things go wrong? I'd rather help the coven on the frontlines and leave the politics to someone else."

"Politics run the coven, you would be the leader," she explained, as if I didn't understand what she was saying.

"I understand exactly what it means," I stated softly. "You wanted to be the one running it when we were little, not me."

"I have very little power, since you seem to have taken it from me," she growled, and I lifted a brow at her anger.

"It wasn't a choice. I wasn't given it, I was born with it."

"And yet you weren't awakened here," she smiled.

"No, I wasn't, but you know that."

"Just take me where I need to go, please," she said softly. "I've been through too much and it's hard to forgive you for what I endured."

"I know that," I whispered through the constricting in my throat. "I didn't know you were there, or I'd have come for you."

"I don't think it would have mattered," she said as she gave me her back and started to dress. I swallowed bile as the angry red scars were revealed. My feet stepped back, away from the guilt that clawed through me.

She'd been tortured because they'd thought she was me. My sister had been impregnated by Lucifer because he thought she was me, and then tossed to his cronies once he'd succeeded.

Her legs were scarred where they'd tied her down, and her wrists carried the same pattern of scars. Whip marks covered her back and the top of her ass as she pulled up the jeans.

"They're tight," she said as she turned around. I lowered my stare to the tiny baby bump that sat perfectly on her tummy.

I couldn't speak past the growing lump in my throat. I wanted to scream that she'd endured it. That she'd taken my place and had gone through absolute hell to get back to us. I nodded and moved back to the small box of clothes I'd brought, pulling out sweatpants. I handed them to her and she changed, then we headed out.

"You expect me to go through there?" she snapped as she took in the moss-covered exit. Spider webs covered it, with decades of dust and other debris.

"You want to go? Because there's no way they are allowing us to just leave out the front door. The other door was damaged in the explosion and instead of repairing it, they sealed it. This is the only exit available to us. The other is guarded since it leads out on the other side of town, close to the Hell Gate. I also don't think in your condition it would be wise to crawl through it. It's over two miles long on your hands and knees, and my car is outside—well, it's technically your car."

"This way works," she said, lifting up her nose as we passed cobwebs and dust bunnies the size of Texas to sneak out.

Once we reached the door, I pushed it open and held my breath. Nothing happened, so we moved past the runes and through the trees until we reached the cars, which were situated a ways from the abbey.

I opened the driver's door and she moved around to the passenger's side. I stood there staring at the closed car door before I climbed in.

"You don't want to drive?" I asked as I put the keys into the ignition and started the car.

"No, of course not," she muttered.

"Are you going to tell me where we are going, then? Or am I just supposed to drive us around in a circle until I guess correctly?"

"I need to go to the Guild in Spokane," she said, and I flinched.

I paused as I rubbernecked at her, sure I hadn't heard her correctly. "You mean the newly remodeled one? The one that's currently being built into a fortress—*that* Guild?" I asked.

"Yes, I know a way inside," she replied, as if she'd said it was a nice sunny day outside, which it wasn't. It was storming and nasty outside. And she wanted to go to the Guild, the same one I'd almost lost my head at, thanks to a crazy blonde with a large sword, who happened to be with the Fae.

"You know they're actually there, watching it," I mumbled. "If they catch us breaking in, they aren't going to like it."

She shrugged as if it was of little consequence. "Whatever comes at us, you can handle," she said after a few moments of silence had passed.

"Uh, no, I can't. They're Fae, Kendra. Like, the

immortal Fae of the world who don't die and are mostly immune to magic—not to mention, they have an actual Fae who trained as a witch and isn't one to be fucked with."

She shrugged again and watched out the window as we passed the town's sign. She turned as we passed it. "Where's the Haven Crest sign?"

I scrunched up my nose, laughing at her. "They took it down when they decided it wasn't needed anymore. It sits in front of town hall. They taught us that in our lessons. It was replaced with the one for Metaline Falls."

"Sorry, I have chunks missing from my memory from before…well, you know."

"Yeah, I know."

We made it to the Guild in a little under an hour and pulled up outside a decrepit old building. I parked the car and we climbed out, eyeing the rickety old thing with unease. It looked as if it had been built when the traders first entered this city and named it.

"You're sure this is the place?" I asked, gazing down the street to where the Guild stood with pristine new doors and stairs that led up to them. That was new, but it had been a little while since I'd been here—or the news cameras had been brave enough to get close enough to get a good image of it, for that matter.

"There's a basement with stairs that lead into the catacombs that run inside the Guild. You can reach the secrets rooms through it. They'll be none the wiser."

"You were here before," I stated, not bothering to ask it as a question.

"Many times," she agreed. "They have archives of the first covens and even more than that. Creatures you cannot begin to believe even exist; their information is also stored in the Guild so that it was protected from our enemies."

"I understand that, but why would you come? You knew it wasn't safe here for you."

"Curiosity, at first, and then I needed facts," she explained as she pushed open the ancient door, which resisted. I pushed against it with her, and together we opened it. I dusted off my hands and then rushed to catch up as she led the way to the basement.

"This place reeks," I said, wondering how her pregnant nose could handle it.

"At one time it was a paper mill used by both the Guild and the newspaper. Then the Guild closed itself off to the other factions, keeping its secrets protected from the outside world." She headed down a set of stairs that looked less than sturdy. I followed her, wondering where her fear had gone. She'd been adventurous, yes, but she was afraid of heights and right now we were walking down the oldest staircase in the world, without a bottom in sight.

"And you know this how?" I countered as the wood creaked beneath us.

"History lessons, where else?" she scoffed as we

followed it down to the bottom.

What felt like an eternity later we reached the bottom, the floor was submerged in water. She didn't hesitate, just moved right through it as she headed towards the Guild.

"What do you need from the Guild?" I asked, and she stopped, swiveling to look at me.

"Why all the questions?"

"Because I'm curious what we are risking our lives for. What could they possibly have that you need?"

"They have a few necklaces, for starters, ones that ward off demons. They also have a lot of items that would assist us in fighting Lucifer, should it come to it. We need everything we can get to protect ourselves against him. You have no idea how evil he is."

"Kendra, he's the devil—it's self-explanatory."

"Actually, he's not the devil. That would be Satan, who is one step up from him. He's the Prince of Darkness, or Lucifer. Secondly, there are worse monsters in the world than him, now that every monster known to mankind can be freed."

"I'm pretty sure he's the worst of our problems at the moment," I said as I pushed against a secret door that popped open, releasing even more water into the already growing pool at our feet.

"These items will help us," she insisted as we stepped onto dry ground as we passed through the doorway.

"Close it behind us."

I closed it and followed her. She whispered the spell for light, and several candles that adorned the shelf-wall exploded with flames. The deeper we got into the Guild, the worse the feeling of being caught grew.

It wasn't until we hit a room that was filled with skulls that I paused, taking in the single coffin, which sat alone. It was old, and it was beautifully inscribed. I shivered as the candlelight bathed the wording, glowing as we passed it. Shivering again, I continued following her out of the room until she stood in front of the room that had held the grimoires inside it.

She waited, eyeing it until she realized it wouldn't open on its own. She frowned, moving to it and pushing it open. Inside, nothing remained but a few trinkets. She spun in a complete circle.

"Impossible," she said, pushing her hair away from her face and holding it back. "There should be stacks of grimoires and jewels in here. The archive said it was rimming with artifacts from the coven's journey here."

"I read that a mad witch placed them here, in care of the Guild," I muttered, and the color drained from her face.

"Mad? She was being hunted, she wasn't mad. She was brilliant, the first to turn dark aside from the witches of old, and she remained so for a time before she caved to the desire to turn fully dark. She wrote about it for others so that we could forge through to become what was needed! They're archived here by the Guild's elders. If they were here, maybe they could tell us who took them?"

"The Guild fell, Kendra. Shortly after you were here, it fell to an evil from within."

"A Guild doesn't fall, it's the Guild."

"You knew it fell, remember?" I asked as she shook her head.

"That's impossible," she argued. "Come; there are other things she left here."

I didn't move. "Who is she?"

"The witches of our coven," she said as if I was a lame child who had been told many times before. "In time of wars, they hid things for the others in case the coven fell." I followed her with an uneasy feeling as she moved back into the room with the coffin. She started at the wall, removing the skulls and, every once in a while, pulling out a piece of jewelry from inside of it. It was going to take forever.

"Isn't this like violating the dead's peace?" I asked, reaching for a skull.

"Not if they gave their lives for ours. Most would have been placed here after death, but in times of discord, it's an honor for a witch to give her life and soul to protect the coven. They hide memories, information, spells, and sometimes pieces of our protection jewels. Once you finish recreating it, you have a powerful charm that can either be of light or darkness."

I offered her a crystal I pulled from a skull and she smiled as I dropped it into her growing pile. Once every skull had been searched and placed into its pile as she'd instructed, she moved towards the coffin.

"Some would even give their life to hunt the coven's enemies into the new world, to revenge her sisters or the one she loved. I read that this one gave her soul to have it attached to another witch…to capture a monster, one she planned to kill."

"That's horrible," I said, noting I'd read the coffin's inscription wrong.

"Why? Why is revenge bad if it saves those you love? I think she was brave; to be soulless isn't something many can handle, and yet hers left her to join with others. So she could never move on, so she slumbers endlessly."

"You mean she's alive?" I asked hesitantly.

"Not quite. Her soul joined with another, therefore she was fractured. If a piece of the soul leaves the body and another piece isn't tethered, both souls leave both bodies. Tethering a soul takes time, though, and isn't an easy thing to do. She tethered hers, which allowed the host to keep her inside of her as this body died. Unfortunately, when she would be reborn, she'd know only that for which she spelled herself to, and those memories would go to the same soul the larger portion died with."

"So she'd take control of the soul and body?" I asked, not following the logic.

"If she was strong enough to silence the host and

eventually kill the soul, yes," she said as she pushed the top of the coffin off and it shattered on the rock floor. I looked around and then stepped back, unwilling to look upon the remains inside the coffin.

She searched it, uncaring of the dead inside of it. I stepped back even further, observing as she pulled things out and placed them into her pockets. I felt them before I saw them. The air sizzled with power and the hair on my nape stood up with awareness.

"Kendra," I whispered as I moved to her and whispered the words to make us invisible. No sooner had I done it than a male with dark blond hair materialized inches from us. Synthia was next, dressed in a flowing white gown. I almost gave a sigh of relief, until a monster sifted in with huge gossamer wings the color of the midnight sky. His irises glowed amber as he stared right at the coffin.

"Lena," Synthia sighed as she pinched the bridge of her nose. "Three seconds, that's how long before I start swinging this time," she growled.

I dropped the spell and exhaled slowly as everyone did a double take of me and Kendra. Kendra threw her hand in the air, intending to cast magic. I pushed her hands down at the last second.

"Why did you stop me!" she demanded.

"Because they won't hurt us," I stated as I stared Synthia down.

"You said they would kill us," she hissed.

"No, I said they wouldn't like us in here to deter you from wanting to be *in* here."

"It's our stuff!" she huffed angrily.

"Synthia," I whispered, trying to fight for calm. The beast moved and my eyes moved up, and up, and up, until my neck was careening to see. I exhaled a shaky breath and stepped back, hitting something solid. I spun around, finding glowing sapphire orbs staring at me with interest.

"Play nice, Zahruk," Synthia laughed. "Change back before you break their poor necks. Fairy, do not growl at me. Lena, explain why you are here. You already…" I shook my head behind Kendra and Synthia's words stalled. "I expect a reply."

"We needed items that the coven hid here so that we can fight the demons," I explained as Kendra scowled at them with disdain.

"And you didn't think to just ask?" she offered.

"No, I don't think we actually put much thought into this at all," I admitted and observed Zahruk's lips as they lifted into a seductive grin. Ryder laughed outright, and Synthia covered her own laughter with her hand.

"I would have to agree; the moment you entered, the alarms were triggered," she said softly.

Power rippled through the area and I looked around curiously, leveling Adam with a cold glare as he sifted in. He smirked nonchalantly, as if he hadn't been all over me helping Lucian.

"Asshole," I seethed angrily.

"Lena, good to see you with more…of your own mind," he replied easily. "Glad to see you made it out of there alive."

"Not with your help—what was the price for helping him brand me? Helping *them* brand me?" I demanded.

"What is she talking about?" Synthia asked, her gaze moving between my stiff anger and his easy grin.

"Lucian asked for a favor and I granted it, so now he owes me."

"And what did you have to do?" she demanded.

"He turned me mindless against their…stuff," I amended at the last moment as heat filled my cheeks.

"Is that true, Adam?" she asked softly, but he stood up straight and had the decency to look guilty as he scratched his head.

"You know what he does, you know what I needed," he explained.

"She didn't deserve that, no woman does."

"You think I liked doing it? I mean, she's hot as fuck, but she's not the one I want—but I needed him to owe me a favor. He'd have found some other asshole that wouldn't have cared if she was damaged in the process. She's alive, she has her mind. She should be happy it was me and not someone else."

"Are you guys brother and sister?" I asked, feeling a tug at my heart as Joshua's image shimmered briefly before vanishing. They stopped, eyeing me as I surveyed them.

"No, but we were raised here together," she said before she moved closer. "You should go, and next time, ask us first. If it is from your coven, it is yours, not ours. I have no issue with giving them to you, unless they will harm you, *Lena*."

"Some witches are born in the fire. Others spend their lifetime trying to grasp it. I don't grasp anymore. I am the fire now." I tapped my head. "I am bathed in fire and born under the blood moon, Synthia. You need not worry about me, not for that reason anyway." Zahruk passed me, moving into the other room as Ryder exited the one we were in. I twisted around, preparing to tell Kendra I agreed that we should go, but she was gone. "What the hell?" I moved to the coffin, finding nothing but artifacts and a staircase that led deeper into the bowels of the catacombs.

"She left you soon after we caught you," Synthia said as she tilted her head. "I, however, needed to know how you did that, so I let her go since I assumed you didn't want her to know."

"Did what?" I asked, feeling an overwhelming urge to follow Kendra.

"Took the grimoires into your mind and are holding on to them. No one has ever done it before and lived," she replied. "There are stories of witches who tried and failed. They died within seconds of it. You still have them and are in control."

"I don't know, honestly. I just touched the pages and they filled my mind."

She narrowed her gaze as she considered my words, and then nodded. "Keep your secrets, Lena, but you should go. We hadn't planned on staying much longer. Until we have guards stationed here, it isn't safe for mortals."

"But Kendra, she can't be alone. She's been through hell, literally."

"We will find her and bring her to the abbey, promise."

I left before they could change their minds. Kendra had ditched me, and she'd left me to face the Fae alone. Not cool. Not when this was her idea in the first place. I got in the car and looked around, hating that she wasn't with me.

I took off for home. As soon as I entered the stretch of highway that led into town, a flash of light hit the car, the sound of glass shattering filled the small space. I didn't have time to react before the car flipped end over end in the middle of the road. My face slammed against the steering wheel before the airbag deployed and the car came to a crashing stop on the roof in the middle of the road.

I could smell the obnoxious odor of gas, but I couldn't move. Pain held me locked there, unable to move or do anything to help myself. I could see the feet of shadowy figures, several pairs of them as they approached the car. I mumbled for help, but nothing came out except a pain-filled gurgle. More shadows approached from the side of the car, moving towards the others, and then they collided. Light exploded, as if they were throwing light at each other.

Strong arms reached for me, pushing the shattered window away as my seatbelt was cut. I could hear other noises—fighting? I could see shadows moving around the car, heard the sound of metal clashing, along with other things. Everything blurred in and out as I blinked. The smell of gas and the sound of it pouring onto concrete made my stomach heave. I felt something tug against the seatbelt as the noise of cloth being cut and the pain sliced through me as someone pulled me from the car. Gentle arms held me, cradling me against a chest. I didn't see who it was, didn't care. We moved away from the car, and then it erupted into an array of lights as it exploded.

The world blurred around me, and pain tore me apart as consciousness eluded me.

CHAPTER
twenty-three

*I'm not afraid of nightmares anymore, not when I've survived enough to know that eventually you always wake up. ~**Magdalena***

My eyelids cracked open as debilitating pain erupted in my entire body as consciousness slowly came back. I groaned as the pain ripped through me. My face ached to the point that I almost gave in to the icy claws that fought to pull back to unconsciousness. I peeked around as best as I could, considering my head felt as if it was weighted down.

I'd been brought to a cottage, one that was covered in a fine layer of dust. There was a picture of an older couple displayed on the wall above a crackling fire that burned in the hearth. Candles fed the room light while the sound of something hitting something else pulled my attention to the dark corner of the room.

I blinked painfully as I inspected cards being flicked into a pail. The man's features were obstructed as the shadows in the room continued, even though he knew I was waking. I felt my body for anything broken or missing, and breathed a sigh of relief when I noted I wasn't chained to the bed or missing anything.

The wreck replayed in my head. The few seconds it had taken for the car to lose control and flip end over end jolted me fully to awareness. The shadowy figures that had fought right outside the doors became clearer now that I wasn't in shock from the pain. Demons had attacked me, throwing those weird energy bolts at me. Lucian had been there. I'd watched him as the smell of gas had made me nauseous. There'd been more demons present than I could count and he and his men had moved them away from the car, away from the gas that spilled onto the highway and away from me.

Someone had grabbed me, pulling me from the wreckage as the gas continued to spread into the roadway. Moments, that's how long it took for it all to happen. The male had saved me from the wreckage, cradling me delicately as he backed away from those fighting in front of the car—and then it happened. Another blue burst of light hit the car and it exploded as the world shifted, and then darkness claimed me. I'd succumbed to the lure of blissful sleep.

I tried to force my limbs to work, to move enough to sit up in bed to face whoever it was that lingered in the shadows of the room, watching me.

"Lenny, stop it before you hurt yourself," Joshua's voice filled the room, and a sob exploded from my swollen lips.

"I died," I mumbled. "This is heaven." I blinked backed tears as he moved closer, his blue gaze holding mine as he shook his head. I started to smile but it hurt too much, and then I winced as I realized that there was pain in heaven.

"You didn't die," he announced softly, ruining my delusion. "You almost died, but I got you out of there."

"Demons," I whispered, unable to say much through the pain.

"Yeah, demons," he nodded slowly, sitting on the bed I lay upon, and looked down at me. "You look like shit."

I snorted and then groaned from the subtle movement. He shook his tawny head and produced a coin from his pocket, moving it between his fingers with skilled precision. I stared at it sadly as it made its way through his fingers as if he was performing a magic trick.

"That bad?" I asked thickly.

"Worse, don't think the fucking airbag in the car worked," he admitted. "I used magic to heal the worst of it, but not even magic would undo it all. Your boyfriend was late getting to you," he growled as he turned towards me. "If I hadn't been tracking that pack of demons, you'd be dead right now."

My heart wrenched as I put it together at who this was: Benjamin. Joshua was dead, and his twin was here, saving my ass instead. It was just salt to the injury at this point. Spokane hadn't been infested with demons as our town was, but then in the larger cities, it would be harder to notice the chaos too. It seemed as if only our world, here in the quiet oasis of the Colville Forest, was the epicenter for everything going wrong.

"Benjamin," I murmured as a tear slid down my cheek.

"There it is, that utter disappointment when you remember I'm not Joshua," he said without cynicism and only a hint of disappointment. "I've never intended to hurt you, Lenny girl. Maybe someday you'll love me as you did him, yeah? Maybe if I save your ass enough," he scoffed as he stood up.

"Why did you save me?" I asked, unsure if he'd done it because we were related, or if he had a more sinister reason for it.

"I couldn't get close to you until now," he explained with a shrug of his wide shoulders. "Lucian made damn sure of that. You know he's not what you think he is, right? Tell me you're smart enough to figure that out."

"I know that," I mumbled as my eyelids grew heavy. "How long have I been here?" I inquired offhandedly.

"Two days, you've been out of it for two days."

"He'll find us," I mumbled as I closed my eyes.

"Why, because he marked you?" he asked. "I placed wards to prevent that from happening. No one knows where you are, little Lenny. This is my father's cabin; it's heavily warded and hidden in the mountains. I had to take measures to be sure we were alone."

"Why?" I whimpered as I adjusted in the bed, sending pain rocketing through my body.

Benjamin stood, moving the pillow to help me get comfortable. He leaned over and kissed my forehead with a feather soft kiss before he pulled back. "Because there are things you have to know, and things you'll have to do if you want to save the people you love. There's more happening than you can see or even begin to understand, Lenny. No one is safe from it, not anymore. Right now, you need to sleep and heal, because you'll need your strength for what I need to tell you."

I didn't fight him, mostly because I couldn't. He was right; I had to heal because the pain was intense, and it overwhelmed my need for anything else right now.

When I awoke the next time, it was to sun beating in from the open windows. Music played outside, and it took a few moments to acclimate and remind myself where I was and who I was with. I slowly sat up and brought my legs over the edge of the bed. I stood, checking my balance as I righted myself and stretched, then moaned as my arms protested.

I limped into the tiny bathroom and stared at my battered face in the mirror. Even after days, it was purple and blue, with ugly red bruises covering most of it. I touched my cheek, where the ugliest bruise had formed with some crude form of stitches he'd used where the skin had torn. Benjamin was right; I looked like hell.

I eased my needs and used my finger with some toothpaste I found before heading out of the bathroom. I followed the sound of music outside and found Benjamin leaning over the engine of a sports car, something Joshua used to do a lot before we'd lost him. I leaned against the door and observed as he tightened things, then checked the oil and whatnot before turning to look at me.

We didn't say anything, just stared at each other until the silence got awkward and I stepped closer. I leaned over the engine as he slowly began to check things again. I didn't know what he intended to tell me, or why he'd assumed Lucian had prevented him from getting to me, but he had a lot of explaining to do.

"I guess I should start with the day you lost your memories?" he asked, tossing an oil rag aside as he gazed at me.

"Probably," I replied.

"You guys were being attacked, but there wasn't shit I could do about it," he said softly as he pulled a coin from his pocket and began moving it through his fingers. "I watched them being locked into the abbey, but there were too many demons to try and intervene. It wasn't until you were brought there that I planned to try to get you out, but he wouldn't leave you more than a few minutes and the other creatures surrounded you once the Fae had used his magic to get you to sleep. I heard you screaming and everything inside of me screamed with you, and then you just stopped. I tried to get away from them, but he sent them to find me. Lucian wanted to know what I was doing there. He held me for a few days, questioning me until he decided I wasn't worth the effort before releasing me in the middle of the mountains in Montana.

"Took a while to get back here, but when I did, I knew why. They were saying it had been an explosion. I knew different. Then I watched you, noticed you weren't yourself at all. I couldn't get close to you, and then I knew why. They'd made you think you were Kendra, and I knew she was where Lucifer took her to. He knew I'd tell you the truth. Guess that's why he left me in the mountains, to buy himself time."

"I figured out that much on my own," I stated as I wiped my hands off onto my bloody jeans. I examined my ripped up clothing and then my arms, which were bruised.

"Yeah, I didn't have anything here that would fit you." He shrugged. "Pretty sure that would have been hard to explain as well."

"It's fine," I said as he moved towards the house. Moving was painful, but after seeing my face, I knew why. I limped back inside, following his stiff back until he pulled out a chair at the small round table. "Your dad lived here?" I asked.

I'd never met their dad, and hadn't heard much about him other than that my mother had once loved him. I'd always assumed we had the same one until my mother had told us otherwise, which I was sure he'd explain soon enough.

"We all have the same father, Magdalena," he grumbled. "Your father is Drake as well, she just couldn't tell you or the others. Why do you think this cabin is so close to your house? Your father, the one they said was yours, isn't," he explained gently, watching me as I absorbed the news. "They were in love, up until he split, anyway. I found his journals when I found this place again. I discovered things, tons of things I wish to hell I didn't know. Things that will change everything you ever thought was true or right. What I tell you won't be easy to believe, but I will prove it to you," he said as he pushed his fingers through his hair. "All of it."

A shiver rushed down my spine, knowing that he wasn't lying. I swallowed slowly and nodded. "Tell me."

CHAPTER twenty-four

*Nothing is ever as it seems, and reality is always colder when you know the truth. ~**Magdalena***

I told Benjamin to drop me off a mile or so away from the abbey so he didn't have to deal with the coven, but also because everything he'd told me was rushing through my mind. He'd had proof of everything he had told me, and it made sense. Everything that had been happening, and everything we knew was still to come…it all fell into place.

That meant my entire life had been a lie, and everyone I loved had lied to me. The things we'd been taught were all wrong, and the consequences, well, everyone would suffer for them. I stepped over branches, hating that every move I made ached. The pain had lessened, but everything I did hurt. Walking probably hadn't been one of my more genius ideas, but had Benjamin come with me, he'd have been an unwilling guest to the abbey.

I cleared the thick brush and stood on the edge of the woods, watching as Lucian and his men argued with the coven. He didn't look happy, but neither did my grandmother. Bags were being handed to his men, which were then loaded into waiting busses.

I surveyed the abbey, noting the black char marks that had created cracks in the walls. The doors were hanging from the hinges. I slowly moved forward as women and children were moved from the abbey into the waiting busses.

My heart leapt to my throat as I took in my mother's face, as battered and bruised as my own. I rushed forward, hearing my name muttered or whispered as I approached those who continually handed off items.

"Lena," my mother uttered, dropping the bags she held as she rushed to me. "Oh, Lena, you're alive," she cried as she wrapped her arms around me and a sob exploded from her. She held me as if she feared I would disappear. I cried out in pain but she ignored it, holding me tightly.

"What happened here?" I asked, but she said nothing as giant sobs rocked her body as she held me even tighter.

"The abbey was attacked last night. The runes and wards failed," Grandma said as she placed a hand on my shoulder. "Are you okay?" she murmured worriedly, taking in the battered bruises from the wreck.

"It looks worse than it is," I lied. "How did they get through the runes and wards?" I demanded.

"We don't know, but they did. We lost a child; he was

taken in the attack and we were unable to follow them. A few witches were killed as well in the initial onslaught. We wanted to follow them to bring the child back. We couldn't chance leaving the abbey unguarded, though, or sending people to chase the demons."

"So no one went after them at all?" I questioned, but even as I asked it, I knew. It had been bedlam, they'd been under attack, and more lives would have been placed in jeopardy if they had. "Nevermind, it doesn't matter right now," I amended as I stared off into the crowd of people who were lining up to get on the busses. Kendra stood at the back of the line, watching me with curiosity.

She didn't rush over, happy that I was alive. Instead, she looked guarded, unhappy I'd turned up at all. "You're sure no one removed the runes?" I asked, eying her suspiciously and then cursing myself for doing it.

"Lucifer was with them," my grandmother admitted. "He couldn't pass through them, and yet his demons did so with ease."

I turned to look at her but paused as an angry obsidian gaze met mine. He'd said nothing, and yet I'd felt his gaze scorching my skin the entire time. No matter how hard I tried to ignore it, I couldn't.

"What did he demand?" I asked carefully.

"You; he said nothing about Kendra, only that he'd never stop until he got you," she murmured for my ears alone, and yet I knew Lucian heard her. "We can no longer take chances, Lena. Lucian has offered to house us in his club until we can find other arrangements. The abbey cannot withstand another attack, not while it's failing from within. The damage is too much for us to handle with our limited resources."

"Failing from within?" I asked softly.

What the hell had happened in the little time I'd been away?

"The heat is no longer working, and without having prepared for winter, there's no wood to feed the smaller fireplaces. The boiler went down two nights ago without warning and it needs parts we cannot easily find. Winter is so close that we cannot chance it."

"We can collect wood," I argued. "There are trees everywhere that have been down long enough that they are dried and easily brought in to burn."

"There's no time, and sending people out to collect it is dangerous and unneeded," she scoffed. "Lucian has enough room to hold us, as well as the other witches who were already heading to the abbey. We will be safer with him and his people."

"We don't know whose side they are on!" I growled angrily, uncaring that he listened as I challenged his loyalty.

"I'm on whichever side Lucifer isn't," he said smoothly. "It's already been settled while you were gone. Tell me, Lena, where were you while the abbey was being attacked?"

"Surviving," I snapped as I turned to face him. His gaze slid over my body, slowly lifting back up to my battered and bruised face. "Is the abbey cleared?" I asked over my shoulder, where my grandmother observed our argument in silence.

"It is, you should pack," she suggested as a sadness I couldn't fathom or deserved crossed her features. "Is anything broken? The car had little left of it when Lucian had it brought to us. We feared the worst had happened."

"No, I'm fine," I said as Lucian's jaw ticked at the mention of the word. "I have to grab my things."

"Lena, take Lucian with you. The rooms have yet to be cleared, but everything was moved to the front of the abbey, minus your belongings, by Lucian's men. We didn't know if you had been taken or if you hadn't…"

"Died," I said it for her. "I almost did." I laughed soundlessly. I ignored Lucian as I entered the abbey, taking in the damage that had been done. The inside looked like a war zone, with black burn marks everywhere. My guess would be it was the same energy like bombs that had hit the car, sending it flipping out of control.

I continued deep into the abbey until my arm was grabbed and I was pushed up against the wall. Onyx eyes stared down at me as I glared up.

"Where the fuck have you been?" he demanded.

"That is none of your business anymore, now is it?" I snorted as I examined the tick in his jaw hammer wildly.

"It is when I scoured Hell to find you," he warned.

"And why would you do that?" I asked, hating that his touch sent my heart beating wildly against my chest as my stomach did little somersaults.

"You fucking disappeared, and both Spyder and I felt no connection to you. That doesn't happen, so fucking elaborate on where the fuck you were hiding and who you were with, now," he growled.

"I don't have to answer to you," I said as I pushed him away from me. I didn't leave the wall; it was supporting my weight and I felt weakened with having walked as far as I had already.

"You don't want to push me right now, Lena," he cautioned. "I have your entire coven on its way to my club and I only offered them protection, nothing else. You want them to starve; you keep your fucking secrets."

"You wouldn't do that," I uttered hesitantly. He would. He held all the cards and he knew it.

"Try me, Lena," he presaged as he stepped closer, forcing me to lift my head to keep eye contact. "I've told you before: I'm not a nice guy. I get what I want, and right now that's answers to where the fuck you were and who you were with. If that means leaving those busses full of your coven here, I'll do it in a heartbeat."

"You're an asshole," I grinded out between clenched teeth.

"That's not the answer I asked for," he seethed as he

lowered his mouth to my ear, inhaling my scent as his hands boxed me in. "Someone hid you from me, and I want to know who it was and how they blocked us from locating you."

"Jealous much?" I asked softly as his lips hovered inches from mine.

"I don't get jealous," he laughed coldly. "I get evil, so tell me what I want to know or go tell your coven to get the fuck off my busses."

I stared at him, unsure what to tell him. The truth put Benjamin on his radar, but the other left us exposed and without a way to protect ourselves. The abbey was in tatters, unable to be defended against an attack from Lucian if he showed up again.

"Benjamin; he pulled me from the car before it blew up," I whispered as his angry glare narrowed at the discovery. "He mended my wounds until I woke up. I don't know how he blocked you, or why he did. If he hadn't pulled me out, I'd be dead."

"And what did he have to tell you, sweet Lena?" he muttered.

"Nothing I already didn't know about you," I growled thickly. "He warned me that you were dangerous, that you'd break me into tiny fucking pieces, but he's a little late to stop that from happening."

"Get your things," he said, pulling away from me as I was left shivering without his heat. "You shouldn't have left the abbey, but you seem incapable of listening to advice."

"It's not advice when it comes in the form of a demand," I muttered as I swayed on my feet, pushing from the wall.

"You're not healed," he growled as he pulled me against his side. "Which room is yours?" he asked, already walking towards it.

"You already know which is mine," I grated out as I rolled my eyes. He knew which one I'd slept in, either by scent or however he knew everything he did. There seemed to be little he didn't know or wasn't aware of anymore.

Once we were inside my room I collected my things as Luna, the little traitor, jumped into Lucian's arms and immediately began purring. I pulled out my bags and filled them with the things I needed before grabbing for the picture of my family we'd taken before Joshua had gone off to war.

With my clothing packed, I opened the drawer and pulled out the small message that had been wrapped and hidden in Luna's collar. I pushed it into my bag and paused looking down, eying my bloodied and torn clothing, then sighed.

"I need to change," I said sternly, hoping he'd take the hint and leave.

"So change," he smirked roguishly.

"I don't suppose if I asked you to turn around, you

would?" I asked.

He grinned and I frowned deeper as I turned around, giving him my back as I pulled out a pair of joggers and a tank top. I carefully pulled my hair into a loose ponytail and set the clothes beside me before I started to peel off the pants. I winced and groaned as I slid them down, ignoring the gasp as Lucian took in the rest of my bruises. I didn't turn around as I felt him closing the distance between us.

"Bloody fucking hell, Lena, you're lucky to be alive," he growled angrily.

"I'm fine, Blackstone," I repeated. I slipped the panties down and reached for the new ones, only to feel his mouth as it kissed my hip where the worst of the bruises were. I stiffened as I tried to ignore the urge to cave and allow him to continue. "Stop," I warned, looking at him as his gaze held mine from where his mouth was inches away from my pussy. He didn't force the issue. Instead, his angry stare took in the other bruises as I lifted my shirt and gave up trying to hide myself from him. Propriety and Lucian didn't even belong in the same sentence.

He stood up, staring at the bruises covering my naked chest as I slowly pulled on a top. I knew I was fucked up; I felt it even though Benjamin had done his best to heal the inside of my body. The outside was only getting worse. The bruises were a mix of reds and blues, and I looked as if I'd been thrown around for fun by a giant.

"They won't get to you inside my club," he murmured as he pulled me close to him, uncaring that I didn't want his pity or attention. His arms cradled me like I was made of glass as he placed a soft kiss against my temple. "If you don't stop taking chances with your life, I will chain you to a fucking bed and keep you there until this ends, or he is dead."

"I'm not yours to protect, and isn't that why we're here in the first place?" I asked, stepping back from his embrace. "Because you fucked me," I laughed coldly. "Maybe we should stop doing that, since it ends up getting me hurt in the long run."

"Get your stuff, we're leaving now," he growled.

"I have to grab some things from the library," I stated firmly as his lips quirked into a seductive smile.

"It's being brought with us, along with a few other things your grandmother requested. If you're good, I may let you read some of it."

"You think you have me right where you want me, don't you?" I mumbled.

"And where is that?"

"At your mercy," I murmured as I stepped closer to him.

"Oh, Lena, I don't have any fucking mercy."

CHAPTER
twenty-five

*When you can fight it, it's normally you that ends up hurting the most. ~**Magdalena***

We stood in line waiting for rooms as Lucian stood mere feet away from me, issuing orders. They were removing items from rooms as each person who waited in line was sent to them. I knew what kinky shit they were removing from those rooms. However, no one else seemed to have a clue what the holdup was. Every once in a while, my gaze would drift to Lucian, who wore a pair of faded, ripped up jeans and a regular T-shirt, something you didn't often see him dressed in. It was a welcome change from the suits he wore.

"Your face is seriously killing me," Kat announced as she slid back into line, handing me a bottle of water. "I think it's gotten worse since we got here."

"Thanks, I had no idea," I deadpanned as I forced my

gaze away from the muscles rippling beneath Lucian's shirt and eyed her with a look of utter disgust. "I wouldn't have guessed it unless you had pointed it out so delicately."

"I'm not going to lie to you, you seriously look like you bounced your face off the floor," she replied flatly. "The guys coming in are all looking at you and it's not because you're hot. More because you look like roadkill," Kat rambled as she did a double take of a group of guys who were passing us.

I'd noticed a ton of witches flowing into the club since we'd arrived. Lucian apparently had a much longer reach than my grandma, because the ones she'd reached out to had shown up less than twenty minutes after we had, and there hadn't been many of them.

I still had to confront them about what I'd discovered. But between the pain and my wounds coming back as if the accident had just happened moment's ago, I'd decided to wait. I wasn't up to it, not with my insides twisting from red hot pain that was making it difficult to remain standing in this never-ending line, let alone dealing with a difficult confrontation.

I leaned over to see how many more people were in front of us and started to fall, only to have a stranger catch me.

"Wow, sweetheart," he murmured as he took in my face with a wince. "You okay?" he asked smoothly. He had dirty blond hair, vivid green eyes, and a smirk that bespoke of sin.

"I'm good," I muttered in embarrassment.

"This is Lena," Kat piped up as she helped me back up against the wall for much-needed support. "Normally she's not such a klutz, but gravity is kicking her ass today. I'm Kat, and you would be?" she asked as she extended her hand and grinned like an idiot.

"Falcon, Falcon Sutton," he announced as he accepted her outstretched hand and placed a kiss against the back of it. "I look forward to seeing you ladies around."

"As do we," she giggled, and I rolled my eyes as his green ones lingered on me longer than I liked.

I would have watched him walk away, but turning my head hurt more than it would have been worth. I did, however, find Lucian glaring at me as he took in my battered face. I dropped my head back against the wall, closing my eyelids as I tried to ignore the burning pain growing inside of me.

"I think he noticed your face," Kat mumbled in warning.

"Who?" I wondered out loud, but didn't have long to wait to figure it out.

One minute I was against the wall, ignoring the world, and the next I was being dragged from the line. I opened my eyes, a shocked cry exploding from my lips as the subtle movement sent pain spiraling through my entire body.

"Stop," I cried out, noting he did as I asked. Everyone

stared at us, and tears rolled down my cheek as the pain became overwhelming. Whatever Benjamin had been trying to do to heal me had failed. I was steadily getting worse with every tick of the minute hand that went by. Lucian's midnight irises ate away at mine and then slowly lifted above my head to where the line of witches watched us.

"You're coming with me; either walk or I will carry you. Choose, Lena," he demanded softly. "You're getting worse; whatever your brother attempted to use to heal you is failing, and I don't give a shit if you want my help, you're getting it. So start walking or I'll put you over my shoulder and carry you."

"Lead the way," I mumbled as I slowly stepped closer to him, wincing as pain enveloped me. I followed him until we reached a hallway without witnesses and then leaned against the wall, unable to go any further. It had taken everything I had in me not to fall on my face as we'd left the club's main room. "Blackstone," I called out when he'd continued walking without a sign of stopping.

He spun around and eyed my weak ass as I started to slide down the wall, unable to even hold myself against it.

"Bloody hell," he growled as he hefted me up into his arms, cradling my body against his chest as we moved through the hallway. "You should have said something."

"I'm not your problem," I stated, hating that I had to be carried, but unable to stop myself from inhaling his masculine scent greedily as my nose touched his neck. My eyelashes fluttered as I gave in to the security he made me feel. I wasn't afraid of him, I was afraid to be alone with him. Something about this man made me need him, want him.

I craved his touch and scent. As if my soul was attached to his by an invisible thread, and we'd been tied together. No matter how much I ignored it, fate kept shoving us together in one way or another.

"Is that what you think? I told you from the start, little witch," he purred smoothly, "you're mine, and I don't care what you say about it. It doesn't matter if I am fucking you, I claimed you. It can't and will not be undone, not even by you. You're mine to protect, and you're safe here. Let those walls down, Lena, and let me inside to help you."

"Those walls? I put them there to protect me from being hurt," I laughed soundlessly as I opened my heavy eyelids to find him watching my response. "I let them down with you last time and you fucked me, so don't expect me to make that mistake again. What you did shouldn't have happened. Not after I let you in and trusted you, only for you to wreck me at the first chance you got. I'm not some stupid girl who falls for the same mistake twice, Lucian," I whispered as I tried to keep my eyes open.

"You're not stupid, but you're already craving what I can give you. You're pissed, so be pissed at me. I couldn't care less if you like me, Lena, as long as you know that you're mine. You were mine from the moment I saw you outside your house staring at it like you were lost in memories. The moment our lips touched, you were a goner whether you wanted to be or not. You want to know why Lucifer wants you. Because you are the first woman I've laid claim to in centuries. So fucking hate me if it makes you feel better, but know this: if you touch another man, he dies. I won't fuck around when it comes to you. I did what I did to protect you. I couldn't lose you, and if that ends with you hating me, fine. At least I know I did what I could to save you. I'm not the guy who gives a shit if fucked up things happen to people, but I cared if it happened to you."

He kicked a door and I cried out as it sent a wave of fresh pain running through me. His words shook me, and yet I couldn't ignore what I now knew. He'd taken my tattoos, my memories of *us*. He'd made me think I was going insane, and worse, he'd fucked me beneath the moon and I remembered everything. I'd kidnapped him, and he'd allowed me to and for a moment, he'd let me come back to him only to push me away again. The things he'd said and done had all come back with a vengeance that had torn me apart inside, leaving me more broken than anything he could have done to me.

The man turned me inside out and watched me fade away as he'd maintained his selfish choices. He'd come here with a goal, one that I didn't fit into, or maybe I did and neither of us had known it.

I hesitated as he sat me down inside his bedroom. My vision moved to the bed, the very one he'd claimed me in as his men had watched us. It took effort to tear them away from it and to stare at him as he moved to the other side of it, punching a code into the wall.

He stepped back as the wide doors swung open,

revealing a secondary room which had been hidden behind the paneling. I wondered how many more secrets this club of his held. Many, would be my guess; he was full of secrets.

"Get your ass in here," he growled when I continued to sit on the bed, hesitating on whether I should ask to go back to the line, or follow his lead. Lucian had healed me before, a few times. Whatever Benjamin had done was coming undone quickly, and that scared me. I had no idea how bad my injuries from the wreck had been when he'd taken me.

I moved, albeit slowly as I followed him into the room. There was a huge tub in the room. One big enough to fit a few people if they wanted to sit closely which, considering where I was, may or may not have happened a time or two.

"Have you…" I started to ask the question and paused. *What, Lena? Ask if he's fucked other women in it. Hey, Lucian, have you happened to have had an orgy in your tub? You know, just checking and stuff? Brilliant.*

"Used it with other women?" he snickered as he turned those midnight orbs of seduction in my direction. "Jealous of them?"

"Envious," I shot back, and then faltered. Maybe I'd sustained brain damage in the accident.

He laughed huskily and shook his head. "Take your clothes off and get in," he murmured as he turned his back on me and started withdrawing items from drawers.

I didn't strip as instructed. Instead, I observed him as he worked, staring at his reflection in the mirror. The moment his eyes lifted to mine, I twirled around with a guilty flush that crept up to my ears.

I started to undo my joggers and then stood upright, grasping on to the wall as my head swam with dizziness. I felt Lucian's hands touching me as he gently pulled on my shirt, allowing me to lean back against him for support as he removed it. His fingers slid over my hips, pushing the panties down until they were around my ankles. I didn't face him, knowing I'd be entirely too close to him if I did. Once he'd helped remove my clothing, I continued to face away from him as his heat comforted my battered skin.

After a few moments, I stepped away from him, touching the cool wall with my forehead as I felt him putting distance between us. The sound of the water being turned on soothed the ache I felt at needing him to touch me. This man, this dark ethereal creature undid me. He unraveled me until I was laid bare to his midnight gaze. He hadn't just broken down my walls; he'd taken a wrecking ball to them and obliterated them without me even realizing he'd done it.

I swung my head in his direction, hesitating to move as he did his best to ignore me. I waited until the water had reached halfway before I walked around it and slipped into the watery depths. I sighed deeply as it soothed the aches of the outside wounds. I didn't bother with modesty; he'd already seen me naked more times than I could count. I slid my legs flat and rested my head against the smooth edge of the tub.

I stared at Lucian's back as he lit candles and placed them around the room until it looked as if it was being set for seduction. Once he'd finished lighting them, he dropped what looked like bath bombs into the water and silently went back to the counter. They fuzzed, sending a multitude of tiny bubbles exploding into the heated tub. The moment it spread across my skin, it numbed it.

"What is in them?" I asked, letting my fingers move through the bubbles.

"Salts from Switzerland, rosemary, peppermint, and my blood," he announced as he spun around and tossed some flower petals in.

"Your blood?" I asked, coming out of the water a little as I stared at the fizzing balls. The petals changed the color of the water as I watched. He pulled off his shirt, which drew my attention to him as he slowly tossed it aside and knelt beside the tub facing me. His smoldering stare ate up the sight of my naked form and then held mine in open challenge, as if I'd try to expel myself from the tub.

"You've had other parts of me inside of you, and yet you recoil from the idea of my blood upon your skin? Need I remind you that when I claimed you, you drank it?" he whispered thickly as he whispered something in another language that caused the candles to leap higher, sending more light into the room.

"Lucian," I murmured as my body responded, not caring that it was covered in angry bruises or that my insides were bruised as well.

"Don't worry, Lena. Not even I am asshole enough to force this when you're injured and covered in bruises I didn't put there. These should help you heal rather quickly, though."

"What do they do?" I whispered, ignoring his hooded gaze as his fingers trailed through the pink-hued water that I sat in.

"The water will heal the outside," he replied carefully, his stare moved from my body to gaze at me. "I'm sorry, Lena," he murmured.

"For what?" I asked, unsure I wanted his apology when I was exposed as I was.

"For this," he said, moving faster than I could respond. I was pushed beneath the water without warning. My response was to scream, opening my mouth as I inhaled water into my lungs. My hands grabbed for his arms, scratching him as I struggled to get out from the watery grave he intended to put me in. When that failed, I grasped for the side of the tub, coming up to gasp as water secreted from my mouth as I coughed and sputtered, only for him to climb in atop me and push me back under.

My lungs were on fire, filling with water. He straddled me, holding me under as I stared at him in horror. I'd trusted him and he was going to murder me with my entire coven just out of reach to help me. My arms grew heavy, and my mind started to shut down when he pulled me out. I grasped for him, wrapping my arms around him as I sputtered and expelled water from my stomach, heaving it out as my body trembled from shock.

"You're okay," he mumbled as he pushed the hair away from my face. I glared at him, pushing him away from me and then shoving him into the water as I held him down. He smiled back up at me through the murky depths as if it wasn't even bothering him. He stayed there, gazing up at me as no bubbles escaped from between his lips.

"What the ever-loving fuck," I uttered as I dipped my head to the water and, before I knew my intentions, I'd placed my lips flush against his and kissed him. He came up, wrapping his arms around me as he deepened the kiss and encircled me with his arms, holding me close against his naked chest.

My hands slowly slid up his back and buried into his hair, threading through it as I held him to me. We were unnatural to want this…this crazy thing that was happening between us. He was the storm out on the ocean, dangerous and deadly, and I was the idiot in the boat who danced upon those deadly waves, sailing the treacherous sea in chase of the adrenaline rush only he could give me.

He lifted us up and my senses came rushing back as our lips parted. He allowed me to slide from his body until my feet touched the smooth surface of the tub. He pushed me down and I didn't argue, didn't complain as he followed me back into the tub still wearing his pants. He reached for a bottle of shampoo and turned me until my back was against his chest.

"How's the pain?" he asked gutturally.

"It's…gone," I murmured as I struggled to ignore

the appendage I felt in his jeans. "You got in the bath in jeans?"

"You want me to remove them?" he asked, and I shook my head. "Didn't think so," he laughed softly.

"You healed me," I pointed out.

"Yes," he responded carefully. "Don't ask it," he started when my lips parted to do just that. "You're not ready for that, and I am barely holding back the urge to tear you from this tub and bend you over that counter. Now, shut up and let me wash your hair, little witch."

He washed it with strong fingers, massaging my scalp as I rested against him as he'd instructed. It was too intimate. The setting was everything a girl could dream up. Candlelight flickered in the dark bathroom and I gazed up, wondering when the lights had gone out or how I'd missed it when they did. Roses mixed with other types of flower petals as they danced on the water's surface around my knees. His hands were magic as he washed my hair with something that smelled divine. I actually let loose a moan as he continued to massage it, sending pleasure racing from my head to my toes.

"Did you have to push me beneath the water?" I muttered as I rested my head against him as I peered up into his onyx depths.

"Would you have allowed it otherwise?" he asked deeply, his deep baritone voice rumbling against my skin. I shook my head, giving him my answer as I watched him lower his lips and place a gentle kiss against them.

I swallowed as tears swam in my vision. I could handle anger. I could handle the hate that burned through me. I couldn't handle this. Not this nice shit, this gentleness from him, not when I wanted to remain angry at him. I lifted my head, moving my mouth away from him as he pulled down another bottle. "Magic is touchy when you use blood. My blood heals; you're no longer bruised or bleeding inside. Unlike Benjamin's clumsy attempt to heal you with white magic, I used the magic of my blood. You'll be fully recovered in the morning, but until then, you'll sleep with me."

"That's not happening," I argued as he finished washing my hair and I faced him.

"It wasn't a question," he growled. "Blood magic has a price, Lena, one that I won't allow you to pay, so you will sleep in my bed," he purred silkily. "You will be the first woman to ever sleep in it without getting fucked, so shut up, get dressed or don't. That one is up to you but I warn you, sweet girl, I'm hanging by a fucking thread and it's about to snap without being able to take what I want. Lucifer is still out there, and he's made it known he wants you. Every fucking demon is itching to get to you to fall into favor with him. So no, you're not sleeping alone tonight or any other fucking night, not even claimed.

"He's lost his fucking mind in his need for revenge, and I promised you that I would protect you. I don't break my fucking promises. I won't force you to be with me, but I didn't go through months of hell keeping my distance to lose you now. I've had Luna and your things brought to my room, so get changed. Seeing you naked is driving me bugfuck crazy and I'm a sinner, and you're no fucking saint. Us naked, beautiful girl? We're explosive, and I crave you like a drug addict on a fucking bender in need of a fix. Go get dressed, now."

I stood up, ignoring him as his hungry gaze trailed down my body, following the rivulets of water. I stepped from the tub, eyeing the mirror as I took in the lack of bruises, leaving behind only the crude stitches.

"I'll remove them when you're dressed and my cock stops aching," he hissed from the tub, where he remained seated. "Clothes, Lena." I grabbed a towel as I darted to the bedroom.

Inside the room, I dressed in a gown and crawled beneath the covers, waiting for Lucian. Luna jumped onto the bed, scaring me as she fried my already frayed nerves. I petted her thick, midnight coat and tried to ignore Lucian as he sauntered into the room with only a thick white towel wrapped around his narrow hips. He moved to the cupboard and withdrew a pair of sweats. I observed quietly as he tossed the towel aside and then faced me.

He clucked his tongue and Luna jumped up, mewling as she slunk her traitorous ass over to the edge of the bed before jumping into his waiting arms. He cradled her as he moved to the closet once more, withdrawing a huge velvet bed and setting it in the chair that sat at the end of the bed. She jumped into it, lying down as she started grooming her paws. He deftly moved around the room, putting out water and the expensive as shit cat food.

"Goodnight, Luna," he purred as she watched him move to the bed.

"Thank you," I whispered hoarsely.

"For what?"

"For taking care of her," I replied. "When I found her she'd been abandoned. She was scared of her own shadow and covered in fleas. I nursed her back to life, and she's been with me since. You've spoiled her rotten, though, and I'm not sure she'll want to go with me now." I laughed as Luna mewled in agreement.

"Do you have any idea how hard it was keeping her from her mother? Anytime you walked in she went crazy. No amount of expensive cat food will replace you in her life. You're her mother, and I don't think you realize that you were never alone. The coven watched you; they protected you even when you didn't know they were. No witch is ever alone in this world. You're all bonded until death, and sometimes not even death can break that bond."

I watched as he pulled the blankets apart before sliding beneath them. His body rippled with masculine power, muscles moved with sinewy perfection as he reached for me. I didn't fight him, instead letting him pull me close as he whispered words that turned off the lights. In the darkness, I prayed to Hecate.

I prayed for the strength to do what was needed when the time came. I prayed that he wasn't what Benjamin said he was, because if he was, I'd fallen in love with a monster from the depths of Hell.

CHAPTER
twenty-six

The truth hurts, but hearing it hurts even worse. Knowing it does things to you. It breaks away at the chips in your armor, until you're standing naked in front of everyone. ~**Magdalena**

The next few days were a blur of activity as more covens showed up, everything moving faster than I could keep up with. Some had come from as far as New Mexico to find protection with our coven. Each was known to us, which at least made it easier to accept them into the fold.

I'd steered clear of most of them, ignoring Lucian as well until bedtime. The latter wasn't as easy since anytime he entered a room, my stomach did a summersault, and my heart sped up a little faster even without seeing him.

Tonight I was hunting my mother and grandmother down for a conversation I could no longer wait to have with them. Our family had secrets, the kind of secrets that left everything upside down and inside out.

Moving through the club's main room, I slowed my pace as I watched Kendra approach Lucian. Her hand touched his shoulder and she giggled as she pulled it back, tucking her hair behind her ear as she spoke to him. I stood there, dumbfounded as she laughed at something he said and then pointed to a booth close to them. Lucian nodded and together they walked to it then slid into the seat on the same side.

Kendra smiled, leaning her shoulder entirely too close to Lucian as she lifted her lips to his ear, whispering into it. I felt my anger rising as if I had a right to be angry over her getting that close to him, but I didn't. Hadn't I pushed him away? My question was: If she'd been battered by Lucifer using Lucian's image, wouldn't she be hesitant or uncomfortable speaking to him? Instead, she looked like she was flirting, and he didn't look immune to it, either. She was flirting with him with my face! Of course he wouldn't be immune to it, she was me. He could easily go with her and just toss me aside because we were literally the same make and model.

I was so absorbed in observing them that I hadn't heard Spyder come up beside me. He pushed me into the corner and laughed throatily as I gasped in shock.

"Jealous, kitty?" he inquired softly as his thumb captured my chin, lifting my gaze from Lucian and Kendra to meet his instead. I pursed my lips together and began to feed him the riot act when he shook his head. "She isn't you," he purred huskily. "He wants your fire, you burn red hot. She's ice-fucking-cold and boring. Don't do that jealousy bullshit. You're better than that. Now run along before more people see you glaring daggers at your twin image."

"I'm not jealous," I lied. I totally was. The pain in my heart ached, and my stomach twirled with a new emotion I hadn't felt in a very long time. Not since my ex had fucked Cassidy on my own bed.

"Liar, it's written in your eyes and the stiffness of your spine. You're pissed," he argued.

"She was taken by Lucifer, and he was projecting Lucian's image, yet she's okay with whispering into his ear as her hand strokes his?"

Spyder paused as his stare turned to look at Lucian and Kendra. Exactly! She seemed cozy with him, and she shouldn't. Not after what she'd endured. Hell, she barely spoke to me more than to order me about. Lately she'd asked me to take her places, places that we had no business being at. Shit, I'd barely managed to call Benjamin and warn him that she'd suggested we go investigate a cottage close to our house where an enemy may have hidden before the demons had been released.

She'd changed, and no matter how hard I tried, I couldn't connect with her. I'd tried to use the mental link—shit, I'd screamed at her through it for hours last night as I lay awake next to Lucian. Nothing, radio silence on her end. Not even the sight of Lucian's bare chest distracted me as my mind replayed everything she'd been up to since she'd returned.

"Has she been different since she returned?" he asked, forcing my mind to focus on him. I wouldn't betray her, not when whatever was going on with her was my fault.

"No, just forget it. I have to find my grandmother," I replied as I moved away from him.

"Does she have a devil's trap on her, Magdalena?" he asked as he grabbed my arm, preventing my escape.

"We all do, even Luna has one," I admitted.

"You tattooed our Luna?" he asked, and I zeroed my gaze on him. *Our* Luna?

"According to what Alden told my mother, not even animals are immune to being possessed," I retorted. "Furthermore, she's mine and it's my responsibility to protect her."

"Calm your tits, kitty. Your grandmother is holding her court in the dungeon, with the other elders. I did supply whips and chains so if anyone steps out of line, I'm sure Sarah can handle them easily."

I smirked as the mental image played through my mind. "That's just wrong on so many levels that I'm not even sure where to start, Spyder," I laughed.

"There it is," he said as he reached up and pushed a stray piece of hair behind my ear. "They should be done soon, and if he doesn't see through her shit, it will be his own fault, and then you and I? We'll play cat and mouse a bit," he laughed as he teased but the heat in his eyes said a totally different story.

I looked away from him to where Lucian had been

watching us together. The look in his angry glare told me he wasn't happy about it, so I did the only thing I could to let him know I didn't care. I stood on my tiptoes, kissing Spyder on the lips before I moved away, leaving him with a dumbfounded look and Lucian with a clear message.

I'd made it to the end of the bar area before Lucian appeared in front of me, and I tilted my head a bit, knowing he hadn't gotten here by walking.

"What the fuck was that?" he demanded.

"You tell me," I demanded back, crossing my arms as I glared up at him.

"You fucking kissed him," he growled.

"I gave him a peck on the lips," I replied easily, as if Spyder's lips hadn't affected me any.

"You want to explain why the fuck you did it?" he asked icily, his jaw ticking wildly.

"You want to tell me what my sister whispered into your ear?" I countered angrily.

He smiled and grabbed my arm, pulling me into the hallway that led out of sight. Lucian pushed me against the wall and kissed me, hard. When he pulled away, he growled long and hard as he stared down at me.

"You can keep acting like you don't want me, but you need me," he whispered hoarsely.

"No, Lucian. The difference is I never needed you.

I wanted you, and there's a huge difference between the two. I wanted you with every fiber of my being and you fucking broke me, like I was some sort of promise you decided not to keep. Do you have any idea how that makes me feel? I feel worthless, like I wasn't worth the chance you'd have taken to trust me to follow your lead. And now, now you're all cozy as a stripper and a dollar bill with my sister. And you get mad when I kiss someone else you forced to claim me? Why are we here right now? Whose choices led us here? Because it sure as shit wasn't mine. Mine would have been by your side, unwaveringly following you into the depths of Hell if you'd asked. So guess what, if I kiss someone else? You deal with it, because I didn't push you away, you fucking threw me away like your unwanted trash."

"I would never throw you away, Lena. I saved your foolhardy life, and right now you're making it very hard not to slam you against that wall and prove it to you. You think I want Kendra? I assure you, you couldn't be further from the truth. She's even colder than she was before, and my feelings for you didn't change one fucking iota when you thought you were her. Staying away from you was one of the hardest things I've had to do, and trust me, I've done a lot of hard things in my lifetime, but none of them affected me as you have. So throw your fucking fit and get the fuck over it, because you and me? We're far from done. You want me and I want you, and that's all that should fucking matter right now. People outside are dying and you're too pissed off to see past your anger to grab what is right in front of you," he seethed as he boxed me against the wall. "There's not another woman that roams this world or any other who I want more than you."

I swallowed as I closed my eyes against the angry tears. "Then why didn't you let me choose? Why did you take away pieces of me?" I uttered painfully.

"Because you would have run right to Lucifer in your pain to get her back, and I couldn't allow that. You think we weren't being watched? You think he didn't have fucking minions up here watching me? I made them keep you away from me until I was sure the glamour we'd cloaked you in had worked on the demons. Once I knew, I made them send you to me every fucking chance I got, every fucking excuse to see you I took. Life isn't fucking black and white, Magdalena, wake the fuck up and get past it. Be pissed, but get the fuck over it."

"You think it's that easy?" I demanded angrily. "You erased my brother, and then you went even further and you erased my tattoos, which meant something to me. They were proof I'd survived something, and you obliterated it from my past like it was written in fucking sharpie. I was falling for you and then you played God in my world; you didn't trust me and that hurts the most. You made me into something I'm not, and now you expect me to just go back to the girl I was before. Why? Because your world didn't change? Mine has been shaken from its foundation and left in a pile of fucking rubble to rebuild alone. You burned my world down, and in the same breath, you didn't let the flames touch me, but in the end, you were the flames that burned me the most. You protected me and let someone I love take the fall. She'll never be the same, and neither will I."

Footsteps sounded down the hall and Lucian took a step away from me as we watched my grandmother and mother converge on our location. I turned my head from them, wiping away the tears before I walked in their direction.

"I need to speak to you, both of you. Now," I announced.

"Is everything all right?" my mother questioned.

"We need to talk about Drake," I growled.

My mother's blue eyes grew rounded as she moved hers between me and my grandmother. She knew that I knew she'd lied to me from birth. My grandmother asked Lucian for a room and he directed us to one, which I entered silently. Once the door had closed, I rounded on my mother and stared at her shaken pallor.

"You need to explain why you would withhold it from the coven and us," I snapped.

"Drake was a born dark witch," my grandmother answered for her sternly. "It was forbidden by the coven. We weren't aware of it when they first got together; he was awakened by the ancestors, or so we had assumed. He used dark magic to make a deal with a witch; in exchange, he was given a mate of pure blood. He got Fiona. We were unaware of what he was, or what he'd done at the time. They conceived the boys on that very night. They fell in love, Lena. You and I both know the heart doesn't care what is wrong or right. It goes after what it wants no matter what the brain says otherwise.

"We didn't know what had happened until it was too late, and even then, they were in love. When Benjamin turned dark, it was too late to drive the darkness out of him. Drake took him to the cottage for a while, hid him from the others. I myself took them food and supplies. Months later, I watched Joshua as your mother snuck up to see him, to tell him it was time to go away from here, as the others had begun to notice his presence, or lack of. Your mother became pregnant that very night as they said their goodbyes. That was why, on summer solstice every year, we took you girls to the seer in the woods. You were both protected from the darkness. So, when Drake and Benjamin disappeared, we vowed to find her another mate immediately and claim he sired you and Kendra."

"You could have told us," I whispered through the thickening in my throat. "What if we'd changed? What if we'd formed a darkness inside of us and had to hide it to remain here?" I asked.

"Then we'd have handled you as well," my grandmother answered coldly. "No witch can be born of darkness without being evil. It's written from the beginning of the tales of witches, Lena. Those born to darkness will destroy us all. They cannot fight the evil within their veins and souls for more than a few years, but as children it's worse. They are the truest form of evil, and why the humans have tales of evil witches from the dawn of man. Understand this: Benjamin should have been drowned to purify and release his soul, yet we didn't have the strength to do it. So we let him live, and not a day has gone by that we have not wondered what kind of monster we allowed to live. He is of our bloodline, which means he is very powerful, and with his father driving him, there's no telling what he has done."

"You think he unleashed the demons on us?" I asked in disbelief.

"Who else would have done this?" my mother finally asked.

"Benjamin is mortal," I announced. "Mortals do not hold enough power or magic to unleash Hell on earth. He didn't do this. He is darkness, but he is not what you think. He pulled me from the wreckage and did his best to keep me alive. He allowed me to leave without any argument."

"But not before he filled you with discord. He told you who your father was, and he probably told you a million other lies. Of course he let you go, Lena. He made sure you were questioning things before he did so, didn't he?"

"What he said to me made sense," I replied. He'd shown me proof, which one of those things had already been proven to be correct.

"He isn't what you think, granddaughter," my grandmother whispered. "He's tried to turn you against us, do not let him win this fight. He showed up right before the gates opened and allowed a few more demons out, and now again as the gates have failed. That is a truth as well. Now, tomorrow we will hold a dance for the new witches and ours to become united in a cause worth fighting for. You will be in attendance, and you will cease leaving this place, do you understand?"

"But I—"

"Enough!" she shouted and glared at me. "I've been

patient with you, Lena. It ends here. You are not to leave here anymore. You will stop forcing Kendra to join you and taking her from the safety of this place in her condition. It's not safe for either of you out there."

"I didn't want to leave, she did!" I snapped, and both regarded at me as if I was losing it.

"Kendra reported less than an hour ago that you forced her to leave here three times. I was also told that you were just witnessed in the club glaring at her as Lucian showed her attention and then we find you and him together, arguing. If you continue, you will be confined to the room you are staying in."

"Yes ma'am," I said, spinning on my heel as I exited the room. That bitch set me up! Maybe she *didn't* have a devil's trap on her body, because this shit? This shit was low, and no matter what had happened, I didn't deserve it from her.

I made my way through the heavily crowded club, full of witches. Once I'd taken a seat at the bar, Spyder pulled up the stool next to me and glared at me. He rapped his knuckles on the bar and I smirked as I gave him my attention.

"You want to explain what the fuck that was?" he demanded as the bartender approached. I shook my head as I gave Vlad a small smile.

"Get me drunk," I said as Vlad gave me a lopsided smile.

"Now why would a pretty girl like you want to get

drunk?" he asked, pushing his long black hair away from his face as he watched me.

"Because I just kissed Spyder, got berated by the High Priestess, and because some people have lost their integrity," I muttered as I stared him down in open challenge. "So get me a drink, please. Something strong," I frowned as I turned back to Spyder, deepening the frown. He had a black eye, which wasn't healing as fast as his other injuries had before. "Someone hit you?" I asked, wondering if I was misjudging it, or if the shadows were playing games on me.

"I ran into a fist," he said before he swung his glare to Vlad. "Jack Daniels, on the rocks," he grumbled as he turned to face the crowd. There was no music playing, which seemed off. Every time I'd been in here the music had been bumping.

I dismissed him, observing Vlad as he poured two fingers of Jack into the glasses and then pushed them in our direction. I took the cup and tipped it up, swallowing it in one gulp before I set it back down and pushed it back.

"More," I said, ignoring the two sets of eyes that stared at me.

After the fourth, I slowed down and turned, taking in the witches who mingled or flirted. There were so many of them that I didn't even know who was who anymore, or which coven they were from. My head swayed as I tipped the glass and swallowed deeply.

"You're not going to drink it away, kitty," Spyder

said as he surveyed me with hooded eyes. "That pain of betrayal, it's not going anywhere."

"I wasn't betrayed," I stated, watching him as his lips tipped up, forming an alluring smile. "I never said anything about being betrayed." *What the fuck, did the walls have ears?*

"You didn't have to," he laughed as Vlad nodded.

"Girl drinks like that, she's either hiding something or she's hurting. Sometimes, it's both," Vlad tossed in.

"What if the girl just wants to get drunk?" I pointed out defensively.

"Girls don't get drunk without other girls," Vlad countered.

"Then there are things like clothes coming off, hooting and hollering, and the fun starts. You're not doing any of those things, and you're drinking with me," Spyder retorted as his forehead creased as he struggled not to laugh at the disgruntled look I gave him. "Go to bed, kitty. Before I end up with another black eye," he warned.

"Fine," I grumbled as I pulled out a few dollars and started counting change.

"I got this," Spyder announced as he pushed the money back into my pocket and gave me a gentle push in the direction of the sleeping quarters.

"He shouldn't have hit you," I said.

"It was fucking worth it."

"If you say so," I muttered as I started to walk away from him.

"I say so."

CHAPTER
twenty-seven

*It's the evil you see coming that should worry you. It's the evil you never see following behind you that sneaks up and hits you head on. ~**Magdalena***

I strode down the hallway, oblivious to everyone and anything happening around me as anger simmered to the front of my mind. I hadn't wanted to leave the club or the security it offered, which was absolute. Lucian was a sure bet against Lucifer, and yet Kendra kept throwing it in my face that I owed her for what she'd endured for me.

The worst part was, I'd thought we had been making progress on fixing what we'd broken, but we hadn't. The first chance she'd gotten, she'd thrown me under the bus. Kendra had forced me to go and then turned it around and made it look as if I had been the one pushing it. On top of that, she'd made a move on Lucian, which I knew I shouldn't care about, but I did.

Watching them together had made me feel eviscerated,

sickened to the point that I wanted to physically hurt her, my own flesh and blood. It shouldn't ever be like that, and yet the red hot rage as her fingers traced Lucian's hand had made my magic unfurl from deep inside of me. As if it wanted release to do harm, which white magic never did.

I slammed into something solid and stammered as I righted myself, holding onto what I had hit. Emerald green eyes watched me as I lifted mine to see what I'd run into.

"Whoa there, little lady," he said with a soft laugh as he held me up. "Not that I mind being ran into by something like you, but you might want to pay attention when you're walking," he joked and I stepped back, away from him. His touch felt oily, as if he was tainted.

"Sorry," I mumbled as I tried to sidestep him, only for him to block my way as I did so. "Problem?" I asked as I gave him a curious look.

"Weren't you beat up the other day?" he asked as he slowly slid his gaze down my face to my breasts which were pushed up by the top I wore. "Damn, girl. You're beautiful."

"What was your name?" I asked as his smile faltered.

"Falcon," he announced as he held out his hand. I accepted it, shaking it as I felt a spark ignite the moment we touched. It was nothing like the one when Lucian touched me; no desire unfurled or unraveled inside of me. It was something else, as if I knew him and yet I couldn't place him anywhere before the day we'd all come to Club Chaos for sanctuary. "And you're Magdalena Fitzgerald, in the flesh. You've caused quite the stir of chatter with your power in the community. One of the strongest witches in the bloodlines to date, or so some are saying."

"Is that what they're saying?" I asked, wondering why this guy's vibes were giving me the creeps and hitting all of my alarm bells.

"And that you're single and unmated," he replied smoothly as he grinned impishly. "Tomorrow I hear we will have a mixer and your grandmother had made it known that she'd like you to be considered as a mate to those of us who hold power, real power," he continued pointedly. "I plan to place my hand in that pool for a night with you, or longer."

"She is telling people that?" I quizzed as I tilted my head.

"Seems she doesn't much care for the one who you fucked, and would prefer you pick from your own species," he replied with a hint of something in his tone.

"Species? I thought we were all human here," I returned.

"Are we?" he countered as he bowed and walked away, leaving me to puzzle over his cryptic words.

Great; so my grandmother, who had begged Lucian to bring us here, was trying to hook me up with some magical dick. Kendra was carrying Lucifer's child, and it was widely known. I was the last Fitzgerald available to carry on the line at the moment, until Kendra birthed whatever she was carrying.

My feet moved as I considered how to get out of my grandma's scheme, which she hadn't bothered to inform me of, when someone stepped out from around the next corner and blew something into my eyes. I coughed as my face burned with liquid fire.

Pain erupted as whatever it was continued to burn as my legs gave out and I hit the floor on all fours. I looked up, seeing Kendra with a male as they watched me. I tried to ask her what the hell was going on, but nothing came out other than a stifled sob.

I rolled to my side as pain burned through me, enveloping my mind until I felt it, a darkness rising inside of me. It fought to save me from whatever was happening to me. Voices began shattering from inside my head, and popping erupted in my ears as if I was rapidly rising in altitude. The voices grew louder, clearer, and then, as the darkness rescinded, so too did they. I lay there on the floor until the whispered voices became further and further away from me.

I pushed off of the ground, touching my face as I sat on my knees in the middle of the hall floor, blinking as my vision swam with the fading silhouettes of my attackers. I used the wall for support as I held myself up, leaning against it as I wiped at the filmy sand that they'd used on me. My hands came away clean and I swung my face towards the laughter that sounded from the end of the hallway.

"Kill them before they kill you," a small voice whispered, and I looked around, peering down the hallway in both directions.

"She is safe from you," a female's voice ran out, echoing inside my head. I clapped my hands over my ears as my eyelids closed.

"We protect her!" another shouted, and I doubled over.

"Who will protect it *from me? You cannot save them both,"* a small voice whispered, and nausea swirled inside my stomach as they chanted.

"Stop!" I screamed and then listened as everything grew silent inside my head. Fucking hell, the grimoires I'd managed to hold silent were now active in my head? How? I'd bound them to be silent, to be unable to communicate, which was why I'd ignored Synthia's warning. I wiped at my nose as something ran from it, drippling over my lip.

I stared at my hand as red flowed from my nose onto it. It flowed steadily, and with effort I managed to push from the wall and head in the direction of my room. My hands dropped as I swayed precariously on my feet, slowing as the wall gave way to another hallway. I stumbled, collapsing onto the floor, and began crawling.

When the wall was back, I grabbed on to it and made my way back to my feet before I heard footsteps approaching. I paused, unsure if I should bolt or if I even could. I turned towards the wall, resting my head against it. Slowly, I crumpled and hit the floor hard.

"Kitty, what the fuck?" Spyder's deep baritone voice filled my ears, forcing me to clap my hands over my ears as his voice echoed inside my head, piercingly loud. I managed to rise again and leaned against the wall. I started to fall backwards, unable to hold myself upright, and felt his hands catching me before I could make it back to the floor. He hefted me up against his chest as he started walking. His hand moved and then he spoke. "We got a fucking problem, meet me in your room, now," he ordered and then pushed his phone back into his pocket.

It took him seconds to reach the room I'd been stumbling so hard to reach. I was placed gently onto the bed, and he loomed above me. His blue gaze stared down into mine with a look of horror as he turned from me as the door opened.

"What the hell was so bloody important... Lena?" Lucian's words trailed off as he took in the blood gushing from my nose continually. "What happened?" he demanded of Spyder, who shrugged and stepped back.

"I found her in the hall by following a trail of blood," he said softly. "That's a lot of fucking blood, and it isn't stopping, Lucian."

"A spell?" Lucian mused as I tried to move my head to look at him, only I couldn't. My strength was waning, and even though I was on the bed, everything was spinning. "Get Vlad in here, now," he demanded as he knelt beside me. "Hold on, Lena, I'll fix this."

CHAPTER
twenty-eight
*If I'm dreaming, leave me the fuck alone. ~**Magdalena***

I awoke to someone touching my face. My eyelids felt weighted but I managed to pry them open. I stared up at a young man, who peered down at me with curiosity. I could feel that my nose had been packed, and Vlad sat beside me, an IV hooked into his arm as he stared at me, smirking.

"You had us worried, pretty girl," Vlad explained.

"Why is there an IV attached from your arm to mine?" I mumbled through the cotton in my mouth. I sounded like shit. My nose had been packed with gauze, and everything sounded off. I brought my free hand up to my ear, finding it packed as well.

"You were bleeding from your nose, ears, and eyes when Spyder found you in the hallway," Vlad murmured as his hand intertwined with mine, holding it still. I started to sit up only for the man who had loomed over me to push me back down.

"You're not well," he stated firmly. "We have yet to figure out what caused this to happen to you."

"This is Eliran, a friend of mine, Lena. He's skilled in healing and one of the most treasured healers of Faery. He saved you, let him do his job."

"Faery?" I muttered at the man working around me. Unlike the others, he didn't have the rings around his irises and he looked exhausted. According to legends, the Fae never aged and yet he looked exhausted, older than the others I'd encountered, including the ones I'd met here.

"Aye, from Faery," he supplied as he grabbed my wrist and took my pulse. "She's stable, but until we know what caused her to bleed so much, she should remain in bed."

The door opened and we all turned to watch as Lucian, Spyder, Ryder, Synthia, and a ton of others poured through it. I swallowed as Synthia's electric blue gaze searched mine. I'd discovered she could change them at will; either that, or they were triggered by her moods. I still hadn't figured her out, or what she was yet.

"She's awake and recovered?" Lucian asked Eliran and I snorted. "Lena, what the fuck happened?" he demanded as his body swung in my direction, changing course. He dismissed Eliran before he could even answer the question.

"I don't remember," I lied. "I was walking and then

everything just went haywire." I wasn't throwing Kendra under the bus; I no longer trusted her, but until I knew why she'd done it, I would keep that tidbit to myself.

"You were leaking blood from every orifice on your face when Spyder found you. If he hadn't discovered you when he had you'd be dead right now," Lucian snapped angrily, as if he could force me to tell him what happened. "This happened inside my club, where I vowed you would be safe, Lena."

"That doesn't change the fact that I can't remember anything happening," I growled as I fought against Eliran to get up. After a few moments of struggling, Lucian traded him places and pulled me up carefully, allowing Vlad to adjust the flow of the blood he was so graciously donating.

I settled into Lucian's body as I stared at where the thick blood disappeared into my vein. Eliran moved to his supplies, drawing my attention back to him and the silent room who watched as he brought a chest over to Vlad and set it down beside him. He withdrew the needle from his arm, softly placing a pad of gauze on his arm before he did the same to mine.

"Apply pressure for a few moments," he ordered firmly as he slowly backed away and placed his hands behind his back, as he began to explain what he'd found. "As far as I can tell, she's fine other than the loss of blood. She has no other symptoms that I can find, or any telltale signs of it being a spell. Whatever happened, it hadn't been meant to kill her; harm her, yes. Murder, there's no proof of; more to the point, it could have been a spell she did herself that went awry. My worry is, without knowing what caused it, or which spell was used, we cannot prevent it from reoccurring."

"You think I did this to myself?" I asked, releasing the gauze as I pulled the others from my nose and ears. The room whirled with sounds the moment I did. I swallowed bile as it struck me on all fronts. The mixtures of smells were obnoxious, overwhelming as I brought my hand up to cover my nose. I could see a thousand times better; everything was brighter, more vivid and the Fae were even more beautiful. "What did you do to me?" I demanded softly as I turned to look at Vlad accusingly, and noted his silver eyes twirled in an intricate pattern that I'd never noticed before today. His skin was flawless, his hair a rich blackish-blue that caught the light and reflected both colors gorgeously.

"I'm a vampire, Lena. You received my blood," he pointed out slowly as to not overwhelm me. "It heals faster than magic could have, and it will rebuild the cells you lost. You will, however, experience things how I do for a little while. My blood should be out of your system within a day or two as it recirculates and you build your own cells and replenish your normal blood volume."

"You smell everyone like this? How do you manage it?" I asked.

"Ahh, there's benefits to that one. Such as smelling a woman who is aroused," he chuckled.

"Enough," Lucian rumbled, and I slipped my hand into his, loving how it fit and hating it at the same time.

"You don't remember anything?" he asked sharply.

"I remember people walking down the hallway, and then someone said something but I didn't catch what was being said. A few moments later pain exploded inside of me and I woke up on the floor, bleeding from my nose, with Spyder picking me up."

"You didn't see who it was who walked by you?" Spyder asked from the shadows and the entire room looked at him. I would never get used to him blending into the shadows, which seemed to caress him as a lover would. "You were screaming for them to shut up the entire time I carried you into the room. You were shouting even when you were unconscious, screaming for them to stop. No one was inside the room with us, and yet you held your ears and continued to beg them to stop screaming."

"I don't remember that," I answered honestly.

"Are the grimoires inside of you speaking yet?" Synthia interjected into the conversation softly. "It's been weeks, Lena. You should be dead by now, by all recounts of history. The only witch to last more than a few hours that we could find was a dark witch, one who had little to no information reported in our history."

"You wouldn't find a history of a dark witch in any records," I admitted, knowing I was spilling information I should be guarding. "It's forbidden to even speak of them once they have died, for fear they will return from the grave. Dark witches were never documented; their entire line was sometimes erased to hide the shame from a coven's past doings. Dark witches are stronger, live longer, and are unnatural. It's for that reason the covens forbid them to be a piece of any history to any coven. Your coven is different, but witches who allow the darkness inside of them and those born to it are different creatures. One is evil from birth, the other is by choice. In the end, no trace of them is to remain in our history. Like a blemish, you remove it."

"And you, Lena, which one are you?" Synthia surprised me by asking.

"I use white magic; black witches are unable to cast such a thing," I pointed out as Lucian's arms tightened around me. "If I was a dark witch casting white magic, you would know. Everyone would know."

"And why is that?" she asked.

"We would know," Lucian agreed. "She would turn dark; thick lines of black poison would run through her veins, and her eyes would turn completely black with the darkness. It would consume her soul and devour any control she held. We would all know if Lena turned to the darkness, because she'd be unable to control it, even with how powerful she is. When a witch turns dark, it's near impossible to hide it from anyone."

"Then let's pray she doesn't succumb to the grimoires, because at least three of those names who once owned them traced back to tainted bloodlines. Everyone leaves a trail, Lena. No matter how hard you work to erase someone from history, there's always something left behind."

I stared at Synthia and struggled to swallow past the

lump in my throat. "If I turn evil because of them, put me down," I whispered, watching her flinch from my request. "I can't be allowed to hurt the people I love. If I can control it, fine. If I can't, you have to end it. Don't make Lucian or Spyder do it. Promise me it; you're trained to kill creatures. If I become evil, it means that I am no longer alive in this body. I will fight until my last breath to remain in control, but if I lose it, it means it eradicated me. No one should ever have to live with that. Lucian doesn't deserve to have to endure it. My family won't be able to, so I'm asking you to do it."

"You are aware that they are not as they pretend to be," she smirked as she sat on the bed and grabbed my hand. "Are you aware of what I am?" she asked carefully.

"Definitely not human and not Fae," I answered softly. "Your eyes change color, and you're married to him," I pointed out with a nod of my head. "He's the Horde King, eyes the color of freshly spun gold thread with the solar system captured in their ember depths. His wings are as soft as gossamer, and yet wield death with their aim, he is final death for mortal and Fae alike. I have heard the tales about him. But you, you are something else entirely. My gut says Goddess, and yet you wear the glamour of the Fae upon your face, which is curious. The others are easy. The last time you came, you left out what you'd become. You only said what you were."

"You are very observant, that is a good thing. It bothers me, though, that you failed to see who did harm to you. Because it makes me think you're protecting someone who tried to hurt you. If they tried to harm or kill you, are they really worth protecting? Unless it was blood? Your sister, perhaps," she thought out loud as she stared at me for any telltale sign I was lying.

"Kendra wouldn't do this to me," I uttered.

"We are discussing the same sister who abandoned you when you snuck into the Guild nearly a week ago, right?" she asked, a saucy smirk filling her full lips.

"She is blood, but she's also my twin. If it had been her, I would know it. We are connected, and unlike your coven, ours is united through more than just a vow. We are one; when one falls, we pick them up. When one strays, we bring them home."

"And yet they left you in Portland," Spyder pointed out with a hiss, and I frowned. I couldn't argue that. But then I'd left on my own and I'd made sure they couldn't follow me.

"She needs to rest. They will expect her to attend the soiree tomorrow," Lucian growled as he pulled me closer as if he thought to protect me. "I would like to extend my thanks and ask that you stay close for the next few days as we discover who it was who tried to harm her. There are over a thousand witches inside this club at the moment. After tomorrow, a few selected will turn to darkness to protect their covens. As you are aware, it can turn deadly rather quickly and I have given my word that we will protect the white witches during the process. I would owe you a favor at your time of choosing," he said carefully. I somehow knew him saying it was larger than he made it sound, as if owing anyone a favor bothered him greatly.

"We will stay, for the witches, of course. You will not owe us for it, Lucian, she will," Synthia said, and Ryder, who had been observing us, snorted. "For the witches, and the ones we could not save of the Guild, I will do what I can to help your coven, Lena. You will owe me something in return, and I will vow that the Fae will protect your family and coven from any harm as the others turn to the darkness."

I swallowed hard and nodded. "I accept."

CHAPTER
twenty-nine

You only have one life, and then it's over. Live it, love, and let them in. ~**Magdalena**

I remained in my room for the rest of the night and long into the morning hours, refusing to see anyone except Spyder and Lucian. Both had stayed close to my side throughout that time. The voices had dulled to a whisper, but no matter how much I tried to ignore them, they never stopped speaking. I couldn't make out their muted words, but if I tried to listen to them, they would go silent. It was as if they knew or felt that I was eavesdropping on their conversations going on inside my head.

Sitting on the edge of the tub, I placed my fingers into the water, testing it. I slowly dropped rose petals and bath salts Lucian had brought into the water. I listened as slow music played in the bedroom; knowing it was driving Spyder a little crazy brought a smile to my lips. Lucian was on witch duty, probably being driven insane by my grandmother and mother.

Letting the silk robe drop from my shoulders and pool at my feet, I stepped in. It took effort to shut out the world, along with the voices. Sometimes it sounded like static and other times it became constant chattering that made no sense. The spell I'd tried hadn't worked, and I was out of options.

The more pages I flipped through, the less confident I became of which spells had once belonged to the dark witches or white witches. Had I accidently already cast a dark spell? It was possible, and what Synthia said could happen. I wasn't sure if I'd be able to control what happened inside of me. I'd absorbed entire grimoires, and now I was faced with the cost of doing my actions.

I knew what was coming tomorrow, knew that I'd pushed for it, and maybe I'd been wrong to do it. Maybe I shouldn't have mentioned it, or lobbied for it. I was newly awakened and yet I'd run my mouth in affairs I shouldn't have. What if my secrets came to light? What if the entire reason I'd fled the coven was revealed, or all my effort to hide it was undone? What if everything went wrong and it was all for nothing? Once you fully embraced the darkness, it couldn't be undone. Death was the only release, which I knew more than anyone else. I'd battled it and won, and I'd paid for it. I'd won, but only because I'd found a way to lock it inside of me.

I sank fully beneath the water, staring up at the ceiling as I weighed the consequences of my actions. The voices got louder, as if they felt my uncertainty and fears. The voices that said the bad things inside my head, were they the dark witches? Was that what my friends and the others would become? I closed my eyes as I released air, slowly letting the fire in my lungs ignite until I rocketed out of the water, gasping for air.

Spyder stared at me as I gasped at him from where he stood against the wall, enshrouded in the darkest corner of the room. "Ah, kitty, that's never the answer," he murmured as he stepped forward.

"I wasn't committing suicide, jerk," I growled as I covered myself the best I could. "I worry about tomorrow. I pushed for this, Spyder. What if I was wrong?" I asked, and he smirked.

"Dark witches aren't evil right away, and we'll put them down if they step out of line tomorrow," he assured me with a shrug, as if he didn't even consider their lives worth anything. "Don't you glare at me like that; I don't want them to die either…Well, most of them, some are cocky little fucks who could probably use a little downtime. But if it's between you and them, they're fucked, kitty cat. Utterly fucking fucked." He knelt down beside the tub and splashed me with a charming smile.

"I like you too, Spyder."

"Finish up, and get dressed." He shook his head as he rose from beside the tub. "We have a party to crash."

Twenty minutes later, I stared at my reflection and the dress I'd decided to wear. One I'd conjured with magic, which flattered my slim frame. The maxi dress was a silky, almost sheer material that draped from each shoulder in a wide V-neck that exposed most of my chest and barely covered my breasts as it dipped dramatically just above my navel. The sides were similarly exposed under my arms. The only thing that kept the fabric from shifting like a wardrobe malfunction was a slender band of black fabric that supported my breasts and kept the sides and chest pieces from slipping.

My hair was loose, cascading down my back, as Lucian preferred it. I had minimal make-up on, preferring to look natural instead of made-up or fake. I'd never used much of it anyway. A little mascara, lip gloss, and cheek blush and I thought I looked good enough to face the world. Kendra would take hours in the bathroom for school, but I was the opposite. I missed her, the old one who used to smile from her eyes when our gazes locked across the room at some boring coven function.

I tossed the brush onto the counter and slipped into the small heels I'd made and headed into the bedroom. The moment I entered it, I heard Spyder's sudden intake of breath and peeked up at him curiously. He stood motionless, his gaze roaming over the exposed skin before they closed and he took a big step backwards, as if he didn't trust himself with me.

"The Gods are fucking fickle bastards," he growled. "Five minutes; that's the time between when he entered that party after you arrived and when I did. It was supposed to be me, but no, I had other obligations."

"What are you talking about?" I asked as I lifted the skirt and stepped closer to him.

He exhaled and shook his head.

"It doesn't matter," he laughed silently as his chest shook but no sound escaped. "Let's go crash the party, kitty," he said as he extended his elbow. "You do know you're probably going to get half the kids out there murdered tonight, right?"

"That's not going to happen," I laughed softly.

"You're beautiful. So fucking beautiful it hurts to look at you tonight," he mumbled as he rubbed his free hand down his face and stared straight ahead.

"Thank you, Spyder. You're pretty fucking hot too," I laughed as we entered the main hallway, picking up some burly-looking Fae, including the sapphire eyed one who had scared the crap out of me at the Guild. He smirked as he took in the dress.

"Poor fucker," Zahruk mused before he pulled knives from their holsters on his legs and slipped them into his sleeves. I swallowed as a nervous flicker started to take hold of me. I could see the weapons he carried, the multitude of them, and yet he was protecting me against Kendra. I didn't know why she'd done it, or if she knew what would happen when she did, but I knew I could no longer trust her and that broke me more than Lucian ever had.

As we got closer to the club's main room, I could hear the noise level becoming unbearable mixing with the noise my head. Vlad's blood kicked one hell of a punch that hadn't released me yet, and everything was heightened;

my senses, my reflexes, my body's responses, everything.

The moment we reached the club's main room, everything seemed to stop. The noisy chatter died down to a minimum as I entered the room, pausing on the edge of it. The assembly turned, staring at me as I stepped from the hallway, followed by the guards who flanked my sides.

My gaze searched the endless sea of faces until I found him. Lucian stood in the middle of the sea of people, staring up at me as I gazed back with a need so raw and red hot that it terrified me. I stood there, somehow managing not to fidget as his gaze swept down my scantily clad body. I found strength and courage in the heat that filled his endless depths.

I wasn't the girl who wore such dresses, not the type that exposed this much skin. I was modest, never needing to show myself off as something I wasn't, but I'd wanted to be special tonight. I was on display, but there was only one man who I wanted to catch. I'd chosen everything carefully, dressing for seduction.

Lucian was dressed in a dashing suit, one that was a mixture of midnight and dark blues to match his alluring eyes. His hair was pulled back, and he still managed to look every inch the predator he was. No amount of expensive suits hid what he was, or ever could. Falcon stepped in front of him, blocking my view.

I tore my eyes it from where Falcon stood, searching the other faces until I found Alden gazing at my mother from across the crowded room with a longing that tightened my chest. Dexter stood mere inches away from him, vying for Kat's attention as men offered for her hand in the next dance. No one had the balls to go for what they really wanted. They wasted time pining away instead of going for it.

Didn't they know how short life was? How precarious it could be, or that in an instant, it could be lost? They ignored what they wanted most, hiding or burying their feelings to protect their heart from getting rejected or hurt. I bit my lip as tears filled my vision as I considered what I had done. I'd pushed Lucian away and he was the one thing that stood beside me.

Yes, what he'd done was wrong, but his intentions had been pure. He'd fought to protect me, and even so, I'd lashed out. And while I had a right to be hurt, did I really want to waste any more time without him? The crowd began to chatter again, and men moved towards me with purpose in their gait.

I stood on the stairs that led into the room and, before the first man could offer his hand to dance, I began moving. The urgency inside of me grew as I started through them, turning sideways to pass as they tried to vie for my attention or talk to me.

Falcon growled when I passed him by, his words of tradition ringing in my head, and I smirked as I headed straight for the one man who held my soul. Fuck tradition; fuck the coven's laws tonight. Life was too short. I knew what I wanted and I intended to take it; nothing else mattered right now. I pushed past anyone who tried to bar my way to the one man I wanted, the one who stole my heart like a thief in the night. He waited in place, not moving as I made the choice on my own, deciding my own path.

I rushed into his arms and kissed him with everything I had. I didn't care who watched us, or if I was disobeying what the coven had laid down for me to follow. The guards had followed me right to him, circling around us as I threaded my fingers through his hair, claiming him in the only way I could. I knew without having to look around us that every eye in the club was on us. It didn't matter; the moment our lips touched, everything else faded away into the background.

There might be no tomorrow for us, just right now. My grandmother's message she'd given them to hand to me was long forgotten, and even if the coven kicked me out, I knew he'd be there to catch me when or if I fell. I didn't need another lover, didn't care to take one. There was this man, and he alone held the key to my heart.

His arms slipped around my back, lifting me closer as our bodies crushed together. Our mouths moved in a dance as old as time as each of us fought to get closer to the other. His hands slid up my back, capturing my face between their warmth as he pulled away and stared into my gaze.

"What are you doing, little witch?" he murmured as his lips touched mine again as if he couldn't get enough of them.

"I'm yours," I whispered as his smile broadened and he pulled me close again, claiming my mouth in a toe-curling kiss. He invaded me, the smell of sandalwood and masculinity unraveling my last shred of dignity as I moaned loudly against his lips. I didn't care who heard it.

The club had started moving around us, dancing as they pretended not to watch us in our brazen embrace as we threw propriety to the wind and basked in each other's presence. He was my perfect. Lucian Blackstone was my own fucked up version of perfection that I craved more than I did the need to breathe. It didn't matter that he wasn't mortal, or that we were so different, or more to the point, that we were all wrong, because together, he was my right.

"Magdalena," he warned as he pulled back and peered down at me. "You were always mine," he murmured before he started moving me around to the music that played in the background. Ed Sheeran's *Perfect* filled the room and Lucian surprised me as he moved us gracefully. We glided around the floor, the men slowly moving around us as we danced to the heady notes of the song. He danced perfectly, as if he'd practiced it a million times. He ignored my clumsy movements and controlled them, which made it appear as though I didn't have two left feet.

"You could have acted surprised," I mouthed off as my brain registered what he'd said.

"Why would I do that?" he countered as his fingers threaded through mine when we stopped dancing and stood in the middle of the dance floor with couples all around us. "I knew you would come around, you needed time. I gave it to you because I know you're one of the most stubborn women on the planet."

"You're a conceited ass," I laughed as I smirked up at him. He shook his head and pulled me with him away from the dance floor. "Hey," I said, pulling back against his hold on my hand as he tried to leave the dance. "Coven rules state we cannot leave until at least the fifth song."

"Fuck coven laws tonight, Lena. I'm seconds away from ripping off that dress and claiming you right in the middle of this dance floor so every asshole in here stops eye-fucking you."

"You wouldn't dare," I challenged. My eyes grew wide as he turned around and grabbed the strap that sat on my shoulder. "Don't you dare, Lucian!" I warned with a giggle.

"I've been patient with you, but it has reached its end, little witch," he warned as he pulled me with him, as we entered the empty hallway.

The moment we were out of view of the others, he pushed me against the wall, trapping me between his hands as he placed his face inches away from mine. His lips touched my neck and I groaned as desire tore through me. My body clenched in response to his hungry mouth as he sucked against the rapid pulse that hammered wildly for his touch. "You're so fucking beautiful, but tonight, tonight you shine from within with a confidence that surprises me. I've never wanted anything as much as I want you right now," he admitted between kisses.

"We need a room," I uttered, breathless from his kisses. He lifted me until I was forced to wrap my legs around his waist. I wrapped my arms around his neck, pushing my fingers through his silky hair as I held his mouth against mine.

He ground his cock against my wetness, uncaring that this position showed my bare thighs or maybe even more to the men who coughed or made remarks as we struggled to get closer to one another.

"We're not going to make it," he growled as he started us down the hallway, not bothering to set me on my feet.

"Lucian," I warned and grinned against his mouth as he kicked the door to the bedroom open. "You undo me," I moaned as he slammed the door in the men's faces, much to their disappointment.

CHAPTER
thirty

*He sets my world on fire, and I always hand him the matches. ~**Magdalena***

The moment the door was closed, flames leapt from the candles that filled the room and bathed it in a soft glow. The music started up as I slid down his body slowly, not missing the ardor that filled him as his hands slowly slid down my exposed sides. Theory of a Deadman's cover of *Wicked Games* started up as he turned me around, cupping my breasts as his lips kissed the back of my neck until my legs grew weak.

He slowly walked me towards the bed, never stopping until we reached it. I expected to be tossed onto it. Instead, he pulled his mouth away from my neck and untied the bow at the back of the dress. His hands came up, warm against my arm as he pushed one shoulder off, kissing it softly with his hungry mouth, only to repeat it with the other. He worked it as if he was opening a treasured gift.

The dress pooled around my feet, and I kicked it to the side as he slowly kissed his way down my spine. The panties I wore were ruffled, which pulled a growl of approval from deep in his chest as he pushed them down.

Once he'd bared me to his greedy gaze, he slowly trailed his fingers up my thighs and side until he stood at his full height. He grabbed my hair, fisting it as he turned me around and then lowered his forehead against mine. He swallowed hard as he searched my face, and whatever he found there made him growl with approval. His lips touched mine and I moaned, leaning forward, only to feel him pull against my hair. He tugged my head back, using my hair for leverage as his lips met mine and his tongue sought entrance. His other hand touched my sex, parting it with his skilled fingers as it slid through the slick readiness he'd created. He rumbled from deep in his chest as his mouth consumed any coherent thought I had. It wasn't just a kiss, it was more.

He backed up, staring down at my naked body as he slowly began to remove his shirt. I was lost in the sight of him stripping so much that I didn't even realize the song was slowly repeating over and over—and I didn't necessarily care, either. He'd picked it; for some reason this beautiful creature had chosen this song to make love to me with.

Once his chest was bared, I lowered my mouth, licking along the lines of each tattoo, unable to stop myself as I lowered myself to the bed, sitting on it as he allowed my moment of weakness. His hands tangled in my hair as he allowed me to continue, his breathy sigh encouraging me as I struggled against his slacks, needing them off as much as I needed him inside my body.

"What the fuck am I going to do with you?" he murmured as I freed his cock and slowly licked down the long length of him until I felt him tense against my seduction. I kissed the thick tip, slowly enveloping him in my mouth until I felt him pushing against my throat. His hold on my hair tightened as I swallowed until my throat relaxed, allowing even more in. When I started to withdraw, he pushed me down, following me as his mouth found mine, claiming it hungrily until breathing no longer mattered. His fingers parted my sex, slipping through the wet folds as he tested the waters of my desire.

My knees dropped, giving him further access to my pussy. His mouth left mine devoid of his heat and I cried out. He nipped at my breasts, slowly licking around the areola before his teeth scraped over the heated peaks. His middle finger entered me and I arched against it for more, his mouth devouring my skin as his finger worked magic on my pussy. I exploded without warning and he laughed against my nipple as his gaze lifted and he bit down gently, nipping my flesh.

Lucian pulled me up until I wrapped my legs around him, poised above his thick cock as he slowly used my hips to push me down onto it. I cried out as he stretched me until my body trembled and adjusted to his fullness.

His arms wrapped around me, forcing me to work against his cock as I rose and lowered my body, his lips once again finding mine. His hands rose, grasping my face on either side and capturing it, kissing me as if it was the first and last kiss he would have. The orgasm built inside of me until it was a storm, threatening to release. The moment it did, I screamed his name like he was my savior, as if he was my God. My hands lifted to thread through his hair, holding him still as my mouth continued to battle against his. With his growl and my moan, the music was drowned out against the fervor in the room, a fever burning that neither of us could control.

"Greedy little witch," he murmured.

He pushed me down, following me onto the bed as he started to pick up the pace, taking what he needed. My hands continued to hold his mouth against mine. His slim hips moved slowly, as if he was savoring every thrust. He broke the kiss, staring down into my face with a look that both confused and undid me. He ate my soul, and never had I felt more loved than I did right now, more cherished than I did as he gazed down at me.

I watched as he lifted his body, supporting his weight on his arms as he started to move faster. My legs wrapped around his waist, giving him more depth as he watched me through obsidian eyes that tore apart my defenses and battered my already fractured walls. I didn't know how to react to this, the slow love that he was showering me with. I could react to hard, brutal sex, but this…this was new to me. This gentleness from him terrified me.

He continued until I cried out with the impending orgasm that lingered just on the precipice of the cliff—and then everything changed. His body slammed against mine and he rolled me, forcing me to rock my hips as I straddled him. His hands grasped my breasts, pulling against the nipples as I clenched around him, my body tightening hard against him as the orgasm ripped me apart. The moment it began to ebb, he rolled us and pushed my legs further apart as he slammed against my body with brutal intensity. It refused to stop; orgasm after orgasm shuddered through me until my body refused to stop shaking with the force as each one grew stronger. His hand lifted, pushing against my throat. I braced for my air to be stolen, but it never came. His thumb pushed into my mouth and I bit down, sucking greedily against it as he continued to ride my body hard.

When he withdrew his thumb, he captured my chin in his palm, cradling my face against his mouth as he lowered it. His body shuddered and I felt him emptying inside of me. He moaned, unable to stop it from finding purchase as he swore and trembled against me.

He lay beside me in the bed, lifting my leg, which he held over his hip as he entered me again. He didn't stop. Hours passed, and every time we came apart, he held me until his cock pushed back into my body.

When we couldn't physically take any more, he held me. We talked and I laughed, something we'd never done before. It was unusual, but I wasn't going to question it. This was a side of Lucian not many got to see, and it was the first time I was seeing him beyond the cold exterior he showed to others.

"I've never been slow with anyone," he disclosed, and I blinked as I turned and looked at him in disbelief.

"Never?" I questioned.

"I've never cared to," he admitted. "I fuck hard. I don't think when I fuck; it's just something I do."

"What changed?" I asked, fishing for the reason. I knew why I'd wanted him. Everything inside of me had cried out of love for him, and he held my heart in his palm whether he wanted it or not. I'd vowed to never love again, and yet with him, I'd fought it and failed.

"I don't know," he murmured. "Something about you tonight made me need this," he said thoughtfully. I swallowed hard at the tension I heard in his voice, the way he stiffened as if he had just discovered something he didn't want to, or liked.

I exhaled and settled against his arms for warmth. We'd talked for hours between bouts of crazy sex and endless passion, but now something was wedging us apart.

"Maybe you fell in love with me," I joked and felt him tense even more against me.

"Go to bed, Lena."

"I love you," I whispered as my eyelids grew heavy, as if he'd used something to force me to sleep, but I fought against it. "I always have."

"Bloody hell," he growled as he pushed his legs into his pants and paced beside the bed. "You shouldn't have said that! Fuck!" His fist hit the wall, sending plaster crashing to the hardwood floor. I swallowed as a tear slipped from my eye. I'd fallen in love with this brutal man, and he'd rejected it.

CHAPTER
thirty-one

*When being strong is the only thing you have left, people should fear what you will become. Warriors emerge from those who have been broken, born from the flames that created them. ~**Magdalena***

We stood outside the club

with the wind howling as the storm clouds moved in. It was as if the world sensed the coming darkness we were about to release upon it. Lucian and his men, along with the Fae, patrolled the club's impressive parking lot where we had set up the altar, along with the blood of the animals they'd sacrificed. They'd done everything as the books had instructed, and yet I felt something was off, wrong.

Something inside of me was screaming to get out as each new preparation was secured and made. I watched with detachment as the morning replayed through my mind. Lucian had been gone long before I'd awoken, if he'd even slept in the bed at all. His things had been moved, and the more I thought about it, the angrier I became.

He'd gone from red hot to ice-cold before I even knew what to think or could figure out what I'd done to deserve it. I watched him from beneath my lashes, noting he acted as if I didn't even exist anymore. Was it because I'd told him that I loved him and he'd never wanted it? Or was it because I was no longer a challenge? I swallowed as Kat and Dexter approached.

"Whoa," Kat announced as she took in the angry look. "You'd think you would be smiling this morning, after that little display last night."

"Yeah, everyone is talking about how you went and threw caution to the wind and fucked him, again," Dexter muttered as he stared at Kat. "Couldn't even care less or see what was right there in front of you," he grouched.

"Just tell her, Dexter," I growled back. "She isn't a fucking empath; what the fuck is with men? You don't tell us and expect us to just know what is wrong. Well guess what, she doesn't even have a fucking clue you like her, and the worst part is she loves you! She always has and yet you say nothing," I snapped, and then blanched as they stared at me as if I was losing it.

I hated that I had ousted him, but then he wouldn't have ever told her he's liked her since first grade. He was shy with her, while he was a total flirt with everyone else. I swung my gaze back to Lucian, only to catch him speaking to a girl who was touching him entirely too much.

"What the fuck, Lena?" Dexter demanded, and I frowned as I took in his pinched features.

"She didn't know," I explained. "You expect her to guess, and she's Kat, Dex. She doesn't take the hints, and you know it. So why beat around the bush? We could all die tomorrow and you'd die without telling her how you feel, so stop wasting time, and for God's sake, just do it!"

"Lena," Kat said as she put her hand on my shoulder, but I shrugged her off. "What happened—and you like me?" she said to Dexter who nodded as his gaze lowered to the ground shyly.

"I told Lucian I loved him," I replied, and she clapped her hand over her mouth.

"That's great, so why aren't we happy?"

"Because he left the bed cussing and then moved his things out of the room," I confessed truthfully.

"That rat bastard," she seethed, glaring at his back across the parking lot. "I say we fuck him up, or cast a spell on him."

"It's fine," I said as I chewed my lip as my grandmother cleared her throat pointedly. "We can't cast on him, he's not mortal, but thanks for that," I laughed soundlessly.

"Once the stone changes colors, if it does, you will then move into the circle of protection," she explained as I stared down at the overly large pentagram that held several in the middle of it. "There you will embrace the darkness, Hecate have mercy on your soul. If you cannot fight it off, you will be handled. We cannot allow those who turn evil to leave the boundaries of the protection barrier. Does everyone understand?" she asked, and we nodded, even though I hadn't been listening to most of what she had said.

"Lena, what if we end up being chosen?" Kat asked as her gaze strayed to Dexter, who hadn't said much since I'd blurted his feelings for her.

"If you're chosen, stay in the group that is good. You will fight the darkness as it grows inside of you. Think of those you love, everything you could lose if you let it take hold and gain control of you."

"What happens if the majority turns evil?" Dexter countered, finally speaking up. "What the fuck do we do then?"

"I don't know," I answered as we started to migrate to the line to pull a rock from the pile. Only those under twenty-five were choosing stones. Plus, any who were pregnant wouldn't be allowed to, which meant Kendra was out of the process altogether. I looked down at my white sweat suit that said *Some Like it Witchy* across the bust line and ass of the outfit in bright pink writing.

Once we'd selected our stones, we moved to the rather large group, which awaited the spell to be cast. Torches and piles of wood were ignited around the protection lines, and jasmine and sandalwood were placed with basil and other dried herbs for protection. Crystals were placed sporadically through the area to ensure the safety of those who remained white, and yet something kept itching against my brain, as if it was trying to warn me.

The moment everything was set up, chanting began

and, one by one, we stepped forward, holding the rock in one palm as we slid a blade through the palm of our hand, leaving a shallow cut in it before we used the other hand to place the stone into the blood.

I watched from the back of the group as each witch moved up with the stone held in their closed palm. The first few passed and went back to the coven that stood off to the side, watching in sadness as one by one, their children and bloodline moved closer to their fate. Within an hour, we had fourteen dark witches, and most of the others remained the same, untouched by the taint that could either destroy them, or save us.

It wasn't until Kat stepped up to reveal her stone that my stomach sank as my grandmother's face twisted in sadness. I swallowed a cry of denial as she twisted her neck to look back at me, a look of sheer panic in her beautiful gaze.

Next, Dexter moved up, mere feet away from me, he too was chosen. His shoulders didn't shrink as Kat's had. Instead, he moved to her in the pentagram and hugged her tightly. The next few were a mixture of white and dark, and then I stepped up to my grandmother. Her vision sparkled with unshed tears as I held out my hand, palm up. The look of relief that washed over her sent a pang of guilt rushing through me.

She exhaled and motioned for the group who waited to see if any of the chosen failed to the darkness. I stared at Kat and Dexter, who embraced each other, and my stomach churned with unease. Falcon looked excited, and I wondered if he hadn't already known his fate. His cronies remained close to his side.

Every one of the men who had remained close at his side had been chosen. An unsettling feeling filled the air, but as I watched Falcon, I noted he anticipated something. My heart slowed as I watched him, noting the thin black pupils that seemed to pulse, as if they wanted to grow.

My mind flashed back to the first few days in Portland, to the clubs that I'd been wild inside of. It was as if memories were slowly coming back, and then something I'd hidden came rushing back. I knew his look; I knew it because I'd felt it before.

I stepped backwards slowly, turning to move to the back of the group. I withdrew the knife from my pocket, slowly cutting open the tip of each finger as I expelled the tiny shard of crystal I'd sewn into them to hold it at bay. I whispered the spell to heal my skin but nothing happened. We were warded against magic, I realized as I stared down at the symbols scribbled on the concrete. I stared at the blood oozing from my fingertips and frowned. I slipped the knife into its sheath and moved back to the front of the group as I pushed my hands into my pockets, concealing the blood.

Kat and Dexter stood with two other witches as the larger group stood on the other side. There were witches from the coven all around them outside the barrier, placing the final pieces to ignite the spell that would force the darkness which had chosen them to come out. My stomach swirled with unease as Falcon smirked at me, and then his eyes blurred, turning black as he tilted his head.

He was already dark. I closed my eyes, remembering the way his skin felt oily, as if he was tainted. I started forward but I was too late. The magical cage ignited, sending a buzzing noise through the air around us.

"He's already dark," I uttered as I looked through the crowd for my mother. I pushed through the coven members, struggling to find her. Once I did, I grabbed her arm and watched as Kendra smirked beside her. "They came to us dark," I announced, horrified that my friends were inside that magical cage with them. They'd slaughter the others before they ever had a chance to fully embrace their own darkness.

"What are you talking about, Lena?" she demanded. I looked past her to Kendra and watched as her face contorted.

"Lena, save me!" echoed through my head so loudly that it almost took me to my knees. *"You have to save me!"*

Something changed in her eyes; they turned darker as her face moved, looking to those who started shouting from the cage. I swallowed and shook my head.

"Kendra?"

"Lena, save me." She sounded weak, almost faint this time she spoke. As if she'd used everything she had to get the first words out. I blinked repeatedly as I covered my ears as the endless chatter erupted inside my head.

"Magdalena!" my mother shouted, grabbing my hands as a scream ripped from the cage. I turned, hating the noise level that rose around me. Sabrina was in front of Kat and Dexter, and she was on the ground, writhing in pain. I looked at Falcon, who was moving his fingers as he stared at her. He was casting…dark magic.

"They were already dark. They didn't turn dark," I mouthed in horror as I pulled away from her.

I stepped forward as blood exploded from Sabrina's nose and mouth. She screamed as Falcon grinned coldly; those behind him joined him as he started to laugh as Sabrina's body jerked, and she screamed louder with pain tearing her apart, literally.

"Stop them!" I screamed and watched as my grandmother turned, staring at me as her complexion turned pale. Her eyes were large, rounded in the horror of watching what was unfolding. "Stop them!" They had to stop this. Kat and Dexter were inside with Falcon, the same monster who had helped Kendra blow the dust into my face.

"No one can get into them, it's sealed, Lena," my mother murmured.

I moved forward as the Fae closed in, expecting the dark witches to escape the cage if my grandmother opened it. I knew she wouldn't. She would be potentially placing the coven in mortal danger if they escaped. Kat and Dexter would die once they'd finished murdering Sabrina. They'd come here to kill us, all of us. They hadn't wanted protection, they'd wanted to take the power the white witches held, the same as the demons we feared. One would use our bodies; the other could steal our power. Both were evil.

Dark witches could siphon white magic as their own, adding it to their power. That's why everyone feared Benjamin, but where he'd helped us, these fuckers had strolled right in—and we'd allowed it. I brought the knife from my pocket when everyone else screamed in fear as Sabrina began bending in weird positions as they broke every bone in her body from the inside.

I slit my tongue open, spitting out the last crystal my body held to keep the darkness I'd conquered at bay. I moved with purpose, watching as everyone stepped away from me. Power erupted from me, sending a wave of it crashing through the crowd as lightning exploded, hitting trees just mere feet away from where Falcon stood. His gaze searched the crowd until they landed on me. He smiled coldly, unafraid of me. He should be afraid. I'd fought the darkness and already won. I'd suppressed it until now, keeping it locked inside and hidden with crystals made directly from the original leylines.

Someone moved to stop me and I disappeared from where I'd stood, popping up in front of Kat and Dexter. Their cage held darkness in, not out. I spun around, staring at my friends as they came up from where they'd been huddling together on the ground, awaiting death.

"Lena, you're...*dark*," Kat whimpered as she stared at me, confused.

"I am not dark, not entirely," I uttered, spinning back around as I felt power rushing towards me. I lifted my hand, easily preventing his magic from touching me or my friends. "Stay behind me," I ordered as I let the darkness inside of me unravel. I'd been terrified of it, of the vile things it had whispered to me. I'd wanted to murder everyone and anything when it had first shown up right after Joshua's funeral. I'd left without a word after that, unable to control it and terrified of what would happen if I couldn't.

The other witches started adding to Falcon's power as he stepped back into their protection. I reacted, moving forward without a thought other than the fact that Kat and Dexter's lives were within my ability to protect them. Coven law stated that we protected our own, no matter the cost. The problem was that I *liked* the darkness. It offered freedom; the magic it released was raw, powerful, and there was no limit to what you could do.

But it came with a price. One I hadn't wanted to pay. Until now.

The first witch stepped into my path, intending to take me down, and I smiled as the blackness inside of me erupted without warning. I reached for his arms, grabbing both as he threw the first punches, which would also be his last. Falcon's magic continued to assault me but it didn't touch me. I'd built a wall between him and us. It was a strong magical barrier that refused to allow him to touch my friends with his tainted magic.

My hands captured the man's arms and I ripped them from their sockets. He wailed and I smiled coldly, using the magic inside of me to finish him. Blood exploded as his body was ripped apart. He dropped and the next one moved to take his place. I kicked him in the nuts, using an uppercut to catch him off guard before I dropped, swinging my leg out to send his out from beneath him. I didn't murder him; I wouldn't allow the magic to do as it wished. I pulled it back and shoved it into the dark recess of my mind as I stood up and stared at Falcon.

My hair floated with the power pulsing through me. I had an endless supply of magic at my fingertips.

"If it isn't a fucking Fitzgerald," Falcon laughed coldly. "Wasn't expecting that," he sneered as his men got closer to him, as if they could save him. I'd been burying my magic for so long that it had built up a dangerous supply. It was why I hadn't been able to release the leyline. I'd hidden it so deep that I'd blocked myself from knowing it was there; unless someone I loved had their life on the line, it would have remained locked inside, hidden from even me. I'd erased my own memories of it, leaving only a few crumbs to lead me back, should I ever need to use it. Not even Lucian's blood magic had found it. Kat and Dexter being placed in danger had made the crystals in my fingertips burn, my trigger to unlock the memories.

They moved as a group, and I smirked as I shouted a spell to make them all float in the air, helpless, unable to cast. They screamed as their bodies became paralyzed in midair. I walked below their floating bodies until I was toe to toe with Falcon.

"You are not welcome here," I growled. "Leave now and I will release those who came with you, but you are not to return here. Your kind is unwelcomed."

"You think you can do a spell and beat me? You're

nothing," he laughed coldly as he moved to strike me. I grabbed through his chest without a thought, withdrawing his still-beating heart as I held it up to my eyes, which I knew were black from the sudden release of raw, dark power I'd called upon. Blood dripped from my wrist and arm and I stared at his useless heart, covered in thick black lines. He'd been dark longer than I had. I dropped it as he fell to the ground. My head tilted and I swung my head to where I felt a heavy stare boring into my head.

Lucian stared at me and I felt nothing; cold and lifeless as he had made me feel when he'd proceeded to remove his things from the room without a word. He'd used magic to make me sleep through it, but like this, I could remember everything. His midnight gaze flinched as he took in my profile. I knew what I looked like: evil incarnate. Blackness swallowed the irises and whites of my eyes, thick veins of dark magic pulsed beneath my skin, and my hair floated like the men I stood beneath. Gone was his little wilted flower who needed to be loved, and in her place was a coldness that didn't want his warmth.

"Put it away, Lena, he's gone."

I stared at him, unwavering as I decided the fates of those who literally hung in the balance. I could hear my mother crying as Alden comforted her with empty words. Synthia inched closer to me, ready to follow through with the promise I'd made her vow to keep. Kat and Dexter begged me to bury it wherever I'd hidden it before, and I ignored them all as I stared into eyes the color of the flames that burned in Hell as he ordered me to come back.

"Kill him," a voice whispered, and I smiled as I considered it.

"It cannot win if you are stronger," a softer voice whispered, and I blinked. *"Do as he says, he's trying to help you."*

"She doesn't need him. He'll kill them all if she doesn't stop him. We all know that lesson too well. He is death; he will take her soul and curse it, as he has done with all of ours."

"She is in love with him."

"And that worked out so well for us, didn't it?"

They were arguing again inside my head. I shoved them all away, the voices, the magic, the power that flowed through me. Grunts sounded as bodies hit the ground and I craned my neck as I watched them get up with horrified looks as they got as far away from me as possible. I slowly moved to see what had become of Falcon and blanched as his severed heart lay beside his head, directly in front of his open eyes. The other body lay in pieces, two to be exact, still where I'd ripped it apart. I knew why those who had welcomed the darkness kept it; it numbed the pain of what you had done in its sickening embrace.

"Magdalena," my grandmother fretted. I turned sapphire blue eyes on her and watched as she exhaled deeply, releasing the fear she'd held. I dismissed her as I moved away from Lucian and Synthia, towards Kat and Dexter and the others from my coven who had awaited certain death at the hands of the dark witches we'd allowed to get close to them.

Their darkness called to mine and I smiled, holding my arms out as they rushed into them. They were my people. I'd given up my secret to save them, and I wouldn't change it. I was born bad, with a sickness that not many could contain, but it didn't change that I was good, too. Had I known who my father was, I could have handled it before it had driven me from town.

I was born into darkness, but so, too, was Benjamin. Unlike him, the moment it had surfaced, I'd been old enough to hide it from others, even the High Priestess. I'd stayed away from them until I knew I wasn't a risk or danger to my coven, but I'd needed my powers awakened. I laughed as I considered what it entailed. I'd awakened to my powers on Lucian's cock, because I hadn't needed to be blessed by anyone; darkness doesn't need the light. The light needed the darkness so it could see the stars and the beauty that the night held secret.

"Magdalena, not a word," my grandmother urged as I released Kat and Dexter to be freed from the circle.

"I know the rules," I said. I spun on my heel, facing the witches that Falcon had brought with him, the dark witches of my own coven at my back. "You can stay and fight the demons with me, or you can run and I will hunt you down and kill you. That choice is yours, only you can make it. Your leader is dead, and he was of weak bloodlines, but I am not. I am Magdalena Fitzgerald, dark witch of the Haven Crest coven, and my coven is ours to protect. Vow you will not harm them and I will allow you to live."

"Falcon promised us power, we're not from strong bloodlines," one announced.

"You don't need to be from strong bloodlines if you are dark witches. You just have to be smart enough to survive. Power comes with time, but the white witches of this coven will keep theirs. No harm is to become of them; vow it, or die."

"You will kill us anyways," another shouted. The others agreed.

"It is possible, but I will make you a promise that I won't do it today. If you decide to leave, you will leave this town and never come back. If you stay, you will promise to protect the coven and in exchange, you will have food and shelter, and you won't have to face or worry about demons as you sleep. Decide."

I waited, not knowing if they would choose to follow me, or if the coven would even allow it. However, we'd only gained a handful of witches who could protect the coven and we needed them all.

"You won't kill us if we remain with you?" one of the younger boys asked. He couldn't have been any older than sixteen. He trembled and I frowned.

"I do not relish the kills, but if the need arises to protect my coven, I will not hesitate. Our laws state that we protect our own, and if that need arises," I moved my eyes to hold my grandmother's, "then we will do whatever it takes to protect them, no matter the cost to ourselves."

They huddled together and we waited; once they'd

decided, I exhaled and nodded. I hadn't wanted to release the magic again. Each time I used it, it became harder and harder to push it away. It was why I'd placed the shards into my skin and tongue, blocking every point on my body that could release magic. Then I'd erased my own memories, which was probably why, when Lucian had erased it again, it had taken so long for them to come back.

I turned and faced my grandmother, bending down until I was on my knees, the others following my lead. I lifted my gaze to hold hers.

"I am yours, you are mine. I give this vow through the blood of mine. You are mine to protect, and I am yours to control. The coven shall accept us, one and all, for this darkness inside should not fight the light. In your darkest hour of need, we will arise, to fight with you by our side. I am given to you in this time of need, do you accept me as yours, to use as you need?" I waited, praying she would accept us.

"I accept, granddaughter mine. Rise darkness, and come to the light, for we have need of you at this time."

I rose and frowned.

"What?" she asked softly.

"That was corny as shit," I laughed nervously.

She laughed and the crowd released its breath, joining in. We'd survived the darkness, and as I searched the crowd for my mother, I paused. Tears streamed down her cheeks as Kendra glowered beside her. Her gaze remained locked on Falcon's remains. I swallowed down the suspicions for tonight and almost jumped out of my skin as my grandmother touched my arm.

"You were not supposed to intervene," she announced. "I am glad you disobeyed this time, but it could have turned out differently for you, granddaughter."

"I vowed to protect the coven at all costs when I agreed to allow the ancestors to awaken my powers. We all did; I made a choice. It's one I will have to live with."

"You didn't make a choice here; you revealed that dark witches can be saved. You used crystals to keep it hidden, to contain it. You have done the unthinkable, but you have also given the coven hope on this day, in our darkest hour."

CHAPTER
thirty-two

Are warriors born, or are they forged through the hellfire that life forces them to walk through? ~**Magdalena**

Life seemed to be placed on pause as everyone scrambled for what would happen next. Days had passed since we'd embraced the darkness, and while only one person hadn't been able to endure or contain it, the rest of us seemed to be managing it rather well. Unless you counted going insane from being locked up in Club Chaos, but that had changed yesterday. We were now patrolling our town, slowly removing the demons who lingered. It was a learning curve we were adapting to rather quickly.

We'd only encountered a few, but one pack had been at least three generations of a family who'd been turned into vile creatures, which attacked us. The blessing of dark magic was the numbness it offered, the blind rage that allowed you to kill without feeling it. That too faded with the power as it subsided. We'd buried the Grangers beside the road in shallow graves, unable to give them more as we made our way deeper into the woods.

I knew the others felt it as deeply as I had. The loss of the family, as if they'd been human. They had been inhabited, and to those of us who knew them, it felt wrong to end their lives. I slowed as the cabin came into view through the woods. My grandmother had requested we check in on the seer, but from this vantage point on the hill, the cabin looked rundown. The runes were outdated, unkempt, and broken. It looked all wrong, and even though my gut told me to leave, I couldn't.

"She's probably dead," Kat pointed out as her hair blew in the wind howling through the valley. I hated to admit it, but she was probably right.

"We still have to be sure," I mused as I continued to survey the decrepit cabin. Parts of the roof were missing, along with the windows that now littered the ground in glittering shards of glass. The door was cracked open, and no sound flowed from within. I frowned as I turned and nodded to the others as we started forward. "I want five of you outside on each side of the cabin. Every entry point gets two guards. If you see anything out of the ordinary, turn dark. My gut says there's something wrong with this place."

"It's all fucking wrong," Dexter agreed as he shivered and slipped his fingers through Kat's before letting them drop. I smirked, knowing they'd shacked up finally. Of course, they were trying to keep it hidden, all things considered.

I stopped at the door, and let the magic from within slither over my skin. Dark magic slinked and crawled in, warming over the uppermost layers of my skin. I gazed inside the darkened cabin and then at the yellowed, discolored grass that held the rune stones. Bending over, I picked up one and touched the red substance used to draw the enhanced protection spell.

"It's not for protection," I announced. The others followed my lead, picking up the stones and examining them as I toed the salt line that should have been whole, but was broken. "They kept something inside, not anyone from getting inside," I mused as I dropped the stone and pushed the door open.

I could make out a corpse placed atop a table. Chains held limbs in place, as if they hadn't wanted her to escape. I swallowed past the lump in my throat as I stepped over the threshold and into the falling down cabin.

Light from outside flooded the room, exposing the skeletal remains that sat in the middle of the room. She'd been dead for a while, according to the yellowing of the bones and the thick layer of dust that covered her. I knew the coven had stopped visiting her a long time ago, soon after they'd brought me here to her.

"That's disturbing," Kat's voice trailed off as she followed me in.

Around the body were dried flowers, enchanted chains, and thin silver lines that went from the body to the wall, where hooks held them in place. The air inside the cabin was stale, as if even with the broken windows no fresh air could get inside. The ropes held charms on them, which were musical as the gentle breeze jingled them. The wind touched them, and yet the air in the cabin was stagnant. I closed my eyes as I mentally flipped the pages inside my head until I found what I was looking for.

"She's spelled, and those charms are as well. Don't touch them or anything else in here," I warned as I walked around the cabin, opening the only other door inside it. The entire house had one closet? I looked around, noting the old cooking stove that sat off in the corner. I walked to the window, peering out and frowning as I saw the old moon-shaped door of an outhouse. "This house is old, really old," I mumbled as I went back to the closet and pulled out the leather-bound journals.

I set them down beside the corpse and opened the first one. "Meet Brenna MacTavish, first wife of Drake Vanderbilt. It says here she was waiting for him to return to her." I swallowed hard. "Ninety-three years ago, Brenna had been shunned by her coven for catching the eye of a dark witch, who poisoned her mind with tales of the coming of Lucifer," I exhaled as I stared down at the corpse. "The charms are used to control the dead," I explained. "The chords are controlled by someone who could be anywhere using them with magic. Which means everything she's ever told the coven was a lie. She was never here. Her last entry states she waited for Drake for days before she lost their child, and then feared she would die of starvation before he returned. Their horses perished in a storm, and she had no way to leave here."

"Isn't she the one who told your mother you were pure of soul?" Kat asked, and I nodded slowly.

"Also the same one who said Benjamin was dark and forced my mother to send him to Drake, Drake Vanderbilt. My father," I snorted.

"That can't be good."

"No, it means that someone has been feeding the coven information from God-knows-where for a very long time. All he had to do was call on her soul, which is trapped here in this cabin. To anyone else, she'd appear alive and well, taking the form of whomever he projected to them. The coven came for a seer, a renowned one who was old. That's exactly what they saw when they arrived here. To activate her, the runes outside the cabin would alert whoever controlled her to the presence of others. They'd use a pattern with the chords to wake her. The charms on her body match to those on the chords, much like those we use to awaken the ancestors for the ceremonies. Only, these ones are controlled with ancient magic, dark magic that controls the soul of the dead it is attached to."

"But why would anyone want to control someone like this? Even for dark magic, this is fucking morbid. And why her?"

"Because she decided who was dark and light from the coven, and also who is thrown out when they are unable to be controlled. When I was a child, they brought me here to her. She told them I was pure of soul, and that Benjamin was dark and tainted, and couldn't be saved. She told my mother if Joshua was to live, Benjamin had to die. Whoever is controlling her had Benjamin removed from the coven," I growled as anger pulsed through me. Someone had fucked with my family; they'd used this poor soul to dispel my brother before he was old enough to defend himself.

"That's not good," Dexter announced as he entered, running into the silver chord before we could warn him. His arm reached up and his hand jingled several charms. The air inside the cabin intensified, growing thick with darkness.

All eyes moved to the corpse as a cackling sound erupted and an arm lifted, then slowly lowered as it went still once more. It hadn't been enough to reanimate her, but it would have alerted whoever controlled her to our presence. I shuffled off my bag and slipped the journals inside before pulling it back up over my shoulders. I looked down at the corpse as her face turned towards me slowly.

I could see her soul and I winced as the evil of an unknown presence shuddered through me.

"You're free, Brenna MacTavish," I muttered before I started ripping the flowers from the table. "Help me free her soul," I demanded, and Kat and Dexter jolted into action. I removed the flowers, and the chains, and then I stepped back as dust erupted into the air and her soul escaped. I exhaled and then jumped as a hand touched my shoulder.

I spun around, gasping as the ghostly figure of a young woman stood beside me. Her hair was jet-black, and she had upturned eyes that told me she had once been part Native American, and utterly beautiful.

"Lucifer comes," she hissed before she began to evaporate. "Thank you, Magdalena. Now run, child," she whimpered as she turned her head, revealing half of it had been caved in.

"Go, Brenna." I said firmly as I nodded. "Find peace."

"Your father…" she tried to explain, but her head lifted and she turned her broken head to the side before a horrified scream tore through her and she vanished.

"My father is an evil bastard," I snorted after she'd vanished. If I was right, Drake was an evil bastard who had lured Brenna to her death with promises of his undying love. He was a dark witch, which was why I'd felt it the moment tragedy had struck. It was the reason I'd fled from the coven, protecting them from me while learning to live with the pain of my loss, but I'd resorted to pretty drastic measures to beat it. Judging by the journal entries, my father had broken more than coven laws; he'd broken the laws of humanity and was somehow immortal.

I withdrew the thin slender blades Zahruk had given to me, along with the smaller daggers Synthia had donated to our weaponry once she'd seen the lacking supplies we had. I pushed the smaller knives into the thin slits in the sheaths of my waistband and retrieved the swords from the table as I stepped towards the door.

"Stay together. No one says anything unless I say otherwise. He wants me, so if it comes to it, you guys run one way, I'll go the other," I grumbled as we emerged from the cabin.

"How does he even know we are here?" Kat demanded.

"My guess? He is the one controlling Brenna, or was. She's free from him now, which I'm sure he isn't going to be happy with." I frowned and then shouted for the others. "Everyone to the front, now, we got company coming."

"If it was him controlling her and meddling with the coven…"

The air grew thick around us, cutting Kat's words off as she stalled as the temperature dropped around us. Demons materializing, power pulsed around us, and then Lucifer was there, standing mere feet away from me.

I let the darkness out, ignoring the others as they followed my lead. His piercing blue gaze slowly slid over my face before his lips lifted with a seductive grin. I stepped forward without fear, without hesitation. He wanted me to cower, to fear him, and I wasn't giving him what he wanted.

"Lena, Lena, Lena," he repeated my name as his finger came up to trace slowly down my cheek. "So beautiful," he murmured as he let his hand drop.

"If you came to rip me to pieces, get it over with," I challenged. "But if you think he will care, I assure you, he won't. You could rip my heart out and send it to him and he'd probably eat it."

"Is that what you think? That I am here to hurt you? I have much planned for you, sweet Magdalena, and it includes you being alive for it. When I start to use you against him, you'll know it," he laughed. He pulled me closer and placed his mouth against my ear. "Have you told him you carry his child yet?" His lips tugged at my earlobe as a shiver raced down my spine.

"I'm not pregnant," I whimpered as desire pulsed through me. "Turn that shit off, asshole."

"Turn what off? Your desire for me? It has little to do with me," he smirked impishly as he pulled away. "I can control a lot of things, Witch, but your reaction to me isn't one of them. Darkness does call to darkness... Maybe yours craves a real taste of it for once. You're toeing the line," he pointed out as he watched me. "You have no idea what you're up against, do you? You're just part of our game, a piece that has yet to be played. We started this game eons ago, he and I. He took away what I wanted most, and now, now I will show him what it feels like. You, you have your part to play in this, but I don't benefit from your death. No, I need you alive for my plan to see its end."

"Then call off your demons," I stated coldly. My body trembled with fear, real fear as his words replayed in my mind. I could feel the fear oozing off those behind me, feeding the monster's ego as he smirked at my pretend bravado. Even with the darkness running through my veins, I feared this creature. He was the Prince of Hell, and he wanted to use me in some sick, twisted game. There was also what he'd said, which I couldn't say if he was right or wrong, or just fucking with me. "They seem hell-bent on bringing me with you, and if that isn't your intention, why the show of force?" I asked with my chin lifted and my shoulders squared. I wouldn't allow him to see how much he'd shaken me.

"He isn't fucking you anymore, is he?" he laughed. "Do you need to fuck, Lena? I can pretend to be him if you want me to. I can make you think I am him again; would you like that?" he purred silkily as he pulled me against his chest and inhaled sharply. "You smell like you want to fuck me."

"I'm not much for playing pretend," I whispered as I licked my lips and lifted my gaze to lock with his. "In fact, I don't much care for games at all. They're too childish for me. I also think you both should grow the fuck up, because the only people who end up hurt are those of us who have nothing to do with it. I'm not part of it, he doesn't want me, and you only want me because he does. That makes a girl feel really shitty, ya know?"

His hand snaked through my hair and he tipped my head back as his mouth crushed against mine. I pushed against his chest to no avail, knowing no matter how much power I used, it wouldn't move him. His hands wrapped around me and I groaned as I bit into his lip. He growled and smiled against my mouth. The coppery taste of blood filled my mouth as he pulled back and his stare went to something over my head.

Power erupted, shaking the cabin; the sound of wood collapsing met my ears as light exploded around us. I was yanked back and thrown to the ground hard enough that the wind left my lungs in a sudden whoosh. Pain erupted as I looked up to find Lucian's midnight eyes glowering down at me from where I had stood, facing Lucifer. Lucian scowled at me with a murderous glint in his depths before he turned around and his hand shot out, capturing Lucifer's throat.

I struggled to get to my feet, only to have strong hands lift me and hold me. I careened my neck and found Spyder smirking down at me. "Bad, kitty," he growled angrily. "You didn't think we'd feel it? Playing around with the devil is a very dangerous game."

"Feel what?"

"You lip-locking that nasty little fuck," he hissed.

"Should I have drawn a sword against him instead? How long do you think I would have lived if I had?" I demanded.

"You should have panicked so we felt it faster," he growled as his arms wrapped around me and we turned back to watch as Lucifer gurgled against Lucian's hold on his neck. I felt his power unfurling, the world vibrating with it. I felt the darkness enveloping us, and it wasn't coming from me this time. Spyder's lips touched my ear and he laughed against it, adding to the vibration running through us.

Metal clashed against metal and I looked around, noting the Fae were battling the demons Lucifer had brought with him. The Horde King zigzagged faster than my gaze could follow, but everywhere he left, bodies remained. Synthia stood in the middle of them, examining her nails as she waited for them to finish. Once the last demon had fallen, he materialized beside her and pulled her close, kissing her hard. As if the battle had turned him on. I blushed, lowering my stare away from their intimate moment.

The darkness inside of me simmered and then released as I let it go to allow my mind to come back. Lucifer made a strangled noise and Lucian snorted.

"She's mine," he snarled, and Lucifer laughed.

"She says otherwise," he coughed out. "You're not even fucking her anymore, why? I'd have that spread and be so buried in her welcoming warmth that you wouldn't find me for weeks. Not man enough to keep her in bed that long?" he sneered.

Lucian released him and his armor materialized. Souls writhed and slithered as he stepped closer to Lucifer, only to have huge wings explode from Lucifer's back as his own armor covered his body, black armor. Lucian slammed into his face with a fist as the other hand produced a sword from thin air and moved to swing it to remove his head, but Lucifer vanished.

I sagged against Spyder in relief until Lucian turned on his heels and started towards me. I tried to back up, only to have Spyder blocking my retreat. The sword vanished and Lucian's hand wrapped around my wrist, pulling me with him into the cabin. He slammed the door behind us and wrapped his hand around my throat. He trembled as he caressed it, not bothering to apply pressure. My hair rose from the power pulsing from him, and the air in the room filled with the raw current he exuded.

"What the fuck were you doing?" he snarled.

"I was doing as the coven asked me to and checking on the seer," I growled back.

His armor faded away and his angry stare ate into mine as he searched my face. "And you had to fucking kiss him to do as the coven bid you to do?"

"Or fight him, yes. It wasn't like I wanted to kiss him; I even bit him to get him to stop," I shrugged. "Not your problem now, is it? He kills me, and you no longer have to worry about the bond. That would probably be a relief, wouldn't it?" I laughed stiffly. "You made it very clear that you don't want me, so I listened to the message, Lucian."

"You think I don't fucking care what happens to you?" he demanded coldly.

"I think you shouldn't," I smiled impishly as I exhaled and pushed his hand away. "I think we should steer clear of each other. Just like you've been doing for the last few days," I murmured. "I don't think we work together, and while it was fun, it wasn't healthy for either of us."

"You don't get to throw your life away, and you sure as fuck don't get to run to Lucifer to get back at me, little girl," he growled.

"I didn't run to anyone, and I don't need him to get back at you. I spilled my fucking heart out to you and you threw it away as if it wasn't worth your fucking time. What happened, Lucian? I submitted and wasn't a challenge to you anymore? Or was it because I had the balls to admit what I felt for you? You know what? I don't even care anymore. I was here, patrolling as the coven asked me to, he showed up, and I used what I had to stall him to save my people. I appeased his fucking ego to survive.

"You think I have anything to get back at you for? I couldn't care what you think of me, not anymore. I know this might be hard to understand, but my world doesn't revolve around you. My sun doesn't set behind your fucking bed, and it sure as hell doesn't rise in your eyes. You walked away from me, and I'm okay with your choice. You and he both need to leave me out of your fucking games. I'm done being used by both of you. Find someone else to destroy; there's nothing left of me you can hurt anymore," I whispered as I pushed past him and exited the cabin. "Fall in," I demanded as I ignored the stares of pity as everyone watched us start back to the club.

"Lena," Spyder growled as he moved to join us as we started out of the clearing.

I made it almost to the tree line before Lucian materialized in front of me from thin air. I slammed against his chest and growled as the darkness escaped in my anger. My black gaze lifted to his and power pulsed through me.

"You're done for today," he whispered as he watched me with something akin to disappointment in his stare. "He's still out there."

"You're not the one calling the shots anymore, not in my world," I warned. "If you think that, because you house the covens in your club, you hold any power over me, you're wrong. I can turn my humanity off, I can shut it down and I won't feel anything for you or them. So let me go, Lucian. You made it clear where you stood when you walked out the other morning. I'm smart enough to take it as it is and walk away, so let me."

"Put the darkness away before you end up hurting yourself," he warned. "You're not scaring anyone here like you do the others."

"No, I wouldn't. Your heart is as black as your soul. It's as black as mine has become, and you really have to stop thinking I do anything for you. This, this is for me so I'm numb. I don't feel you anymore. Like this, you can't hurt me."

His gaze searched my face and his hand left my flesh. "Is that why you chose to go dark?" he murmured.

"You think I'd do this for you?"

"Why else?" he muttered as he stepped closer, inches away from me. I felt his heat; his earthy masculine scent filled my senses, and I swallowed against the groan that lodged in my throat from needing to touch him.

"Because someone I loved was in danger and there's nothing I wouldn't do to protect those I love," I stated, hating that unshed tears shone in my gaze as I stared him down.

"And what if you had to push them away to save them, Lena? Would you do it to protect them?" he murmured as his hand lifted and his finger trailed slowly down my cheek. "Even if it was the hardest thing you've ever had to do?"

"Yes," I replied at his cryptic meaning. I scanned his face before I stepped away from him, turning on my heels to leave him and his fucking riddles. "Let's go," I said as I felt the others closing rank around my back and we ignored the others who watched as we left the clearing to slink back into the woods as we made our way home, to Club Chaos. Not that they left us alone. Instead, they trailed after us to ensure we made it back.

I walked into the club and searched out my grandmother and mother. Once I'd found them I pulled them aside.

"I need your help," I uttered as my heart hammered wildly against my chest.

"What's wrong?" my grandmother asked as she placed her hand on my shoulder.

"I need you to run a test on me," I whispered so low I wasn't sure they'd hear it.

"What sort of test, Lena?" my mother queried, her voice just as soft.

"A pregnancy test," I answered as unshed tears threatened to fall.

CHAPTER
thirty-three

I've met my demons, turns out we like the same music.
*So we're cool now. ~**Magdalena***

We had found a room that allowed the privacy needed to run the magical pregnancy test. I paced the floor as I waited for them to finish with their part. I couldn't have a child now, not after I'd turned dark. Dark children were banned, as Benjamin had been. If I was pregnant, I'd have to leave to have the child. I'd be alone raising a child of God-knew-what species. I had no idea what Lucian really was, and that only added to the stress of what could happen, or what would happen.

"Magdalena, calm down," my mother instructed softly as I growled as the idea of being knocked upped forced the dark magic to the surface. I turned on my heel, staring at her and watched as she shrunk back away from me.

"I'm sorry," I said as I struggled to keep it at bay.

"It takes time to get used to…seeing you as such," she mumbled as she stepped closer to her mother. "You said Lucifer told you this was true? That you were carrying Lucian's child?" she asked.

"He whispered it into my ear, yes," I admitted as I watched my grandmother pour the ink into the sand inside the stone bowl used to determine pregnancy. Once she'd finished, I stepped up to it and held my hand out for the small delicate dagger that was used to pierce skin for the blood of the woman being tested.

"Lena, if you're pregnant…" My grandmother's words trailed off.

"I'll be shunned," I answered. "My child will be removed from the line, and any trace of him will be removed. I know the laws," I muttered.

"No, not with the changes we've made. It was considered that some of the chosen could have conceived before they'd turned. We ruled that those who have will not be removed, nor their child. However, there will be no record of the birth. With Lucian being the father, though, with us not knowing what he is, there is danger in it. The unknowns are always the hardest to foresee playing out."

"There's the seer," my mother said from where she'd begun to pace behind me.

"The seer was dead. She's been dead a very long time. Long before you were even born, mother. Her name was Brenna MacTavish, born in the 1800s. Her husband's name was Drake, Drake Vanderbilt. He left her to die alone in that cabin with her unborn child. She left journals. When we found her remains, it had chords tied from the wall to her corpse. Each one contained a magical charm. Someone else controlled her, but when we touched the chords, Lucifer showed up."

"Drake Vanderbilt?" my mother gasped as she moved to the couch and sat down. "It would have to be one of his ancestors."

"Unless he is immortal," I replied, frowning as my mother covered her mouth with her hands. "You wouldn't have known otherwise. It's not easy to know what someone is, trust me," I said, comforting her since I was in the same boat.

"I took you to that seer, Lena. I took Benjamin to her, what if he wasn't bad? What if I gave him to that monster and he wasn't bad?"

"Benjamin is dark," I confirmed. "I don't pretend to know why they wanted him sent away, but I do know he is dark. They wanted us to think she was real, that she was there to help the coven this entire time. I released her soul; her only warning was about Drake, but she vanished as Lucifer showed up and couldn't tell me anything. I brought her journals back with me for the coven to look through. Maybe there is something inside them that will ease your guilt."

"And you, you're dark too!" she accused as she stood up and backed towards the door. I didn't argue it or point out that I hadn't fully accepted the darkness inside of me. The crystals had slowed it down, forcing it to remain dormant inside of me. I'd fought it hard when I'd first left Metaline Falls. I'd discovered information via the web and tried several things before I'd placed the crystals of purity into my flesh at every point that cast magic. "You could be with them, filling us full of lies, Lena. How can we trust you when you did this?" Her hands indicated all of me, as if all of me had turned against her.

"Fiona, calm down right now. She's bound her life to ours in protection. She's your daughter!"

"Is she? Because lately I don't even recognize her anymore," she cried as she left the room, slamming the door behind her.

"She didn't mean that," my grandmother mumbled as she stared at me with regret.

"Yes, she does," I laughed soundlessly. "I hardly recognize myself anymore, either. I used to have it together. I knew what I wanted, and now everything is falling apart. Kendra is distant, and she refuses to speak to me now at all. Mother is right, I've changed."

"We all have," she huffed as she slipped her hand through mine. "Evolution does that to us; we adapt to what this world throws at us. The Fitzgeralds have withstood the test of time, but now we have one who carries the devil's bastard, and another who is standing tall as she learns her fate. The women of this family have always held to the laws, but those laws often change because the world is always evolving. Now, let's get this over with so I can go calm your mother."

I held out my hand as it trembled. The knife sliced through my palm and I held my hand over the stoneware and made a fist, squeezing it into the dish. My heart leapt to my throat as we waited for the lines to move. The blood turned black, slowly combining with the ink inside the dish. It separated into a web, splitting and twisting until two vines moved, and I held my breath. The potion hardened, turning to a sand like substance, and the thick black blood branched off, and then stopped as the other continued to move.

"No," I cried as tears formed in my eyes, running down my cheeks. "No, it's wrong. It has to be, do it again!" I demanded breathlessly as my throat constricted and my stomach flipped as I stared down at the time sand, which refused to move.

"Dear Gods," Grandmother whispered as a tear rolled down her cheek. Pain gripped my heart, as if someone had a fist tightening around it. She lifted the dish and shook it, and once more, the line refused to move. "No, oh, please, no," she said as she set it down and tried to touch me.

I jerked my hand away from her as I lifted the dish and smashed it upon the floor. "No, no, that's not fair! Not after everything I've been through."

"We can help you, there has to be a way," she whispered through mumbled words as she tried to hide her fears.

"No one else is to know, do you understand me?" I demanded.

"Lena, he's the father. He may know how to help us."

"He can't know, ever. It is my right to withhold it; it's my right, Grandmother. No one is to know; it doesn't leave this room. Nothing that was revealed is to leave this room."

"I can't stop it alone," she whispered as she wiped at the tears.

"No one can stop it, you know that. Fate can't be changed, only altered, but in the end, it comes and you damn well know it. This stays between us. No one can change it, there's no reason for them to even know. You know as well as I do that if the sands say it is going to happen, it will."

I moved to the door, blindly leaving the room as tears fell. I rushed through the hallway, ignoring Spyder, who paused as I passed him. I didn't want to see anyone. How could the Gods be so cruel? How could I be carrying Lucian's child after I'd made a choice to save people I cared about? He'd said numerous times that he couldn't have children, and yet here I was, pregnant with *his* child.

Once in the main room, I pushed through the crowd, ignoring my mother as she called my name over the music. I didn't stop until I was inside the bedroom with the door closed. I slid down it until my ass touched the ground and my head leaned back, resting against the door. I hugged my knees as tears fell unchecked until my body trembled as I screamed with frustration.

I wasn't an idiot. No child born of darkness would be

accepted by the coven, no matter how much my family tried to make it otherwise. It would be no better than being born with leprosy.

Why me?

What sort of fucked up shit had I ever done to deserve this?

I pushed off the floor and headed to the bathroom, tearing my clothes off as I stared in the mirror at my stomach. I didn't look pregnant, but then I'd missed my period twice now, which of course I'd blamed on stress. My hands slid over it, closing my eyes as I imagined what a child of his would look like. Would it have its father's eyes, or mine? What would it be other than half of me? I glared at my reflection, knowing it was my fault. I'd been careless. I'd been so hyped on his fucking addictive kiss that I'd thrown caution to the wind once he'd said he couldn't have children.

Turning on the water, I pulled out rose petals and dried lilacs before tossing them into the water. I sat on the edge of the tub, dipping my fingers through the water as the flowers swirled and I became lost in my thoughts.

Could I willingly bring a child into a world like this? What if everything Benjamin had said came to pass, or was true? With the world as it was, with the gates to the worlds opening, could I bring a defenseless being into this mess? Lucian would protect it, wouldn't he? I mean, he'd have to, right? I stood up and slowly stepped into the tub.

I was pregnant. I was having *his* baby. We'd created

life together, and he'd never know it. He didn't need to, not with all of the cards falling into place, not with everything Benjamin had said would happen, happening. The sand was never wrong, ever.

I slid beneath the water, letting it fill my lungs until it burned. I stared up at the ceiling, watching the petals as they floated into my line of sight and out of it. Emotions ebbed and flowed like the ocean, crushing down on me until I sat up, sputtering as I coughed up the water.

The pregnancy was the least of my worries according to the sands, and I didn't dare to think of it. Not now, not ever. The coven came first, it always had. I'd been immature when I'd returned to town, but sometime during coming home, and everything that happened. I wanted to be a mother. I wanted to hold my child in my arms, to feel its heart beating against mine.

I wanted to create life.

Fate was fickle at best, but this…this was a nightmare that I knew I wouldn't awaken from. The coven needed refuge. The Guild wasn't ready to house them yet, and even though Synthia had offered to take some, we all knew they couldn't accommodate the masses. It needed the witches, we needed the shelter from the storm that was brewing as the gates of the other worlds began to open, letting even worse creatures into this one.

If we were going to stand a chance at winning, we had to combine forces, which meant they would need to start moving witches to it as it was finished. They didn't have the numbers to fight yet, but we did. Together, maybe we could make a difference. This world needed us, even if we hid in the shadows. We kept the balance of magic alive through the bloodlines; we meant something.

It didn't matter what fate was throwing at me, I'd find my own way around it. My grandmother had to remain unbiased; she had to think of the greater good. Humans were dying by the handful every minute that ticked by.

I rinsed off and wrapped a towel around me before strolling into the bedroom with puffy eyelids. I felt his power filling the room and peered into the shadows, watching as Lucian stepped forward.

"You want to explain what is going on?" he purred as his gaze slowly slid down my body.

"I don't know what you mean," I countered as I moved to my bags, which I'd packed once he'd left the room. His eyes didn't miss a beat; he zeroed in on them and a dark brow lifted.

"Going somewhere?" he asked.

"Preferably to a room that doesn't carry your scent," I answered as I withdrew a pair of joggers and a tank top. "You shouldn't have to give up your room, and I'm sure there's somewhere else I can be moved to."

"You're not going anywhere. I like you in my room, Lena," he said in a hoarse tone before he rolled his shoulders and spoke again. "What's upset you?" he asked as he moved closer.

"And why would you think I'm upset?" I returned,

irritated that it was written on my face from the red puffy eyes to the fat lip that I'd bitten so hard that it bled.

"You don't cry in crowded rooms. You hold it in. You just ran through the entire club crying, Lena. So what has you so upset?" he asked softly.

"I'm fine," I stated as I moved into the bathroom, dismissing him as coldly as he'd been dissing me. I didn't see him for days, and now he seemed to be everywhere again.

I slipped on my panties and stared at the mirror as I imagined growing round with his babe inside of me. I shoved the image away, burying it as I finished dressing for bed. I pulled the tank top on and dried my hair, exiting the bathroom to find him sitting in the chair with his elbows resting on his knees as he stared me down.

"Do you need something?" I asked.

"I'm not leaving until you tell me what the fuck is going on with you," he growled low and pointedly.

"I can't add to my bloodline now," I lied.

"Kendra is carrying on your line," he said softly.

"Kendra is carrying Lucifer's child," I countered coldly, accusation tainting my tone. "You think they'll give it our name?"

"Lucifer was an angel at one time, now he's fallen. It doesn't mean his child will be evil, Lena. It's only a child."

"And what about you, Lucian? Do want children?"

"No, never," he snapped angrily. "I told you, I cannot have them, and therefore have never wished for one."

"You should go, I'm tired," I replied evenly, somehow managing not to break down into tears.

"Would it matter if I did?" he asked.

"No, not for me," I stated slowly as I watched him stand and shove his hands into his pockets. "What we had is broken, so if you are thinking to fix it…"

"I didn't come here to fix it," he growled.

"What did I do wrong?" I asked offhandedly.

"Does it fucking matter?" he snapped. His gaze lingered on me and I lowered mine as I chewed my lip.

"No," I replied before I continued. "If you knew someone you loved was going to die, and you could stop it, would you?"

"Yes."

"What if it cost you everything? What if the price was more than you could pay?"

"There's nothing I wouldn't do to protect someone I love, even if that price was to walk away and pretend I didn't care, Lena. Sometimes you have to die a little to save or protect those you care for, even at the cost of yourself."

"Did you ever care for me, or was I just something you wanted to play with?" I asked softly as I lifted tear-filled eyes to his.

"Go to bed. You look exhausted, Lena," he ordered, and I watched him stroll to the door and pause there, as if he'd planned to say something else. He stared at me for a long moment before he pulled the door closed behind him.

CHAPTER
thirty-four

When all else fails, chuck it in the fuck it bucket and move forward. ~***Magdalena***

Long after Lucian had left the room I remained awake, poring through the journals inside my head. I ignored the witches who pointed things out as if trying to divulge information to me as I studied every journal and every entry in detail. I discovered things, old things that happened during their lives as I read about those who had lived before me. My mind continued to fill up like a filing cabinet as I processed each of them. In every journal, towards the end, one name repeated: *Katarina.* She'd been the first journal I'd read, and in every one since, she reappeared. Her name and the initial L continued until the very last one.

I'd discovered the seal, an ancient thing believed to open the doors to the other worlds. My heart had skipped a few beats as I'd learned of it and what it did, considering our world's current situation. Then…then I learned about a witch who had stolen it. Katarina had taken it from her lover, L. She'd done as her coven had bid her to, betraying him, and since then, it seemed she played a part—or more to the point, her curse did—through every generation of witches born since.

The last journal held more information than any before it. It told of a woman, who had been half-witch, half-nymph. She had been possessed by the seal, but when she bore her lover a child, it somehow tethered to the child's soul. It was murdered soon after birth, a fate no infant should endure before he'd even experienced life.

I slept restlessly as nightmares plagued me. I dreamt that I was the nymph, forced to birth a child only to be slaughtered as it took its first breath. I awoke, drenched in sweat as I fought off the tremors of the nightmare that lingered. Katarina had cursed the coven, of that I was sure. She'd betrayed L, who I assumed was Lucifer, and I wondered if that made Lucian the hunter who slaughtered her time and time again to protect it from falling into the wrong hands. Was he its keeper, forced to hunt it down to protect it? How did he fit in?

I dressed and moved around the room, pushing my things into a pile as I readied to go out and face the crowd. I eyed the clock, noting it wasn't even nine o'clock yet. I shimmied out of the sweats and into a skirt, one that hugged my figure and flowed to my ankles. I picked out a camisole, white and soft that flattered my complexion. I piled my hair into a messy bun and stared at my pale complexion. I looked ill or exhausted but honestly, I felt it to my bones.

I picked up the notes I'd scrawled in bed, along with the journals from the seer's house, and headed out to find my grandmother. I entered the main room and stood still for a moment, watching as everyone moved around, laughing and dancing as if the world wasn't going to hell outside. Kat and Dexter slow danced together, ignoring the others and the fact that it was a fast-paced song playing. Synthia and her group were present, some dancing while others watched them with annoyance, as if they'd rather be out destroying something.

I started forward the moment I caught sight of my grandmother. She was looking over the crowd, and the moment she saw me, she waved frantically. I increased my pace as I lifted my skirt and moved towards her.

"Lena, have you seen your mother?" she asked.

"Not since she left the room earlier."

"I have not been able to find her since earlier, either. I've sent others to find her and no one has been able to locate her yet."

"Maybe she is somewhere with Alden?" I offered.

She waved her hand in the direction of the bar, where Alden was resting his arms against the bar as he stirred a drink and spoke with Vlad. My gaze searched the crowd and then rounded on my grandmother.

"Her room?" I asked.

"She's sharing one with Kendra, and we can't locate her either," she admitted.

"She wouldn't leave the club." I frowned as I considered the fact that she would. If Kendra had left, Mom would have followed to protect her, and neither of them had very strong magic. "I have the journals for you." I held the bag up and she nodded.

"Let's go somewhere quiet," she said as her brow creased with worry. "I feel like something is about to happen... Something is off, I just know it."

"Everything is off," I said, and she laughed nervously.

"Oh, Lena, it is, isn't it? How are you feeling?"

"I'm fine," I groaned as I watched her gaze dart to the crowd again.

"You're always fine, aren't you? My brave girl," she uttered as she pulled me close and hugged me tightly. "Even as a child, you were always the one who never complained and remained in the back while Kendra took the spotlight. You and Joshua were always getting hurt, and yet you never fussed or wanted holding when it happened. You'd just puff up and tell us you were fine."

"Mom wouldn't have left the club, not after dark." I pulled back and smiled at her. "She was terrified of the trip over here from the abbey. She hasn't wanted to be outside since."

"She didn't want to come after you either, but she did. You're her child, she'd have gone to hell for you..." She paused.

"Before I turned dark," I finished and smiled tightly.

"Am I so different now?" I asked, wondering if I changed that much in so little time.

"No, but you hold yourself away from us, as if you are protecting us from what you've become. You all do it now, like you are unsure of your welcome and, my darling... You are of my line and so loved. If I had to choose from a million other souls to be mine, I would always choose yours for its purity."

"Thank you," I replied.

"Let's find somewhere without ears, shall we?" she said, and I nodded, following behind her until we were alone in a small room. "So, what did you find out?"

"I went to the Guild a little over a month ago, almost two months now. Inside the Guild was a room, one that was filled with artifacts from our coven. They were old artifacts, some over a hundred years old or more. Inside the room were journals and grimoires, several of them. I touched them and the words and spells left the grimoires and entered me. I have everything that was inside of them in my head."

She sucked in her breath as her eyes grew wide with what that meant. "Lena, that is deadly. Grimoires don't just enter a soul unless they have a need to. I am going to guess that it wasn't your intention to take them, but to only read them?"

"Yes, but as I read, they slid from the page onto my skin and disappeared. Now they're in my head. I can use them as if they're my own personal grimoires. Only the journals aren't mine and each one says a name, Katarina. She was in love with someone named L, and hunted by a monster. Only…I don't think the monster is as she says, I think he is protecting or hunting an object that can open the doors to the other worlds. She took something from him, like a seal of some sort. There are sketches and ideas of it, or more to the point, what it is. I think it is evil, as in it changes people once it inhabits them or is activated. The creature hunts it, to keep it from anyone who would use it to open the worlds. Once the seal passes through a world, it unlocks it. Or so I think, or maybe all of them at the same time, but that part was unknown.

"I think when Kendra and I were in Hell, one of us unlocked it. Before I turned, when I was speaking to Mom, Kendra shouted at me inside my head to help her. I thought I imagined it, and now, now I think Kendra is being controlled, or she is the seal and is in trouble." I explained the journals, and how the nightmares we had suffered had been mentioned over and over again, and how every time it replayed, a new curse was put into play somehow.

"You're saying that she isn't your sister anymore?"

"I don't know," I admitted. "When has she ever told on me, though? When has Kendra ever been able to hold a grudge for more than a day? She isn't the same, and I know she's been through a lot, and it's different than when we were little, but something is wrong with her. My gut is telling me that she isn't Kendra, not anymore. Whoever it is, it's not my sister."

"She has a devil's trap on her body, she isn't

possessed."

"If it was a demon, we'd know. But I don't think it is a demon that has control of her. Too many things are adding up to be wrong lately. The seer in the woods, the news that our birth father played a part in it, and the fact that Kendra might not be Kendra, and that is worrisome, especially with Mom missing," I admitted. "I'm going out to find her."

"If what you say is true, then we need to be very careful. There are too many unknowns unfolding, and it's moving faster than we can stop it," she muttered softly as she watched me.

"I should go; it's dark and the temperature is going to drop soon."

"Lena," she said, grabbing my hand to stop me as I moved to the door. "I love you. I need you to know that in case anything happens. The sand isn't always right. It's been wrong before, when you were born, and the boys. You should go to Lucian and tell him what is happening. He will help you. You're carrying his child now."

"He doesn't need to know yet." I chewed my lip. "If and when I tell him, it's my choice. No one deserves to believe something good is happening only to have it torn away from them." Not that he'd consider it as much.

"He left a mark upon you to protect you," she acknowledged. "If you're in danger, he can find you?"

"Yes, he can. So can Spyder, so if I don't come back, you can go to them for help."

We left the room together, and no sooner had we stepped out than one of the new kids handed me a phone and ran off. I frowned as I looked down at it and back up as the kid retreated out of sight. The towers were down, which meant no service. I started to put it in the pocket of my skirt when it rang. I stared at the screen, then slid my thumb over it and held it to my ear.

"It's time to move your piece into play, sweetheart."

Ice rushed through my veins as Lucifer's voice whispered through the phone. My heart leapt to my throat as blood pounded in my ears, drowning out his words.

"I told you, Lucifer, I'm not into playing games," I muttered as I bit my lip as my grandmother covered her mouth with her hand to keep from gasping. My mother screamed in pain and I closed my eyes as Kendra's laughter followed it. "Where?" I asked without hesitation. I fought a sob that constricted my throat. Tears entered my vision as I watched my grandmother put it together.

"We are at your house. Lose your guards, Lena, or I'll show you what it is like to watch the flesh be ripped from someone while they still breathe. If I see anyone else with you, she dies. Be a good girl and play your part, and your mother can live."

The phone went dead and I turned it off as I moved to my grandmother. I hugged her as she struggled to keep it together. Lucifer had my mother, and worse, if I was right, Kendra had taken her to him.

"I need you to distract Lucian and the others so I can

sneak out," I said firmly, managing to keep the fear in my voice hidden. "I won't lose them. I will fix this, no matter the cost. I will end this game of theirs once and for all. You have to trust me on this. Give me at least an hour to reach them. After that, tell Lucian where I am and who I am with. The Fae will follow him, but I need you to stay here, do you understand? Promise me you will stay here where it is safe," I urged.

"I can't promise you that," she said as she tugged me into her arms and held me. "You will not make it out of this unscathed, Lena. If you can't save Kendra and your mother, get out. Don't be a hero like your brother was. You are the power that holds this coven together; you hold us up right now and keep us safe. If she isn't our Kendra, she isn't worth dying for. You have to live, do you understand me?"

"I'm not planning on dying," I whispered against her ear.

"They want her, right? This Katarina?" she asked.

"Something like that, and the seal she holds. I have to go," I said.

"No, not yet," she mused as she touched her index finger to her lip. "If they came for her, why do they need you there? You said the journal mentioned the nightmares the coven suffered and how they mentioned runes, right?"

"Yes," I mumbled as I checked the time on the phone I held.

"Come with me," she said as she tugged on my arm.

"I don't have time!"

"You do for this," she countered. "They need you for something, or they wouldn't have taken my daughter. If I am correct, you play a big part, and in case that is what I think it is, I need to do something. If we end it, the next generation will not suffer from their deadly games anymore."

I followed her into the room and once she'd finished doing what she needed to, I gently kissed her on the cheek. "I love you; if I had to choose a family to be mine, you'd always be my choice too."

CHAPTER
thirty-five

*You're always one decision away from a totally different life. ~**Anonymous***

I slowly rounded the corner of the house, gaze darting around as I searched the chaos going on for my mother. I found her atop the pile of drained bodies, tied to a corpse. My stomach dropped and my knees threatened to buckle as I took in her disheveled appearance. Her clothing was ripped, her hair mussed and covered with dried blood, which I prayed wasn't hers.

Her eyelids opened as if she sensed me, and she lifted her tawny head, shaking it and using her bruised arm to shoo me away. I wasn't leaving her. She was my mother. Fate had brought us here; for whatever fucked up, twisted reason, we were here facing down the devil and creatures that shouldn't even be in our world.

I exhaled and struggled to gain what little courage I could as I stepped forward, revealing myself. No one turned or even looked at me as I walked to the circle. It was drawn in human blood and I swallowed the bile as I looked at the pile of bodies and realized they'd been sacrificed. Innocent lives had been lost to create a protection circle which couldn't be broken. The same one Katia had used, only thicker this time.

"There's our girl," Lucifer said without turning around. When he finally did, I swallowed hard to keep from crying out as I took in his appearance. Gone was his mask of civility and humanity. His piercing blue eyes took in the swaying skirt and my disheveled appearance from the trek over here. I hadn't bothered wasting time changing. I'd simply slipped a small knife into my pocket and had headed out the moment my grandmother had created a small scene and distraction.

The icy wind bit into my skin as it howled and sent my hair whipping into my face. The skirt lifted, revealing my legs as I slowly stepped forward until my toes touched the line.

"You will let my mother go and I will enter the protection circle. You cannot force me to enter it; I know how it works, Lucifer. Once you have let her go and vowed that she is not to be harmed, you can have me to do as you want," I said without letting the tremor that rocked through me show in my voice.

"You're fire and ice, Lena. You surprise me," he chuckled as he moved to the pile of bodies and kicked a young woman's corpse. "At first I wondered how he could be drawn to you, but as I've learned, you're special. You break the rules, and yet you have an honor code you follow, just as he does. You're selfless, which you shouldn't be. You weren't created to be selfless; you were created to be dark and deadly. Yet here you are, coming to me to save a worthless human."

"You didn't create me," I growled, but his lips thinned as they lifted into a beautiful grin that made my heart pause before pounding faster. "Let her go," I demanded adamantly. "You said if I came, she could go. Let her go and give me your word that she won't be harmed, and I will enter the protection barrier you've created. If you think to harm her after I am inside, I will hurt myself and Lucian will be here within moments. Do you understand?"

"We made a deal, Magdalena. There's no reason to get angry," he purred as he pulled my mother from the pile, the ropes disintegrating. She shook her head as he pushed her towards me. Tears streamed from her eyes as she rushed to me, only to be thrown back as she crashed into the barrier. Lucifer laughed and I exhaled slowly as I struggled to remain composed.

Demons moved closer to where I stood, smiling at Lucifer as I released a pulse of magic, enjoying their screams and the heavy scent of sulfur as they burst into ashes. I didn't back down as he snarled and pulled my mother up by her hair.

"You have a thing for killing my friends," he snarled.

"You need new friends."

He shoved my mother through the barrier and I breathed a sigh of relief as she rushed to me, hugging me tightly.

"Lena, don't go in there," she pleaded as I embraced her tightly and then pulled away.

"Go into the house and activate the wards," I uttered as I pushed her hands away as she tried to hold on me.

"Lena, no, please. They are going to kill you!" she screeched as tears flowed relentlessly down her face.

I stepped through it and spun around to stare at her. "I love you," I said through the tightness in my throat. Strong arms grabbed me and I closed my eyelids.

"That was fucking stupid, girl," a deep voice growled against my ear. I was turned to face Lucifer and I paused, mentally calculating how the fuck someone else was in the circle. Kendra moved into my line of sight and frowned at me briefly before she concealed it with an aloof look. She smiled coldly as she moved closer and frowned.

"You're sure the spell will work?" she asked, turning to glare at Lucifer.

"It will work," he assured her as she moved away from me and started to drop items into the cauldron, which boiled as steam rose from it.

"Have you told her what she is yet?" she laughed mirthlessly. "How she isn't even real?"

"I figured you wanted to tell her, love," he mused. "How's our little one?" he asked, ignoring her as his gaze latched onto my midriff. "Did you tell Lucian he was going to be a father?"

"No, I didn't. What was the point?" I asked. "You think he cares, but he doesn't. I keep telling you this, and yet you refuse to listen to me."

"Because I know he cares." Lucifer touched my cheek as the arms released me and the man walked to where Kendra stirred the cauldron. "You've met Hades before, kind of. He's the one who lapped at that pretty pussy of yours. He's also the one who prevented me from getting you pregnant."

The man turned violet eyes on Lucifer and narrowed them. Power erupted from both men as if they'd fight, but then Kendra reached over and slammed her palm against his chest and the man went to the ground. Violet eyes stared up at Lucifer.

"Oh, don't be so surprised, Hades. I knew whose side you were on," he laughed coldly. "I knew Lucian had someone on the inside, someone who reported to him. You tipped your hand when you didn't fuck Magdalena. I had my minions following you, and when they reported back to me that you'd gone aboveground, I had enough proof. Don't worry, old friend. The spell will only render you paralyzed until I've finished here."

I was pushed closer to the cauldron, which released a putrid scent that made it almost impossible to breathe. I covered my mouth with the back of my hand as I glared at Kendra. She exhaled and shook her head.

"He only liked you because he thought you were

me," she said in a deadpan tone. "He thought you were pure, but you're nothing more than a selfish bitch. You left me down there to endure what should have been your torment. But I guess I should thank you for that. It was so much easier to get your sister to agree to allow me to endure the pain for her." My heart hammered against my chest as tears burned my vision. "You see, I've always been a part of her. Just as you were never meant to be born," she said cryptically. "You didn't just come to be, you were created from magic. Your father helped me; he planted the seed, and I divided it. Everything that was dark inside of me is now yours. You're nothing but the parts I didn't want. You see, after so many centuries of being chased and hunted, I made a deal with Lucifer that he couldn't pass up. Revenge against Lucian in exchange for my life back," she cackled, and I narrowed my stare on her coldly.

"You cannot intervene with life," I growled. "Magic has rules; there are boundaries that no witch can touch."

"I wasn't bound by those laws in death. A child isn't alive until its heart begins to beat anyways. Just as your child's does now inside your womb. I divided the egg in your mother's womb, cutting away bits and pieces, and then there you were. It was the same for your brothers, which was how we knew it would work the second time. One twin born of light, and the other of darkness. Drake, of course, figured out that my intent was to kill Benjamin and hid him from me, but then that little problem solved itself, now didn't it? Joshua was slaughtered in a war, far from home. Not before they were once again tethered, thanks to Lucifer. You see, if one of us dies, the soul returns to the other, becoming a whole. Unfortunately, the spell must be finished first, or both of us perish. Nasty hiccup, so don't get any ideas or you will die with me, along with your unborn child."

"You're insane," I muttered.

"No, I've spent centuries planning this, and you? You played your part beautifully, Magdalena. You were created to lure him to you and keep him occupied as Lucifer laid down the trap to ensnare him. But you, you little slut, you couldn't stay off of him. I guess it's not really your fault. You are every part of me that ever loved that monster."

I trembled as it hit me. Lucifer wasn't L. Lucian was L, and Kendra had been taken over by the dormant soul of Katarina.

"You won't keep her," I seethed. "She's my sister!"

"She's already gone," she laughed as she watched me. "She's now the dormant soul, fading away as I take full possession of her. Poor thing; she couldn't handle what was being done to her, but when Lucifer showed her you in his bed and projected the image of you being slaughtered, she had handled everything we'd done to her at that point. You helped us break her. Once she watched you being fucked and murdered by Lucifer, she broke and begged to not feel it anymore. So I made her an offer: I'd feel everything and she wouldn't ever have to feel it again."

"You made her think I was dead," I mumbled as I struggled to imagine what she'd gone through. They'd raped her night after night, until she was pregnant with Lucifer's child, and then I'd walked into his club in my dream and he'd made her think I'd been murdered before her eyes as she was raped.

"She wouldn't break," she growled as she tossed the hair of the dead into the pot. "I whispered to her, promising her escape, and yet she held on. You're both so fucking stubborn and think little of tradition. Neither of you deserved to live, which makes this easy."

"And you? What about you, carrying Lucifer's bastard in your belly?" I asked.

Her hand moved faster than I predicted, slapping me across the face. I slowly brought my gaze back to hers and smiled. For someone with so many years on her, she hit like a bitch. I stepped closer, only for Lucifer to growl in warning.

"You shouldn't have done that," he hissed as the air around us grew thicker, power erupting as trees cracked from the pressure of the wind. The flames of the fires around us leapt and his scent rushed through my senses. "Stupid bitch! You've brought them right to us before we're ready," he snapped as Lucian appeared inches from the circle with Spyder beside him. One by one, they appeared around us. The Fae sifted in, bringing those of the coven with them. I winced as Synthia brought my grandmother and then pushed her carefully, using her own body as a shield.

"I warned you last time to stay away from her," Lucian seethed. "There won't be another time."

"She came to me of her own free will, Lucian."

I flinched from the anger I read in his eyes as they locked with mine. My mother rushed from the house, having watched everything from inside. Alden caught her as she rushed into his waiting arms. I swallowed the pain as her battered face was examined, but Lucian's gaze moved from my mother, to me, and then to Kendra.

"Let the girls go, now," he demanded.

"I don't think so; you see, we've been planning this a very long time."

Katarina glared at me before she swung her matching eyes to Lucian and scowled at him. A hungry look filled them as she slowly let her heated gaze slide down his hard, sinewy body that rippled with strength and power.

"I have them both," Lucifer laughed. "I have Magdalena and her sister," he purred as he grabbed our hands and pulled us closer to him. "One carries my child, the other carries yours."

"Impossible," Lucian snapped as his stare moved to me accusingly. "I cannot sire children; Katarina saw to that."

"Actually," Katarina laughed haughtily. "You can have children; you just have to care about her enough to ignite the curse. Of course, the moon had to shadow the sun and day had to become night with Venus in her closest position to the earth. I made sure the curse couldn't be broken until I was ready for it to be, Lucian."

His gaze swung to hers and he swallowed hard. I winced as a look passed over him that I'd never seen before. His eyes filled with pain and something else, something that drove a blade through my heart. He'd loved her. My hand tightened against Lucifer's as I struggled to get it free. I was in their fucking game, not because Lucian had brought me into it, but because his lover had.

"Lena," Lucian growled, and I swallowed hard as I brought my tear-filled gaze to his. He flinched as he read the truth of their words on my face. Lucifer dropped my hand and moved behind Katarina, placing his hands over her womb. Lucian's gaze left mine, burning a hole into where Lucifer touched his lover.

The nightmares, the one the entire coven had endured, were of him. He was the monster who hunted the cursed witch through every lifetime, and also her lover. I'd given him a piece of me, the one piece that hadn't been hers: My heart. I no longer wondered why he walked out; he'd never stopped loving the original witch, and now she was here, inside my sister.

"Katarina, sweet girl," Lucian whispered, and as his words soothed and caressed, my heart shattered a little more. "Come to me."

"Not this time, Lucian. Not anymore. You see, I've already won. Everything that loved you inside of me is now in her. Your precious Lena. Even your precious seal," she purred as she laughed as his eyes widened and slowly moved to my stomach. "You're getting it. I have ensured that you feel pain like you've forced me to endure time and time again. You let me come back long enough to seduce me, and then murder me. I am free of you; Lucifer has made sure that you can never hunt me again, monster. I have won."

My heart sank and my knees threatened to give out. *I* had the seal inside of me? *I* had it? No. I smothered a sob with the back of my hand. I didn't have it, my child did. Lucian's child held the purest form of evil in his tiny soul. I stepped back as I shook my head. This wasn't happening.

"You cursed an innocent child to death?" he demanded.

"No, I cursed you to take your own child's life. You want it so bad, Lucian, take it."

"And what happens to Lena?" Spyder asked as he stood inches from the circle, as if he intended to bust through it, which was hopeless. No one could get through.

"She dies, of course," Lucifer answered. "Katarina will need the rest of her soul back. By the way, Lucian, it's a boy. The son you always wanted and never could grasp. It's too bad you'll never get to see him grow as I will watch mine and Katarina's child do."

CHAPTER
thirty-six

While I thought that I was learning how to live, I have been learning how to die. ~**Leonardo da Vinci**

I continued moving backwards until I was inches from the cauldron. One kick, one kick and the potion to remove the soul would seep into the earth. I let the darkness slither over my skin, knowing what I was about to do would be suicide, but it was the only chance I had to get everyone out of this without leaving them broken or worse.

Katarina started in on Lucian, and he argued facts with her, which seemed mundane now. They'd pushed innocent lives into their deadly game time after time again. I turned, intending to push the cauldron over, but Lucifer slapped me, appearing in front of me. He sent me sailing to the ground, and I lay there, dazed, as I regained focus. I shot up the moment he dropped his guard, thinking I was subdued. I heard Lucian scream as my grandmother and mother cried out with him.

I pushed my hand through Lucifer's chest, intending to remove his heart. Light flashed around us and the ground trembled, but the further I dug inside his chest, the less I found. He bellowed and slammed me against the ground; my vision blurred as my head hit against something hard. I gurgled as I fought to get back up, but couldn't.

"You stupid bitch!" he snarled as he straddled my body and gripped my head, slamming it down on the ground over and over again. I heard it crack as it bashed against the hard ground and darkness threatened to consume me. I struggled to get free, but I couldn't move. Something moved beside me out of my peripheral vision. Screaming continued, light exploding as the sound of trees hitting the ground filled the area. One minute I'd been expecting certain death, and the next something slammed into Lucifer.

I heard more screaming; Kendra?

Light exploded, and someone shouted for Lucian, and my instincts said to get up. To fight. I rolled onto my stomach as I watched Katarina slapping Hades as he drove his fist into Lucifer repeatedly. They disappeared after Hades shouted something to Lucian, but he wasn't listening. His midnight eyes watched as I struggled to get up.

Katarina moved her assault on me, kicking me and screaming blurred words that I couldn't hear through the drums beating in my ears. Everything sounded far away, even my own cries as she kicked me. Sound came back at a deafening roar and I grabbed her foot, pulling her down.

I got to my feet, barely. My body felt wrong, and my hand touched my head, coming back covered in blood. My skull felt soft, broken. I watched as Katarina got to her feet and stumbled towards her. My first attempt to get her was clumsy, as if I'd drunk too much whisky. I lunged again, letting the darkness take a little more control than it ever had before.

Lucian spoke to Katarina, distracting her as I moved closer on clumsy feet, my equilibrium fucked.

"Let me help you, Katarina. We can be together again, but this time free of the seal," he murmured, and tears swam in my vision. "We can kill her and make you whole again, and we can have a child together. We can be everything you ever wanted."

"You kill me every time! In every life! Do you know how frustrating it is to discover who I am and who you were to me, only for you to strangle the life out of me the moment I do? I loved you more than life and you, you killed me. That wasn't enough for you, you couldn't let me go. Instead, you cursed me to relive this one, this cursed life where I fall in love with you and then you murder me. This time, though," she seethed. "This time, I get here and you don't even notice me. You go for her, everything that was wrong in me that I put in her because that is what you love, and it's why you love her! She's just a piece of me. You didn't even look at me when I threw myself at you. I came to you naked last night and you threw me out of your room because I wasn't your precious Lena. Well, look at her now! Is she still everything you wanted?" She laughed.

I lunged without thought. I grabbed the sides of her face, capturing it as I held on to her with everything I had.

"Kendra," I mumbled, unable to get words to come out right. I let a little more darkness in. "Kendra, please."

"She's gone, you stupid whore!" Katarina screeched as she struggled to get away.

"Kendra!" I screamed, and it echoed through the clearing, bouncing off the mountaintops as I started to fall to the ground, losing my hold. I pushed everything I had into the words, the spell, fighting for Kendra to come back, even if only for a moment.

"Lena," she whispered as she held me up. Her gaze looked at my face and she turned white. "Oh my God, Lena, what did they do to you?" she whimpered.

"I'm…fine," I uttered as I held on to her.

"I knew you would know it wasn't me," she whispered as tears rolled down her cheeks. "I knew you would be able to tell. I couldn't fight her. I'm so sorry for the things she said to you, they weren't true."

"We don't have time for that, Kendra. I need you to listen to me. We're not both making it out of here alive," I mumbled brokenly. "I love you. I love you so much," I cried as I leaned against her for strength. "We have to take care of Mom, you understand?"

"You will," she said softly. "You can't separate me from her; you will live, Lena. I love you more than life. I understand what you have to do. Tell them I love them, all of them. You will be okay; I will stay with you, always."

"Kendra, I'm so sorry," I sobbed as my hands held on, knowing the moment I stopped holding on, she'd be gone from me.

"I understand; it is okay. I know what you have to do," she replied through tears. "It's okay, it will be okay."

"No!" my mom screamed, and I couldn't look at her. I didn't have the strength to do what I had to do *and* look at her. She was losing a daughter tonight. "Lena, you stop! Get away from her, she's your sister!" Mom screamed through the pain as she figured out what was happening.

"I have to end the game," I said softly. I felt blood dripping from my lips. My body was going numb; if I was going to have the strength to end the game once and for all, I had to do it soon.

"You're going to be a mama," she said as a giant sob tore through her. "You tell him I loved him, that I would have been the best aunt in the world. You tell him about me, Lena. Promise me?"

"He'll know," I said as I started to falter, only for her to help me stand. "I'm sorry, I'm sorry I didn't realize it sooner."

"I don't blame you, for anything. I know what she said, but you didn't know. I never blamed you. When you think of me, know I'm with Joshua and that I'm okay. I love you, Lena. You're not just a piece of that bitch, you're my other half. You're my sister."

"I can't fight her off any longer," I sobbed as I tried to hold on. "I love you, I'll always love you. Death isn't the end, Kendra. You will be okay," I whispered as I stepped back, swaying on my feet.

Katarina backed up, screeching as she took control. "You stupid bitch, you can't kill me!"

~Lucian

I watched, unable to pass the fucking protection barrier. Lena's head was bad, so fucking bad that if we couldn't get to her soon, she'd die. She'd somehow managed to get to her feet, but I could feel her fading, unable to get to her. My heart pounded for the first time since I could remember. My chest ached as I screamed out in frustration.

"Katarina, come to me. I can help you," I lied, my throat clenching against the blood that was trailing down from Lena's head wound. I'd watched her with Lucifer, fighting to survive, and those around had felt the world tremble at my anger, felt it quake in my presence.

I paced the line, watching as Lena backed away and turned towards her mother. She was going to kill her sister, and then she'd want me dead when I told her of the child and what it held. She'd hate me, and this fucked up game would replay because now it's inside of her. My child, my child held a monster inside of him. He held my seal in his tiny form, already being overtaken by it before he ever got to draw a breath.

My eyes burned and I lifted my hand, pulling it away after I'd wiped whatever the fuck was on it. I stared at the moisture, blinking.

"Look away!" Lena whispered and I turned, looking at her mother who already hated her for what she'd become even though she tried hard not to. She'd hate her for what she was going to do: free her sister. "Please look away," she begged brokenly, and her gaze skimmed over me. "Make them look away!" she screamed, and Alden moved into action, pulling Fiona against his chest. She fought against it, slapping him as she struggled to get away to see what was happening with her children.

My gaze slowly drifted back to Lena, who nodded softly at her grandmother and then almost collapsed from the small motion. Her hand slipped into her skirt's pocket and she stood taller, prouder as she faced Katarina.

Spyder inched closer, as if he'd catch her once she fell. She wouldn't fall; she was Magdalena, fierce and strong even though everything was stacked against her.

"Lena," I whispered, and her gaze lowered to the ground before her eyes lifted to me and held mine. Her pupils were blown, but the look in her eyes made my stomach churn with unease.

"You think you can kill me?" Katarina growled as she seethed her anger at Lena. "You can't even fucking stand up! You ruined everything. You are nothing; without my soul, you are empty and devoid of life. You were created to die; you're not even worth the air you breathe."

"I don't have to kill you, Katarina," Lena whispered as she tore her gaze from mine and lifted her head.

"The only way you can kill me is if you…you can't!" Katarina screeched as she watched Lena in horror.

"I win. Lucian will not kill our child, and you will no longer control my sister. This ends here, now. You will never be reborn to hurt any other witch ever again," Lena brought the knife up to her neck.

"No!" I screamed, sending the world tilting as anger pulsed through me.

The blade slit through her flesh, opening her neck to the bone. The knife dropped to the ground, bouncing against it. I struggled to remain upright as I watched her hands grasp at her neck. Her legs gave out and she hit the ground, kneeling on them. Her body crashed against it as her blood seeped into the ground.

"Let me in!" I demanded, but it was still Katarina in the body. She took in the morbid scene before her; Lena was gasping and making noises, but it was the only thing coming out as blood bubbled from her lips.

"Lena!" Kendra screamed as she rushed to where Lena was on the ground. "No, stay with me, oh, God, stay with me. This wasn't the plan," she sobbed as she picked up Lena and rocked her in her arms. The coven was silent, everyone in shock; no one was putting it together. Lena's hand touched the ground as her eyes fell vacant, lifeless. I screamed as I fought the protection barrier, and then

Spyder was kneeling, pleading to Kendra to bring Lena to us.

The moment she'd been moved out of the circle, I fell to my knees, holding her as Vlad sliced his wrist and pushed it against her mouth. It was useless, she was gone. The moment the soul expired, she died. Tears formed in my vision and I buried my face against her blood-covered chest as the Fae and everyone worked to save her. The witches chanted, Kendra screamed hysterically, pissed that she was still here, but her sister wasn't.

Lena gave her life to save her. She gave her life to keep me from killing our child. She knew she wasn't living, and she was aware that half her head was crushed. She'd shielded Kendra and everyone from seeing it. She'd fooled them all.

"She's not coming back," I muttered as I lifted my head, pushing Vlad away. "She has no soul. She can't be saved," I said, but they continued to try. "Get the fuck off her!" I snapped, watching as Spyder touched my shoulder; he'd felt it too. The bond was gone. It had left with her. I knew I'd feel it if she was lingering, but she left us. She freed me, but the cost for it was her life, and I'd have played this game until the end of time to spare it.

"Lucian, she has to be shrouded in the cloth of purity," her grandmother whispered as she stood mere feet from me.

"She's gone, there is no rebirth for her," I growled coldly. "She released the little bit of her soul Katarina planted, and in doing so, she can never be reborn. She can never come back. She's just fucking *gone*."

"I'm aware of it, but that of the child she freed isn't. It deserves to be buried and have a chance at life, whenever Hecate chooses it."

"Fuck Hecate," I snarled. "The child is mine; it holds something I have to get back."

"No, it doesn't. We placed runes upon her skin to free the innocent soul from the seal. It is dormant inside of her body. It has no soul to attach to. Lena knew she would die when she came here; the sand foretold her death. She made a choice to save her family and protect you, so let us finish what she started. Let her not die in vain."

"She knew she would die and she still came?" I demanded.

"It was her choice to make," she said, her tears running freely down her cheeks as I rocked Lena's lifeless body. "She told me to tell you if it should come to pass, that some love is worth dying for. That she gave her life so that you would be free, and that every curse upon your skin will leave with her death. Katarina is no more, nor can she ever be born again. Her soul is fractured. She cannot ever be reborn. You are free of her forever."

"That was my price to pay," I seethed.

"And you are paying for it," she pointed out. "You should respect her sacrifice, for you are not the only one who is mourning her."

My face turned to her mother, who was screaming

against Alden's chest as he held onto her. Kendra was numb, staring down at her sister's lifeless corpse. Her friends remained off in the distance, hugging each other as they cried without care of who saw them.

I stood, carrying her with me. "You can place the shroud around her, but I'm not leaving her fucking side until she's placed in the ground. I don't give a fuck about your traditions or laws; I'm not leaving her alone."

CHAPTER
thirty-seven

Kendra Fitzgerald

They say dying is hard, but it's not those who leave us who are forced to go on living. They're just gone, finished, their story ends. Fuck people who say that. Living is harder, waking up every morning and pretending that life is normal. Somehow we do it, we rise and place one foot in front of the other. We pretend that there isn't a void inside of us, a place that died with the one we loved.

Others expected us to get over the grief, but for me, it was as if I was missing a piece of myself. My other half had just ceased to exist.

They told us that she'd want us to be happy, but how the fuck would they know? Grieving was normal, it was the hearts way of reminding us that she'd been loved. It was the price we paid for loving them so much that we could never fully let them go. It was how we kept them alive inside of us, that pain; it reminded us that they'd lived.

I'd stayed away from the main hall for the most part, walking through the empty halls like a ghost as I worked through everything that had happened. I hated their pity, their looks of sadness as they whispered behind their hands of what she'd been, or what she'd done.

They had no idea of what she was, or who she was. She was my sister, the most powerful witch in our coven because, unlike us, she hadn't had a soul to hold her back. She'd been a conduit of magic, an endless force that couldn't be held back by mortal limitations. Not like the rest of us, no; she'd been fearless in her own right. She'd been selfless in both loving us and protecting us.

Day after day I'd wanted to lie beside her and just give up. I was tired of pretending that her loss wasn't tearing me to bits and pieces.

Grief didn't get easier; that was a lie to appease those left behind. You got stronger; you found ways of living with the never-ending pain in your chest. You learned to breathe again, to draw air into your lungs even though it hurt to do so. Lena had said it once, that death broke you, it stole a piece of you when it visited, and she'd been right. She'd stared down at Joshua's casket when they'd carried it in for the service and said, "*Fuck death; it fucks the living more than the dead. Life ends, it isn't the dying who hurt, it's the ones we leave behind.*"

The day she died it had taken them hours to cease trying to save her as Lucian held her corpse. They'd tried everything from magic to vampire blood to bring her back. He'd fought against them, screaming as they tried to take her from him. In the end, only their unborn child's soul swayed his hand. He released her body, and yet he'd refused to leave her side even now. Days had passed as the child's soulless body was purified with his mother's.

Lena would never be reborn. Only one soul had been allowed to find passage with the spell they'd cast, she'd given it to her child. She'd taken what little chance she had at being reborn and sealed her fate. Of course, she'd sealed Katarina's in the process. She'd freed Lucian, something he hadn't been able to do himself.

I'd stood with him as her body had been cleaned of the blood, revealing the extent of her injuries. She'd known she was dying, she had to have. The entire back of her head had been cracked open. Both pupils had been fully dilated, revealing a massive hemorrhage. How she'd managed to end the game was a testament of her strength and desire to free both Lucian and me from Katarina's clutches. I'd watched as the runes were revealed, something she'd allowed Grandmother to do before she'd left the club, knowing that she'd never return to it.

Lucian had worried about the child being alive inside of her womb up until that point. He'd given a short explanation of what she'd held inside of her. She'd held pure evil inside of her that not only opened the gates to other worlds, but tore through them, destroying everything that was good. Somehow, even with it inside of her, she'd remained pure. She'd remained devoted to those she'd loved.

Lena had been a bright light in a world filled with darkness, and somehow, she'd shined brighter than any of us.

I was angry at her for it, for taking the choice away from me. She'd fooled us all, made us think that I wouldn't survive, and then she'd done it. She'd taken her life and with it the light she held.

Lena was buried beside Joshua beneath the giant oak that lined the property. There was no music to lessen the blow or lighten the crowd that had gathered. Her casket was carried by Lucian and his men, placed upon the ground beside where she would be buried. The coven chanted for her soulless body to find peace in any way it could. She'd given her life for mine, and I'd never forgive her for it. Lucian had placed her beside Joshua's memorial and then moved to stand at a distance. No one followed him, but like me, he was probably angry that she'd made the choices for us.

As coven law dictated, Magdalena Fitzgerald would be removed from the history, fading away into the past as so many before her had. My hands slid to my belly and I wondered if Hecate would bless me with a daughter, one as strong as my sister had been.

"Kendra, it's time," my mother said as she placed a gentle hand on my shoulder. She had gone into a deep depression with Lena's death, but then we'd known she would. Not even Alden could bring her out of it. It had only been two weeks since she'd died, and in all that time,

Lucian had remained true to his word, never leaving her. It was as if he expected her to wake from a deep slumber, or maybe turn into something else.

She belonged in a better place, somewhere that souls could find peace. It was hard to think of her as soulless when she'd been so full of life. She'd been my other half and now…now it was gone.

We stepped back as they lowered her body, into the ground, covering it with a green tarp once they'd placed the earth upon her coffin. She was right where she'd want to be, beside Joshua. Unlike his embellished headstone, she had a small concrete slab that merely held the initials MF and Unborn Son.

Flowers were placed on the ground above her body along with wreaths for protection. Candles and other things were lit, giving some resemblance to a normal coven burial. Once we'd finished, we started towards the cars that lined the field along the property. Lucian was the only one to remain as we left her at peace.

The club was a reminder of what had transpired. The atmosphere was sober, silence reigning throughout it as we waited to see if Lucifer would return, or what other creature crept from the few worlds which had been unlocked. The Fae had brought the word to us that there were a few unsealed portals which, of course, led into this world.

Life seemed to be at a standstill, as if everyone held their breath as they waited for something to happen. Me, on the other hand… I felt numb, unable to ignore the emptiness Lena had left without her bond to let me know she was there with me. The finality of it reminded me every day that she was gone; every moment was empty, and every time I reached out for her, she couldn't reach back for me.

"After a time, we will remove any sign that she ever existed," Grandmother said, and I watched as my mother broke down, and had to be helped from the room by Alden. My hands smoothed over my belly and I excused myself to do the same.

I walked through the hallway and Lucian stopped, staring at me with a look I didn't understand. He backed into the wall and shook his head before he turned around, leaving me to ponder his reaction. I lifted my hand to my face and exhaled. I had her face, her beauty, but I lacked her fire; the fire of life that burned so brightly from within. They could try to remove her from history, but I was a constant reminder that my sister had lived, that she existed and had been real.

CHAPTER
thirty-eight
I'm not done yet. ~*Magdalena*

Dying sucked, but then I'd known it wouldn't be easy. I'd died to save those I loved, to protect them from what would happen if a sacrifice hadn't been offered. I'd made a choice, one I intended to live with. I'd known going in that it would be my grand finale, my big bang, if you would. The sands had foretold it, and I'd known that everything I'd been told was real. All the facts had lined up.

I couldn't die. I had no soul to take. I'd gone in with that knowledge, that power to face Lucifer. I'd died with dignity, for a good cause. Saving those I loved? I'd do it a million times over.

My brother had explained what happened when souls fractured. He'd told me everything, and how not having one would save my life. You cannot kill something that never existed in the first place. I was never born, I was cloned. Katarina had been correct about that, but not about everything.

I hadn't come out unscathed. I'd killed my child to protect him. I'd made my first and only decision as a parent alone. I'd freed him to be reborn, to find life again with a new family. I'd spared his father the unspeakable choice of murdering his own child to save this world. I would carry that burden alone, the loss of his life before it had even begun.

I wasn't a saint. I'd known heaven would never want me and Hell couldn't hold me. I had no soul for them to take. Much like my brother's, it had left him, and in its place was power, untold power that made the world ours. We had nothing holding us back now.

When it came down to it, I'd made my choice knowing that the reason the sands had shown my life line ending, while my son's had been never-ending, was because something else was in him. When the sand had turned around and moved back towards my line, I knew it was evil driving him. Good keeps moving, it keeps going to help the next one in line. Evil turns around when it's finished its goal—it goes back to the familiar things it's known or loved to destroy them in the end. I'd protected the coven from it, and its father.

That's okay, though, I'm not done yet. My life has just begun.

I opened my eyes as soft steps approached the water I floated in. Opening my eyes, I peered at my brother's disheveled appearance.

"Hey, Lenny girl," he laughed as he bent down and touched my cheek. "Please tell me my funeral wasn't that miserable?"

"Worse, Joshua, so much worse," I laughed as I stared into his loving face.

"Few more days and you should be healed," he said as he examined my head and throat. "Next time, no dramatic bullshit," he grumbled as he lifted the cloth from my neck. "That is going to scar."

"Scars are fine, Josh," I uttered. "They just mean I lived."

"Soon as you're healed, you need to meet the others. They're dying to meet you," he announced.

I winced at his words and shook my head carefully. "Too soon," I whispered.

"It's never too soon, not when we have eternity," he replied.

~The End For Now~

About the Author

Amelia lives in the great Pacific Northwest with her family. When not writing, she can be found on her author page, hanging out with fans, or dreaming up new twisting plots. She's an avid reader of everything paranormal romance.

Stalker links!

Facebook: https://www.facebook.com/authorameliahutchins
Website: http://amelia-hutchins.com/
Amazon: http://www.amazon.com/Amelia-Hutchins/e/B00D5OASEG
Goodreads: https://www.goodreads.com/author/show/7092218.Amelia_Hutchins
Twitter: https://twitter.com/ameliaauthor
Pinterest: http://www.pinterest.com/ameliahutchins
Instagram: https://www.instagram.com/author.amelia.hutchins/
Facebook Author Group: https://goo.gl/BqpCVK